Praise for the *Wars of Vis* series by Tanith Lee:

"The drive and inventiveness which made Lee's *Birthgrave* remarkable are in evidence in [*The Storm Lord*].... The unnamed world in which the story is set is as richly varied as Middle Earth."　　　　　*—Publishers Weekly*

"Fans will savor her original, and sometimes frightening, characterizations and careful world building."
　　　　　—Booklist

"The language is very rich, evoking a world of almost Byzantine splendor and complications.... Lee is always a persuasive writer, and her imagination is compelling."
　　　　　—Locus

"An epic fantasy of immense proportions.... Suffice it to say that *The Storm Lord* is a book I would recommend most highly, and Tanith Lee is definitely a writer who knows her craft."　　　　　*—Tangent Magazine*

"Truly a feast for the senses. The lush sensuality of her prose envelops the reader in a magical ambience."
　　　　　—Rave Reviews

"First-rate fantasy adventure.... A complex plot ... peopled with Lee's unique creations and superior storytelling ability."
　　　　　—S. F. Chronicle

"In terms of what it takes to make a great fantasy novel, *The Storm Lord* has it all. I recommend it highly."
　　　　　—The Diversifier

DAW Books presents
classic works of imaginative fiction
by multiple award-winning author
TANITH LEE

THE BIRTHGRAVE TRILOGY

THE BIRTHGRAVE
SHADOWFIRE
(originally published as *Vazkor, Son of Vazkor*)
HUNTING THE WHITE WITCH
(originally published as *Quest for the White Witch*)

TALES FROM THE FLAT EARTH

NIGHT'S MASTER
DEATH'S MASTER
DELUSION'S MASTER
DELIRIUM'S MISTRESS
NIGHT'S SORCERIES

THE WARS OF VIS

THE STORM LORD
ANACKIRE
THE WHITE SERPENT

AND MORE:

COMPANIONS ON THE ROAD	CYRION
VOLKHAVAAR	SUNG IN SHADOW
ELECTRIC FOREST	TAMASTARA
SABELLA	THE GORGON AND OTHER
KILL THE DEAD	BEASTLY TALES
DAY BY NIGHT	DAYS OF GRASS
LYCANTHIA	A HEROINE OF THE WORLD
DARK CASTLE, WHITE HORSE	REDDER THAN BLOOD

DAW is proud to be reissuing these classic books in new editions
beginning in 2015.

The Storm Lord

TANITH LEE

DAW BOOKS, INC.

DONALD A. WOLLHEIM, FOUNDER

375 Hudson Street, New York, NY 10014

ELIZABETH R. WOLLHEIM
SHEILA E. GILBERT
PUBLISHERS

www.dawbooks.com

First Printing, May 1976
First New Edition Printing, July 2017

1 2 3 4 5 6 7 8 9

DAW TRADEMARK REGISTERED
U.S. PAT. AND TM. OFF. AND FOREIGN COUNTRIES
—MARCA REGISTRADA
HECHO EN U.S.A.

PRINTED IN THE U.S.A.

TABLE OF CONTENTS

Book One

The Amber Witch

THE GREAT UPTURNED BOWL of the Plains's sky was drenched with the blood of sunset. The sun itself had fallen beyond the Edge of the World. Now, before the rising of the moon, only a single scarlet star gemmed the cloak of gathering twilight.

A group of about twenty men were crossing the arid slopes—hunters, but not of the Plains. They rode thoroughbred animals, with here and there a light hunting chariot of Xarabian design, yet they were not Xarabians. They moved with a special, almost a specific, arrogance, which pronounced them alien to this landscape far more than did their black hair and black-bronze burnish of skin. Yet it was the scale markings of their metal that told the precise nature of their menace, for they were Dortharians, dragons, and they carried a High King in their midst.

Rehdon, King of Dorthar, the Storm Lord, that god-given title which essentially meant mastery of the entire continent of Vis, this now darkening planet: a king, ruler of kings. Even the hunting helm bore the spiked Dragon Crest. Beneath it, age had infected, with its own reptilian markers, a pair of eyes that were staring upward, toward the gem of the scarlet star.

Zastis. In Elyr, the withdrawn and euphemistic, they

called this the time of marriages. But it was more vile and prosaic. It was the time of greatest sexual need, the tyranny of the flesh, strong in all, but in the royalty of Dorthar a domination brooking no denial, a bizarre badge of the line of Rarnammon.

The moon rose. A moon red from the star.

Rehdon's charioteer glanced back at him, a thin graceful man with a face which, at no time, said anything, except where the long narrow slits of eyes led down into a machinery of intellect. His position as chariot driver was misleading. This man was Amnorh, King's Councilor, the Warden of the High Council of Koramvis, in certain ways the nearest power beside the throne.

"Amnorh, we're far from Xarar," Rehdon said suddenly. He had a king's voice—deep, resonant. He had in fact every appurtenance suited to a king, but it ran shallow. Amnorh knew this well.

"My lord's restless? There's a village near here. The serf we questioned mentioned it, you'll recall."

"This accursed No-Land. Why do we hunt so far from the borders of Xarabiss?"

"I hoped your lordship would get better sport here in the Lowlands. The borders of Xarabiss are hunted out."

"This place," Rehdon said again. The star made him uneasy, peevish, as always. "What name did you give it before?"

"Oh, the native name, my lord. The Shadowless Plains."

Abruptly the land dipped. They were among sparse grain fields, blush-colored from the red moonlight. A small shrine appeared between stalks and was gone—probably a field altar to the Plains goddess Anackire, half woman and half serpent. Amnorh knew of such things. He glanced back again, this time beyond Rehdon, to the place in the party where the Prince Orhn rode with his men. Orhn, Rehdon's cousin, had little time for Xarabiss and her elegant ways. He would be happy enough to pitch a camp here for the night.

As for Xarar, Rehdon's visit of courtesy to his king-held fiefs was almost at an end.

Presently, Amnorh made out a flicker of lights.

It was one of the Lowland villages indeed, an uneven track, groups of poor dwellings, a dark religious building with a grove of red trees.

The hunting party drew to a halt.

Three or four women stared from the grove. Unlike the Vis, the master race, the Plains People were pale, light-haired, yellow-eyed. No children showed themselves, and no men. Perhaps a disease had taken them or they were away, hunting plain wolves—those the Dortharians had un-successfully tracked all day—or the venom-clawed tirr that shrieked from the forests at the Edge of the World.

"Where are your men?" Amnorh called out.

The women remained blank-faced, and immobile.

"We are Dortharians," a voice said harshly. "You'll give us the best you have to offer for the night, and be honored."

Amnorh turned and saw Prince Orhn. The racial intona-tion amused Amnorh, also the great and powerful body on the granite-black animal, a symbolic strident aggression, achieving apparently nothing. More softly, Amnorh said:

"We're in need of food. And the Red Moon troubles us."

The women stared unflinchingly back, but he guessed this threat might have touched them. The Lowlanders were immune to Zastis, it was said.

Rehdon moved impatiently behind him. The reptilian eyes ran over the women, already hungry, already dissatis-fied. Irritably, he turned his head.

He saw, framed by the uprights of the temple doorway, a girl.

Motionless, expressionless, she seemed carved from white crystal, translucent eyes, like discs of yellow amber, open wide on his, the tawny cloud of hair fixed as frozen vapor.

"You. Girl," he said. "Come forward," and his voice held

all the majesty of thunder, was even echoed by thunder low above the dune-dark slopes. If it spoke power to her she did not show it, but she obeyed him. "Tonight you lie with me," Rehdon said. There was the briefest pause, a drop of silence, like the first drop of a great rain.

"Yes," she said then. And strangely, for there was no other answer she might give, her voice carried all the meaning, all the accepting in the world.

They pitched their camp at the edge of the straggle of village, small owar-hide campaign tents; the grooms and charioteers would sleep in the open. They had taken what they wanted in the way of food and drink, careless that their demands would make the thin yield of the fields harder for the village to bear. Vis servants had slaughtered a cow in the temple square, and roasted it whole above a pit of coals.

But, unlike their King, they did not take the women, although the need was already on them. Even the coarsest groom had shied away from a vision of white-limbed passivity and wide eyes. Plains women, it was rumored, knew strange arts. Knew, too, how to stare in at a soul stripped naked by the pleasure spasms of the flesh. So the women slipped unmolested away, and not a light showed from their hovels, not a sound came out.

In Rehdon's tent the meal was finished. Amnorh leaned forward, filling the King's goblet with the stolen bitter potent Lowland wine. Orhn was absent — his animal was lame and must be seen to, he had said, but it was Amnorh's presence he abhorred. Amnorh half smiled at the thought. Orhn Am Alisaar, waiting on a tyrannical sire who would not die and give up his kingdom for his bevy of sons to fight for. Orhn sought power rather at the side of his cousin, and Amnorh, sly Amnorh, came between them in subtle ways. And not only between cousin and cousin, for there was also the matter of Rehdon's Queen.

The man posted outside the tent showed himself.

"Storm Lord, your pardon. There're priests here from

the village, asking for audience. Do we send them packing, my lord?"

"They were hiding in their temple until now," Rehdon said. "What reason to emerge?"

"The girl your lordship honored with speech."

Amnorh said:

"Your lordship might be amused by them."

Rehdon, oblivious of most things save his waiting lust, nodded to the guard.

The man ducked out. A moment later the priests entered, three in all, long black robes, faces blanked out by shadow from their hoods. Priests in Dorthar were gaudy, vivid with their oracles and their miracles and the corruption of a thousand greeds. These intruders carried their own mystery, they seemed to have no presence, as if some smell of humanity were absent from them.

"We thought no men were in the village tonight," Amnorh remarked smoothly.

"Among us a priest is not numbered as a man."

"So we see. Well, you're here. What causes you to trouble the Storm Lord?"

Without seeing them, he sensed the six eyes of the priests fixed on him. He was not as contemptuous as he seemed, knowing as he did of certain powers sometimes manifested in these serfs, and peculiar magics. He wondered if they now conferred together inside their heads as they were reputed to do.

"Your lord desires to lie with Ashne'e. We ask him to take another woman from the village."

So she was called Ashne'e. A common enough name among Lowland women.

"Why?"

"The woman belongs to our temple. She is ours, and Hers."

"Hers? I take it you mean your serpent goddess."

"Ashne'e has been given to the goddess."

"So. The Storm Lord will pardon you that the girl's no longer virgin. I imagine this is what you intimate."

He thought they would speak again, but they were silent.

"Go back to your temple," Rehdon suddenly snarled at them.

In the bowl sky, thunder burned.

Without a word the priests turned; making no sound, they slipped one by one into the dark.

The fires were almost out, smears in the night world, when they brought the girl to Rehdon's tent.

In the half-light she was unhuman. The low flame of a tent torch filled one eye with gold, freckled her cheek as though she wept fire.

The men sidled out and were gone.

Rehdon trembled with his need. He took the edge of her robe in his fingers, recalling what Amnorh had said to him.

"You're from the temple, Ashne'e?"

"Yes." There was no color in her voice.

"You know the bed lore of the temple women then."

He pulled the garment from her. She stood before him naked. His hand moved on her, hesitated on her chill breasts. He drew her to the torch, examined her. An evanescent beauty, which a very little would swiftly destroy. High breasts, cold, for they were capped with gilt. In her navel a drop of yellow resin spat. The resin excited him unreasonably; it might have been a third eye, this time of her sex. He cupped her sexual hair, rough as the spun metal it resembled.

"Are you afraid of me?"

She said nothing, but her eyes expanded as if with tears.

Unable to resist the impulse of the star he pulled her down with him on to the couch, but somehow she twisted as she came and was above him. He saw then the expansion of her eyes was pure luminosity, they were glowing, awful as the eyes of a tirr, or a banalik crouched now to suck out his soul.

His head reeled with amazing fear, but he found in a second more that she knew those things which Amnorh had promised. He could not evade her will, floundered gasping in her snake's coils, until the night became a dream of fire between the surges of which came the intoxicated thought he must keep her by him forever after, to terrify and delight him and pull him struggling and groaning into the spinning pit of her womb.

Dawn came, cool before the day's heat, with a beat of bird's wings over the trees.

Amnorh folded back the flap of the King's tent, and stood a moment regarding the sleeping girl, her face turned into the cushions, first light licking her bone-pale back.

The King lay on his side, apparently locked deep in sleep, yet, as Amnorh had already noted, his black eyes were wide open. Amnorh crossed to him, reached and shook the Storm Lord's shoulder, presently slapped the bloodless mouth. The glazed eyes were fixed far beyond this insolence. Rehdon, Dragon King, whose new heir had lain two months in the body of his queen at Koramvis, whose other earlier heirs by lesser queens slunk about the palace courts in dozens, lay dead apparently from a casual Zastian coition.

Amnorh left the tent. He cried out wordlessly into the morning air, rousing men bleary-eyed from the embers of their fires. Two guards ran to him.

"In the tent," Amnorh said harshly. "Our Lord Rehdon is dead. The bitch-witch is still sleeping. Bring her out here."

He saw the horror start up in the guards' eyes. They ran into the tent, the flap did not fall back into place. He saw them balk at Rehdon's corpse, then lean and drag Ashne'e from the couch. She seemed limp, yet when they dropped her before him on the ground, her eyes came open, staring up into his. She made no move either to rise or to cover herself.

"Abomination," Amnorh hissed at her, "you have murdered a King."

One of the guards lifted his spear.

"Wait!" Amnorh rasped. "There's more to this."

"No doubt."

Amnorh glanced up and registered the tall figure of Orhn Am Alisaar, fully alert, a drawn knife ready in his hand.

"What's this panic for?"

"The Storm Lord is dead," Amnorh said, his eyes reduced to slits.

"Damnation take your tongue. I'll see that first."

"My lord prince is very welcome to judge for himself."

Amnorh stepped aside from the tent mouth; Orhn strode by him and inside. Amnorh watched him shake Rehdon's body, speak to it and finally let it subside. Orhn straightened, turned and came out. He glared for the first time with dry pitiless eyes at the girl Ashne'e.

"Who?"

"A whore from the temple. Has your lordship forgotten—"

"Yes. I'd forgotten."

Orhn kneeled abruptly, caught her face in a cruel grip so that her eyes were forced to his.

"And what did you do, temple witch? Do you know who this man was before you killed him? Storm Lord, High King—*Look* at me!"

Her gaze had slipped to Amnorh, and then, suddenly her eyes turned up and the lids fell over them as if in a fit. Orhn felt her skin grow chill under his hand and let her go, thinking she had fainted. Amnorh knew otherwise, said nothing.

Orhn got to his feet.

"No time for ceremony," he said, "I'll dispatch her now." He stared upward at the pale sun newly risen, which already masked the inflamed star. "The Red Moon was a curse to Rehdon," he said. "He was no longer a young man." The knife shone in his hand.

"However, lord prince, there's one thing we forget," Amnorh said softly.

Orhn looked full at him.

"I don't think so."

"Oh, yes, my lord. It's possible—merely possible—that Rehdon's child is planted in this inferior body."

A deeper, more intense silence fell around them. The men stiffened in attitudes of almost superstitious unease.

"She may have used the way of women to stop it," Orhn said.

"How can we be sure? There is no suitable test, lord prince. And permit me to remind you, my lord, that the last child conceived before the death of the king becomes, by the laws of Rarnammon, his ultimate heir."

"Not a by-blow on a peasant—the yellow scum-race of the Plains—"

"Indeed, my lord, but dare we alone decide the matter?"

Orhn's eyes were flint; the contemptuous distaste he felt for Amnorh suffused his face like a blush.

"My authority should be enough—"

"Lord Orhn!" a man cried suddenly.

On a low scarp a few yards away a guard waved his arm, then pointed off across the fields.

Orhn turned and saw a dust cloud whirling up from the slopes.

"What now?"

"The village men," Amnorh said softly, "perhaps returning?"

Orhn moved with long strides up the side of the scarp and stood beside the guard, Amnorh following more leisurely.

Sunlight touched the dust to silver, made it hard to distinguish shape inside the shining blur.

"How many men to kick up that much dust?" Orhn snapped. "Fifty? Sixty?"

"But they are only serfs, as you pointed out, lord prince," Amnorh murmured succinctly.

Orhn ignored him. He shouted down the hill: "Captain, get your pack into weapon drill."

Activity answered him about the smoking fires.

"Men from more than this one village," Orhn said. "Why?"

"Possibly the priests called them," Amnorh said.

"Called them? Because of a girl?" Orhn cursed. "You profess to know a great deal about these Plains scum, Amnorh. What'll they do then, do you suppose?"

"They're known for their passivity, lord prince. Probably nothing. But under the circumstances I think you'll agree the girl should be spared your knife."

Orhn sneered, sheathing the blade.

"For once, your counsel carries some weight. See, I've put the toy away. What now?"

It was plain he had no enjoyment in deferring to Amnorh's judgment, yet Amnorh did indeed seem to have some curious grasp of this unlooked-for situation.

"I suggest this: Tell the village of Rehdon's death, laying no blame on the girl. Say that she will in fact be honored as the vessel of the King's heir."

"Heir!" Orhn spat. "Can you see any faction in Dorthar upholding such a claim?"

"That scarcely affects us, lord prince. These are ignorant people, as your lordship has been heard to mention. It's quite probable that they'll accept such a story. It has a certain mythological quality that should appeal to them. Once in Koramvis, let the High Council decide what's to be done."

"You'd take her to Koramvis?"

"It's always best, lord prince, in the face of the unprecedented, to be as cautious as possible. Who knows what view the Council would take of any hasty action?"

Orhn frowned toward the dust cloud. He could make out zeebas now, and fair-haired men riding them.

"There's one small problem," Amnorh said. "The girl must be seen to comply."

Orhn looked down at her, his dark features fraught with disgust.

"Difficult, when to all intents and purposes she appears dead."

"Merely a trance state, my lord. Some Lowland acolytes are adept in such magics. I think, if you'll permit me privacy with her, that I can bring her out of it."

"I bow to your wisdom. Do as you think fit."

Light the color of a dead leaf circled in the brazier.

Out of it Amnorh drew a flame-tipped brand, shook off candescent fire flakes that settled in the air above the girl's naked body. She lay on his sleeping couch, where the two grooms had placed her, a white stasis in the darkly glowing tent.

"Can you feel the heat of the fire, Ashne'e?" Amnorh murmured. He bent to her ear. "Let me tell you, Ashne'e, what I'm about to do to you." Whispering like a lover, he scorched the down about her navel, but no more. "If I hold the torch to your throat the flesh will char to the bone. But you have presumed to kill a king of the Vis, Ashne'e, perhaps I should make you linger. Begin with your breasts—"

Pearls of moisture broke on the girl's forehead. With a sudden eruptive motion life regained possession of her. Her eyes opened and focused instantly on his.

Amnorh smiled. He had outwitted the spark of her consciousness in its blind craving for existence—once the body was threatened she had fled back to succor it.

"Did you think I'd do that? Scorch the gilded nipples from your white breasts?"

She spoke for the first time.

"You would do as it pleased you."

"Very perceptive. I would indeed. Most recently it's been my pleasure to save your flesh from the Prince Orhn's knife. Can you imagine why? No, I would think not. Prolonging your life will be more difficult. It depends in point of fact on whether or not Rehdon's child is in you. With the Am Dorthar the last male conceived before the king's death generally becomes his heir."

"Yes," she said, "I am with child by the Storm Lord."

"Your brave self-confidence inspires me to help you."

The tent was filled with blind crimson light.

He reached out and stroked her inert body. She seemed to have three eyes as she looked at him, two golden eyes set in her face, the third eye sputtering in her navel.

"I have told you. The King's child is in me."

"If not, there's still time."

The urging of the star was on him, yet he was subtle, as in all things. But his caresses, which had pleased even Rehdon's queen, were wasted on stone. The Lowland girl lay like a corpse beneath him, while her hair seemed to set the pillow alight. So he used her, and found her spoiled for him, and drew away, his eyes only showing how it might be at another time.

The dust cloud had settled on the fields, subsided like a swarm of insects in the grain.

The Lowlanders sat still on their zeeba mounts. Not a sound came across from them to the Dortharian camp. The hunt guard stood in formal lines, an impassive defense formation, weightily outnumbered, yet supremely confident of superior military skills. What did they face, after all, save a rabble?

"The Councilor takes his time," Orhn remarked impatiently. The captain turned to send a man up the scarp to Amnorh's tent, but Orhn caught his arm. Amnorh had requested absolute privacy, claiming his esoteric work to be a dangerous affair, and Orhn could do little but leave the matter in his hands.

There was an oppression of waiting in the air. The staring sun laved the Plains with its furnace heat.

"Movement from the temple, lord prince."

Orhn glanced aside.

"A priest."

The black muffled figure slid across the track, as if on rollers, along the slope toward the Lowland men.

"Some new scheme hatching," Orhn said.

He watched the hooded priest make some form of silent

contact with the foremost rank of riders, and almost instantly a man came out to stand beside him. Man and priest then began to walk back, crossing between the grain at a different angle, making directly toward the Vis camp. Orhn followed their progress intently. He made out the man to be young, unremarkable; tanned, muscular, gaunt-boned, a boy whose body and mind had long been exposed to unluxurious hard living—good military material had he been born of Vis stock. The priest at his shoulder glided like his black shadow.

At the outskirt of the encampment a guard stepped in the way, blocking their path.

The young man stopped, amber eyes fixed on Orhn. "Storm Lord, you have kept a woman here to please you. Let her return to her people."

The guard struck him with contemptuous lightness on the chest.

"Kneel when you address the prince, Plains dog."

The young man knelt immediately, not looking at the guard.

"I ask again, Storm Lord."

"I am not the Lord," Orhn barked. "The Lord is dead."

"That is sorrow. But I ask again for Ashne'e."

"Ashne'e possibly carries the King's heir. Do you understand? She must go with us to Koramvis."

The young man stared back at him with pale immutable eyes.

"Will you kill her there?"

"If she carries, she'll be honored."

"Why are you so concerned at what we do with Ashne'e?" a voice demanded, Amnorh's voice. So the Lord Warden had at last emerged from seclusion, successfully it would seem. "She belongs to your goddess, not to you."

"My sister," the Lowlander said slowly, "she is my sister."

"Very well. Follow me and bring your priest with you. You shall speak to Ashne'e. Ask her if she desires any greater joy than to enter the city of the Storm Lords."

The statement, brusque, imperative, seemed to strike responsive, relevant nerves. Orhn saw the Lowlander accepted at once both Amnorh's authority and his words. Amnorh went up the scarp, the boy following; at the top Amnorh let him alone into the owar-hide tent.

Orhn waited, and it was not in his nature to wait gladly. Would the girl speak as Amnorh instructed her? Damn her, she would have been better dead before talk of conception and the Council had clouded a perfectly clear issue. And what, in all this, were the Lord Warden's personal motives?

The Lowlander came out from the tent. Orhn saw at once a change in him—he seemed astonishingly blind and old, groping, not through a physical but a psychic darkness. He walked down the scarp, among the Dortharian lines into the sketchy wilderness of the fields, all the while the priest keeping like a black crow at his shoulder.

A simultaneous movement ran through the Lowland ranks. Men and zeebas broke formation suddenly, wheeled, a flurry of fresh dust surging up to mask their departure.

The captain swore beneath his breath.

Orhn glanced at Amnorh.

"Very clever, Councilor, very clever."

And Amnorh allowed himself a moment of childish answering inner scorn: "Certainly too clever for you, lord prince."

As a form of inescapable etiquette, a messenger was sent ahead of them to Xarar. Consequently, Orhn grit his teeth as they passed beneath the white Dragon Gate and entered a city plunged into deep and poetic mourning.

"Damn their mewling," he thought as the women howled in the streets for Rehdon, whose momentarily glimpsed person they had most probably forgotten.

Their host in Xarar, the King Thann Rashek, whose name in certain circles was Thann the Fox, sent a procession of embalmers to anoint and bind Rehdon's body. Rashek's numerous queens, women of Xarabiss, Karmiss and Corhl, and the troop of daughters, appeared in profound funereal magenta, while bards wailed of invented heroics—there had been no full-scale war since the time of Rarnammon in which a lord might earn or buy a hero's name. The mummery sent Orhn into a tight-held towering rage. He gathered up the disorganized factions of Rehdon's entourage with brutal haste. Within four days he had shrugged off the pomp and drama, the ubiquitous pale faces ready with histrionic tears and the eight-stringed laments.

He moved the Dortharian party swiftly out across Xarabiss, the corpse as the excuse, and left her crystal cities in a pall of offering smokes.

They entered the narrow land of Ommos, death in a closed golden Xarabian bier. Ashne'e—kept in exotic captivity in Xarar like a wild yet interesting beast, peered at, no doubt, through spy holes in the drapes—now dwelt in windowless gray rooms, and was spat at from low hovels flanking roadways. At twilight, in a white-stoned fortress by the sea, the warden personally killed a newborn child, brought into the world mere hours before their arrival by one of his dull-eyed wives. It was to mark his sorrow, he told them, yet it had been a girl and not a son and so, particularly in the case of an Ommos, no great loss to him.

Not long after, Orhn heard the mother shrieking somewhere in the darkness, and for some barely explicable reason his thoughts turned to Rehdon's Queen.

Val Mala, Dortharian princess of a minor House in Kuma, raised to her position as Jointress of Koramvis because of her beauty and Rehdon's weakness.

How she would detest the Lowland girl.

Orhn permitted himself a grim smile at the thought of the cruelties Val Mala would devise for her; in particular quarters Val Mala's name was already a byword for cruelty. Certainly no woman who had maligned her in her early days of power was now to be seen about the court. He recalled her chosen pet—a white kalinx, a tuft-eared cat, devil of incalculable viciousness—which roamed her apartments more or less at will, and was a symbol to Koramvis at large of her own glamorous and inventive spite. Val Mala indeed would be an intriguing study on their return.

And if the Lowland bitch were seeded? If there was to be public proof of the Vis Lord's extramarital lust? Orhn wondered, with a not entirely idle malice: would the embraces of the Lord Councilor be sufficient consolation?

2

DORTHAR, THE DRAGON LAND, Dorthar the dragon's head, the mountains its jagged crest, the lake Ibron its white eye, Koramvis its thinking jewel of a hub, the heart-brain.

The city lay on the foothills of the crest crags, elevated like a gigantic pure white bird on a nest of fire. Her foundations, bisected by a river, lay in the farthest recesses of time; like the Dragon Gate of Xarabiss, she was in part a remembrance, a physical creation burdened by essential legend, her ancestry a charred place where the Storm gods had come out of heaven, riding in the bellies of pale dragons.

At mid-noon, in the first Zastian month, her watchtowers spoke to her across the plain, black scavenger clouds of death smoke, and Koramvis opened her gates to admit her King.

Val Mala's apartments were filled with a dim smoky incense-light. Candles fluttered, her women were dressed in black. The girl who conducted them there had silver tears painted on her cheeks.

Val Mala made them wait a good while, Amnorh the Lord Councilor and Orhn prince of Alisaar. When Orhn grew impatient, the girl stared at him and murmured: "The Queen mourns."

Orhn made a sound of derision, but presently the mourner came and he bit back his curses.

Val Mala. Her Vis coloring was startlingly disguised by a creamy unguent, the Dortharian ebony of her hair hidden under a wig of hyacinth blue silk. She wore a funereal gown but the mood of it did not reflect in her face or her kalinx eyes, though they were as black as moonless lakes. She was far younger than her dead consort, had never loved him. Even her pregnancy was as yet invisible. She seemed to have rejected every vestige of Rehdon, and the ritual phrase — "the Queen mourns" — had all the absurd obscenity of something scribbled on a wall. Yet her beauty had lost none of its familiar edge, its stunning magic, despite that faintest hint about her of a high-class whore, that pinpoint glint of something vulgar and unrefined.

She glanced at Orhn, and then away.

"Where is my Lord Rehdon?"

"Coming unconducted through the palace courts since you, madam, called us to wait on you," Orhn growled.

"It's a pity, Prince Orhn, that you didn't conduct him better while he lived. He might, perhaps, still walk among us."

"It's at once apparent, madam, how grief overwhelms you at your loss."

She flinched at his irony and clenched her ringed hands in a convulsive, furious spasm.

"Oh, I am indeed overwhelmed. Overwhelmed by your malicious impropriety. You bring a gift for me, I hear."

"A gift, madam?"

"So I hear. Your notion of a *gift*." Her voice rose. "His whore! This filthy temple slut. A snake-worshiping devil-bitch he took for his pleasure because he couldn't have me."

Am Alisaar said nothing, his face stony with his own anger.

She spat at him: "You will not speak of this problematical child she carries. I won't have her live! *I* am the mother of the King's heir — I, and no other."

"You and many others, *madam.*"

Her eyes grew suddenly enlarged and blank as if they saw in terror those other lesser children clamoring for their birthright. She turned and crossed to Orhn and looked in his face.

"I," she said, "I, alone. Your King is here, Orhn Am Alisaar," and she snatched his hand and laid it over her belly. He felt the gentle swell of her body, the ribs of some jewel set in her navel beneath the folds of her dress. He felt, too, the blood thicken immediately in his temples and surge in his groin. Val Mala saw his breathing quicken and abruptly pushed his hand away. "Your King, to whom you will kneel," she said, smiling contemptuously at how she and the star had moved him. "And now you have my leave to go. The Queen-widow, I believe, can give such an order to a mere prince of Alisaar."

Orhn stiffened, his mouth set. He bowed as rigidly as an automaton and strode out. The great cibba-wood door crashed behind him.

Val Mala glanced at Amnorh standing in the shadows.

"So much for the upstart."

"Indeed, my goddess. So much."

"I'm not certain what you mean, Amnorh. Possibly you should be thankful," but she laughed and pulled the wig from her head. Her hair flowed black over her shoulders. "And has a physician examined the girl?"

"As soon as she reaches the Palace of Peace."

"And Rehdon," she said— "and Rehdon. When did he die?"

"A little before sunrise, I would judge. The girl was with him."

"Foolish Rehdon, to need women so greatly and have such fear of them. Always fear. Even in lust, fear. An inadequate, hollow King."

"He no longer troubles you."

"No." She bent close and her astonishingly white hand gripped his shoulder. "How?"

"I gave it to him in the bitter wine they brew in the Lowlands," he said evenly. "The Red Moon was in his body. He didn't realize what he was drinking."

"I wanted him to know. I wish I could have seen him drink it and die."

"Impracticable, my Queen."

"And is Koramvis payment enough for you?" she hissed.

"In excess of what I ask," he murmured, and reached out to caress her body already moving against his in awakening desire.

A man in a black robe hurried out from under the wide portico of the Palace of Peace. Behind him, high up in one of the bowl-topped towers, the room from which he had just come burned with a yellow light. Dusk was well advanced over the silent gardens.

He passed two sentries, whose eyes squinted after him when he had gone by.

In the shadow of the broad gate a strong hand came from the dark to seize his arm.

"What do you want with me?"

"News of the Lowland temple girl."

"On whose authority do you ask me that?"

"The Lord Amnorh's."

The physician hesitated. At last he said: "It's too early to judge her condition with certainty."

The voice in the dark was insistent.

"Come now, physician. You think your own thoughts."

"Then . . . I think she has conceived."

The hand let go of his arm and someone moved soundlessly away. The physician shook himself as if to be rid of a shiver, and turned toward the sweep of the city, where lamps were lighting like stars.

Night flooded Koramvis, her bright palaces and narrow murderous ways, night and the star throbbed and faded and sank before the scarlet eruption that was dawn. Thereafter other nights and other dawns followed.

Somewhere a stringed bell began to rasp and toll.

Similar bells echoed it.

As the disc of this new sun steered above the horizon, gouts of smoke burst from the black temple of the Storm gods and drifted in gauzes over the river Okris. This red, scalding day would see a king finally carried to his tomb.

The sky cooled to darkest indigo.

From the Storm Palace, the temples, the Academy of Arms, moved black and glittering worm trails, converging and uniting on a white road flanked by gigantic crested dragons of obsidian—the Avenue of Rarnammon.

The High King is dead, the sun is eclipsed, the moon falls, the earth quakes.

A hundred priestesses were the prologue, wailing the mourning chant; a cry from hell it seemed, it was so full of emptiness, despair, pain. Their robes the storm-red of dragon's blood, their eyes streaming tears from the citrus juice they had splashed into them, their bodies punctured and streaked with self-inflicted wounds. After them the priests, purple robes and a humming disquiet of gongs and mask faces caught in a congested rigor.

Rehdon's Dragon Guard carried in their midst the embalmed death. Among their black, clashing assemblage, framed by the dipped rust banners and the trailing tassels, rolled a gilt cage with a man sitting up in it. He wore full armor. The great spiked crest flamed on his head, the eyes stared straight in front of him. He might have lived, yet death breathed out from every pore of him, an odorless stink of corruption, and the black eyes refracted and flashed and blazed, being constructed now not of tissue but onyx and crystal. Behind him walked princes like serfs, a king or two and after these their women and their wives. And Rehdon's Queen in her black velvet and fantastic jewels, her skirt also trailing in the smoking dust. Her eyes were blank

as the gem eyes of her dead and hated husband. Her wish
had killed him, yet she must mourn him through the city
like a slave. She recalled the greetings of the Zakorian
princes—"Honor to the heir in your womb"—and fury
burned bitter as the dust on her tongue.

At the tail of the worm marched the endless ranks of
soldiery. Drums thundered across the streets and thunder
answered dully from the panting sky.

The crowds trembled, hearing this sullen roar of gods in
anger. Women fell to their knees weeping as Rehdon's
death cage passed them. Soon a shout rose, a shout to kill
the witch, the banalik of the Lowland-Accursed, the mur-
deress of the Storm Lord: Ashne'e.

The Hall of Kings stood on a terraced bank of the Okris,
and its entrance was a marble dragon's mouth.

Between those upstrained jaws the shimmering worm
ran, flaring now with torchlight. The sky had turned black,
and spears of pallid light flickered beyond the river; rain
began to fall in huge molten drops, and the river boiled.
Thunder cracked in fragments.

The priestesses raised their rain-and-tear-dashed faces,
quivering terror and exaltation.

In the shell of the sepulcher the torches quavered and
dug blue and red light from the rubies and sapphires of
rearing mausoleums, from the eyes of carved monsters and
hiddrax, and ran in silver pools between the limbs of metal
guardians.

A line of priests marked the way to the newest tomb. In
the breath of sweet-smoke and incense the body of Rehdon
was lifted from its cage and carried into its heart. Prayers
moaned among the sarcophagi and were lost.

Val Mala followed the kings and princes into the silent
place. Long ago she would have been walled in beside her
lord, his thing till eternity or decay, and a dry raw fear rose
in her throat as she thought of it.

He lay before her on his couch, on his back. Fear was

replaced by contempt and scorn as she recalled that never again would he lie thus in life before her. She reached to take his hand, to press her lips to it in a mockery of the traditional kiss of sorrow. And was turned to scarcely breathing stone.

There was a snake.

It stood straight upright on her husband's breast, wickedly thin, yellow gold, splattered with a coiling black design. Its tongue flickered like a black flame in and out of its mouth.

She could not draw back her hand. She could not call out.

She held out her hand for the snake to strike her with its needle teeth, and for the poison to fill her veins. Its head recoiled and she knew her last instant of life was on her.

Lightning. It seemed lightning had struck through the roof into the tomb. But it was the glare of torchlight on a sword, the sword, in fact, of Prince Orhn, which had moved a fraction more swiftly than the snake and struck off its head.

Val Mala pulled her hand back as if from a sucking, reluctant clay, and fainted.

The silence in the tomb broke into shouts and imprecations, communicated rapidly to the throng outside.

Orhn wiped the blood slime from his sword and resheathed it methodically.

"Find the master mason of this tomb. He has some questions to answer." As guards moved to oblige him, he motioned to Val Mala's women, then stepped over her body without attention and went out.

It was no comfort to Val Mala that she was not required to walk back across the storm-choked streets. She lay like the brief vision she had experienced of her own death, and after oblivion came pain and sickness and alarm: physicians scurried to her, there were a hundred remedies and prayers. But the feared miscarriage did not occur; she held to her child with a furious, frightened vigor, and after the panic was done more than one surgeon howled under the whips of her personal guard.

She lay in her darkened bedchamber beneath the glittering coverlet embroidered with marigold suns and ivory-silver moons, and her eyes scorched her own shallow brain with their hate. Never had she known such terror, few times would she know such terror again.

"Bring me Lomandra," she said.

Lomandra the Xarabian, her chief woman, came like an elegant and slender ghost into the shadowy room.

"I am here, lady," she said. "I rejoice at your safety."

"My safety. I almost lost the child, the King within me, Rehdon's seed. My only hope of honor—she wants to take it from me—she sent the snake to kill my son."

"Who, lady?"

"The whore Orhn brought here to spite me. The Lowlands worship the serpent, the anckira. That witch, that she-devil—I prayed she wouldn't live. I swear she shan't."

"Madam—"

"Quiet. This is all you must do. You must go to the Palace of Peace."

"Madam, I—"

"No. You'll do as I say. Remember, I trust you completely. You'll wait on the bitch, and then we shall see. Take this."

Lomandra stared at the Queen's extended hand and saw what Val Mala offered her—a ring of many precious stones, a beautiful and valuable ring.

Lomandra seemed to hesitate, and then, softly, she drew it off and placed it on her own finger.

"It becomes you," Val Mala murmured, and Lomandra was wedded to her scheming.

Outside the casements, thunders crashed and galloped across the city, the black animals of the storm which was to last three days.

After the long rain, morning heat fell more sweetly into the gardens of the Palace of Peace.

The eyes of the guard turned sideways. A woman was

coming up between the tall trees and the topiary, a woman with golden ornaments and wearing palace black. They knew her by sight: she was the Queen's chief lady, Lomandra the Xarabian. She walked past them, up the pale steps, under the portico.

Inside, a coolness in the corridors, and mosaic floors. In a room sat a girl with lank hanging hair that was the exact hue of the rarest amber. Her belly was already enlarged with child, but her body did not seem to have grown with it; rather, it appeared shrunken away, as if all her flesh, all her being had concentrated itself in this one area of new life, the rest of her merely a shell, a housing.

Lomandra halted. She stood quite still, she stood with all Val Mala's pride and contempt apparent in the lines of her, for she was at this time a total emulation of Val Mala.

"I am sent to you by my mistress, the Queen of the Am Dorthar and of all Vis, the Lord Rehdon's widow," she said coldly, stringing the titles like rare gems.

"For what purpose?"

Lomandra was startled by this directness, but only for an instant.

"To serve you. The Queen honors her husband's child."

Ashne'e turned and looked at her. She was a pathetic creature, Lomandra thought, with merciless distaste. Except, that was, for her eyes. They too were amber, and quite extraordinary. Lomandra found herself staring into them and looked quickly away, disproportionately unnerved.

"How long have you to wait for your labor?"

"It will not be long."

"Precisely how long? We understand the Lowland women carry their children for a shorter time than the Vis."

Ashne'e did not answer. Lomandra's hauteur crystalized into anger. She went forward and stood over the girl.

"I'll ask you again. How long before your child is born?"

Yes, the eyes were perfectly— Lomandra searched her mind for a suitable word and could not find one. Perhaps it was merely this alien racial coloring that made them seem so—*preternatural*. Small veins stretched across the white like paths into the golden circlet of the iris, the vortex of the pupils. The pupils expanded even as she gazed at them. They seemed to pull her down into a whirling lightless void. In the midst of the void Lomandra was assailed by a foreign emotion which was pure horror, pure dread and a misery beyond endurance.

She fell back gasping and caught at the chair to steady herself.

When next she looked down, the Lowland girl was sitting with her head bowed and her hair falling over her face.

Lomandra stared about her, confused. "I am ill," she thought.

"In five months I shall bear the child."

Lomandra recalled putting a question to the girl; this then must be the answer. She had asked about the birth. Her reason steadied suddenly about her; she was reassuringly calm, almost amused, at her brief hysterical disorientation. "I must be more careful of myself." It was the heat, or possibly . . . Lomandra smiled, remembering that tonight she would lie with Kren, Fourth Dragon Lord, Warden of the River Garrison, whose lovemaking always pleased her.

The girl Ashne'e had already dwindled, guttered like the flame of a candle.

Lomandra forgot at the Garrison high table, and later, when the night dripped redly black through the open windows and she lived through the world of a man's body under the auspices of the star. But when she slept, she lay with the great swelling of her own imminent labor before her, and felt the terrifying movement of foetal life within. Then there was a crowd screaming, and she stretched naked in an open place, pegged out under the cruel sky, and a blade was thrust through her, through her sex into her womb—the most ancient, unspeakable punishment of the Vis. She screamed, she heard the embryo scream. She saw her own corpse, and found it was not hers. It was the corpse of Ashne'e.

Kren woke her. She turned her face into his chest and wept. Lomandra had not wept since, long ago, little more than a child, she had left her own land for the crags of Dorthar. Now, rivers ran from her eyes, and afterward she trembled, fearing herself possessed.

At first she considered revealing to the Queen her fear, asking that some other woman be sent in her place to watch the Lowland witch, but when she attended Val Mala, bringing her the answer to her question, all hope of it left her. Since the serpent, Val Mala's beauty had been gradually demolished by the tyranny of her womb; her whims were peevish, and she was at her most temperamental and dangerous.

So Lomandra returned to the Palace of Peace and found only a thin and wasted girl chained to the parasite of creation.

A month passed. Lomandra dressed the girl in rare fabrics that hung like sacks on her body, and combed out her lifeless, fulvid hair, and observed her closely, never once looking into her eyes, which now, correspondingly, never turned to hers.

And Lomandra marveled. She came to know the fragile body intimately, yet, knowing this much, Lomandra felt she knew nothing; the soul within the body was dumb and locked away.

The physician, the black gown flapping round his thinness like rags on a skeleton, came and went. At the end of the month, Lomandra approached him in the twilit colonnade.

"How are things progressing, lord physician?"

"Well enough, though she doesn't, I think, seem well made to bear a child. Her hips are very narrow and the pelvis like a bird's."

Lomandra said then, as Val Mala had told her to: "It will happen soon?"

"Not for some months yet, lady."

"I would have expected sooner," Lomandra lied, the Queen's words. "Milk pap comes out of her breasts on occasion. She's complained of sharp pains in her lower back. Are these not signs?"

The physician appeared startled.

"I haven't noticed that. She's said nothing."

"Well, I'm a woman. She's peasant stock, unsophisticated, afraid perhaps to speak to a man of such things."

"It may be sooner, then."

He seemed troubled as he turned away and vanished between the pillars like a tattered shadow.

Lomandra, her hand already on the curtain, paused. She had guessed long since the Queen's intent; but it came to her now, for the first time, to recoil from what she had made herself accomplice to.

In the room, the girl sat before the oval mirror drawing a comb slowly through her listless hair. An inexplicable pity choked the Xarabian. She went forward, gently took the comb and continued its movement.

"Lomandra."

Lomandra was startled. This voice had never before spoken her name. It had a curious effect; for a moment the pale drained face in the mirror became the face of a queen who had bound her in service. Her eyes met Ashne'e's in the glass.

"Lomandra, I have no hate for you. Fear nothing."

The words fitted so perfectly with the overlaid image of royalty that Lomandra's jeweled hands shook and she let go of the comb.

"Xarabiss lies beside the Shadowless Plains, Lomandra. Though you are Vis, the blood of our peoples has mingled. Know me and yourself, Lomandra. You will be a friend to me."

The soul of the Xarabian screamed suddenly within her. Only fear of Val Mala kept her from crying aloud what she knew must happen.

The girl seemed to hear her thoughts, without surprise.

"Obey the Queen, Lomandra. You have no choice. When her work is done, then you will do mine."

The moon hung, a red fruit in the garden trees, as Amnorh passed the uncrossed spears of the guard with a noncommittal: "I am on the Queen's business." Inside he climbed the darkness of a tower and pulled back the curtain of Ashne'e's chamber. Only moonlight defined the room.

"I see you always as I see you now. Lying on a bed, Ashne'e."

Her eyes were shut, but she said: "What do you want from me?"

"You know quite well what I want."

He sat beside her and put his hand on her breast. It was obvious to him, even in the dark, that her beauty was both eradicated and unrecoverable, but it was not prettiness he desired.

"I want the tricks you taught Rehdon, the murdering tricks. You'll find me an apt pupil."

"There is a child in me," she enunciated clearly, "the Storm Lord's heir."

"Yes. There's a child. I doubt it's Rehdon's. His seed wasn't overpotent."

Her eyes opened and fixed on him.

"Do you imagine," he said, "that you'd live now if I hadn't planted you with the excuse?"

"Why does it matter to you that I live?"

"Ah, a profound question, Ashne'e. I want your knowledge. Not only the love you teach between your white thighs, but those powers your people play at in their dunghills. The Speaking Mind: yes, I have mastered your terminology. Instruct me how to read men's thoughts. And Her Temple—where is that? Close?"

"There are many temples."

"No, not those. This is Anackire's place. I am aware the ruins lie in the hills of Dorthar."

"How do you know this?"

"I have had other Lowlanders at my beck from time to time. Some are looser-tongued than others. But none was an acolyte of the Lady of Snakes."

"Why do you seek this place?"

"To despoil it of its monetary and spiritual wealth. This no doubt distresses you, but I assure you, you've no choice. There are a million subtle ways in which I can distress you more violently should you refuse to assist me in everything I ask. It would be easy to instigate your death."

He needed no answer. She gave him none.

"Now I'll have what I came for."

She made no protest or denial, but reached for him and twined him at once in her limbs and hair, so that he also was reminded irresistibly of serpents in the moon-tinged blackness.

The Queen had summoned Lomandra to the palace; certain of Amnorh's men had relieved the scatter of external guard at the Palace of Peace. Amnorh took the Lowland girl to his chariot and drove with her by circuitous routes toward the skirts of the mountains.

A silver dawn was replaced by a pitiless lacquering of blue as the towered city fell behind. Birds loomed on broad wings, casting ominous shadows.

"Stop at that place," she said to him.

It was a cleft in rock; below, he saw the dragon's eye, the lake Ibron, a gleam of white water.

"You must leave the chariot."

He obeyed her, pausing only to tether the restless animals, and followed her along the bony spine of the hill.

And then she vanished.

"Ashne'e!" he shouted. A furious conviction took hold of him that she had duped him, escaped to some lair like a beast. And then he turned and saw her pallid shape, like a dim candle, burning in the rock beside him. It was a cave with an eye-of-a-needle opening. He slid through, and at once felt the dampness in the air, the chill and the encroaching, almost tangible dark.

"No trickery, Amnorh," she said, and there was a subtle difference in the way she spoke to him. "All that remains of the temple hill-gate is here."

"How can you be sure of the entrance?"

"I, like you, have been told of this place."

The back of the cave fell away in a corridor of blackness into which she turned and he followed. Once the blackness enclosed him he felt immediately reluctant to proceed. He struck sparks from a flint to tallow and held it burning in his hand, but the small light seemed only to emphasize the impenetrable shade.

The corridor ended in blank stone. Ashne'e reached out and her fingers ran in patterns on the stone. He tried to memorize what she did, but the shadows confused him. The stone shuddered; dislodged, an ancient dirt cascaded, and there was a groaning of something old disturbed. An opening appeared grudgingly, low and slit-thin.

She slipped through it, a fluttering pale ghost, and seemed to fall in slow motion into a bottomless pit. Amnorh maneuvered after her and found a stairway, a great jagged pile of steps pouring down into the lightlessness below, and sinking in the inky sea was Ashne'e, an impossible fish.

As he watched her, there came a stifling urge to turn back. This was her element, it absorbed her, incorporated her into its being. From the Vis it drew away, amused but intolerant of his greed for substantial things. Yet his lust for the riches of the temple hurled him forward.

He followed.

Curious sounds stole into his ears.

There seemed to be a tingling, the rippling of unimagined instruments; it was the ceaseless dripping of blue water onto silver stone. The shivering damp steamed and slithered on the steps. A vision infected Amnorh of a screaming man who was falling, falling, falling into the depthless dark.

But though trembling and cold, he reached the bottom, and found another arch-mouth. He went through it, after the girl, unprepared by anything any terrified bleeding serf had ever babbled to him. Out of the black sprang a flame, and horror. He felt his tongue thicken and his joints melt like wax.

Anackire.

She towered. She soared. Her flesh was a white mountain, her snake's tail a river of fire in spate.

No colossus of Rarnammon had ever been raised to such a size. Even the obsidian dragons could crouch like lizards by her scaled serpent's tail. And the tail was gold, all pure gold and immense violet gems, and above the coils of it a woman's white body, flat belly empty of a navel, gold minarets of nipples on the cupolas of the ice-white breasts. The eight white arms stretched in the traditional modes, such as he had seen on little carvings in the villages, casting ink-black chasms of shadow. The arm of deliverance and the arm of protection, of comfort and of blessing, and also those terrible arms of retribution, destruction, torment and the inexorable curse.

At last his eyes pulled themselves like tortured flies on to her face. The hair was all golden serpents, twisting, spitting to her shoulders. But the face itself was narrow, pale, long-lidded, set with a devouring yellow stare that might have been hewn from topaz. Or amber.

Ashne'e's face.

He turned, and saw they stood in the great pool of shade that spread from the anckira, and it occurred to him that the cave was full of light, though no source was apparent.

"Who made this?"

When the girl answered, he could not repress the shudder that took hold of him.

"It has been said, Amnorh, that this is Anackire herself."

And then sanity came back to him abruptly, for he saw the carved doorway set in the lowest coil of the tail.

"The hub of the mystery," he said, "the treasure hoard."

He went by the girl and strode to the door, ignoring what leaned above him. It had no secret machinery, giving at a thrust. Rusty metal swung inward, and he looked down into the eye of a great pool. Another deeper cave, filled by water, probably some entrance into the lake of Ibron. He stared about him, raising the burning tallow. There were no jewels, no religious amulets set with diamonds as the old stories had suggested; neither were there the great books of the lore and magic of the psyche and all the forces it might conduct and control. Only a cave smelling of water and filled with water. Anger lashed its thongs in his brain. So he had been tricked after all.

He turned and looked at Ashne'e.

"Where else do I search for what I want?"

"There is no other place."

"Did you know there'd be nothing here? That all your legends were merely the dung of time?"

His hand closed viciously on her arm. He saw the blue circlet his fingers made, but no sign in her face that he caused her pain.

"Perhaps I should abort my child from you and leave you to the gentle mercies of the lord Orhn."

Incredibly, a smile rose like dawn over her white face. He had never seen her smile, nor any woman smile in this fashion; it seemed to freeze his blood. His hand fell away from her.

"Do so, Amnorh. Otherwise he will be my curse on you."

A curious sensation gripped him, so that he felt he looked at her not with his open eyes but with a third eye set in the center of his forehead. And it was not her he saw. Standing where she stood was a young man, indistinct, spectral, yet Amnorh could make out that he had the bronze skin of the Vis and, at the same time, eyes and hair as pale as the Lowland wine with which he had poisoned Rehdon during the first nights of the Red Moon.

The apparition faded and Amnorh staggered back.

"There is nothing here for you," Ashne'e said.

She turned and began to cross the cavern toward the

archway and the steps, and he found that he must follow her
for he could no longer bear the singing silence and the presence of the creature in the cave.

He should then indeed have had her killed. She was no longer useful to him, a dangerous embarkation which had
failed. And yet his lusts still drew him to her swollen ugly
body, long after the star Zastis had paled and fallen from
the sky. There was, too, the remembrance of the child in her
which might so easily be his own. Would he, if Ashne'e were
allowed to bring it forth alive, stand to benefit from this
thread of his lineage woven into the royal line of kings?

The temple also haunted him.

Months after he had fled it, he had surveyed his terror
and gone back. By then, the High Council, which he held in
his palm, had voted him to the position of Warden of
Koramvis, that title which ultimately and tactfully would
ensure that he attained the regency. It had been the blood
price he had earned from Val Mala, and her network of
bribes and threats had not failed him. So long as he could
amuse her he would do well, and Orhn, now redundant in
the palace, deprived of honor and to a large extent of funds,
afforded Amnorh a faint, aesthetic pleasure. Yet it was a
season of waiting. And in the waiting, the urge came on him
to return to that place.

Night was drowning the sky when he took the chariot
and rode out of the River Gate, out of Koramvis, into the
barren hills. The mountains, still tipped with the last light,
were a monolithic desolation crowned with blood. A mad
wind, the first voice of the cold days coming, howled among
the rocks. When he came to the cleft, he left the chariot as
before, and, taking a light in one hand, he followed the path
the girl had shown him. He searched a long while. The
moon appeared overhead, the stars came out. The narrow
arch-mouth eluded him. Everything seemed to have become a fantasy, the hallucination of a dream. He recalled

the peculiar moment when he had seen a man stand where Ashne'e had stood.

He turned back to the chariot, but checked a few yards off. The team was trembling and sweating. Amnorh looked about him. It was possible the night had called some animal out of its lair to hunt.

Then he saw it. A huge shape, with a glistening along its back from the moon. It eased over the rail of the chariot and slid away. A rock snake most probably, absorbed now into some hole. Yet Amnorh, voyeur of a superstition, had caught the imprint of the superstition like a disease. Had She perhaps sent it, he wondered with inadequate cynicism, that woman underground?

3

L OMANDRA HEARD A VOICE calling her name.
　　She turned to look down the dim corridor, which was
empty, and the voice seemed to come again—inside her skull.

Ashne'e.

Lomandra hurried up the marble flight of the tower,
drew aside the curtain and stood staring. The girl lay white-
faced and expressionless, yet, through the thin shift, Lomandra saw the running stain of blood.

"Has it begun?" Lomandra cried hoarsely, sick with fear.
Then: "The child has come early." They were ritual words
merely. Lomandra knew well enough, and without surprise,
why the child came. She had mixed the Queen's medicine
with Ashne'e's food and drink for three months now. "The
bastard will tear its way from her body," Val Mala had murmured, "and be stillborn." "Will it kill her?" Lomandra had
whispered. And Val Mala had said, very gently: "I shall pray
that it does."

"Are you in pain?" Lomandra asked uselessly.

"Yes."

"How close together are the pains?"

"Quite close. It will be soon."

"Oh, gods," Lomandra cried out in her soul, "she will die,
she will die, in agony, in front of me. And this is my doing."

"Where is the physician?" Ashne'e asked tonelessly.

"At the Storm Palace. Val Mala summoned him a day ago."

"Then send for him."

Lomandra turned and almost ran from the room.

The Palace of Peace was in pale darkness, caught in the pulsing blue afterglow of dusk.

Lomandra leaned on the balustrade a moment, trembling. She made out a girl moving below, a brown moth fluttering from lamp to lamp, lighting each with the firefly taper in her hand. Lomandra shouted to her and the girl froze, wide-eyed, then fled away through the colonnade, calling.

Lomandra moved slowly up the stairs, hesitant, dreading to return to the room above. In the doorway she halted. It was very dark.

"I have sent for the physician," she said to the white blur on the bed.

"The waters have broken within me," Ashne'e said, "just now, while you were gone. How long before he comes?"

Lomandra shuddered. Words flooded from her mouth before she could control them.

"The Queen will delay him. She and I have poisoned you. You'll lose the child and die."

She could see nothing of the girl except the dim whiteness. She gave no sign of her pain or any fear; it was Lomandra who writhed in terror.

"I understand all this, Lomandra. You have done the Queen's work; now you must help me."

"I? I know nothing of midwifery."

"You shall learn."

"I can do nothing. I'd only harm you."

"I am already harmed. This is the son of the Storm Lord. He will be born alive."

Abruptly Ashne'e's body arched in a great paroxysm on the couch. She let out one single mindless animal cry, so solitary, unhuman and remote that Lomandra wondered wildly who it was that uttered it. And then, wanting only to run out of the room, she ran instead toward the girl.

"Take off your rings," Ashne'e gasped. Her mouth was a great tragic rigor of struggling breath, above which her eyes were blank and empty as glass.

"My—rings?"

"Take off your rings. You must thrust into me and seize the head of the child and draw him out."

"I can't," Lomandra moaned, but a desolate power converged and overwhelmed her. The rings fell glittering from her fingers, with them the jewels Val Mala had bought her with. She found she had bent to her task like a peasant woman, felt her whole stance and physical presence alter, now rough and capable and indifferent, while in the core of her wailed the trapped court woman in horrified loathing.

There was a welter of scalding blood. The girl did not shriek or spasm but held quite still, as if she felt nothing.

Into Lomandra's narrow hands emerged the brazen head, the wrinkled demon face of birth, and then the body on the dancing cord. In the uncertain dark, Lomandra saw the girl reach up and snatch at the cord, knot it, gnaw it through like a wolf bitch in the Plains.

The baby let out an immediate scream. It screamed as if at the unjust bestial world into which it had been dragged, half-embryo still, blind and unreasoning, aware, nevertheless, of all the agony which had been, the agony which was to come.

"It's male. A son," Lomandra said.

She shut her eyes and her tears fell on her bloody hands.

The physician hurried into the Palace of Peace in the first cool breath of day.

A woman, like a ghost in a dark robe, emerged from the colonnade. He had a moment's difficulty in recognizing her as the Queen's chief lady, Lomandra. Brows creased in anticipated distress (for some idiot of a servant girl had delayed the message, and he feared the worst), he asked: "Is the girl dead?"

"No."

"Then she's still in labor? Perhaps I may be able to save the child. Quickly—"

"The child was born some time ago, and lives."

The physician found that his hand had moved unbidden in a gesture of ancient religious significance as he stared incredulously in the Xarabian's face.

With a flick of her fingers, Val Mala dismissed her attendants, and Lomandra stood alone in the room with her.

The Queen was big with child, overblown and beautiless; the loss of her looks made her the more terrible. And Lomandra, who had felt herself too weary to be afraid, became afraid as she looked at her.

"You've come to tell me some news, Lomandra. What?"

Harshly the Xarabian said: "Both the child and the mother live."

Val Mala's bloated face squeezed together in an ecstasy of malice.

"You come to me and dare to tell me that they live. You dare to tell me that you were present and they lived—both of them. The witch that sent a snake to abort me and her offal. May the black hells of Aarl swallow you, you brainless bitch!"

Lomandra's heart raced desperately. She met Val Mala's blazing eyes as steadily as she was able.

"What would you have had me do, madam?"

"Do! In the name of Dorthar's gods, are you a fool? Listen to me, Lomandra, and listen carefully. You will return to the Palace of Peace and wait until the physician leaves her. Oh, don't tremble, you can dismiss the whore from your mind, I'll deal with her. Merely attend the child's cot and see to it that it smothers in its pillows. It should give you little trouble."

Lomandra stared at her, the blood draining from her face.

"I begin to wonder if I can trust you, Lomandra. In that case, I shall require proof of what you've done." The Queen settled back into her chair and her face took on a look of impenetrability. In that moment Lomandra despaired, for she felt she was no longer communing with anything human or rational, but rather with some she-devil from the pit.

"Bring me," Val Mala said, "the smallest finger of the child's left hand. I see you will like this task even less than the first. Consider it the punishment for hesitation. You understand the alternatives, I think. Disobey me and you'll live the rest of your life with every manner of scar on your body that my whip master can devise. Go now. Get it done."

Lomandra turned and went out, dragging herself like an old woman. She scarcely knew where she was going. With dull surprise she reached the curtain of Ashne'e's room and could not remember how she had come there.

The child lay sleeping in its cot beside the bed; the mother too appeared asleep, and the physician had taken his leave. Lomandra went to the cot, stood gazing down with burning, half-sightless eyes. Her hand went out and touched the pillow's edge. Easy, it would be so easy. The pillow slid half an inch from below the head of the unconscious child.

"Lomandra."

Lomandra turned swiftly, and the girl's eyes were open and full on hers.

"What are you doing, Lomandra?"

The Xarabian felt the impossible compulsion grasp her.

"The Queen. The Queen has instructed me to smother your son. As proof that I've carried out her wishes she desires the little finger of the baby's left hand."

"Give me the child," Ashne'e said. "On that table the physician has left a sleeping draft in a black vial. Bring me that also."

Lomandra, moving in a dull and soulless incomprehension, did as she was told. Ashne'e took her baby in the crook of her arm, bared her breast, and smeared there a little of the dark liquid before giving the child suck.

"Now," she said, "fetch me a knife."

Never in all her life had Lomandra witnessed such an adamantine ruthlessness. Beside this, Val Mala's malice became a scattering of dust.

It seemed to the Xarabian that she moved like a doll to do what Ashne'e directed, as though some puppet-master brought about all her actions by the twitching of silver strings.

A man in the Queen's livery bowed low before the Queen.

"Madam, the Lady Lomandra begs to present you with this token."

"Indeed? What a pretty box. Elyrian enamelwork, I think."

The Queen eased up the lid of the box a little way and gazed inside. Not a muscle moved. Only the sight of her personal blood distressed her. She had that true stamp of Vis royalty which made her consider all others, particularly those born from the lower echelons of the people, to be progressively more and more subhuman. She shut the lid with a snap.

"You may tell Lomandra that her gift delights me. I shall remember her kind thought."

Val Mala rose and went into the privacy of an inner room, where she tipped something from the box into an incense brazier.

Moments later her women were brought running by a sharp cry. The Queen's labor had come upon her, somewhat prematurely.

Five physicians and a flock of midwives were summoned.

The birth was uncomplicated, but Val Mala forgot she was a Queen and screamed like a street whore, cursing them, and complaining to the gods that this affliction was not to be endured. At last a drug was administered, and the child born as its mother lay insensible.

White birds were slaughtered on temple altars, offering-smoke lay like river mist over the Okris, stringed bells rang, blue signals shot from the city's watchtowers.

The Queen woke.

Her first thought was of her own body, free now from its enslaving ugliness, the tyrant plucked out. Second, she thought of the King, the man she had created and would eventually rule as he sat on the throne of his hated forerunner, Rehdon.

Several women stood beyond the bed; low evening light caught ornaments glistening like rain and showed, too, a certain unease on the dark faces.

"Where is my child?" she asked them.

Nervously they glared into each other's eyes.

A fat midwife approached the bed.

"Majesty, you have a son."

"I know." Val Mala became impatient. "Let me see him. At once."

The woman backed away, was replaced by a man in surgeon's robes who leant over her and breathed: "It might be best, gracious madam, if you were to recover a little of your strength before we bring the baby to you."

"I will see him now. *Now,* fool, do you hear?"

The man bowed low, gestured and a girl came from the end of the chamber carrying the white bundle of the infant in her hands.

Val Mala stared about her from her cushions.

"Is the child dead?" The sudden question sent a pang of terror through her. This was her only key to Dorthar and the power of Dorthar; if this were a stillbirth—Oh gods, what would she do? She snatched the baby in its dragon-embroidered mantle, and it was warm and feebly moving, though it gave no cries. She unwound the cloth. Why did the thing not cry? Was this unhealthy? No, now it sat naked in her hands she saw that it was perfect. And yet, what was—?

Val Mala screamed. The discarded baby fell tumbling down the bed, the midwife and the girl rushing to catch it up.

A monster, she had birthed a monster. Waves of insane rage and fear pounded and smashed in her body like a boiling sea.

*   *   *

A pale bird, sacrificed on the altar of Amnorh's palace, would not die. It screamed and fluttered, its breast sliced open, until all the birds in the cages of the aviary court were shrieking and dashing themselves against the bars. It appeared the gods were loath to accept the offering.

At noon a flight of white pigeons, winging up past the windows of the Storm Palace, redrew the incident clearly and frightfully in his mind. An omen. Yet what place had omens in the Warden's scheme of things?

Val Mala came into the room a moment later.

Her beauty was restored. It had taken her one month and the arts of a hundred women and slaves, masseurs from Zakoris, beauticians from Xarabiss and Karmiss and an astrologer-witch out of the Elyrian lands. She wore a gown of amethyst velvet, a girdle of white gold, and jewels scorched in her hair and on her hands.

"My greetings, Lord Warden."

"I have been in darkness without the lamp of your loveliness," he said.

"Pretty words, Amnorh. Did you buy them from a minstrel?"

Amnorh stiffened. He felt a sudden obtrusive coldness in his loins and around his heart. She had changed toward him, then. He must tread softly now, very softly. He thought of certain rumors he had heard concerning the birth of the prince. Certain rumors, too, that certain people present at the birth were strangely no longer seen about.

"I seek your counsel, Lord Warden. Your advice on a delicate matter."

"I am your servant, madam, as you know."

"Do I, Amnorh? Well."

A low white shadow drifted through the open doorway. The kalinx had followed her in. The sense of cold griped in Amnorh's vitals as if this creature were the presage of some disaster. It rubbed its face against her foot and sank down beside her, and she, seating herself in a low chair, began to caress its head. Her familiar.

"I am troubled," she said, "deeply troubled. I've received curious reports regarding the Lowland girl. No one has seen her baby for many days, and she will say nothing. I think she's killed the child and hidden the body."

His narrow eyes studied her expressionlessly.

"And why, my peerless Queen, should she do that?"

"I'm told she suffered unduly at the birth. Perhaps she's deranged."

Amnorh gambled.

"Perhaps there's a beautiful woman who hates her." And saw at once that he had lost a good deal on this one cast. She stared at him with her black-as-venom eyes and said without inflection: "Never be too sure of me."

"Madam, I speak only as your servant—one who would guard you whenever possible."

"Really? You'd guard me, would you? Haven't you known how this Lowland witch has practiced against me with all manner of diabolical magics and foulnesses?"

"Radiant Queen—"

"She is a sorceress and shall be punished as such," Val Mala cried out in sudden fury, and the kalinx lifted its icy head and snarled.

Mastering himself, Amnorh tried a new tack with her.

"What you do is dangerous," he said. "All high positions make enemies. Beware of those who will seize any opportunity to destroy you."

"Who?" she said, almost in a caressive tone. "Tell me."

"You yourself should be aware—"

"I am aware of more than you think, Amnorh. And why is it that you want the Lowland bitch to live? Was the body of the Queen not enough for you?"

"The nucleus of her spite," he thought, "merely jealousy? But such dangerous jealousy."

"There's a reason why the girl should be spared. She has knowledge of peculiar powers. They would ensure you complete and unassailable rule. The throne of Dorthar would be safe for you and for your son."

"I don't need your safety," she said.

Silk rustled in the doorway.

"Majesty, the Lord Orhn still waits on you in the antechamber," a woman said.

"You may tell him I shan't be long."

Amnorh held his breath, weighing the feel of a balance in his mind. Val Mala rose.

"Go now," she said, and she smiled at him, "go and enjoy your skinny little Lowland whore while you are able."

"You misjudge me, madam."

"I think not. I've heard you've often been a midnight visitor at the Palace of Peace."

The coldness filled his mouth, and he shivered. Flinging the last dice, knowing already everything was lost, in a measured voice he said: "You forget the service I did you, Val Mala, in the Shadowless Plains."

"Oh, but I do not."

His tongue grew large in his mouth as it had when he looked at the white and golden nightmare creature in the cave. He bowed, turned silently and left her, knowing very well what she had promised him. In the anteroom he passed the tall figure of the Prince Orhn Am Alisaar, but did not see it.

Orhn, however, marked the Warden's going and waited no longer.

He came into the room, and the kalinx lifted its head, lifted its lip and bared wicked ivory at him.

"Keep your place, you filthy abomination," he said to it, and the kalinx sank, tail twitching, eyes a livid blue.

Val Mala turned.

"I didn't give you leave to enter."

"We'll dispense with this playacting, I think, madam. I have entered and am here, with your leave or without it."

"I'd heard, Orhn, that we were at last to be blessed with your departure."

He grinned unexpectedly, but it was a wolfish, menacing grin.

"I'll *depart,* madam, all in good time. But I seem to remember, madam, I did you a kindness which hasn't been repaid."

"Ah, yes. The prince rescued me from a serpent. What do you want, then? The usual mercenary's fee?"

"What I have in mind I don't imagine you spend on hired soldiers."

Val Mala's eyes widened. She took a step back, and he several steps forward. He reached out his large hands and gripped her velvet arms.

"Before I leave, I've promised myself something. And I calculate you know precisely what."

"Your insolence is disgusting."

"I always appear to disgust you, but you graciously granted me this audience. And so beautiful and elegantly dressed you are for it. Or do I mistake? Did you pretty yourself for Amnorh instead?"

"Let me go."

He pulled her against him and thrust one hand inside the neck of her gown, his fingers closing like five claws of hot metal on her right breast. She reached up and raked the point of a ring down his cheek. He came away from her in a second, but caught her wrists in his hand and struck her across the face without hesitation. The blow chopped her to one side, and only the grasp on her wrists kept her from falling. A weal of dark blood appeared like a brand on her cheek.

"Hell take you for that!" she screamed.

He swung her up struggling.

"What dulcet tones my lady has," he said, and he was very jovial. He carried her across the floor, and she shouted at him and fought against him all the way. He kept her hands tight and a distance from his eyes. Her spite was entirely impotent.

A brief colonnade led to the door of her bedchamber. He thrust the door open and then shut, and dropped her down onto the coverlet, where the embroidery of suns and moons flared up shocked eyes at him.

"Do this to me and I'll kill you," she hissed.

"Try by all means. I've slain men in single combat sixty times, each one fully armed and skilled in weaponry. Don't think you could do better."

He bent over her and began to unlace her bodice but she scratched at him. He immediately struck her hands away and effortlessly ripped the material open and the lacy undergarment with it. The false paleness of her unguent faded into copper on her breasts. He slid both hands to cover the erect red buds at their centers and felt them harden, like warm stones, against his palms.

"Now," he said, "this isn't Zastis, madam. You've no excuse for that. And I am so disgusting to you. Let me disgust you a little further."

He pushed aside the heavy folds of her skirt.

When he entered her she made a sound in her throat far from anger, and her arms came clinging to his back, but he pushed her away and held her still, totally passive under his riding. Not a long but a hard ride. At her abandoned cries of ecstasy he slipped the tether and fell plunging in blind convulsions of pleasure through the golden thunder of her body.

"You hurt me," she murmured. Her soft hand slid over him, finding out his hard muscular body, its plains and crevices, the core of his loins, which stirred faintly, even now, beneath her touch. "You're well endowed for this work."

"And you are a whore," he remarked.

She only laughed, and soon he pushed her back and took her again.

The blue dust of night settled in the room.

Orhn left the bed and stood against the open windows, a towering male symmetry composed of darkness. Lifted on one elbow, Val Mala considered him.

"You abuse me, then leave me, Orhn. To Alisaar?"

He did not reply.

"Do me a service before you go," she said, and caught

the glint of his eyes turning to her. "Help me rid myself of the Lord Warden of Koramvis." Unable to see his mouth, she surmised he might be smiling. "And also of the she-witch who practices sorcery against me."

He came back to the bed and sat beside her, and now she saw the smile. Still he said nothing.

"Orhn, might it be possible that the girl's baby wasn't Rehdon's seed ... perhaps some priest, before he used her—"

He stretched out and cupped her breasts.

"Val Mala, when we found Rehdon dead, the Lowland girl sent herself into a kind of trance, which Amnorh claimed himself able to revive her from. He was alone with her in his tent for some time."

The breath hissed between her teeth.

"So."

"So. I've answered both your questions, I think. And the child which troubles you so greatly is no more than rotten fruit."

"Amnorh shall be killed."

Orhn shrugged. She caught the lobe of his ear between her teeth and bit it viciously. He pushed her away with an amused curse.

"Do as you like, gadfly. You've only the gods to answer to."

"And you. Is it the regency you want, or me?"

"The regency. You, sweetheart, are the worthless dross that comes with it."

White stars clustered in the sky, swung in the stained glass of the river, on the brink of which black hovels craned up to the moon. Some way off, on the opposite bank, the glow of a temple's lights spilled down narrow steps into the water.

Lomandra moved along avenues of old cobbles, between the rat-infested remains of walls. Often she glanced nervously from side to side. Earlier a man had come out at her from a rotten doorway, thinking probably that she was a prostitute searching for custom.

"Let me by. I am summoned to the Garrison," she had managed to choke out, and this invocation of the name of law deterred him.

She came to the place this time on foot, the hem of her cloak wet with mud from the filthy gutters, she, who had always in the past ridden here in curtained litters. It was a large formless building, white walls soiled with dirt and night. The guard at the gate blocked her path with a slanted spear.

"What's your business?"

Lomandra had no presence of mind left to her at this moment.

"I am here to see the Dragon Lord, Kren."

"Oh, are you, miss? Well, the dragon is busy, too busy to be interested in your sort."

She felt her body wilting with weak hopelessness, but another man spoke from the dark beyond the gate.

"You, sentry. Let the lady through."

The guard swung round, saluted, moved aside. Lomandra came into the dingy, damp court. She could not see the man's face, but his voice had seemed familiar. He took her arm gently.

"The Lady Lomandra—am I correct?"

He led her beneath the pulsing splutter of a grease torch, and, looking up, she was able to identify him. His name was Liun, a man of Karmiss, one of Kren's captains.

"Yes, I see you are." His mouth took on a scornful slant. "You must have missed him unbearably to come here alone. These streets are no place for a court woman, particularly after dark."

"I—have to see him. . . ." She halted, uncertain as to what he would do, how much credence he would give her. If he judged her a pestering fool, no doubt he would do his best to keep between her and the Dragon Lord. But there was an unexpected warmth in his tone when he spoke again.

"If you'll forgive me, you seem unwell. Come inside. The place is grim enough, but at least impervious to river damp."

They passed between a row of sentries at perfect attention and in through the studded cibba-wood doors. Too casually he said to her: "Has he given you a child?"

"No," she said. Her eyes watered with tiredness. "No. And yet," she thought, "it's because of a child that I've come." Ashne'e's child, taken in the concealing dark from the palace, now hidden away in one of the dank houses by the river and fed on pulps. The old woman who rented out the slum had scarcely glanced at the baby's tiny damaged paw, but no doubt she was inured to the injured brats and frenzied mothers among the poor. Lomandra struggled against a sudden dreadful urge to weep. She seemed to have lived a year without sleep. Why she had done as the Lowlander told her she hardly knew, and did not permit herself to seek for an answer, afraid of what it might be.

She felt the young man's grasp on her arm increase.

"You aren't well. Sit here, and I'll go for Kren myself."

And she was seated in a small lamplit room, where a fire smoked dully in the grate.

It seemed a long time before he came, a tall broad-shouldered man, dressed informally in brown leather and the dark red cloak of the Garrison. He had a tough intelligent face, scarred, like his body, in his earliest youth from border fights in the Thaddric mountains and sea skirmishes with Zakorian pirates. But the face was dominated by a pair of observant and remarkably steady eyes. His smile was concerned and friendly but no more, for there had never been sentiment between them; only in a bed had they been lovers.

"How can I be of service, Lomandra?"

She opened her mouth but could seem to get no words out. In the pause, he saw the oldness in her face. Her eyes were sleepless and unpainted, her beautiful hair hung lankly on her shoulders.

"Liun seems to think you have my child."

"No. Besides, it would have made no difference to us."

Again silence choked her. He went to a table and poured

wine into two cups. She took the goblet, and when she had swallowed some of the drink, words came into her mouth.

"I need your help. I must leave Koramvis. If I remain, it's likely the Queen will kill me."

He looked at her for a while, then drank.

"I've told you of the Lowland girl Ashne'e."

"The enchantress who poisons your sleep with bad dreams," he said quietly.

"Yes, perhaps. . . . Her child was born a month ago."

"I'd heard of it."

"Val Mala had medicines mixed with the girl's food—she hoped the child would be stillborn. When it lived, she ordered me to kill it—smother it. She wanted the small finger of the left hand given her as a token of its death."

Kren's face darkened. He drained the cup and dashed the dregs into the fire.

"The bitch is insane. Does she think you're her butcher?"

"I didn't do it, Kren. Ashne'e—cut the finger away—I—have never seen such a savage purpose. I sent Val Mala what she asked. But the child is still alive."

Her whole body drooped on the narrow soldier's couch. He set down his cup and sat beside her, putting a gentle arm about her.

"And you have this child hidden somewhere."

She was very glad of his perception.

"Yes."

"You're a brave woman to go against Val Mala."

"No. I'm afraid to my very soul. But Ashne'e—she asked that I take the baby out of Koramvis, leave it in some Lowland holding on the Plains. The Queen will murder her as soon as she has the means, and the child, too, if she can find it."

"Then she must be positive it's Rehdon's work."

"It has the skin of a Vis," Lomandra said softly, "but its eyes—are her eyes."

"I'll help you get safely to the Plains," he said. "A traveling chariot and two men—more would arouse suspicion. I'll make certain you can trust them."

"Thank you, Kren," she whispered.

"And you," he said, "what of you, Lomandra?"

"I?" She looked at him distantly, finding she had not thought of herself, only of the child. "I suppose I shall return to Xarabiss. My family are dead, but I have jewels I can sell. Perhaps I'll marry into some noble house; I've been well-trained in aristocratic etiquette."

He touched her hair lightly, got to his feet once more and went to stand beside the smoking fire.

"I'll see to it that there's transport ready in the morning. Sleep here tonight. There are several private chambers you can choose from."

She saw that it was solicitude prompted him to make this offer that she sleep alone. Perhaps, besides, he had already made arrangements with a woman of the Garrison to share his bed. She felt too weary not to be glad, yet, at the same instant, vague regret, for she would not see him ever again.

4

THE CITY WAS ROUSED at midnight by an apocalyptic blaze of watch fires, running torches and the clangor of bells. Men in the black and rust livery of the Storm Palace stood shouting in the public places of Koramvis, riders galloped through the avenues and alleyways, bawling their proclamation as if the end of the world had come.

It was to be a night of fire and terror.

Treachery. Blasphemy.

Amnorh, High Warden of Koramvis, Councilor of the dead Storm Lord, had the curse of the gods on his back. He had taken the Lowland witch, whose evil had first slain Rehdon, and used her as his harlot. His bastard, not the Storm Lord's heir, had thriven in her devil's body.

The work was done well. The absurd pride of the Dortharian rabble, who believed themselves, even in extremes of poverty and unprivilege, to be in some remote way fathered by gods, soared to fever pitch. In the streets they bawled for Ashne'e's death, for the spike to be driven into her womb, and howled too at the gates of Amnorh's palace, for they fancied themselves tricked and had been given the power of revenge.

A party of soldiers, the mob behind them, strode into the Palace of Peace, their mailed feet ringing in the corridors.

Two of them came to the room where the girl lay and entered a little uneasily. She was, after all, a sorceress; she might turn into an anckira when they touched her. It was said she had devoured her own child.

But she lay quite still. The torch glare seemed to shine right through her, as though she were made of alabaster.

She had not waited for them.

The soldiers carried out the corpse, nevertheless, and showed it to the people. A pyre was roughly but enthusiastically built in the Square of Doves. The populace dragged out willingly items of furniture and clothing to solidify its structure. Ashne'e's white body was carried by a grinning baker to the top and slung down naked on the heap. Torches were applied. A black column of smoke towered into the lightening sky.

The mob broke open wine shops and became drunk. When the charcoal struts collapsed, they ran again to Amnorh's palace and tossed blazing brands over the wall into the trickster's court.

"My lord," a man shouted, "the trees at the wall are on fire. The gate will go next. Once that's down the mob will surge through, and the house guard can never hold them."

"Is my chariot ready as I asked?"

"Yes, Lord Amnorh."

The servant hurried ahead of him into the courtyard. The dawn air was already thick with smoke and the charred smell of burnt wood. Outside he heard an unmistakable crowd noise.

Amnorh mounted the chariot alone and took up the reins of the skittish team. He felt a certain bleak satisfaction in himself that he could turn his back so completely and promptly upon the entire sum of his power and wealth and leave it to the flames and the greed of the Dortharian scum.

"Aiyah!" Amnorh cried to the team and drove them along an avenue of smoldering feather trees, straight toward the gate. His own guard scattered, slaves pulled the gate wide for him.

Torch flare and smoke and mass, and foul stink and an impression of a single creature with a thousand yelling mouths and clawing hands. He plunged into it, the chariot's bladed wheels spinning, and the foremost rank of the crush toppled and spread before him, screeching. It seemed for a moment the chariot would overturn or at least be halted by the mash of fallen human flesh, but the fleet, neurotic animals, blowing, and terrified by the fire, dashed on and pulled the car after them, while Amnorh slashed from side to side with his knife.

A man leaped in next to him, shouting obscenities, but Amnorh, with a swift half-turn, slit his vocal throat and thrust him out. A severed hand clung on the rail until the chariot's uneven progress shook it loose. Women wailed curses and agony.

A rush of sweet air, and the crowd was behind him. A few ran baying after him like dogs, but could not match his pace and presently fell back. The chariot was spattered with blood, and his hands also.

The white road spun beneath; gardens and buildings were flung away on the burning wind. He glanced back. A glare lit the dark half of the sky; flying sparks must have homed at last into his tasteful rooms.

The wheels rattled across the great south bridge, and the Okris shone below like clouded wine in the sun's first rays.

One of the black palace chariots was behind him.

The charioteer, a man in the Queen's livery, raised his hand and yelled for him to stop. Amnorh raked the backs of the team with his whip and saw flame strike under their hooves. From the mouth of a turning in front of him a second chariot leapt into his path.

"She has my measure," he thought in a moment of leaden anger, but he pulled the animals around and hurled to the right of the opposing vehicle. The wheel blades churned through their near axle; the car tilted and spilled its contents on the road. "But not quite, my lady," he thought, "not quite."

The city streaked behind, and the hills opened like honeycomb on either side. One black chariot was still at his back.

"I should have reckoned on the advent of this day, and planned for it," he reproached himself.

Between cleft rocks he saw the sudden pearl gleam of water: Ibron far below.

At once he visualized the cave. Could he but have found it now.

"What do I offer you, Anack, to persuade you to reveal your hidden ways to me?" his thoughts whispered with a bitter humor. "My Vis soul?"

There was a bend in the road. A great bird fled up before their coming, and the animals swerved madly at its passage. Rocks struck the wheels and flew off into air. Amnorh felt the chariot give a great lurch, then sky and earth were momentarily juxtaposed, after which there was only sky.

The black car careered to a halt. The two men jumped down and ran to the lip of the road, staring over at the mangled remains of the broken chariot and team caught on the teeth of the scarp some way below.

"Where's the Warden?" one asked the other.

"The lake. He'll die just the same."

"It's a better death than she would have allowed him."

The wind shrilled. The burning whip of the wind had beaten him semiconscious. He turned in mindless spinnings toward the great mirror which would swallow him.

At the last instant, a thought—death.

Amnorh struggled with his numb flesh, striving to arrange his body for that moment when it would cleave the water. He took huge gasping breaths at the air.

The impact was of a white hot furnace. His bones seemed to run like molten gold. Stifling ringers probed in every orifice. There was no sound.

Deep below the surface now, Amnorh turned more slowly, a foetus trapped in a womb of inky sapphire.

Death.

"I lie soft," he thought. "I am no longer a man but a piece of this water."

A pain flared in his chest. His lungs convulsed uselessly on nothing.

"Let the water in and die."

But he could not.

There were bubbles lisping upward through the dark; he felt dimly the pull of a new current and let it take him. He shut his eyes, lifting so gently. Presently raw light pierced his lids and stone thrust against his inert body. He floundered like a fish in a net, all instinct suddenly to achieve the light. His hands grasped the stone and air splashed on his face.

He lay by the brim of a great pool, breathing, spent, the terrible spasms of coughing and retching past, and his body a lifeless heaviness containing the pale flickers of his thoughts.

"There is a door. A rusty door. She is all about me. I am in Her entrails like Her egg, Her child. When I reach the door and go through it and crawl out into the cave, I shall be born of a goddess."

After a time he got to his feet and staggered to the stone wall of the pool, edging along it until he found the door. He pulled and the door gave, but he fell to his knees with the effort and crawled, as he had fantasized, out of the golden tail of Anackire.

He opened his eyes and saw the narrow pale mask of a giantess gazing down at him, framed by a gold seething of serpents. And he thought: "The face of my mother."

And grinned, thinking of the Iscaian slut who had conceived him in a wine shop under a minor Dortharian prince. Bastardy had been useful, as Amnorh had realized when he climbed the first rungs of the social ladder. She might so easily have brought forth from a respectable marriage to a hod carrier.

He got to his feet. His wet clothes clung unpleasantly, for it was chill in the cave.

"So you saw fit to save me, Anack," he called out at the statue, "and now I'm your firstborn. My humble thanks."

Her eyes bored into him.

"What gifts will you give me, Mother, now that I'm cast penniless on the cruel world?"

He went forward and laid his hands on her fiery tail— a million scales, each a plate of hammered gold.

Experimentally he grasped one of the plates and wrenched at it. How long ago had she been made? Too long—she was in sad need of repair. The plate came away in his hands, and Amnorh let out a bark of wild derisive mirth. Again and again he wrenched. A rain of gold fell round him, and he plucked violet jewels like grapes from a vine.

When he had stripped her as high as he could reach, he made a bundle of his cloak and slung the riches into it.

"So I despoiled you after all, Mother mine. Unwise to take such a thief to your bosom."

He fancied impotent rage on the white face, and at the arch he turned and saluted her, crazy from the water and the falling gold.

In the dark he moved with inadequate care. The bundle bumped and clanked. This time he had no flint and no guide. He did not reach the steps.

At last it grew apparent to him that he had taken a wrong turning somewhere in the blackness.

He stared about him but could make out almost nothing. He became aware in that moment of the far-off, high-pitched singing note that he had heard before. And, as he moved on in his blind search, the sound seemed to grow fuller, as though several more voices had joined the first.

"Anackire weeping," Amnorh mocked aloud.

But sweat broke on his forehead and his hands. He moved more quickly.

The stairway was lost to him for sure. What then? Retrace his steps? Somehow the thought of turning back toward the cave repelled him. And the sound, the sound was louder. It penetrated his skull like a knife.

Amnorh turned to look behind him.

There was a man in the passage, distinctly visible against the dark. A man with black-bronze skin and yet pale hair and eyes—even as Amnorh stared the hair and eyes spread and merged like flames; the whole face melted and became Ashne'e's face. The mouth opened, and out of its serene pallor burst the singing scream of the cave.

His own cry mingled. He ran. The bundle in his hands doubled, trebled its weight—he almost threw it down and left it there, but somehow could not despite himself. The walls bruised him, and colored sparks exploded before his eyes.

Suddenly daylight.

He flung himself into it, blind and moaning, and the ground left his feet and he fell.

"Wake up," said an insistent female voice, as it seemed mere seconds later.

Amnorh turned his head and saw a girl kneeling beside him. She had a brown peasant face and too-big, simple eyes.

"I thought you were a devil out of the hill," she said conversationally. "I went in there once, and there was a light, and I ran away." She ogled him. "But you're only a man."

He sat up. The hot sun had already dried his garments. How long had he lain here with this laborer's bitch watching him? He glanced apprehensively at the bundle of his cloak, but it seemed undisturbed.

"Are you going to Thaddra, across the mountains?"

"Yes," he said shortly.

"There'll be men going there over the pass. Our farm's just down the slope. Will you wait there for them?"

Amnorh looked at her. It would be reasonable to travel in company. He had no provisions, and an early snow might soon lock the mountains in walls of ice. There were also bandits on the mountain shelves.

The farm was little better than a hovel. A bony cow picked at yellow grass outside, and there was an old man minus eyes sitting like a dried-out insect against the wall.

Amnorh waited in the shade of the house while the girl went about her tasks. The traders did not come. He wondered if she had dreamed them up to keep him here for some villainous purpose, but she seemed too stupid for that. He tried to question the old man, but he was apparently deaf as well as eyeless.

In the cool of evening the girl gave him bread and cheese and watered-down milk. When he had finished, she sat close to him and put her hand on his thigh.

"I'll be friendly with you, if you like. I'll do whatever you want if you give me something."

So, she was whoring to supplement the leanness of the living. He gripped her shoulder roughly.

"Were you lying to me about the travelers?"

"No—no—tomorrow they'll come."

"You'd better be speaking the truth."

He pushed her away and lay down to sleep, the bundle an awkward pillow under his head.

He slept long and deeply, weary to his bones. Near dawn there was a dream.

The Lady of Snakes came out of the hill and slithered down the slope into the hut. She wrapped him in her coils and in her arms and in her spitting glinting snake-hair, and he played with her the games of lust which Ashne'e had taught him.

A fierce needle of sunlight burned on his eyes and woke him; the travelers had come.

"There was rioting and a fire in the city," one of the men said to him.

Amnorh glanced back toward Koramvis, a toy of white towers between the jut and fall of the hills. He turned away, and for the first time an anguished frustration and a bitter despair ignited in his heart. The Lord Warden had indeed perished beneath Ibron.

"Everything is lost," he thought. "Only I remain. And I—I no longer exist."

The seated Garrison chariot rattled from the Plain Gate of Koramvis in the black hour before dawn. Amun, a charioteer who had once won races in the arenas of Zakoris, by-passed the ways of the riot, yet they heard the distant belling on the wind and smelled the smoke. Liun's face was set and unreadable, but he muttered: "On occasion a man wishes the gods had made him a rabbit or an ox—anything rather than a man."

Lomandra held the child close to her, but it made no sound. She felt some dim yet awful presence over the city. "This act will bring its own retribution," she thought. And she prayed the girl had been dead when the mob came for her, as Ashne'e had told her she would be.

They traveled across Dorthar, arid and golden in the last conflagration of the summer, across the broad river into Ommos, where perfumed pretty boys squealed at the chariot, and the Zarok statues now and then consumed in their furnaces the flesh of unwanted girl children. At a little eating house they saw a fire-dancer strip her flimsy garments from her body with a live brand.

"A symbol," Lomandra thought. "So it is with my life."

Yet, as they passed into Xarabiss, the tension and the sourness left her. She felt liberated, almost at peace. As so often before on the journey, she examined the child, and no longer observed it with fear. What would it become? she wondered. Most probably some peasant—hunter or farmer—sweating out its days, unaware of the turmoil and ancestry that had formed it. Or perhaps it would die young. Should she herself keep it, she asked herself now, rear it and give it whatever status and wealth she could acquire? She felt an immediate aversion to the plan. Despite the compassion she experienced, there was the imposition of another's will, a sort of geas laid on her. This baby was not Xarabic, nor hers. She had no place in her life, whatever that might be, for this curious and terrible stranger. And Ashne'e, it seemed, had known and approved that fact.

The first cold rain of the year came at sunset in Tyrai, about ten miles from the border.

She had fed the child with milk, while the storm beat like birds on the shutters and finally fell quiet. Red slanting strokes of the tumbling sun pierced afterward into the room. A knock came on the door, and when she opened it, Liun stood in the doorway. It was the first time either of the men had come to find her after the day's traveling. She thought something must have happened and alarm clutched at her pulses.

"Is anything wrong?"

"No, nothing at all. I'm sorry if I made you think so."

He came into the room with a directness that was at the same time somehow diffident, and crossed to the cot as though this were an excuse for entering.

"A quiet child, thank the gods."

"Yes, he has always been quiet. As she was."

"And you," he said, exactly as Kren had said it, "what of you?"

"I shall make a home in my own land when I've done what she asked me."

"Xarabiss. Yes. You should never have left it."

"Perhaps not."

He opened a shutter on the cool red air. Awkwardly he said: "Did you wonder why I was the second man in the chariot?"

"Kren promised me an escort I could trust."

"I asked to accompany you."

She looked at him, surprised.

"Why should you do that?"

"I suppose I'd be a fool to suppose you'd understand such a thing. I never dared to speak to you in Koramvis."

"Speak of what?"

He flushed slightly and smiled without humor, still not looking at her.

"That I desired the Queen's chief lady. What, after all, was the use? A mere captain existing on army pay."

A flood of quite unexpected warmth ran through her. Something she had never considered before, she found, had the power to lift her off her feet. She felt like a very young girl, a ghost of herself in Xarabiss. Her hands trembled and she let out an unconsidered sparkling laughter.

"But I have nothing now," she said.

He looked at her then, his face full of amazement.

"Kren would release me," he said breathlessly. "I have enough put by to get a villa-farm, to hire men; it could be a good living, here or in Karmiss. But such a life would be horrible to you."

"Dorthar was horrible to me and the things of Dorthar. Oh, yes, Liun, I could breathe in the life you offer me. And I can get money to help you."

They were both laughing, unreasonably, happily. He came to her and his eyes were very bright.

"Oh, what am I doing?" she asked herself, but nothing seemed to matter except this strong young man with his bright eyes and the sense of hope that clung about him. He was younger than she, but it was irrelevant suddenly. "You are not a thirteen-year-old virgin to tremble like this," she thought as a little clumsily, yet gently, he lifted the thick hair back from her cheek and kissed it. How could she have longed for this and not known it?

"Lomandra," he said, and kissed her mouth not clumsily at all.

The next day they passed through Xarar under a metallic sky. By afternoon the wind was full of dust.

"Storm coming," Amun said. He spoke little; when he did, it was generally about the weather, the state of the chariot or the animals.

"Do we call a halt, then?" Liun asked.

"There's a small town, outpost of Xarabiss, a few miles

west of the Dragon Gate. I reckon we can make that before
the worst of it breaks."

So they went on, and the two white pillars of the Gate
passed behind them, and the roll of the Plains spread out
their barren amber flanks under a purple canopy of cloud.

Presently it grew dark. There came a wind like a bolt of
black cloth, whipping and screaming across the slopes. Lomandra held the child close to shelter it as whirling grit
slashed their faces. They seemed to be driving straight into
the mouth of a ravening, spitting, roaring beast.

A pale blue flash hissed overhead. Instantaneously thunder pealed. The animals flung up their heads and pranced
with fear. She heard Amun curse them: "Damn half-bred
team to dance a pimp to his fancy boy's couch!"

Another lightning skewered toward the plains. The chariot jounced and rumbled, and the animals careered ahead
of it, their manes streaming back in black whips. Amun's
face was fixed with rage as he held to them; he had been
used to something better, his whole stance proclaimed, in
his racing days.

A copse of dark and ragged trees sprang suddenly up in
front of them on the livid skyline.

"Pull their heads round," Liun shouted.

"Do you think I'm asleep, you puppy?"

In that moment the world cracked open on a white and
blazing void.

Lomandra felt a great cold heat rush by her like the
breath from a demon's mouth. She lost all sense of place
and of self and seemed to be flying until a wedge of pain
slammed into her back.

She discovered herself lying on the ground among drifts
of dead leaves, the child at her breast. Her own body had
cushioned its fall, but its face had screwed into tears. A
white glare came and went on her eyes and then was blotted out as Liun bent over her.

"Are you hurt?"

She shook her head, giving herself no time to think

whether she was or not, and he half-lifted her to her feet.
She stared about her wildly.

"Lightning," Liun said brusquely. "It struck the trees and
the team. You and I were pitched clear, and the brat."

"And Amun?"

Liun's face was set.

"His gods were sleeping."

Lomandra looked away, unable to bear his stony grief. A
dreadful guilt came down on her like the weight of the icy
rain which was now pouring over them. She turned a little
and made out the shape of the chariot trapped in the black
and white flaring mosaic that was the burning trees.

"Don't look." He put a hand on her arm almost formally.
"We'll have to walk the rest of the way to the town."

One slope was very like another in the cloud-sealed darkness. Muddy banks ran up a little way, dripping with sparse
wet vegetation, though the rain had stopped. Liun had
taken the child from her, but she walked with that other
irrational weight fastened to her body.

It was her guilt perhaps which made her unnaturally
aware of menace in the gloom. For a long while she quivered with the knowledge and kept silent until at last the
sensation became unbearable and uncontainable.

"Liun," she said softly, "there is something behind us."

It surprised and strangely pained her when he said: "I
think so too. We've had company for about a mile."

He put his free arm about her and did not turn to look
back.

"What is it, Liun?"

"Who knows? Perhaps only a dust rat or two."

The undergrowth was thicker here, steaming with moisture. Through the narrow stems she caught an abrupt and
ghastly glimpse of light—a pair of incendiary eyes, first scarlet, then gold. He heard her gasp, but only glanced aside.
Casually he said to her: "Take the baby, Lomandra. And get
ready to run."

She took the bundle from him in blind obedience.

"Tell me why."

"Our admirers are dangerous."

"What—"

"Tirr," he said without expression.

She felt the blood abandon her heart and stood paralyzed.

"Then we're dead."

"Not inevitably. I can delay them and you can run for
your life. A hero's death. I never thought the gods had
marked me down for that."

"Liun—Liun—"

"No, my darling Lomandra. They haven't left us the
time."

He pushed her. There was the sound of tearing foliage
above, and a shape arrowing down. An awful screeching cry
burst from the dark and stench filled her nostrils. She saw
the bald flanks, the jutting face and the envenomed claws. A
second cry sounded, and a third. Two others anxious not to
miss their kill. And—though she knew he must die, this man
who had thrown away survival for her, who she might so
easily have come to love—she fled.

She ran on in nightmare, feeling death hanging on her
heels, and far off, as she ran, she heard a no-longer recogniz-
able voice calling out in agony.

At last she could run no more.

She fell and lay still and waited for a smell of corruption
and a rending which did not come. The child whimpered at
her breast, demanding milk she could not give.

There was an itching discomfort in her shoulder. Gradually, as she lay there, a dull and numbing ache began to
spread across her back and upper arms. A little blood ran
down her side. She did not remember a paw striking at her
or the penetration of the single claw, but she saw now that
her flight had been entirely useless after all.

The Xarabian got to her feet, the child locked in her
freezing arms, a cradle of already annihilated flesh.

"You," she thought, "you."

But she did not particularly hate the child.

"Where shall I die? Which is the spot where I shall fall down and you at my breasts? And how long will you outlive me in these foul and empty Plains?" And again she thought: "It will die young." And began to walk toward the moonless horizon.

BOOK TWO

Ruins and Bright Towers

ALL HEAT WAS DRAINING from the year and the sky was like unpolished brass as the ten or so villagers followed Eraz to the temple. She lay on her death bier, very white and still, conforming like any corpse to the pattern expected of it, but her hair was still tawny for she was not beyond her middle years.

A hunter held up the front of the bier. Like all the rest but one, he was quite without expression. No Lowlander reckoned on longevity, for life was hard and mostly fruitless. But the young man who supported the lower poles of the stretcher was staring at the dead face, his own working with the effort not to weep.

It was the bits of amber in her ears. He had seen them gleam so often in and out of her hair; it was perhaps his earliest childhood memory. Now they moved him unbearably, and he did not want to shed tears in the midst of these people. They seldom if ever wept for their dead—he had never seen it. They showed no emotion: no pain, no sorrow and no joy. They. He tasted an old bitterness in his mouth, for though he was in part one of their own, yet he was a stranger and an alien. She had understood, Eraz, his foster mother, and she had given him what demonstrative love she could and such intimations of a locked-up sweetness.

They came into the grove of red trees and up to the black oblong of the temple door. Two priests emerged. They moved like lightless ghosts, one to either end of the bier, and took the poles from the hands of the hunter and the young man. Without a ritual word the priests bore Eraz into the gloom. The villagers stood immobile for a moment, then turned and slowly dispersed. Only the hunter, passing him, murmured: "She is with Her now, Raldnor."

Raldnor could not speak. He found his eyes were burning and wet and turned his head, and the hunter moved away.

Soon she would be ashes mixed with the soil beyond the temple. Or would the essence of her truly rest in the arms of Anackire? The tears ran scalding down his face and left him oddly purged and empty. He walked away from the temple and began to retrace his steps toward Hamos, the village of his fostering, below the slope.

When he reached the little two-roomed hovel, he pushed the door shut and sat alone in the deepening shade of evening. Before, this place had been his home. Despite all differences and all self-searching, he had never questioned that. But now, now he questioned. Naturally he could stay among them, work in their fields as through the preceding years, hunt with them in the lean times, eventually tie himself to a wife and produce children. So far, from the few casual couplings, there had been no births. As well. They would not want another cripple in their midst.

He got up suddenly and went to the round of polished metal Eraz had used for a mirror and stared in at himself.

Vis.

Vis, for all the light gold eyes and the sun-bleached yellow hair. It was physically apparent in the dark bronze sheen of the skin, the tan which did not fade in the cold months, and also in the strikingly handsome face, the arrogant mouth and jaw that had no place set on a peasant. He was taller, too, than the average Lowland man, very wide in the shoulders, very long in leg and lean of hip. It was an unmistakable mark on him: this man was at least half-bred from a line of strong forebears who have never starved on the unnourishing acres of the Shadowless Plains.

He said suddenly aloud: "Why was I moved by the death of a woman who wasn't my mother?"

For his mother had been a Xarabian, he knew. A man of Hamos had found her near dawn, a few miles from the Vis town, Sar, which perhaps had been her destination. A beautiful woman, he said. She lay on her back with the last wisp of moon hanging over her like a drop of milk. There was an oozing tirr scratch on her shoulder and a mewling baby held tight in her arms.

In memory of her they had given him a Sarish name. But she had marked him already. It was her ancestry betrayed him. Yet he had a Lowland father, for his eyes and hair spoke of that. He thought of the woman with disturbed emotions. It must have been a casual Vis mating, for the dark races shunned the Plains people by all accounts. And she had left him a dreadful legacy. Her Vis sex, for one. He, like they, roused irresistibly at the coming of the Red Star. It had been the dreadful shame of his childhood till Eraz had explained it to him. Later it sent him prowling like a wolf through nights of sleepless blind desire when every dream was an unsatisfying frenzy. The girls of the village, unsensual at any season and quite immune to the Star, cost him endless effort, each coition preceded by intolerable seduction. That he gave them pleasure he only knew by the almost grudging soft cries wrung out of them on occasion. He felt they went with him from pity, and were amazed by the effect he produced on them, and every coupling was ultimately soured for him, for it was basically unshared, and he to himself seemed bestial once the Star had faded.

Yet this legacy was not the worst. It was his crippling which was hardest to bear. At the remembrance of it now, here in the dark hovel, he smashed his fist against the metal mirror in senseless anger.

He was both deaf and dumb. Not physically, that was, but in his mind.

They, the pale-skinned people all about him, could listen to each other's thoughts, project their own. There was a silent murmuring always about them, like invisible swarms of bees. And he stood, unconscious and mute, on the fringe of their society, a tolerated idiot—outcast, not by them, but by his own deformity.

Outside, above, the white pitcher of the moon poured black night into the sky.

A wolf howled faintly across the distances of the Plains.

Soon it would be cold. Snow would come. Thick stockades would be dragged about the village, and they would be trapped within until the second thaw.

Resolution came on him suddenly. He took from the chest the thick cloak of wolf skin, and from the wall hooks his hunter's knife and the pouch of small copper counters that was the sum of Eraz's wealth. He felt like a thief.

There was no one else about in the night. He strode along the straggling earth road, up the slope, by the temple, and away toward the south.

"Where are you going?" he asked himself.

Not to Xarabiss, certainly. Automatically, it seemed, and resentfully he had turned his back on the north.

Something came into his brain.

Somewhere ahead there lay the ruins of a city, a Lowland city, Eraz had said, a relic of a past completely blotted out. Why not there, then, to this hulk of the Shadowless Plains.

He felt insecurity and liberty mingle in a peculiar sensation for, whatever else, he was free. He would not have to endure again and again the same excluding faces; at least now they could be different ones.

And he grinned as he walked, at his pleasureless joke.

He lived where he could off the wild, shunning the occasional impoverished signs of habitation. He kept toward the south. He became lightheaded at his journey—this slough-ing of all responsibility—and the city assumed vast meta-physical proportions.

After about nine or ten days he came to a hovel with an old woman outside it. She was patching a garment, her long colorless hair hanging over her face. He asked her for a drink of water from the well, and then about the city. She pointed without words, southward. So he went on.

"A mirage," he thought, "a phantom I don't even see."

The winds blew very bitter.

He had never been so long alone.

It was early dusk and there were leafless trees. He came out of them and looked down and saw a shallow valley set in the slopes, already swimming with shadow. And in the val-ley and the shadow a progression of shapes—runnels, chan-nels, flat projections—like something a child might build out of the rain-moist dust. The City.

He did not believe in it at first. He began to walk down into the valley, expecting at any moment that it would van-ish, a trick of the fading light. But it grew more solid and more real. Quarried black Lowland stone like the stone of the temples.

Half a mile away, it occurred to him that no sound came from the city, no light, and not a puff of smoke showed. It was deserted then—quite feasible considering its dilapida-tion. Still he went on. A great ruinous wall loomed pres-ently above him, and the vault of an open defenseless gate. He went into the gate, and was at once almost overpowered by a sense of enormous age and enigma—the city's person-ality.

Beyond the arch a stone terrace led down in broad steps to a dim, shadow-filled square. His boots sounded on the stone, and a purple gust of birds flurried up from the dark into the sky, startling him.

As he crossed the square, there was a flicker of sudden light from under an arch-mouth. A woman with a tallow lamp and hair like the lamp flame was drawing water from a well. She did not look at him. So, there were inhabitants after all, lairing like beasts in the ruins. Well, he too could make a lair.

He walked the cold oppressive streets as the white embers of stars formed in the sky. He saw no other living thing abroad, though bird wings sometimes fluttered on the tops of ancient houses, and now and then he made out a trembling obscure light behind narrow latticed windows.

The moon was rising as he climbed the steps of a dark palace.

Sitting, leaning against a pillar, while the moon splashed white on the cracked mosaic of the floor, he ate the last meager ration of his fire-cooked meat. Shadows slid all about the roofless hall. They were very deceptive. He did not for a long while see that one of them was a man.

"Don't be alarmed," the figure said, moving forward into the moonlight, "there's no need of your knife."

He was in middle age, wrapped in a ragged but serviceable cloak, and at his heels padded a black velvet beast with glowing eyes.

"Sit, Mauh," the man said, and the beast sat. "Yes, she is indeed a wolf, but mine since birth and therefore will do you no harm."

"Then you needn't fear *her* harmed," Raldnor retorted sharply. "I've killed wolves often."

"Yes. So much is evident."

The man squatted by his animal and looked into Raldnor's face. Although plainly a Lowlander, his countenance was unusually open, promising to be expressive.

"Your mind is shut to me, and you are dark-skinned," he remarked after a moment. "Perhaps that's why you're here. There are many mixed births in the city. Men with light eyes and dark hair, blonde-haired, black-eyed women."

"You give sanctuary to misfits, then?" Raldnor said sardonically.

" 'You,' " the man repeated, considering the word. "There

is no collective 'you' in this place. No Authority. In the temple villages there are the priests, but here—here there is only the city. We are all a scattering, all strangers to each other. Why did you come up here?"

"To eat," Raldnor said shortly.

"This is the palace of Ashnesea, a princess who ruled before time as we know time. You see bits of her still there in the mosaic on the floor, musing with the goddess."

Raldnor said nothing. The man troubled him; besides, his days of lonely traveling had made it additionally hard for him to communicate.

"At night," the man said abruptly, "in the cold months, wild beasts run into the ruins. It would be best if you found some house to hole up in."

"Thanks for your advice."

"No thanks are asked, or indeed given, I think." The man rose and the black wolf rose with him. "My name is Orhvan, and you're welcome to share our hearth—the hearth, that is, of my little family, my kin by choice not blood."

Raldnor hovered between embarrassment and reluctance. Yet it would be better to rest in reasonable comfort tonight than roam the city searching for some bleak cranny. He felt at once intolerably weary, as if all the exhaustion of his spontaneous flight had suddenly caught him up.

"Come," Orhvan said.

"I have some money. I'll pay for anything I have."

"Money? Ah, the city doesn't recognize such things. All is barter here."

Raldnor got to his feet and let the man Orhvan lead him down the palace stairway, the wolf loping ahead.

He woke to the clear cold hyacinth sky of late morning from a bewildering welter of dreams. He lay on a firm pallet stuffed with straw, a faded brocade cushion under his head, a generous pile of furs and blankets over him. It took him a moment to remember he was in the house of Orhvan. At least the house Orhvan had appropriated for himself. What ancient family had originally dwelt in these dark impressive rooms and glided up and down that imposing staircase, only She knew.

Raldnor left the bed and began to dress again. The air up here was freezing, coming in through broken shutters and cracks in the ceiling. He recollected that last night there had been a fire below in the grate of the round hall, barley bread to eat and a hot soup. A young man with a gaunt narrow face and deep-set eyes had been sitting in the firelight, plaiting baskets. Set aside on a bench was a fine, as yet unpolished carving in light wood of a slender epicene girl. Orhvan had taken it up, remarking on its beauty, and the young man had shaken his head with a half-smile of abnegation.

"This is Ras, who doesn't understand his own talent. And here's a symptom of the way we live. We all plait baskets from time to time and exchange them for food and other luxuries."

Later, as they ate, a whispering movement came from above, little more than the stirring of a large moth.

"Yhaheil," Orhvan said. "Yhaheil's father was an Elyrian," he added with a measured bluntness, "and he has their leaning to astrology. He spends most of his days in the tower room of the house."

Orhvan had allotted Raldnor this small chamber, and the pallet and coverings had been provided and also the cushion, a product of Xarabiss, Orhvan informed him. Raldnor wondered how it had come here. In the dark on the stairs a shadow brushed by him—Yhaheil? He had only the impression of some creature with an unhuman lisping dream-quality about it, yet he glimpsed dark hair above the dark robe, and was curiously comforted. Perhaps the astrologer also spoke only with his mouth.

Dressed, Raldnor went down the staircase and into the hall. A little albino snake, of the kind that lived in the stone walls of houses, was squinching gracefully under the door in order to sun itself outside. There was no other company. Neither Ras nor Orhvan was here, and he saw that the heap of baskets had vanished with them. There were slices of bread left under a cover on the age-pocked table, and a little pitcher of milk. Raldnor ate and drank sparingly, conscious of the poverty of these people, which seemed worse than, yet strangely not so depressive as, the poverty of the villages—perhaps because they had presumably chosen this warren in preference to field labor.

A fire was still burning in the grate, and he added a few sticks to it. As he was doing this, he became intensely aware of another presence in the hall. He straightened and turned slowly, and found a girl had come in from the street. She carried one of their baskets with a cluster of eggs in it, and Mauh, the black wolf, stood at her heels. He found himself astonished, almost absurdly awe-struck, for she seemed quite unreal, a kind of apparition of pure light, like something cast from milk crystal. She was all whiteness—even her ragged dress seemed caught up and filtered through her glow, and all of her framed by hair like blown and nacreous tinsel.

But she also was startled, almost afraid. She clutched the basket to her.

"Orhvan offered me shelter," he said to reassure her, wondering if she too were one of Orhvan's "family of choice."

She lowered her eyes, saying nothing, and came into the room to set down the eggs on the table. As she passed by him he felt an unmistakable twinge of desire—but it was her rarity he wanted more than her flesh.

"My name is Raldnor. May I ask yours?"

She said something he could not catch, and hesitated at the table lip, not putting down the basket. He came and took the basket out of her hands and set it down.

"Who did you say you were?"

"Anici."

"That's a pretty name, and suits you very well."

"It's a corruption of Ashnesea," she whispered, like a nervous yet erudite student, "as is Ashne'e."

"Oh, really? Well, I like your name the best."

She blushed at once, and her blush stirred him. He reached out and gently silked a strand of her white hair through his fingers.

"I thought at first you were a ghost. Or a goddess."

"I must go now," she said breathlessly.

He saw she was trembling, and this response to him of shy fear, he found, excited him in a most extraordinary way, perhaps simply because it was a response. He slid his arm beneath her head and leaned to her mouth, but in the final moment some sentimental regard for her obvious innocence stayed him, and it was a very chaste brief kiss he delivered to her lips before he let her go. He saw tears in her eyes, nevertheless. The full intention of his body had communicated itself quite clearly. And, with a lazy disdain, he said: "I beg your pardon. You were entirely too much for me."

She jerked about and fled toward the door, provoking in him at that moment a sort of scornful amusement. And then, without warning, his head reeled and he staggered against the hearth as if drunk. An agony, bright and unbearable, pierced through his skull so that he let out a cry of pain. She halted in the doorway, staring at him, and in that moment he felt his mind touch hers.

Shaken, he leaned against the stone, gazing in her face almost pleadingly, but she had somehow shut him out. Next moment she turned and was gone out the door.

Orhvan and Ras came back at noon, having bartered all the baskets but three for provisions and a woolen shirt.

"Anici came and brought us eggs," Orhvan said. "And how is my guest today? Did you see a white-haired girl?"

"Yes," Raldnor said, but no more. He had sat before the fire a long while, lost in a dazed frustration after she had gone.

"No other visitors, I trust? No. As well. It's better I deal with the Ommos when he comes."

They ate some of the food Orhvan had brought, and the wolf gnawed delicately on a bone at Ras's feet.

"This is how it is," Orhvan said. "We sometimes take our wares across the border into Xarabiss, to Xarar or Lin Abissa. Ras's carving fetches a good price, despite his modesty, and Anici is a cunning weaver. The profits are more than useful in the cold months. Now suddenly we find there is a new law—no Lowlander can leave the Plains without a permit signed by a Vis." Orhvan's face had, like his tongue, gradually fulfilled its early promise of expressiveness: he frowned. "There is a Vis merchant here in the city, an Ommos with his household. Oh indeed, a curious phenomenon. But, as you will unfortunately see, he uses largess to manipulate the city dwellers, for who has much pride when they're starving? Now we have to ask him for a permit, in exchange for which he will take a commission on our sale amounting, as I understand it, to over half. I expect his steward today."

Raldnor felt a stirring of anger, and these first intimations of racial sensitivity were strange to him.

"Why let him exploit you? Can't the people here band together against him?"

"That isn't our way, Raldnor. We Lowlanders are a passive breed. You perhaps may not quite be able to accept this."

"Because of my mother's blood? Maybe. I don't dispute the fact that if a man strikes me in the mouth, I'll strike him back with interest."

"There you have it," Orhvan said.

"Possibly it was your philosophy that frightened Anici away. She generally waits for us."

It was the first thing Ras had said, though he had looked at Raldnor intently from time to time since they had come in. Raldnor met his deep-set shadowy eyes. In the depths of them he thought he glimpsed a love-haunting. With contempt Raldnor said: "She seemed a timid girl. No doubt well taught by example."

"Anici is a child still," Ras said quietly.

"And you are ambitious that she remain one."

Orhvan spread his hands.

"Be still, my friends. You bring discord on my house."

"I apologize," Raldnor said stiffly.

"No need, no need," Orhvan said, but his heart troubled him. "You are Vis," he thought. "Like the chameleon, you have assumed some of the color of your situation, but under all, you are a dark man with black hair, and a package of lust and anger and arrogance in your soul." And then he thought with compassion: "Poor boy, poor boy, to be pulled thus two ways at once. There is a look there too, the pain of the blind and dumb."

"It is the Storm Lord who makes these permits necessary," he said aloud, deliberately ignoring the brief disturbance in the conversation. "He has no love for the Plains people. I'm afraid we shall suffer for that."

"Storm Lord," Raldnor said, "the Vis High King."

"Yhaheil says," Ras murmured, "that he has the scales of a serpent on his arm because a snake frightened his mother as she carried him." His impenetrable gaze leveled, "and he has, so Yhaheil says, an extra finger on his left hand. An irony you will appreciate, Raldnor."

Raldnor felt the malice sting him. Before he could answer there came a loud knocking on the street door.

"Orklos," Orhvan said softly, and rose.

The open door revealed two thin Lowland male children dressed as pages, and behind them the looming figure of the unwelcome visitor. He moved into the room and seemed to fill it up with his scented smell and his well-fed body, and the barbaric-colored cloth of his robe.

"Good day, Orhvan."

His speech was curiously slurred by his thick Ommos tongue. A ruby glinted in an upper canine. His black eyes rolled languidly toward the unknown face.

"Who?"

"My name is Raldnor."

"Indeed. I have a message for this house. From my master, Yr Dakan." He yawned and glanced again at Raldnor. He saw the stunted left finger and pointed at it immediately. "You gave it to a god?"

"No."

"No. Well, well. In my land it is customary for a man to dedicate something valuable to his gods. Often it is more precious than a finger, hmm?" Orklos turned as if remembering Orhvan. "My message. Tell Orhvan the basketmaker that he is invited to dine at Yr Dakan's house tomorrow night."

"Thank your gracious master. But I asked for a permit."

"So, so. You will not refuse a dinner. The permit will be granted, perhaps, after the food. You are all welcome. The little pale girl also. And this young man too. The hour after sunset."

Without waiting for an answer, Orklos turned and swayed through the street door, the two pages running after him.

Through the afternoon Raldnor walked about the streets in the grip of a desolate and panic-ridden anguish. At first he could think only of the girl Anici and how, in that astonishing instant, his mind had seemed open to hers. If only—ah, goddess, if only. Might Anici be the key for him? Yet as a leaden sunset darkened the sky, he began to think again, and with increasing distress, of his foster mother Eraz. He felt, in some irrational way, that he had abandoned her. "I must find her," he thought and was unsure if it were Anici or Eraz he visualized.

He made a vow to leave his copper counters on Orhvan's table and be gone, and then remitted the vow at once.

In the night he lay awake on the pallet and heard the dim dismal wailing of wolves which seemed often very close about the house. He remembered Orhvan's warning that wild beasts ran into the city in the cold.

"Perhaps she'll come in the morning, as today. Perhaps. Perhaps," he could not help hoping.

Finally he left the pallet and went down to the hall. Mauh widened her opal eyes at him from her place by the hearth, and he scratched between her ears, still unable to quench his instinctive reaction to her ancestry. A polite reserve existed between them.

It was not for some time that he realized there was another in the room. As before, it was a faint, moth-soft movement that gave away the presence of Yhaheil the Elyrian.

The man was seated on Ras's bench, his dark hair falling round a waxen face.

"Raldnor," he said, and his voice was a whisper that shivered on Raldnor's spine.

"Yhaheil."

"I've seen strange pathways in the stars on this night. The man who knows fear, who will comfort him?"

Raldnor flinched at the unemphatic doom of the words, but he was also suddenly heavy with sleep.

"Predictions are subject to error," he said, but Yhaheil ignored him.

"It's her doing. Ashne'e. She reaches out of time and stirs the world."

"He's eccentric or else mad," Raldnor thought, but was not convinced of this.

Yhaheil went on murmuring. Buzz, buzz. A velvet bee droned round and round in Raldnor's brain.

"Sometimes a light-haired girl is born with the face of Anackire. For her there is always a destiny. The Storm Lord took her from her temple, mounted her and died. The dragons carried her to their city, which is called Koramvis. She brought forth a child. Whose child? The King's? Or the Councilor's? The mob killed her and nothing is known of her child."

Yhaheil folded his pale hands and was still. He saw that the young man had fallen asleep. What had he spoken of?

He could not recall. In Elyr they had wanted to train him in the ways of a mystic, starve him and paint his eyes and feed him incenses so that he would fall down and babble intimately of psychic realms. But Yhaheil had been too swift for them, flying by night across the Elyrian wastes into the land of the Snake, from which his mother had come.

Remembering this, he gathered in his hands certain charts and stole out of the hall and up the stairway to the tower and to his stars, leaving the stranger sleeping below.

Yr Dakan's house lay in the upper quarter of the city, a tumble of weather-blackened stone like all the rest, but, unlike all the rest, blazing with light. An alabaster lamp hung over the portico, reflecting on the imported brass gate pillars—shapeless logs to a height of eight feet with, as a capital, the hideous convulsed face of Zarok, the Ommos fire god.

"To that, they sacrifice their children," Orhvan murmured.

They had all dutifully answered Orklos's summons— even Raldnor. He felt he did not really know why he was here except, perhaps, that by coming with them he would see the girl once more. As they went through the gates and into the burning vestibule, he watched her walking close beside Ras. It made him angry to see this closeness, angry as the withdrawal of her mind made him, for he was aware of her mind, acutely aware now that she was near to him, yet only in the sense of being conscious of something locked away—a bolted door.

"What are they to each other, those two?" he wondered. Not lovers certainly, even though Ras plainly adored her— or would worship be a more suitable word? And he visualized Ras kneeling at an altar in submissive contentment, never even thinking of touching the image, and another man with dark Vis skin dragging down the white goddess and remaking her into a woman.

An Ommos porter in the vestibule picked his teeth. The ancient stone of the walls had been disfigured with an obscene fresco of Ommish sexual and cannibalistic mores.

Orklos appeared, smiling and heavy-lidded.

"Ah, the Lowland guests. We have been waiting on your arrival."

He ushered them into the circular hall which was full of the wine-red light of lamps in ruby glass. A Zarok statue towered in the center of the room, a low-banked blare of fire in its open belly.

Orklos sidled to Raldnor's elbow.

"You gaze on the flame god. It is customary to sacrifice to Zarok, or he may grow angry. It is usually a young woman that we offer him, for in my land, as you may know, they are mostly expendable. But now we are here, we discontinue the practice. The Plains people might find the rite offensive."

Raldnor discovered himself paling with anger, and only the allegiance he felt he owed Orhvan kept him from violence. He fixed his eyes on nothing and remained silent.

"And Anackire, does not Anackire demand a tribute?"

"Anackire asks nothing because she needs nothing, being everything," Raldnor said tightly, using a quotation of the temple.

The Ommos laughed gently and shook his head.

"Such undemanding gods."

There was an obese man in a scarlet robe seated at the low table, already eating and drinking. He snapped his fingers, and Orklos guided Raldnor and also Anici forward to stand before him.

"Like slaves at market," Raldnor thought, his rage almost unendurable. But in that moment he felt the little tremor of fear that stole from her unguarded mind to his as she stood so close, at last, to him. Not fear of him now but of Dakan. Dakan uttered a low belch and grinned. He was almost bald, and his face and body gave evidence of a hundred debaucheries and misuses. His gelid eyes fastened on

Anici, and Raldnor half wished he would reach out and
touch the girl, for then he knew his control would entirely
snap and he would probably kill the man. But the fatty
hands stayed in the plate.

"Welcome, Ralnar. And little Anci." The Ommos tongue
mangled their names in syrup. "You shall sit with me. The
young man to my right. And you to my left."

They were seated, Orhvan and Ras placed opposite and
food brought in. Orklos, the steward, moved about stealthily among the Lowland servants, snarling or slapping at
them when he considered their work ill done. The Lowland faces were quite blank, but Raldnor wondered what
insupportable hardship had brought them to sell their
souls.

The dinner was good, doubly good because they were
hungry, had always gone without quite enough and were
now invited to eat their fill, indeed, to bloat themselves.
Through it all, Raldnor was nagged by the question of what
payment would be expected.

There was no conversation during the meal. Finally Dakan signaled—another snap of the fingers—and the last
dishes were carried out. Two men entered, bearing a semi-
opaque bowl on tripodal legs which they set down beside
Dakan. Inside the bowl was a dim swirling movement of
small water creatures.

Dakan rose, held out a hand. Orklos placed in it a long,
thin-bladed knife.

Raldnor tensed with a new and helpless anger. A Lowland man killed animal life only for food or in defense. This
live sacrifice, perpetrated before them, was not merely a
means of horrifying them but of humiliating them too, for
who would protest?

The knife was thrust into the bowl, withdrawn and a
speared thing came from the water, doubling and twisting
on the blade, and screaming also the screams of a tortured
child.

Dakan laughed. He strode to the belly of the flame god

and shook his offering into fire. The screams rose and presently stopped.

"My tribute to you, mighty Zarok," Dakan said, and wiped his knife on his sash.

Orhvan, Ras and Anici were staring at their hands, and Anici's face was gray. Raldnor rose.

"Lord Dakan, you promised us a permit to cross into Xarabiss," he said, hard and very cold, noting vaguely that he had included himself in that "us."

Dakan turned and looked at him, the smile slipping a little on his pudgy face.

"You speak out of turn, young man."

"Your servant told us that the permit would be given us. Is he the liar, or are you?"

Dakan's face fell entirely. His eyes narrowed, yet Raldnor glimpsed a fleeting alarm.

"You shall have your permit. There is no hurry."

"There's great hurry. There are wolves in the city by night. The sooner we leave the better."

Dakan waved a hand.

"Fetch what he asks."

Raldnor felt his pulses thud with triumph. The man seemed unnerved by him—probably no Lowlander had ever insisted on anything before.

Orklos approached Dakan and handed him a slip of reed paper. Resting it on the table, Dakan added his scrawling signature and the imprint of his seal ring.

"There. It's done. You may still your impatience. Speak, Orklos."

Orklos smiled at Raldnor.

"My master offers you all the hospitality of his house tonight."

So there it was. Secured by wolves in the Ommos's house, the girl would be prey to any scheme the merchant had in mind for her. His lust was all too obvious. And for that matter, his servant seemed interested in Raldnor himself.

"Our thanks, Dakan," Raldnor said acidly, "but we've abused your hospitality long enough."

He picked up the permit.

"But these wolves—Orhvan, are you in agreement?"

Orhvan had risen, white-faced.

"I think that I am, Dakan. We'll thank you, and leave."

Dakan's countenance grew very ugly.

"Please do. And remember, if you reach Xarabiss, the terms of this contract. I trust your wolves avoid you."

They passed through the foyer into the cold black night.

A hand brushed Raldnor's arm.

"Why go with them?" Orklos hissed from the doorway. "You endeavor to act as one of these Lowland serfs on whom the Vis spit, but you—you have the way of a Vis and a face I have seen on the statues of Rarnammon. What do they offer you, these people? Stagnant ruins, filth, poverty. My master can be generous, I assure you, to my friends."

Raldnor shrugged off the hand.

"I'm not your friend, Ommos."

The door thudded shut behind him.

At first they traveled the dark streets in silence, the small lamp Orhvan carried casting an erratic pallid light.

Raldnor, walking a little to the rear, stared at the girl's silver fountain of hair. The Ommos wine and his victory had made him slightly drunk.

"Perhaps you were too brisk with them, Raldnor," Ras said eventually, not looking back. "It's not good to fall foul of Yr Dakan."

"You'd have preferred to stay then, and have your girlfriend taken into the slug's bed."

Ras turned and glanced at him: a look turbulent with unreadable yet disconcerting emotion.

At that moment a wolf howled not twenty yards away. It was a peculiarly resonant sound, too big for the silence of the night.

They froze like a tableau.

"That's the white one. I know his voice," Orhvan said

softly. "He came last winter and killed five men in the streets."

Raldnor's hand slid to the hunter's knife and pulled it free of his belt. He felt a corrosive scorn for the three in front of him, passive with inevitable despair. He went past them and was in front as the white shape ran suddenly out between two crumbling walls, and paused, its eyes intent on him.

It was hunting alone, then. He was arrested by its unexpected beauty and its colossal size, for this one was two wolves made into one. He had heard hunters' tales of similar monsters, mutations of strength, but never seen one before. Its massive head would reach as high as his ribs. But such grace it had. He caught the dull calculating flash of its eyes, and its open mouth looked full already of blood.

And then it seemed he toppled into its black primeval brain. Dark, ancient, elemental, a dank forest full of merciless things, steaming swamps and torpid rivers, where sudden sparkling drives and lusts darted and flamed.

It leapt at him, but he had seen the diamond firework of its thought. His hand moved even as its glorious body slammed against him and its stench and insolence choked his throat. He buried the knife to the hilt in the eye of a demon which went immediately out.

He lay then very still beneath the coverlet of the wolf, racked with an abrupt impossible sorrow. Buried by its magnificence, he could only mourn. It was presentiment. There was a sound of distant voices shouting in his head. He opened his eyes and saw the girl Anici kneeling by him on the street, her face a rigid mask of fear for him. He smiled at her and, thrusting aside the corpse of the wolf, sat up and took her hand. "You care for me, then, do you?" he thought, and she hung her head, for there was no longer a bolted door between them and her mind was open for him to invade all the fragile private dusts and dreams inside it. He felt as though he walked on a splintering crystal, entering her mind, and a protective tenderness surged through him.

He got to his feet and, still holding her hand, drew her up also. Then he lifted the dead wolf in his arms and glanced at Orhvan and at Ras.

"Something else to sell in Xarabiss. This pelt should fetch a good price."

Ras's face was blank; Orhvan looked at him, wearily nodding. They sensed how he had usurped them.

6

TO BEGIN WITH HE had turned his back on Xarabiss. Now there was a craving in him to cross the border into Vis lands, to find towns seething with life, and dark-haired women resembling his lost mother. It came on him suddenly, he was not certain why, the day after he had killed the wolf and skinned it of its beauty.

Orhvan took two days hiring a wagon and two zeebas from the lower alleys of the city. Ras and Raldnor fetched the many-colored weaving from Anici's house, the wreck of a palace haunted by the girl's grandmother. They left Mauh here also, sniffing after rats among the fallen columns.

The old lady seemed suspicious of Raldnor. She snatched Ras's sleeve and whispered at him, and Raldnor's face burned with anger. He followed Anici into the ruinous garden and caught her hand.

"Come with us to Xarabiss."

"No. I couldn't leave her alone here."

"Surely there's someone else who could look after her, and Mauh would be protection enough."

She hesitated, her eyes lowered. He sensed a malleable quality and said: "I want very much for you to be with me."

She looked into his face, and her loveliness and innocence brought his heart into his throat. She was very precious to him; his ability to enter her open mind, the look of love in her eyes, were salves for his bitterness. She was his link with his people. He did not want to lose her even for a month.

"There is a woman in the third house," she said tentatively.

Later, as Ras and he walked back across the streets, Ras broke his silence to say: "We've spoken hard to each other, you and I. I saw the way she looked at you, and I was envious. My fault, Raldnor. I ask for peace between us now, and wish you both happiness."

Unexpected warmth moved Raldnor. He made his own verbal reparations, after which they were friendly enough, though Ras's friendship was subdued and reserved, in the manner of the Lowlanders.

They traveled under blowing dark roofs of skies, and at night ringed the wagon with fires. Once they saw tirr crossing a plateau beneath, and Raldnor felt old implacable hatred rise up in him, thinking of the dead Xarabian woman and that lost finger he surmised they might have bitten off.

They drove most of the day, taking this task in turns, huddling at dusk to eat by the fires. In the dark of the night he would lie awake and listen to Anici's breathing behind the curtain she stretched midway across the wagon. They were all too close for him to go to her. He wished there had been more sexual complicity between them, for then it might have been managed. The Vis sex in him was hungry for her, the hunger made more greedy by every day spent in her presence, seeing the look of shy loving in her eyes. Even the sounds of her soft breathing inflamed and curdled in his loins. And yet he had had nothing from her except those gentle and unsatisfying kisses, for she was very timid and nervous—a delicate, difficult pupil of his desire.

On a day of harsh silver light they crossed the border and reached Sar, that small Xarabian town so near to which the Hamos man had found the dead woman and her child.

Their permit was shown at the gate, yet the sentries seemed indifferent, and there were many yellow-haired people moving about the streets. At the town's center a terrace climbed to a small shrine dedicated to the wind gods who beat about the hill, and near this place they found cheap lodgings.

Raldnor lay on his back in the male dormitory he, Orhvan and Ras had settled for, while two or three prostitutes plied their trade from pallet to pallet. The bestial grunts and mutterings of the Vis about him both sickened and excited him. At last, seeing his companions asleep, he got up and slipped out of the long room, following the narrow corridor to the tiny cell where Anici had been housed.

He thought she might have barred the door, but she had forgotten.

Inside the room he stood a long while looking down at her as she slept. Moon shafts described her body and her drifting hair. He woke her with the softest touch of his mouth, yet she stared at him in fear.

"What is wrong?"

"Nothing, darling Anici. Nothing."

"Then why are you here?"

Her naivety served only to increase his need. He sat beside her and stroked her cheek, then took her face in his hands and kissed her, no longer with the familiar childlike kiss.

She did not resist him, but she gave a series of tense nervous shudders, and when he let her go, she began to weep very softly to herself.

"I'm afraid."

"I won't hurt you, Anici. I only want you to be happy. I want to share what I feel with you." And at once he found the stale words again in his mouth from those endless courtships at Hamos—stupid, superficial sentences masking a lust, always impatient, now virtually agonizing. He found he could not bear to drone through those ritualistic phrases again, not with this girl with whom he had mingled thoughts.

He moved close to her and began to caress her trembling body. She lay like stone and merely suffered him, and suddenly a rage took hold of him that he could not keep control of. He gripped her shoulders and snarled: "You forever say you love me. I think you lie to me."

"Oh, Raldnor—you know my mind—how can you say these things—"

"Then you're a child. They kept you a child in that pile of ghosts and ruins."

The tears ran down her face and ended his patience. He found he despised her, hated her passive endurance. He felt that urge come on him that was like a possession—the Vis part of his body ravening to be free. He experienced a total loss of will to it.

When her hands came thrusting at him in terror, he held her more cruelly, and his brain was flooded by her frenzied inner cries. But she was no longer anything to him except an object that in some obscure way represented all the frustrations and tortures of his life. He remembered only partly that she was a virgin, and so, while he did not exactly force her, yet it was an effective and bloody rape. And not once did she cry aloud, only inside her mind, and it was these cries that finally brought him to his senses. His horror then at what he had accomplished was the more intense because he himself had done it. For it seemed to have been another man, a man he would hunt out through the byways of the inn and beat to a pulp. He held her and tried to comfort her, appalled by her anguish and her blood. And as he grew more panic-stricken, she faded into an empty and desolate calm.

"What have you done to me?" she eventually asked, the pathetic seal on her poor ignorance so thoroughly wrenched away.

He bathed the hurt and wrapped her in the blankets of the bed, and finally she fell into a dreary sleep.

He did not leave her until near dawn, when he wandered the streets of Sar as the sun rose, feeling as if some sort of murder had been committed in the dark by a man who had been his friend.

Somehow she kept from the others what he had done to her, but she kept herself from him also. And he found he was like a shamed child in her presence.

They came to Xarar at midday, showed the permit, and sheltered in a dismal eating house from a barrage of hail. The town seemed curiously inert and empty.

As they sat at the trestle over their muddy inexpensive wine, a young man came through the door, shaking hail from his cloak, cursing the weather in a colorful, altogether rather humorous way. He stayed drinking for a while, in a corner by the fire, but Raldnor was aware of his steady, dark, Xarabian gaze, and presently the Xarab rose and, bringing his wine jug with him, came and sat beside them.

"Pardon the intrusion, but I see our friend has served you the worst wine in the house. Permit me." Whereupon he took up Raldnor's cup, dashed the contents on the ground and refilled it from the jug. After which he repeated the performance with each of their cups in turn.

"I must protest," Orhvan said, startled.

"Well, if you must, you must."

"We've no means to repay you," Orhvan said simply.

"I am already paid, twice over," said the stranger, kissing Anici's hand.

They seemed instantly in the young man's power. He had a sorcerous personality, an indefatigable, oblique sense of fun.

He bought them dinner and they learned his name was Xaros. He was the agent, he said, of a miser in Lin Abissa. He seemed to know that they were not merely sightseers but had wares to sell, and later Orhvan took him to look at the colored cloth and the carvings and the few glazed pots that were their inventory.

"You'll sell nothing in Xarar," Xaros decided. "Lin Abissa's the place."

"We've had trade here before."

"Haven't you noticed, my friend, how empty the streets are? I see you Lowlanders get no news on the Plains. The Storm Lord is the guest of Thann Rashek at Abissa, and the whole of Xarabiss has crowded in after him to stare. At Abissa there is endless custom, therefore, from all the holiday-makers. In addition to which, my despicable master will get you a better price if you deal through him."

"You were on the lookout, then, for Lowland traders," Raldnor remarked.

"To be frank with you," Xaros said, "I came to Xarar to visit a lady with whom I am slightly acquainted, at a time when I should have been on my employer's tiresome and unimaginative errands. If you decide to deal with him, I shall use this as the excuse for my absence. Otherwise it's the begging bowl and the open road. Don't think for a moment, however, that I'm trying to influence any decision you might make—"

"What price could your master obtain for our work?"

"Name what you ask independently."

Orhvan and Ras conferred and produced a sum. Xaros gave a bark of derision.

"No doubt you're renowned for your charity, but how do you live? You'll get three times that, even after the swindler has taken his share. And I suspect your permit's been signed by some filthy Vis thief—some excrement of Sar, or worse, an Ommos. Think how delightful it will be to pay the vileness only the half of your expected profit, and keep the excess yourselves. Don't be afraid. I make a very fair counterfeit bill of sale."

It was a two-day journey to Lin Abissa. Xaros rode in their wagon. He had ridden a coal-black zeeba to Xarar, but subsequently sold it to buy his "lady" a present.

His company lifted all the sense of reserve and gloom from their party. He spread a kind of ubiquitous lightness. Raldnor found he could even be easy with Anici now, and she, beneath Xaros's deluge of undemanding flattery, began to smile shyly and seem again like a sweet and untroubled child. Raldnor felt a warmth and a gratitude toward Xaros, but also a twisting of remorse inside himself, a pang of realization he refused to admit. The Xarabian's freedom had been transmitted to him. Now he must ask: Might his true place be here, in Xarabiss, among Xarabians—his roots and all the leanings and cravings of his spirit and flesh? And it was Xaros who spoke it for him, the second night as they sat by the fire.

"The piece of your mother in you feels herself home."

Raldnor stared at the flames and said: "I've lived a Lowlander all my life till now."

"So the worm lives in the chrysalis till the sun bursts it. Then out pops the brilliant flying insect in amazement and mutters: 'Well, well, I've lived in a chrysalis all my life till now.'"

"Not so easy to discard my father's half, Xaros."

"Easier than you think. The Plains breed a gentle and worthy people. Let's admire them, but be honest. You're not a Plains man. For one thing, I see you don't use their mind language."

Raldnor flinched involuntarily at this new knife piercing of the old wound. Besides, he had always heard the Lowlanders tried to hide their telepathy from the Vis. He said nothing and Xaros let him be. But his own brain took up the discussion and gnawed on it.

The first flakes of snow were feathering down as they rode through the broad red gate of Abissa. The guards, with the dragon woman of Thann Rashek's emblem on their breasts, made much of the permit, passing it along their hierarchy to a captain, who finally came out and stood in the snow, examining their faces. At last he called to Xaros: "Will you take responsibility for these people?"

"I will. But what need? As you can see, they're full grown and out of diapers."

The captain cleared his throat and with a stony face waved the wagon on.

"Idiot," Xaros said. "He fears the Dragon King."

"The Storm Lord?"

"You have it. It's well known Amrek hates the Lowlanders. There's always been the story of the curse on him of a Lowland witch, and a prenatal curse at that."

"A Lowland witch?"

"A temple girl, reputed to have slain the father—Rehdon—with sexual acrobatics, and then set the malignancy of Anackire on the unborn prince. Truly a woman of many talents—one I would like to have met."

Something moved uneasily in Raldnor's mind: A Lowland temple girl—someone had spoken of such a one in the city. Or had he dreamed it?

"And of what nature is the curse?" he asked, partly to divert his own unquiet. "Ras spoke of snake scales."

"Apt, but unproven. Who knows? It gives mothers something to scare their children with."

The snow was falling thickly, obscuring the towers and marble vistas of the city, laying on all immobile things an anonymous white pall.

"There's a reasonable inn hereabouts," said Xaros, but when they reached it, the inn was full.

It began to grow late. Overhead the oil-fired street torches of Vis cities flared and smoked. There were three more inns, all with the crimson flag at their doors to show they were crammed. There were soldiers in the courtyard of the last. Big braziers burned there, lighting up five or six of them laughing about the porch. They were very tall, wide-shouldered, plated with a bizarre reptilian armor—scale on winking black scale, each a cresset of dull flame—the dragon mail of the Am Dorthar. Cloaks of rust color, sprawled with black dragons, roped in the wind. The crests and mask-pieces of their helms made their faces fabulous. Lizard men.

As the wagon trundled by, one of the dragons glanced their way, the laughter still playing round his lips. Carefully and elaborately, he spat.

Raldnor felt horror take hold of him. He was made to know abruptly his powerlessness, not only before the armor and the spears, but before such unthinking hate. What did that man hate them for? Only because his Overlord hated? Or was it some old primitive fear ready to ferment in all the Vis, merely because of a difference in pigmentation and the stories that had grown up round it?

Raldnor glanced at Xaros. He seemed to have missed the incident. Was that possible? Or was Xaros, too, a potential enemy?

Finally they found a dilapidated hostel in a narrow alleyway known as Pebble Street. A few Lowlanders sat by the fires in the hall. The dragons did not come here; it was too far from the palace and their King.

Xaros departed into the snow, having arranged to return in the morning with his miser-master's offer, and they made a drab meal—most provisions in Lin Abissa having gone to feed the Dorthanians—and took the creaking stairs to the narrow bedrooms. Raldnor, the old restraint on him again, touched the girl's hand briefly in the dark and left her, unable to speak. In the night he lay and thought only of her and the thing he had done to her, and regret was mixed now inextricably with lust. Lust was a granite barrier between them. And Anici for her part dreamed confused and terrified dreams of a faceless man with a deformed arm. The talk of Amrek and the curse on him had inflamed ancient horrors, begun when, as a child, she had heard from the old women who drifted with her grandmother about the courts of the bleak palace the brief mentions of his name, his nature and his crippling.

Outside the snow sugared the world with its leveling pallor.

*   *   *

Xaros came back in the morning.

"My master's beside himself with voracious joy. Can you take the wagon up Slant Street at noon? He has a hole in the wall in Goldbird Walk."

Orhvan clearly knew the route.

"Hardly a district for holes in walls, I'd say."

Xaros dismissed this with a shrug.

"Only one item—keep the wolf pelt back. It's too good to waste. You can try a furrier later."

It seemed almost prearranged between them that while Anici remained at the inn, Orhvan and Ras—the Lowlanders—should take the wagon, and Xaros and his part-Xarabian brother, Raldnor, should walk together like citizens. Raldnor found himself obscurely troubled by this, yet he was sick enough of wagon riding, and so it was.

"Our poor friends will take at least twice as long," Xaros remarked as they reached the broad snow-white streets of the upper quarters. "Half the roads are cordoned off, the rest choked with sightseers. There's a procession route from the Yasmis's Temple to the palace—the Storm Lord giving his devotions to the goddess of love and marriage. There's a betrothal in the air, it seems; Amrek and the Karmian, Astaris. You've never heard of her, of course."

"Never."

"I thought so. One day the earth will crack in half without the Lowlanders noticing. Well, I'll enlighten your vile ignorance. Astaris is the daughter of the last king of Karmiss, now deceased, her mother being a Xarabian princess of Thann Rashek's stable. She's said—said, mark you—to be the most beautiful woman in the world. She's been in Xarabiss a year, in her grandfather's house at Tyrai. She came to Abissa, once, since when I and half the city have been unable to call our hearts or loins our own."

"So she's beautiful, then?"

"Superb. Have you ever seen a red-haired Vis woman? Oh, no, you head-in-a-bucket Plains man, you wouldn't have. Well, they're pricelessly rare. And this one—a mane the color of rubies. Here comes Lamp Street," he added. "The law here is the law of the wolves. Smile tiredly at the prostitutes and watch your pockets."

There was a great noise in Lamp Street when Xaros was spotted. Clearly, he was well known. Villainous-looking bearded men, probably robbers or hill bandits, clapped him on the back and whispered chuckling nefarious anecdotes at his ear; madams blew him kisses and invited him to bring his handsome self and handsome friend inside to give the latest batch of virgins a taste for their trade. At the end of the street a snake dancer from the Zor twisted an amber python around her bronze flesh.

"I see a hungry man," Xaros said. "Tonight, I think, we'll visit the Pleasure City."

Raldnor colored slightly. Xaros said: "My unfortunate Lowlander, transparent lust is the hallmark of the Vis. Give in. Your mother has you by the heels and is roasting you over a slow fire."

"I've no money—only a few copper bits."

"So, I'll lend you something. The wolf pelt will make you a good deal or I'm very mistaken. Owe me till then."

"Anici—" Raldnor began, and stopped.

"Anici's a delicious child who, like all females, will react favorably to a little competition. Tomorrow you can buy her a dress and some jewelry to ease your conscience and ensure her forgiveness."

"And Ras and Orhvan?"

"My master's certain to invite them to his house tonight. He likes to show off his liberality and his furniture, and they'll get a good dinner—he has a splendid cook despite his other numerous failings."

They arrived at the shop a little after noon, and it was one of the largest and most elegant in Goldbird Walk. The master himself was portly, alert, and as humorously capricious as his offspring. For Raldnor soon discovered from certain intimate references and wild slanders, and the amazing display of affection between the two of them, that Xaros was his son.

It seemed there was a demand for Lowland craft at the moment, and they did on the whole rather well. The dinner invitation was also forthcoming, though Xaros promptly excluded Raldnor from it, declaring that he did not want all his friends poisoned at one sitting.

Xaros remained at the shop, and Raldnor drove the others back in the wagon via byways. Yet he was in a lighter mood than he had been for many days.

There was an incident to mar all this waiting for him on the road.

Trying to avoid the increasing crowds and at the same time to follow Xaros's directions, he came finally, by a wrong turn, to the great intersection of the Avenue of Kings. Without understanding any of the geography of Lin Abissa, he saw at once that they were on the brink of the processional route the Storm Lord would be taking.

The wide street, with its flanking statuary and pillared buildings and towers flashing like diamonds against the sky, had been swept clear of snow. Banners drooped from a hundred cornices. Spectators milled about, and the wagon was trapped immediately in the press. Ahead he heard the distant pulse of drums and the wail of horns.

There came a voice suddenly from the crowd, yet not of the crowd—a harsh, commanding, terrible voice: "Get your rubbish off the road, hell blast you."

Raldnor looked down, his guts lurching with a recognizing fear.

A giant in brazen scales, his helm mask and his scarred coppery face all one. He brought his spear butt sharply against the nearest zeeba's flank.

With a dry mouth and no possible answer, Raldnor pulled hard on the reins. The wagon began to move backward.

"Hurry! Hurry yourself, you brainless Lowland filth."

Behind, the crowd scattered, cursing.

The soldier chopped with his hand, signaling a halt.

"Far enough. Now. Let's see your permit."

"I don't carry it," Raldnor said. Before he could explain that Orhvan had it, the soldier had reached up and dragged him from the box. Raldnor felt the jarring impact of the ground and caught the wheel to steady himself. Next came the soldier's mailed fist aiming for his mouth.

There was a scream from somewhere, and next minute he found that he had ducked the blow and was facing the Dortharian with his hunter's knife poised in his hand, ready to kill him through all his armor. Then the bizarre happened. A tangle of people swept between them and the blade was plucked from Raldnor's fingers. The soldier parted the crowd roughly, but he was smiling.

"You pulled a knife, you clod. Let's see it, then. Think you can nick me, do you, before I break your neck? Besides, it's a hanging offense to resist the Am Dorthar."

A voice called out: "He hasn't a knife."

Other voices yelled: "We'd've seen, wouldn't we? You imagined it, Dortharian."

The soldier's face darkened. He spun to the crowd, snarling, but another soldier shouted for him abruptly from the road. With an obscene curse the Dortharian turned and glared briefly at Raldnor.

"Sometime I'll settle with you, dung-creeper."

He swung aside and shouldered through the press to his station.

A hand slipped Raldnor's knife into his grasp. One or two people were going past; he was not certain who did it. He climbed back on to the box, shaking with a horrified sick fury, and saw Orhvan's white face at the wagon flap.

A burst of trumpets. Dimly Raldnor became aware of the advent of the procession. He had a fine vantage point, which went mainly unused. He registered only a vague blur of dark soldiery, the colors of Dorthar and Thann Rashek, and the priestesses of Yasmis in their carmine garments, while the brass music howled in his ears. But then he saw the chariot.

For some reason all his senses sharpened and centered on that chariot—the vehicle of the Storm Lord, jet-black metal drawn by a jet-black team of animals. Perhaps it was the animals which first caught his attention, for he had never seen their breed before.

The man in the chariot had the Dortharian black copper skin and the black hair. His face was curious, a strangely distorted face—as if it held, half concealed, a cauldron of inner violence—though externally well-formed and boasting the large ebony eyes of his mother, Val Mala. He wore black, with a gold chain slashed across his breast. He held the reins in his right hand, in his left a gold handled whip. And that left hand had on it a gauntlet, with a smoky sapphire on the smallest finger.

And this then was the High King. This dark and odd-faced man was the royal Enemy.

Until this moment he had been merely a phantom; now, as if fated, all Raldnor's hate transferred itself to him.

At the rose heart of Lin Abissa lay the Pleasure City, that area dedicated to the more carnal side of Yasmis, goddess of love. Xaros came in the blue dusk for him, and they soon left behind them the almost empty hostel and the pale girl sitting at the fire.

She had not wanted to go to the fine Xarabian's house; she equated that dinner with the food and fear offered by the Ommos, Yr Dakan. Yet neither did she want to be alone in this creaking shadowy room, with its smoking, barely hospitable fire. On the hostel stairs she had brushed Raldnor's arm.

"Must you go with Xaros?" she faltered.

"You know I must. I explained to you—we're to see a furrier about the wolf pelt."

"But must it be tonight?"

"Why shouldn't it be?"

She could not tell him.

Soon he grew impatient. She tried to repress her tears for she knew that he hated her to cry. In his eyes there came that look which appalled her. She gave him no pleasure—how could she when she did not understand how? So he must look elsewhere. For she realized already that it was to a brothel he was going.

Now the tears ran down her face freely, and she did not wipe them away.

The narrow streets glowed with hot windows. Spangled women flaunted their sensual wares on high booths—fire dancers from Ommos and Zakoris, snake dancers from Lan and Elyr. Pimps roared out the virtues of their most expensive whores.

"Such breasts—such thighs—"

"Three of each," Xaros remarked to the immediate crowd.

They came to a tinsel doorway and went in.

There was a naked Yasmis statue in the middle of the room, and a girl acrobat was contorting herself about it; prisms were pasted over her nipples and between her thighs a piece of mirror. Various customers were scattered here and there, drinking and observing her.

They sat down in an alcove, and a man brought them wine unbidden, and charged a ridiculous amount for it. Discomfort took hold of Raldnor. Presently two girls came drifting across the room.

They might have been twins—both pretty, both the smoke and honey shades of Xarabiss, their blue-black hair in heavy curls, gold sequins at the corners of their eyes. Their dresses were transparent gauze, cunningly pleated to opacity at breasts and pelvis, yet revealing a red gem set in each navel and a gold sunburst raying out from it across each softly curving belly.

They greeted Xaros with chirruping affection, but one sat dutifully by Raldnor and poured him wine.

"You're very handsome," she whispered to him over the cup, but it was a mannered sweetness. "My name is Yaini. And you're a Lowlander."

"Yes."

"There's love in the wine," she murmured. By this he understood her to mean that it was laced with an aphrodisiac, and he set down his goblet untasted. She looked at him curiously, then smiled. "There's a room above."

He rose at once, embarrassed by this sexual etiquette of which he knew nothing.

He followed her to the room, which was only large enough to accommodate a bed. In the dim lamplight she reached to embrace him with a delicate, well-simulated passion. There was magic in her mouth and light-fingered hands, and, as he caressed her pliable and willing body, she seemed to quicken too, though possibly it was part of her training to seem to do so.

Much later, as they lay together in the golden gloom, it came to him suddenly that perhaps his unknown mother had been a prostitute with a sunburst painted on her belly, and he grinned maliciously at this.

"You're smiling," she said, raising herself on one elbow to look at him. "Why? Did I please you?"

"Naturally you pleased me. You're very lovely and also very well instructed."

"That's a cruel thing to say to me after love."

"You must think me very naive," he said. "Am I the first Lowland peasant you've entertained?"

"You're not like a Lowlander at all. Neither like a peasant. You despise me as a whore. You think you bought my pleasure automatically."

He looked at her, and she was clearly angry. Her responses had seemed genuine enough certainly. He drew her toward him and kissed her coral mouth and honey breasts.

"Again and again and again," she whispered breathlessly. "You're indefatigable, a Storm Lord—" He scarcely heard that hated name. "If I please you so much, will you visit me later?"

But he did not answer her except with his body.

A hurricane rent the darkness in his skull.

He woke, crying out, and the Xarabian girl caught his shoulder.

"What is it? A dream? It was only a dream. You're awake now."

"No," he said, his eyes wide, "not a dream."

And in his brain the alien terror thundered, making him giddy, sick and afraid. He flung himself off the bed, snatched up his clothes and began to dress.

"Oh, what is it?" she sighed frantically. "Let me help you."

But he was at the doorway and suddenly gone. Distressed, Yaini huddled on the bed. He was the first man who had ever totally pleased her. She had not expected such strength, such passion and such exquisite lovemaking from one of the moderate Lowlanders. And now he had left her—she did not know why—as if some demon had suddenly driven him mad.

Outside he shouldered through the idling customers and their whores. Of Xaros there was no sign. Intolerable waves clashed in his head. He ran from the brothel.

A black velvet night, towers stitched golden on it now, and lamp shine on snow. He thrust between knots of people, who laughed or cursed him. He lost his way and found himself in a desolate alley, sobbing and clutching at his skull like a drunkard in a fit.

"Anici," he moaned, "Anici, Anici—"

He saw a tall portico of twisted white gold, and shapes of men, and he shouted at them to let go of her. He blundered down the alley, through a yard, calling out, so that faces appeared at windows.

7

THE METAL PILLARS WERE twisted like strange sweets, and torchlight flared from the iron gates. Beyond, a dark avenue, lines of bare trees white with snow blossom.

The chariot wheels sizzled.

One of the dragon men reached out to fondle her right breast.

"And how do you like Thann Rashek's palace, eh, little Lowlander?"

The other man laughed, turning the chariot now toward the temporary Dortharian barracks. A spear with a red drying tip leaned on the rail. It could be an amusing night. But abruptly there were new torches on the road and an imperious order to halt. The soldier pulled his chariot to a standstill; the other muttered an oath under his breath. Dragon Guard. On their black cloaks he could pick out Amrek's personal symbol, the white lightning.

A Guard captain detached himself and came up to the chariot. He looked first at the two uneasy soldiers, next at the pale, ash-faced girl.

"You've got a Lowlander there, soldier."

"Yes, sir."

"How d'you come by her? The truth."

The soldier scowled.

"There was Lowland scum on the procession route to-day, sir. Caused me some trouble, but the crowd—these damned Xarabian sheep—milled about and made things awkward. I went looking for him to teach him some manners. Easy enough to find him, sir. There's only a few places dare to take the yellow rats in, with King Amrek here."

"Did you find him, soldier?"

"No, sir. No such luck. But I found his wench, as you see."

The captain smiled without mirth.

"Well, soldier, I have good news for you. All this time you've been on a mission for the Storm Lord and never knew it. Someone overheard your plans, man, kept an eye on you and told the High Lord. He wants to see this girl himself."

The soldier's face collapsed in a mixture of alarm and vindictive frustration.

"Right, soldier. Hand her over. Don't weep, man, he'll let you have her back when he's finished with her."

Argument would be fruitless and dangerous. The two soldiers thrust the girl out, and the Guard captain caught her and set her on her feet.

"Lucky lass that you are," he sneered, "destined after all for such a high table."

She hung her head and walked in the company of black, iron-faced men into the palace halls. They left her in a glare of torches, swaggering past her. She was briefly alone, except for the two giants who guarded the entrance with crossed spears. Then a tall woman in a diaphanous robe came. She gripped Anici's shoulder in a ravening grasp like eagles' claws, and escorted her along corridors and through anterooms. At a carved cibba-wood door, she halted. Her Dortharian face was a mask—black caves of eyes where unmined diamonds glinted, the blood-red mouth of a vampire.

"You go to the Storm Lord. Please him."

Her claws rapped on the wood and it flew open. She pushed Anici through.

Anici stood like a statue, almost blind, almost deaf and dumb with fear, while the walls reeled and the floor tottered, but it was the earthquake of her fear.

A huge shadow evolved from the light. She felt herself choking on the poisonous vapors of terror. She spread out her hands to save herself from falling into the dragon's pit, but clutched only empty air.

"So this is a Lowland girl," a voice said. She could not calculate the whereabouts of the voice; it seemed everywhere. "Take off your pathetic rags and show me the rest of you."

But she only stood clutching at the air and gasping. She saw him now; at least, she saw the gauntleted left hand come reaching for her, and already she invested it with the marks of damnation. The curse of Anackire. The moment it touched her she would die. So she had always believed in her nightmares.

"Oh, gods, is this what killed my father? Don't you comprehend, girl, the honor extended to you? You, the fruit of the mating of some obscure Lowland filth. What are you afraid of? This? Well, well, there's justice in that. The blasting of the women of your yellow hell now brought home to roost on your innocent, no-doubt virgin flesh."

He pulled her toward him, and the hand of her death settled over her heart. A knife of fire impaled her like the water creature in Yr Dakan's house.

Amrek lifted his mouth from her skin. He looked at her. When he let her go, she fell at once. Under the dull bleeding of the incense braziers, she lay like a white inverted shadow, stretching out from his blackness on the floor. He bent over her and found that she was dead.

Raldnor opened his eyes and knew neither where he was nor how he had got there.

After a little he moved slightly, fearing some injury had

immobilized him. Yet he was unhurt and soon sat up. There was faint, cool fire in the lower sky. All around were twisting dirty alleys, littered with refuse. He thought: "Have I lost my mind in Xarabiss?" And it seemed he had lain all night in the shelter of a rotting hovel.

His head ached dully, and he remembered suddenly an unprecedented terrific blow bringing darkness. Someone had clubbed him then—some thief. Yet his knife was still in his belt, and what was left of Xaros's loan after he had paid the girl. He got up and began to walk along the nearest alley. An old woman emptying slops cursed him for no apparent reason.

At the turning of the alley lay a broken doll on its back with its arms flung wide. The moment he saw it he remembered, and a pain like death surged up into his throat. He leaned on the wall, trembling, muttering her name. What had become of her and the frantic unconscious signalings of her mind? And what, what had brought the dark down on his skull?

A man came shuffling up the alley. Raldnor caught his arm, and before he could struggle free, asked: "Do you know the way to Pebble Street?"

The man grumbled sullenly. Raldnor thrust a coin under his nose. The man responded with vague directions, grabbed the coin and hurried off. Raldnor began to run.

The sun rose, a dim red bubble, as he negotiated the tortuous byways of Lin Abissa, asking again and again for directions. Finally he came to familiar streets and at last stumbled into the courtyard of the hostel.

Catastrophe was at once apparent.

Great wheel ruts—the marks of a chariot—gouged across the snow, and near these were other marks, as of something dragged, and a brown stain.

Raldnor moved like a somnambulist across the yard and into the hall. The fires were out and no one there. He propelled himself through the hall and up the stairs, and stopped outside the door of the tiny cramped room which had been hers. There was no sound in that room, yet there was a presence. He pushed at the door, which swung noiselessly open.

It was very dark, for the shutters were still closed on the windows. But he made out a girl lying on the narrow bed and a man sitting by her. The man looked up and straight into his face. It was Ras.

"She's dead."

"No," Raldnor said.

"She is dead. If you'd gone with us to the Xarabian's dinner, she would have come. If you'd asked her, she'd have gone with you. But you went to the brothel and left her here alone, and they came for her while you were with your harlot." His voice was quite expressionless and very even. "Orhvan and I came too late. His soldiers brought her back after. He told them to. Amrek. She was to have pleasured Amrek, but she died before he had any pleasure from her. As a little girl, she was always afraid of him, I remember. You took her, I let you take her. I couldn't stop you. But why did you take her, Raldnor, when you didn't want her? She was a child, Raldnor. Why didn't you leave her as she was?"

Raldnor stared at Anici, wanting to go to her, to touch her, but there was such an awful stillness about her. Her white face was empty as an unworn mask. He turned and walked back down the stairs, across the hall, out into the courtyard. Who was it that had tried to protect her? Some other Lowland man, perhaps, had spilled this blood.

He went through the gate and began to walk, not knowing where he was going.

At last he found himself seated on a low stone wall, and a man was insistently talking to him, urging him to get up and go to some meaningless destination. After a little he looked at this man, and it was Xaros.

"It's my fault she's dead," Raldnor said. "It should have been my blood on the snow."

But Xaros somehow got his arm and had him on his feet, and now they were moving through crowds, and he thought that Xaros was taking him back to the brothel and began to shout at him. Xaros called to a burly cutthroat lounging in a doorway: "Svarl, my friend's sick. Give me a hand with him."

The cutthroat obliged with competent roughness, and Raldnor discovered they were hauling him upstairs into an unknown building. A door opened on an exotic apartment he scarcely noted at the time, and he was hustled onto a couch. A slender, dark woman came into the room.

"Oh, Xaros, you promised you'd be gentle with him."

Raldnor could not understand the woman's concern, for she was a stranger to him, but when her cool hand brushed his face, her touch seemed to unlock the most bitter grief, and she held him and let him weep against her as if she were a sister.

He did not know if it was Anici he wept for or Eraz—the shadow image of his mother who, nevertheless, had been exclusively dear to him, or the beloved with whom he had shared thoughts, and for whom, intrinsically, he had felt nothing. For even in his bewildered pain he understood this, and understood, too, that the white-haired girl would be his penance.

Anici bent over him and touched his shoulder. He got up in the darkness, and she stood waiting, the wind washing through her silver hair. The white moon shone behind her; he saw the shadow of her small bones beneath the skin. As he approached her, she raised her arms, and long cracks appeared in her body, like ink lines on alabaster. Then she crumbled all at once into gilded ashes, and the ashes blew away across the moon, leaving only darkness to wake him.

There were evenings, nights, dawns, other twilights and suns rising. He grew accustomed to Xaros's elegant rooms as he sat in them, eaten alive by a mindless, creeping lethargy.

After three or four days Orhvan had come, his expressive face showing now only a hesitant empty sorrow.

"Raldnor—the thaw will begin in a little while. Tomorrow even, or the day after, perhaps. Then we'll be setting out for the Plains."

Raldnor said nothing at first, but Orhvan stared at him as mutely, and finally he said: "Why are you telling me this?"

"Because we have to go now—before the second snow. You understand that traveling becomes impossible after that."

"Why are you telling me?" Raldnor repeated, "I'm not going with you."

"You've no choice. Oh, Raldnor, you have to come with us. Haven't you seen what's beginning here—Amrek's work? Even the Xarabians have begun to hate and fear us. Every day there are men in the market places and squares, muttering about Lowland perversions and sorceries . . . You have to come—"

"No, Orhvan. You thought of me always as a Vis. And I am Vis. She—she might have altered me, molded me to be a Lowlander like you, if she'd been stronger and more able than she was. And you don't have to reproach me for those words. I comprehend perfectly every atom of my guilt."

He felt then the lightest touch against his thoughts, as if the mind of Orhvan, like hers, had brushed against his own through the crippling veil.

"Come to the Plains when you can," Orhvan said, "when things are better for you. You know you'd be welcome—"

Raldnor shook his head. With unsmiling lacerated amusement, he said: "Don't ask the thief and murderer back into your house, Orhvan. He might steal and butcher some more."

Orhvan lowered his head and turned, and left him.

After this Raldnor had only two visitors. One was the Xarabian woman on whose unknown breast he had wept. He had expected at first, confronted with her in the aftermath of this hysteria, to be embarrassed and ill at ease, but in her gentle courteous way she somehow made him able to accept his own actions. It seemed she was Xaros's mistress, though she lived in her own apartments somewhere in the building. She was always very quiet, yet her presence was unutterably soothing to Raldnor. She would bring him things to eat or occasionally read to him in a cool lilting voice. Her name was Helida, and her interest a maternal rather than an amatory one, for clearly she loved Xaros a great deal in her own reserved and essentially sophisticated fashion.

The other, second visitor was less welcome; she came in the night and crumbled across his dreams in the consuming fire of her burial. He began to dread sleep. Orhvan had left the wolf pelt when he came, and sometimes in the dark the glimmer of its whiteness seemed like her hair across his bed. Her very innocence had grown evil with the haunting.

Immured in the apartment building, he heard nothing of the city outside. Even Orhvan's ominous despair had had no impact on him, and, besides, alienated from his people as always and for the first time befriended by a Vis, he felt himself truly Xarabian and one with the crowd of Lin Abissa.

Yet on the eighth evening of his lethargy, a boy came running up the stairs and pounded on Xaros's door.

"What's this, you hooligan?" Xaros demanded, and Raldnor thought he recognized the child as the son of the landlord and his wife, who lived a flight down.

"Xaros—soldiers—Dortharians—"

"Certainly. Get your breath back."

The boy gasped a little, swallowed and resumed:

"Svarl saw Dortharian soldiers on Slant Street, asking for a Lowland man with a finger missing on his left hand. He told me to tell you someone directed them here."

Xaros gave the boy a coin and packed him off; then, turning to Helida, he said: "Sweetheart, go and appropriate old Solfina's hair dye," and Helida went out, presumably to obey this curious order, without a word.

"I'll leave at once," Raldnor said, starting up in a sort of sick madness of action.

"And meet the dragons on the street? Oh, no, my impetuous friend. From this moment you'll do exactly as I say. Oh, my darling Helida, how swift of you. Now we'll make this yellow stuff a respectable color."

Raldnor protested as Xaros plastered the jet black paste onto his hair, and Helida applied jugfuls of barely warm water.

"He struggles like an eel. Keep still while I attend to your eyebrows."

"Will this paint wash off?" Raldnor demanded, stunned and made almost submissive by indignity.

"Wash off? Gods and goddesses—Do you suppose all the elderly black-haired ladies you see in the street would pay out their funds to be unmasked by the first rain?"

They toweled his hair before the fire.

"A rough imperfect job of work," Xaros commented. "Now into your bed, under the covers and shut your eyes. It's true certain Dortharians have yellow eyes—their famous king Rarnammon for one—but I can hardly pass you off as him. And say nothing, though an occasional groan I will allow you."

At which moment, new and heavier footfalls, the unmistakable sound of mail, clashed on the stairs.

The imperative knock came seconds later. Xaros opened the door and feigned amazement.

"To what do I owe this honor?"

"No honor, Xarab. You've a man here—"

"Why, yes. How singularly clever of you to know—"

"A Lowlander."

Xaros raised his eyebrows.

"Indeed no, soldier. I spit on such scum."

"Oh yes? Then who's the man?"

"My brother, sir. Prey to a strange affliction; the physician is entirely baffled."

The two Dortharians thrust by him and flung open the

door of the second room. They saw a dark-haired man, apparently asleep in the bed, and a Xarabian woman drooped at the bedside in an attitude of weary despair.

"I must beg you, sir, not to disturb the poor fellow. Additionally," Xaros muttered with pathos, "the fever is highly contagious."

The soldier nearest the bed checked his stride.

"Have you reported his sickness to the authorities?"

"Naturally, sir," Xaros murmured.

"Damnation," snarled the Dortharian in the doorway. "You were born of a lying race, Xarab. I'll skin those rats in Slant Street if I catch them."

"Liars abound," Xaros remarked sententiously.

The two men pushed their way past.

"What had the Lowlander done to displease you, magnificent sir?"

"That's my affair. I owe him something."

Xaros ushered them out and called solicitously after them to mind their step on the lower stairs, then shut the door—and leaned thereon in the helpless mirth of self-applause.

"I'm in your debt for my life," Raldnor said. It had been easy enough to feign illness in that room, so close to a piece of death.

"So you are. But, more to the point, don't you think, Helida, that he makes a remarkably good Vis?"

And later, when Raldnor stared at himself in Helida's glass, another man looked back at him. Something irreparable had occurred—it stretched quite beyond the incident. For it seemed to him he was no longer Raldnor, certainly no longer the Raldnor he had known. And the planes of his face were comfortable and apt, their hauteur set now in this darkness. He seemed to discover himself for what he was. "I am easy with this stranger," he thought. "He never knew the crippling of a deaf mind, nor the unwilling Lowland girls; not even the white crystal girl of the Lowlander's sleep. I am Vis now, truly Vis. Is this the legacy my mother intended? Out of an old whore's dye bottle?"

He took up the wolf pelt in the morning and went out to sell it. The streets ran with the rain of the thaw, but he did not think of Orhvan's wagon negotiating the unfriendly mud, nor of the ruined city; in a way he had renounced them. And he walked arrogantly, unafraid. Since he had seen the Dortharian soldier spit from the courtyard after them, a hidden part of him had been uneasy to move about these streets, though he had not owned this.

Yet near the furriers Xaros had recommended, he passed across the Red Market and saw five women up for sale to the whorehouses.

Four were pert faced and untroubled enough, flirting with the crowd—black-haired tarts already from the look of them. The fifth was a Lowland woman, dressed in a coarse shift.

Raldnor stared at that familiar and unreadable face he knew so well from the villages. And then, incredibly, it seemed their minds touched, for her head jerked up and she scanned the crowd. Yet he was not strong or adept enough to hold their accidental contact; he did not know how. And she, seeing only dark men about her, relapsed into gray immobility.

Yet the mob, mostly louts with some Ommos and Dortharian men among them, began to jeer at her.

"Looking for me, you yellow mare? I'll ride you!"

Sudden cold fear dropped over Raldnor. He began to shiver. With an impulse of agonized cowardice, he turned and pushed a way across the square.

He reached the furriers with a sense of horror still on him.

The shop was lofty and dim, and smelled of its wares. He snatched up a handbell and rang it sharply, and the merchant emerged like a shade from a crevice in the wall.

"My lord?" His voice was oddly fawning, unctuous. Raldnor was marvelously surprised to be addressed in such a voice.

"This," he said; he opened the cloth and spread the pelt on the counter in a spool of icy flame.

The merchant betrayed himself with a sharp intake of breath. Then, mastering himself, he said: "A fine skin. Indeed yes. You bleached it?"

"I didn't touch it. This was a white wolf."

The merchant gave a little laugh, as if amused by a favorite child.

"Ah, my *lord*. A wolf pelt of this size, and so white?"

"If you've no taste for my goods, I'll go elsewhere."

"Wait, my lord—indeed—you're too hasty. Possibly it's as you say. But I've no recollection of a hunter trapping such a thing for years."

"Not trapped. Pierced through the eye. The pelt's unmarked."

The merchant hastily examined the hide, then, shaking his head, he murmured: "Of course, it would be difficult to sell so large an article, the times being what they are. I could offer you fifteen ankars in gold."

"Offer me thirty," Raldnor said, well instructed by Xaros and inflamed by loathing to boot.

"He deserves more for his impertinence alone," a new voice said.

Raldnor turned and saw a man had come out of the hole in the wall. He was a Dortharian, there was no mistaking it, yet he did not wear the dragon mail. He leaned on the counter, looking at Raldnor.

"You should have called me sooner, merchant." The merchant began to speak, but the newcomer overrode him. "Tell me, where did you kill your wolf?"

Cautiously Raldnor assessed his own words.

"In the Plains."

"The Plains? A long way surely from home? You're from the cities of Dorthar, are you not?"

This ghastly irony brought the blood singing to Raldnor's ears.

"I'm no Dortharian."

"How quickly you disclaim the High Race of Vis. Where then?"

"I come from Sar," Raldnor said, "near the Dragon Gate."

It was where his mother had been making for, so his foster village had thought, thus it carried a kind of truth.

"Sar, eh? And the wolf, where did he come from?"

"Out of the dark, on to my knife."

The man laughed.

"Fifty gold ankars for that pelt, merchant." The merchant gobbled. "But you're too late. My master will buy it. It's better than anything you showed me. Come aside." And he drew Raldnor into the dusky twilight of the shop—the merchant, for some reason intimidated, not following. "Well, hunter, so you can kill wolves. Ever killed a man?"

Raldnor stared at him in silence.

"Oh, it's a good trade, the trade of soldiering. Your mother was Xarabian, was she? Know your father, do you?"

"You insult me," Raldnor said coldly, a burning nausea in his throat before he knew the reason.

"Not I. Your father was a Dortharian for my money. And that, lad, is a compliment. Well, would you like to soldier for an exceptionally generous lord who holds a high place in Koramvis?"

"Why should I want such a thing?"

"Why indeed? Why not scratch out a life in Sar?"

"Who is this lord?"

"You go too fast. Take this and spend it, and think about spending such a sum more regularly in Dorthar. Return here tomorrow at noon. We'll talk then."

Raldnor took the bulging money bag, opened it and saw the gold pieces shining up at him. He felt once more a shifting in the planes of his life.

"You're very sure of me, Dortharian."

"That's how I earn *my* gold. By my unerring sense of a willing quarry."

Raldnor turned and walked between the heaps of furs, leaving the pelt for the stranger who had bought it. At the door he heard the Dortharian call after him: "Noon, hunter. I'll be waiting."

Outside the rain still ran in the gutters, but a dark shadow of change covered the landscape. Raldnor considered: "I'll go back. Why? A soldier in their corrupt armies. I, the impostor, Lowland scum. And Dorthar—that reeking tomb of dead kings. What's that dragon place to me?"

8

SHE RODE INTO LIN ABISSA, her grandfather's capital, on the back of a rust red monster.

She and it were a dual thing of fire in the white afternoon, the apex of a procession made up of gaudy acrobats, fantastic dancers and incredible creatures dressed to resemble Xarabian legend. Amrek's betrothed was piped, sung and magicked through the streets like a goddess from an era before time.

The beast that carried her was a giant palutorvus from the steamy swamps of Zakoris. She sat in a golden contraption with a roof of plumes. She wore a dull red gown, trimmed with chestnut fur and cut low in the neck, an orange jewel clenched between her breasts. From a tower of golden flowers at her skull fell a smoky drift of scarlet veil. Her hair was the precise color of blood.

The crowds murmured and craned up to see her. And, as with all things flawless, she seemed unreal. Instinctively they searched her person for humanity, some hint of dross, but this was a salamander beauty, burning, mythological, unbounded by any laws or levelings.

She rode without a glance to either side. She was an image of herself.

* * *

The procession halted on the avenue before the palace portico, and the red beast knelt.

A man took Astaris's hand as she stepped from her gilded ladder of steps and bowed low.

"Madam, I welcome your grace to the Storm Lord's court at Lin Abissa. I am the Lord Amrek's Councilor, Kathaos. Account me your slave." His voice was slightly slurred with the accent denoting Ommos or Zakorian, yet the triple-tailed dragon of Alisaar was the emblem on his robe.

She said nothing to his courtesy, and, meeting her eyes, he had the impression of endless depths of beautiful opacity.

Amrek waited for her on the palace steps in order that the crowds at the gates should get some oblique glimpses of their meeting. Kathaos led her to the King and stepped aside. The woman was confronted by the man who was to be, from this moment, her lord.

He was dark and cruel in his exterior, like an emblem of himself and his reputation. He leaned toward her and placed on her lips the traditional kiss of greeting that marked his approval.

Her mouth was very cool, and she seemed to wear no perfume, despite her finery, as if she were merely a doll that had allowed itself to be dressed. Something about her angered him. He was subject to such angers. Ostentatiously ignoring his Councilor, whom he hated for many various reasons, he took her hand roughly and pulled her into the palace with him. She made no complaint.

"Madam, I am unaccustomed to dangling women on my arm. I walk too fast for you, I think."

"If you think so, you should walk more slowly," she said. Her remark had a combination of insolence and wit, yet he sensed that both were somehow accidental. She had simply made a statement.

"So you have a tongue. I thought the swamp beast had bitten it out."

They came into a huge room, the retinue left behind. He moved her to look about at things.

"Do you know what happened in this room, Astaris Am Karmiss? A woman died here because of her fear of me."

"Did it pain you that she died?"

"Pain? No, she was a Lowland whore. Nothing. Don't you want to know why she feared me? It was this—this gauntlet. But you, Astaris, have no need to fear it. I wear the glove to hide a knife scar—not a beautiful thing."

"What is beauty?" she said.

Her curious responses disturbed him, and she also, this impossible jewel cast into his gloomy life to blaze there like a comet.

"You, Astaris, are beautiful," he said.

"Yes, but I'm not a measure."

He let go her hand.

"Were you afraid on the monster's back? You must blame Kathaos if you were. His ideas become a village circus-master."

"What should I fear?"

"Perhaps, despite what I said to you, you should fear me a little."

"Why?"

"Why? I am the High King, more, I am *her* son—the bitch queen of Koramvis. I inherit all her foulness and her cruelty. And now I am to be your lord. While you please me, you'll be safe enough. But not when I lose interest—unsurpassable loveliness might evoke boredom after a time, even yours. Especially yours. Your perfect symmetry will grate, madam."

She only smiled. It was an enigmatic smile. Was it her hubris, her self-assurance, or was she perhaps unable to grasp his meaning? Either she was obscure or she was slightly insane. Perhaps this was the flaw—an imbecilic queen to rule Dorthar by his side.

Moving with unbelievable grace, she began to look at frescoes. He felt fleetingly unreal in her presence.

"Astaris, you'll attend to me," he shouted.

She turned and looked at him searchingly, though her eyes, as Kathaos had noted, were pools of bottomless dark amber glass.

"I attend," she said, "to you."

A late afternoon light was settling on Lin Abissa as Kathaos Am Alisaar crossed from Thann Rashek's major palace to the guest mansion adjoining it. Such was Am Alisaar's status as Councilor to the Storm Lord that the entire scope of the latter house had been given over to himself and his household.

Which was as well, Kathaos's household being of an immodest yet clandestine nature.

Particularly, there was his private guard. Not that this was, in itself, an unusual acquisition; most nobles amassed them. Yet the dimension and ability of Kathaos's guard would have been found notable had it been investigated. Chosen by Am Alisaar's agents at random in the thoroughfares of several cities—a method which successfully evaded Amrek's direct notice—they came from among the ranks of fortune hunters, thieves, malcontents. Once under Kathaos's yellow blazon, however, they were arbitrarily amalgamated, specifically trained in the fighting techniques of the Imperial Academy in Koramvis and led into collective though no less dangerous modes of living. Not many rebelled or abused their school. Those who did vanished mysteriously, yet suitably, into the dark to which such men were subject. Those who persisted at their new trade did well by it, becoming almost inadvertently part of a large and well-oiled machine. For Kathaos's aim was to possess at last a defense as traditionally geared, strong, elite, and deadly as the Dragon Guard of a Storm Lord.

Kathaos had, as it were, hereditary reasons for his ambition.

His father had been Orhn, ultimate King of Alisaar. Though it was generally said that by the time that Orhn moved to take Alisaar from the dying grasp of his sire, he had in truth lost all interest in her—for by then the reins of Dorthar were firmly in his hands. He had fathered Kathaos on a minor Zakorian queen during one of his brief forays to Saardos, but he was never away from his regency, or his mistress Val Mala, for long. Only death put an end to his to-ing and fro-ing. And now, ironically, it was Kathaos who was Val Mala's lover—a pleasant enough situation, for the queen had taken care to age as little as possible and extended favors to those who amused her.

He wondered if Astaris would amuse her, and decided emphatically that she would not.

The junction of the palace and the guest mansion was marked by a pillar forest of crimson fluted glass, which now throbbed with mulberry embers of the low sun and clotted incarnadine shadow.

"Rashek's architect seems to have had a certain vulgar genius," Kathaos remarked.

"If you say so, my lord."

Kathaos's Guard Lord, Ryhgon, striding half a pace behind him, was not as a rule addicted to long sentences.

A huge Zakorian, his true addiction, which was a form of authoritarian brutality, showed in every line of body and face. His giant's nose was smashed into unrecognizable shape, and a white scar jumped from jaw to oxneck. A vicious leader for Kathaos's personal guard, a leader not to be crossed, with the power of six apparent in his abnormally developed sword arm. Kathaos found him excellent.

"There are twenty recruits from Abissa, so I hear," Kathaos said. "You, of course, will manage them superbly."

Ryhgon gave a grim smile.

"Trust me."

At the portico the Zakorian took another smaller entrance and advanced down the corridor of the mansion to

that long hall where the recruits were waiting for him. Firelight seeped about the hall, casting up a huge familiar shade
behind Ryhgon. The men fell silent at his approach, their
facial expressions ranging from nervousness to bravado.
This was to be one of the few times when Ryhgon spoke at
any length. It was a well-known speech to him. He had used
it on several battalions of untried adventurers such as these,
and the unpleasant smile was still on his scarred mouth.

"So, this is the latest filth they've given me to hammer
into men. I say 'hammer.' I choose the word with care. You
see this arm? This is the arm I hammer with, if I have to."
He moved to a table and poured himself wine, and the silence prevailed about him. "Your profession from today is
that of house guard to the Prince Kathaos Am Alisaar. The
least witless of you may have gathered already that there's
more to it than that. But you'll keep your tongues quiet or
someone will quieten them for you. I hope you understand
me. If it's gold pieces you're wanting, there'll be plenty. If
you feel the need to screw a whore, you'll find those provided, too. If you've any other bedroom habits, settle them
elsewhere and pray I don't catch you at it. For the rest, you'll
discover the discipline is savage and I'm not a gentle master. Do as I tell you, and work yourselves sick and you'll live
till Koramvis." He drained the wine without swallowing and
banged down the goblet. "Any of you that find occasion to
want a quarrel—seek me out. It'll be my pleasure to accommodate you."

Lightly, Ryhgon flipped the short sword at his belt, then
turned and left them.

A man at Raldnor's side said, very low: "Zakorian
midden-keeper."

At dusk the first white birds settled on Lin Abissa. The thaw
was ended. Soon the three-month snow would hold all the
eastern segment of Vis under its inexorable seal.

The Lord Kathaos's new recruits ate their meal at a long
table, separated from the more seasoned guard. The guard

paid them no attention, it being their unwritten law to show no interest until training and probation were done. And there was a deal of sullen silence and covert gossip at the long table. Ryhgon had already established himself as he had chosen to be established—a figure to be hated and inordinately feared.

"That man's no lover of gentle ways."

"Zakorian whore's mistake."

"Watch yourself. Walls have ears."

"Did you get a look at that sword arm? And the scar on his face? Gods!"

Later they sought the narrow pallets of a bleak dormitory.

Raldnor lay a long while on his hard bed, listening to their mutterings and to his own thoughts.

Outside the snow fell in silver flickerings. The siege snow.

"So I've locked myself in with strangers and with uncertainties, instead of with the known village and its familiar hopeless ways," Raldnor thought. He recaptured Hamos under the snow, the purple snow nights and the howling of wolves, and he thought of Eraz beneath the white layerings, returned to the stuff of the Plains.

He had paid his debts. He had given back to Xaros all he owed while Xaros protested volubly, but he had told neither Xaros nor Helida of the man in the furrier's nor, later, of where he was going. And they had respected his silence, probably imagining he would be returning after Orhvan to the Lowlands and the ruined city. He had found a shop in the back streets of Abissa and bought himself a supply of black dye with which he subsequently attended to his body hair. With this bizarre sorcery committed, his life and his soul seemed to slip into a curious interim, a limbo. He had worked a spell of change upon himself, and he had unleashed, like magicians of old, ungauged elemental forces. Now, anything might happen.

Yet there were remnants of ancient magic still clinging. She came, for the first time in many nights, here, to this

Xarabian palace in the dark. The white moon shone behind her, and the cracks appeared in the broken vase of her milk-white body, and she blew away like ashes or like snow.

The bed was an oval of beaten silver, shaped to resemble an open flower, for, like the procession which had brought her here, it was deemed proper that all things surrounding Amrek's betrothed should be fantastic.

And in this flower Astaris opened her eyes at midnight.

There had been a dream. An unaccountable dream. A woman blowing in ashes across the face of the moon, all negative whiteness.

Astaris left the bed and crossed the room, throwing open the draperies and shutters, moving out on to the icy, snow-capped balcony. The cold was only a half-felt suggestion at the edges of her thought. Her entire consciousness seemed centered at the core of her brain, more so now than at any time before. She felt herself listening, yet not for any kind of sound.

And then she saw a man lying before her in the dark. Yet she did not exactly see him or even sense him. She felt, but rather, she comprehended. She did not ask: "Who is this?" There was no need. At that moment it was herself.

Instinctively she withdrew, flinched aside from the contact, and the formless image of the man was gone.

The secret of the enigma of Astaris was only this: She lived within herself, and no part of her reached out to commune with others. It was not pride or fear, but simply the most pure, the most unhuman introspection. She could not believe, or barely, in the external world and its characters; she did not even believe in her own physical self. She was an intelligence shut inside an exquisite mummy case of flesh, a creature in a shell. Now, by accident, a note had woken her, a resonance no longer outside her, but within.

Like a citadel invaded, she was at once full of alarm, but there was yielding also. She understood nothing of what had occurred, but did not need to. This was not the sort of questioning she used. She understood merely that, for an instant, the coiled sea creature which lived in the shell of her and was herself had been discovered by the wandering somnambulist impulse of another.

"Something has come near me," she thought in strange stilted wonderment. "Something has found me out."

BOOK THREE

The Meteoric Hero

9

Enclosed in the white womb of the cold, the eastern lands waited in their three months' chrysalis. Pragmatic winter exchanged their contours for a geography of snow marble, wind-stenciled ice, and the inexorable silence of the desert. Nevertheless, the sun waxed as ever, encroached as ever. The sudden, bright, sounding first rains of a Vis spring shocked and cracked the alabaster seals, as they had always shocked and cracked them.

In Lin Abissa the gutters foamed, and the ornate gardens quickened.

Twilight oceaned about the towers of Thann Rashek's guest palace, bringing an old nostalgia to Yannul the Lan as he sat cleaning his soldier's gear in the uninspiring and impersonal barracks. Impersonal, despite the fact that in three months Am Alisaar's recruits had littered it with certain personal things—their blunt but sentimental knives, some girl's favor, trophies, knickknacks, memories from previous lives. For it seemed to Yannul that they had all been cursorily reincarnated into this soldiering under Kathaos's yellow cloak, made new men with discarded pasts, about which many were very reticent. Raldnor the Sarite, now. He and Yannul seemed to count each other friends, yet what did they ever really say to each other about their earlier days? Both had been village farm stock to begin with—Raldnor, he said, on the perimeter of Sar, Yannul in the pendulous blue bosom of the Lannic hills. Later, both had made their way to the towns of Xarabiss: Yannul to be a juggler and acrobat in the markets, Raldnor to spend a nebulous time about which he said nothing—until Kathaos's scouts found both of them and lured them under the yellow blazon. Yannul rubbed a troubled hand across the nape of his neck. Soldiering had meant a barber for the shoulder-blade-long Lannic hair. "No barbarians in *this* service," the man had clacked. And "slash" those knives had gone, and a part of his supposedly barbarian pride with them. He saw Raldnor looking at him then, across the shadows, so he set nostalgia aside and said: "Koramvis soon."

"Yes," Raldnor said, "the city of Rarnammon, under the protection of the Storm gods of the Am Dorthar."

It had puzzled Yannul often, the pains Raldnor had apparently taken to discover the bits and pieces of Dortharian religion and myth, for under the curiosity and the lip service there seemed to be another emotion—dislike. There had been, too, an incident once—some low muttering at table about how Kathaos was intent on toppling Amrek the Storm Lord. Men had sat, stony-faced, keeping their own counsel and wary of Ryhgon's spies. But Yannul had seen Raldnor's hand clench on his cup until the knuckles went white, and on his mouth there had been a hint of the grimmest and most macabre grin—almost the grin of a madman—before the Sarite had mastered himself.

"It pleases them to say so," Yannul said lightly. "I think Kathaos fears no divine forces."

"Then he's a brave man."

"Oh, men make their own gods," Yannul remarked. "I have a god with a fat belly, and a house full of expensive women to attend his every need, and I call him Yannul the Lan in Five Years from This. Well, that's done," and he laid aside the knives and other metal duly polished. "What now? Neither of us has watch duty. We could try the wine shops of Abissa."

Raldnor put down his own gear and nodded.

"Why not?" Like most people confined inside set limits, they were glad enough to get out of them whenever possible and by whatever excuse. "But we'll need a gate pass, Yannul."

"No. Lazy Breon's in charge. Remember, Ryhgon eats at Kathaos's table tonight. And Kathaos has my profound thanks."

None of them had much cause to love the Guard Lord. He had proved himself all he had promised to be three months before. Yet he had taught them well. The knowledge of the fighting academies of Dorthar, Alisaar and Zakoris was ingrained in them by now, for Ryhgon had flayed them with it, given it to them in place of bread. And there was a bonus, too, for with his absences, however brief, there came a sense of holiday.

Yet the thaw dusk had laid a strange hold on both of them for all that, and they idled only slowly down toward the outer court.

Kathaos glanced across the lamplit room at Ryhgon and said, with irony far too subtle to offend his guest: "I trust the dinner found favor with you."

Ryhgon grunted.

"Your lordship keeps a generous table."

"Good fortune grants I can."

"Your lordship's no believer in fortune."

"Perhaps not, but in this world of euphemisms, you'll permit me mine."

"As your lordship likes."

"Well. And do you have any news of my guard?"

It was customary for Ryhgon, after these excellent dinners, to make some report. Responding to the signal, he laid out his inventory. Things were well enough. The latest recruits from Abissa had shown reasonable aptitude and had been split up among the first and second companies. By the time they reached Koramvis he would have cut them into shape.

"Be careful the knife doesn't slip," Kathaos said.

"Your lordship doubts my ability?"

Kathaos smiled.

"You're a harsh master, Ryhgon."

"Do I claim otherwise? Don't worry, my lord. I can sort the metal from the dross. It's the dross that suffers."

"There was a man with light eyes—I saw him at drill yesterday," Kathaos said unexpectedly. "What about him?"

"The Sarite?" Ryhgon gave a short unpleasant laugh. "He's the unquiet sex of a dragon. The women your lordship supplies have been unusually busy. They seem to like it, too."

"What's his measure as a fighter?"

"Fair." In Ryhgon's terminology this was high praise. Kathaos judged it accordingly.

"That interests me. I want you to keep a watch on him. He has an uneasy resemblance to the royal line of the Am Dorthar."

"I hadn't noticed it."

"I would never expect you to. However, I am perhaps more familiar with that face. Don't you think it unusual that such a Dortharian brand should be set in Sar?"

"A by-blow. Some passing Koramvin."

"Then that Koramvin would need to have been a prince."

"Unlikely."

"Quite. Which leads me to a theory that perhaps your Sarite comes from a higher bed altogether, in Koramvis itself."

Ryhgon's eyes widened.

"Belly of earth!"

"I may, of course, be mistaken," Kathaos said dryly.

"He would have had to know where your lordship placed your scouts."

"Possibly he does. There is a certain careful enmity between Amrek and myself, yet I'm useful to him and not overt in what I do. But if this Sarite is some half-brother of Amrek's, put here as the King's spy—I think you understand me, Ryhgon."

There was a light, indeterminate, white moth snow blowing on the wind, melting colorlessly on the pavements of the city.

Still absorbed by the melancholy dusk, Raldnor and the Lan had settled on the lower and more obscure ways of Abissa. The first wine shop they came to was unknown, but they pushed in out of the snowy dark to the murky light of greasy candles. The place was deserted.

Yannul took hold of the handbell hanging by the grate and rang it, and out of the silence of the shop came the rustling of a woman's skirt in answer. But it was a threadbare skirt, and she little and thin and very young. As the shadow left her, Raldnor saw that she had yellow hair.

She did not speak. Yannul asked her for wine; she nodded and went out. As soon as she was gone, he said: "A Lowlander!" His voice was full of amazement. "Does she know how close she is to Amrek's nest? How has the persecution passed her by? She must be a slave." And then, with surprising gentleness: "Poor little mite, she looked barely old enough to couple."

Raldnor said nothing. As once before, a terror of betrayal came on him. Then it had been the woman in the market at Abissa, but fear had found him more expectedly, and so less painfully, at that time—the physical change he had wrought on himself being still new. He saw now that in the three months of the snow he had come to think of himself as a Xarabian, and as a Vis, despite the subterfuge of the dye. True, he had nursed the old hatred for Amrek, but that had become an almost abstract thing, an emotion sufficient unto itself, a reason no longer essential. Even when she came to him in dreams, and he woke sweating on the couches of the whores, thinking himself once again in the Pleasure City, the agony of despair beginning in his skull, the focus of Anici's death was dissociated from race. Could not a Xarabian love a Lowland girl and lose her to a monstrous perverted King? It had bitterly pleased him to study the ways of the Am Dorthar, to read their legends, and somewhere in this morass of beliefs, he had mislaid the pure monotheism of the Plains. It had been easy, in the end, to swear by gods and not by Her, the Lady of Snakes, who asked for nothing, being all.

And now this girl in her rags, a figment of his lost unhappy past, conjured to torment him with remembrance.

She returned and set cups and a stone jug on the table, and then took their payment in her chapped hands. Raldnor turned away, but even when she had gone the room seemed full of her.

Yannul gave him a brimming cup, and they gulped the raw strong drink. He noticed the Lan's eyes on him.

"Finish your wine. This is a gloomy place, and there's a love house five doors up," Yannul said.

There was a sudden noise outside which did not somehow belong in these streets. The door burst open and the fire leapt.

Six men entered. They wore the black tunics and black hooded cloaks that were the casual wear of the Storm Lord's Dragon Guard, and worked in silver upon breast and back was Amrek's lightning blazon. They cast half looks at the house's earlier customers, discounting them as of no importance. Kathaos's badge was ignored. One of them spoke in a low voice. They laughed.

"A strange haunt for Amrek's Chosen," Yannul said softly. "Why here?"

The dragons had sat down at a trestle and, disdaining the bell, began to beat with their mailed fists on the table top.

"Let's go," Yannul said.

But Raldnor found he could not move. He sat like stone, staring at the inner doorway, and a moment later the Lowland girl came. She walked quietly toward the noisy table, as though unaware of any enmity in the world.

Silence fell at once. The Dragon Guard sat, their eyes riveted on her. One of them, the tallest, eased back his hood.

"Wine, little girl. And make sure you bring it yourself."

Expressionless, the girl turned and went away. A dragon laughed.

"Spawn of the snake goddess. So the rumor was correct."

Raldnor felt Yannul grip his shoulder.

"Let's be on our way."

"Wait," Raldnor said and set down his cup; the blood thudded in his temples, and a taste of dry bone was in his mouth.

The girl came back shortly, a jug in the crook of her arm, cups caught by their stems between her fingers. She poured their wine, then stood waiting for payment.

After a while a dragon looked round at her.

"What do you want, girl?"

One of his companions leaned forward.

"She's demanding money."

"Money for what? For the wine?" He drained his cup and held it out to her, empty. "See, you didn't give me any."

A slow cold laughter circled the table.

The girl turned, presumably to go in search of the proprietor. The dragon swiftly caught her, swung her about and pushed her against the trestle.

"If you want money, little girl, you'll have to earn it. Yes, struggle all you want. You won't get away. Besides, you struggle very nicely." Holding her easily with one arm, he pealed open the bodice of her dress, revealing the beautiful yet immature breasts of barely quickened puberty. "I've heard all you Lowland bitches are virgin. I've never had a virgin. How do you think that'll compensate for the wine you never poured me, you slut?"

But something like a vise caught his shoulder and dragged him round from the girl with a force that utterly surprised him. Next came a blow of darkness in his throat and for a time the world stopped spinning. He fell across the table and was still.

The other five stared at this tall, light-eyed house guard of Kathaos Am Alisaar, who could not be anything but insane.

"Foolish," one said, but he was smiling.

They began circling, two to get behind him, three content to wait on his capture. Raldnor understood very well that he had given them the right to kill him, but he was indeed mad, in a way. Like them, he felt a strange joy at the prospect of violence, and the big men were dwarfed by his mood—a pack he could toss off his back like beans. Then there was a yell from behind him. Yannul, it seemed, had joined the fight.

Raldnor snatched the wine jug from the table and flung the liquor in the nearest dragon's face, leaving the two behind him for the Lan. As the man cursed and clawed his eyes, Raldnor sprang, knocking his legs from under him and sending him crashing into his neighbor. Rolling clear of the struggling heap, he brought his fist into cracking connection with a gaping jaw and kicked the other deftly with a light yet almost deadly accuracy over the heart. In the background he heard the blows of the Lan's own iron juggler's knuckles, and to this continuing music the third Guard slung himself against Raldnor, a short knife blazing in his hand. But he met Raldnor's foot before his body, and next got a concussion in his guts that sent him retching and reeling to the ground. The handy stone wine jug added the finishing touch, and his knife fell harmlessly on the flags.

Raldnor turned with an irrepressible brutal laughter.

"Ryhgon taught us our trade immaculately," he called to Yannul. "A harsh but an excellent master."

Then he looked fully at the second Guard the Lan had felled and saw from the angle of him that his neck was broken.

Yannul stood staring at the body, his face pale.

"He's dead, Raldnor. I wasn't as elegant as you."

"The blame's mine," Raldnor said sharply. "My fight. You came to help me." Yet a dark and dismal quiet had settled in that place. Who knew better than he that death was promised to any who killed one of the Storm Lord's Chosen? It had been Dortharian law for a thousand years or more. But he took Yannul's arm. "Out of here. Who saw?"

"She did."

Raldnor turned and noted the Lowland girl standing motionless at the grate.

"She won't tell any tales." Harshly he shouted out to her: "Go back to the Plains before they eat you alive in this stinking city."

But her golden eyes stared blind as stones into his, though he felt a curious fluttering like a bird in his brain. He turned, put his arm over Yannul's shoulders and drew him out into the cold and empty streets.

"Well Ryhgon, what is this so urgent news?"

"Your pardon, my lord. There's been a brawl in Lin Abissa. The Storm Lord's Guard. And two of my men. One of the dragons is dead."

Kathaos's face was blank.

"You have this on good authority?"

"Would I accept it otherwise? The owner of the wine shop reported the incident. A sniveling sot, frightened of what would be done to him, spying behind a curtain. He described your guard—the Lannic acrobat was one. The other—a pale-eyed man, missing a left finger."

"The . . . Sarite. Is he the killer?"

"I don't know as yet, my lord."

"Discover. What began the trouble?"

"The Xarab fool who runs the shop keeps a Lowland mare as a slave. The dragons were unlacing. The Lan and the Sarite were pleased to take exception to rape."

"Something you find hard to believe," Kathaos remarked.

Ryhgon said: "You know my views on women, my lord."

"Her race is at present more interesting than her sex. How many Vis defend Lowlanders with Amrek here?"

"Xarabs and Lans have soft ways for the Plains."

"Yet our hunter may not be Xarabian, as we discussed before. Where have you put the two?"

"A cellar room below the palace."

"Let them sample a night there. Bring me the hunter here at noon tomorrow. Find out what you can between now and then, but restrain your arm. Is there any word from Amrek?"

"None."

"As well. But not illogical. No doubt he would dislike the incident widely broadcast. The Guard of Kings, after all, is supposed to be invincible, and myth should never be reduced to a mere technicality."

After the darkness of the cellarways, the midday light in the upper rooms of the mansion hurt his eyes. His guards had left him in a small bright chamber, unbound, and presently Kathaos entered.

It was the first time Raldnor had come close to him, this man who had owned him through these three months of hard-bought living. Ryhgon had been the harsh symbol; here stood the actuality. A well-controlled face, blood lines too mixed to give him any hint of his royalty beyond the finecast good looks.

He seated himself and observed Raldnor with an unfathomable expression that might have been the mask for anything and was almost unarguably the mask for something.

"Well, Sarite, what have you got to say to me?"

"Whatever you want me to say, my lord, to amend my fault."

"An elegant speech won't mend anything, Sarite, I assure you. Do you know what you've done? You've offended the King. Of all men, the Storm Lord's Dragon Guard can do as they please; their rights are second only to his. And you, hunter, have hung them up by the heels. Not a good thing to do."

"Your lordship is, I believe, aware of my reasons."

"Some wine girl . . ."

"Little more than a child, my lord. They'd have killed her."

"She was a Lowlander. The King tells us Lowlanders are of no importance."

"A child—" Raldnor broke out.

"Instruct me," Kathaos said, and his voice had grown harder, "which of you broke the dragon's neck?"

"It was my pleasure."

"Your pleasure. Why kill this one man and leave the rest alive?"

"He was their leader."

"He was not." Kathaos paused deliberately. "The shop-keeper saw the Lan catch the guard's neck in his hands and break it like a fowl's."

Raldnor did not speak. At last Kathaos said: "You extend your altruism too far, and anything stretched too far loses its edge. Nevertheless, I am not going to make you the meat for Amrek's anger. Yannul the Lan will do well enough for that. Ryhgon will see that he's punished for his offense. You will shortly receive a pardon."

Raldnor stared at him.

"Punish me too. The fight was mine."

Kathaos lifted and rang the small bell at his elbow. Doors opened and guards reentered.

An empty disdain shook the last dregs of hope out of Raldnor. Buried in his own guilt for Yannul, he ignored what Kathaos offered him, finding it valueless.

"I thank your lordship," he said quietly, "for this impartial justice."

It was enough to hang him, but did not. The guards merely marched him back to his dungeon, from which Yannul was gone.

Yet Kathaos sat on in the upper room for some while. The whole episode had seemed curious; who knew what lay

behind it? From the first he had considered it best not to
thrust the man in the path of royal fury. That would be to
force Amrek's hand, and if the Sarite were a spy, then he
would only, at some future time, be replaced by another,
less detectable one. As things stood, he had become a sort
of game piece between the King and his Councilor, and
there might be uses for him later.

"And I was not mistaken," Kathaos now thought. "This
naïve fighting cock is one of the princes of Koramvis."

It was the sudden icy gust of imperial arrogance that had
convinced him. A fool might be stupid enough to spit in his
lord's eye, as Raldnor had done, yet not with that aura of
incredible assurance and contempt. Kathaos knew that
look very well. He had endured it from his earliest conscious hours. That look had, in part, been the foundation of
his lifestyle, and now, coming unexpectedly as it did from
the eyes of a man who should by rights have been pleading
for his life, it had breached all defenses. And Kathaos Am
Alisaar had inwardly cringed, a fact that interested rather
than distressed him.

The night passed in a black fever as Raldnor paced his
prison, half mad with anger. More guilt. Had there not been
enough guilt for him to bear? The rat thoughts scuttled and
gnawed.

In the morning he woke out of a stupefied sleep and saw
the iron door left open for him.

He climbed the stairways up into the light. He passed
guards and servants with blank faces. In an upper corridor
he saw one of the barrack whores, a pretty sloven, who nor-
mally liked him well enough. But when he caught her arm
and asked her: "Do you know where Yannul is?" she shook
her head and hurried off.

In the dormitory he and Yannul used he found a man
untidily penning a letter, who looked up immediately and
said: "You've heard how Yannul was punished?"

"No. You'd better tell me."

"He was a fool to set on the Chosen. So were you to follow him. You can take friendship too far."

So that was the story Kathaos had put about. Raldnor let the man's meddling, worthless advice go by like so much chaff on the wind.

"Yannul's punishment," he reminded harshly.

The man shook his head.

"That bastard Ryhgon had him dragged into the hall and had them hold his right hand up against the chimney column. Then he took a cibba staff and smashed it across the back. Must've broken every bone. That's Zakorian justice for you."

"Ryhgon," Raldnor said very softly. That was all. Then: "Where's Yannul now?"

"The gods know. Not here, that's for sure. What will you do?" the soldier added curiously. Raldnor knew him well enough for a gossip.

"I? What can *I* do?"

All that day the anger mangled him. The pivot of the anger—Yannul—became a secondary thing. Though he did not analyze this, part of him knew why he no longer sought the Lan or asked questions as to his whereabouts. Yet he had no thoughts beyond his anger. He was quite absorbed in it.

Evening came, and the evening meal at the long tables.

"Look out for yourself, Raldnor," a Xarabian muttered to him. "My gods tell me Ryhgon hasn't quite finished with you."

"My gods tell me things too," Raldnor said.

Another man glanced his way and said: "I see no justice in breaking a man's right hand so he can do nothing to make himself a living. A juggler, wasn't he? He'll juggle nothing now."

A sudden thick quiet fell. Ryhgon, a latecomer, had just entered the hall, his officers about him. He did not sit at once, but struck the bell by his place, and the last vestiges of chat and stirring died out in the room.

"I've something to say to you. I don't doubt you know two men here saw fit to cross Amrek's Dragon Guard. That they live is due to the mercy of the Lord Kathaos and the present good humor of the King. The Lan was punished. The Sarite, as you see, received his pardon. My lord the prince chooses to be lenient with fools, but you've all had fair warning before of my dislike of foolishness. You can thank your gods, Raldnor of Sar, that I too am in a pleasant humor. And in future, Sarite, you'll work twice as hard and watch your manners twice as carefully as any other man here. Am I understood?"

The hush of the room was intolerable. A sense of impending drama had come on it at the last instant, and the eyes of every soldier present were fixed on Raldnor as he sat at the end of the bench. Not turning yet, he got to his feet. His face was quite unreadable, but he reached and picked up the great meat knife off the board, and a hiss went up from the hall as if from icy water thrown on burning tiles.

He turned then and walked up the room toward Ryhgon's table.

"Put that back, Sarite," Ryhgon said.

"Give me back my knife then, Zakorian."

"You'll get your knife when the prince Kathaos thinks fit."

"Then I'll make do with this. Or would you feel safer if you used a staff on my hand first?"

Ryhgon gave an ugly grin.

"You seem over-touchy at the punishment I gave the Lan. I wonder if there was more between you than friendship?" The Guard Lord turned, silently ordering laughter from the crowded benches. Few men laughed, and the mirth that came was false, dry and isolated.

"Words, Zakorian," Raldnor said and, halting a yard or so away, he addressed the jagged point of the meat knife to Ryhgon's breast. "Are you only going to offer me words? You once promised to accommodate quarrels. I've a quarrel, Guard Lord. Accommodate me."

Ryhgon's huge perversion of a right arm moved slowly until the great hand found the sword hilt. The action should have been enough.

"I'll accommodate you, Sarite. Throw down your toy and I'll give you a taste of thong. I think you'll like it better than what I have here."

He saw the movement in the air and swung to avoid it, but he had expected nothing and so was sluggish. The edge of Raldnor's butcher's blade caught the Zakorian's un-scarred cheek, and blood ran bright.

In that instant Raldnor knew death was as near as Ryhgon himself, but such was the madness on him that he welcomed it, for he could outwit death as skillfully as he had outwitted the Vis.

However, he seemed light as air while Ryhgon was a lumbering elemental force all about him, the dragon sword in the giant's grasp lusting after him. Raldnor dropped down to the side and the massive blade swung by him, re-sounding on one of the stone pillars of the hall. Ryhgon used no guard. He wheeled the sword like an ax; the vast sweeping blows were hypnotic and paralyzing. He fought contemptuously, a machine that knows it is invincible and does not have to think. "But the master should be careful of his pupil," Raldnor thought quite clearly, and in his spar-kling rage he saw only a reputation behind the sword, some-thing that expected to be feared and was not essentially fearful.

"Look at me, Ryhgon," he thought, "how I freeze with terror," and he fell back before the giant as if afraid, and the storm came on, its teeth a glimpse of lightning. The great arm lifted the sword, and on the end of that soaring hung Raldnor's death dangling like a doll.

Raldnor thrust beneath and up to meet the descending arm. It was a swift almost casual stroke that severed the Guard Lord's wrist. Thick blood spurted, the ox muscles spasmed and the sword dropped from Ryhgon's impotent fingers.

Ryhgon fell to his knees, clutching the shorn-off hand against him, shouting and drooling in agony. No one moved to help him. They sensed perfectly that his rule was over, yet more than this, they were appalled by the sight of the monster on its knees, reduced so simply and so totally to its basic animal parts, emptied like a broken jar of all its power.

But in Raldnor the silver rage did not abate. He saw they would be on him in a moment and there would be more of Kathaos's justice. So he leaped across the room, over benches, toward the outer doors. No one stopped him; he seemed to be moving in a different time, and outside the corridors were empty.

He ran in smoky lamplight over mosaic floors, looking for an exit point. But there was no cool reasoning left to him—only instinct. At last it was a window, not a door, he found—a window with dry creeper, half dead from the snow, coiling away from it. He took its withered brown claws in his hands and climbed downward into a court of shadows and a forest of columns of poppy-colored glass.

"What now?" he asked himself, and then came a black absorbing dreariness: "Nothing now."

But there was something. A light. It sprang up ahead of him, and where it shone through the pillar stems it was a pale carnelian fire. He pressed backward, but the flame found his face.

There was a girl, carrying a lamp. She was the sort of girl he had grown accustomed to seeing about the walks of the major palace in the past three months—gliding always in the distance, accompanied by servants, hair intricately dressed, jewels on her fingers. Yet this one was alone. She tilted her head a little to one side and gave him an inquisitive, dangerous smile.

"And what's your business here, Am Kathaos? An illicit love affair with some Dragon Lord's wife? And you so breathless to get to it."

The abrupt transition from anger, blood and flight to this

could only stun him. The madman's plan came out of his mouth before it was fully formed in his brain.

"I seek an audience with the Storm Lord."

Her eyes widened, but she gave a little false, elegant laugh.

"Indeed? You're very ambitious."

"Where do I find him?"

"Oh, you don't," she said haughtily. "Your request must go through the proper channels and will take several days. After that you will probably be granted a moment with some underling, if you're excessively favored. And I doubt, soldier, if you will be."

Raldnor felt his head spin from fatigue. He considered thrusting by this doll creature into the courts of the palace, but where could he go? Besides, he could see that expression behind her eyes that he had grown used to seeing in Vis women when they looked at him. He chanced his luck with her, having no other choice.

"I've killed a man. If Kathaos's guards find me, I'll be finished."

"If you're a criminal, no doubt you deserve to be punished," she said, but she was neither afraid nor anxious to see him taken away to a gallows.

"Self-defense," he said.

"Oh, so they all say. What do you expect I should do with you?"

"Hide me."

"Oh, indeed? And why should I? I am the chief lady of the Princess Astaris Am Karmiss, and what are you, I wonder? Some riffraff off the streets of Xarabiss under the Lord Councilor's badge."

Behind him, from the tiers of the guest mansion, came a sudden sound of shouting and red torchlight moving on the colonnades.

"Decide now, princess's lady," he said. "Your mercy or their justice. If they take me, I'll be fit only for worms by morning."

Her eyes flickered and her cheeks paled with excitement. She had made her decision.

"Follow me," she said.

And turning, she and her lamplight drifted between the pillars and into the dark garden walks of Thann Rashek's palace.

Overhead the moon was a smudge of ivory, and near at hand fountains arced among the vegetable statuary. The scene, so incongruous to him now, affected his draining insanity and anger so that he had a crazy urge to laugh. He slipped an arm about the woman's small waist, and she pushed it away, though slowly.

"Don't be insolent with me, soldier."

"Your beauty precludes all restraint," he said.

She heard the laughter in his voice and glanced at him curiously.

"Banter, and you in fear of death? Stop here now. This is the place."

"The place for what? Am I to be so honored—"

This time she did not thrust him off, but said tightly: "You see that avenue? He'll pass along it when he comes from Astaris's rooms and then go by you here."

"Who?"

"The one you say you seek; Amrek the Storm Lord. It's a route known only to a few. I risk my life telling you."

"I'm humbled by your supreme bravery," he said and kissed her. When he let her go, she trembled but said in a measured, cool little voice: "Time enough for that if you survive the night. And remember, you never met me."

And, taking the lamp, she slipped away, leaving him alone in the black velvet garden, the scent of her costly perfume lingering on his hands.

Amrek sat staring at the woman who was to become his wife. "I am mesmerized," he suddenly thought, "gawping at her like a fish on a cold slab." But oddly, neither this realization nor the analogy he had produced made him uneasy.

"Well, she was meant to be looked at, devoured with the eyes. The eternal feast." He could imagine her losing none of this, even with age. She would die at thirty, or else she was immortal, some sort of goddess mistakenly at large. These fancies spread across his mind in many colored fans, evoking no particular emotion. It was on the whole very strange; he had been the subject of violent tearing rages since childhood— the present of his mother, he bitterly supposed. They came on him in white hot waves, like a recurrent illness. More than once he had cowered, suspecting himself mad, before the great and overweening pride of his position swept fear into the underlayers of his consciousness. And yet, with this woman, a stillness had come into his life. Simply to be able to sit like this, quite motionless, as she had been in her carved chair for so long, was a kind of surprising peace. What kept him so still? This banquet of loveliness? Or did she extend some part of her own immobility to the things about her? Certainly it was no gift she brought him on purpose. She was curiously impersonal in all she did, almost unaware of her surroundings. The sudden twinge of nervous jealousy tore him; she might be so easily unaware of him along with all the rest.

"Astaris," he said. Her amber eyes lifted their inner lids like a cat's—yet not entirely. She looked at him, but did she see him? "What are you thinking?"

"Thoughts are very abstract, my lord. How should I express them to you?"

"You're devious, Astaris. When I ask a woman what she's thought or done and she answers in this way, I invariably conclude that she's hiding something."

"We are all born with armor," she said.

"Riddles."

She turned her head again and presented to him the profile of an image. He seemed always to see her in these terms—something unreal, an artifice.

"Well, I won't tax you with it. I'll tell you instead what I thought as I looked at you. You see, I'm altogether more explicit. Every day, I thought, free men and women make slaves of themselves to please me. And you, merely by your presence which denies me its thoughts, please me more than anything in the world."

She looked at him again, and said: "When you speak like this, I wonder what you want from me."

Her words unnerved him. He had never grown accustomed to her directness and her forms of logic.

"I want a queen, Astaris, a woman to give me sons."

"Perhaps I'll fulfill neither of these requirements."

Her calmness stung him. He rose and stood over her, then reached and half lifted her to her feet and moved her body against his.

"Then it must be you I want, must it not? This Karmian flesh."

Yet he had never lain with her, despite the bed rights given him by their betrothal. He had never analyzed his reserve—it was not, certainly, any kind of fear, yet somehow her serene unreality had held him off. Now, quickened by her nearness and the faint pure scent of her unperfumed skin, he nevertheless felt not the slightest desire to satisfy himself with her. Perhaps she would be disappointing, yet somehow he did not think so. Perhaps rather she was like that treasured gift, guessed at but avoided until the last moment.

Now he kissed her, and his need increasing, only drew back from her and looked in her face. She smiled, a peculiarly sweet smile.

"You inspire tenderness in me," she said, as if it surprised her as much as it surprised him to be so told. Surprised, and oddly hurt him, too. Desire was transmuted into a sort of disorganized spite. Wildly and blindly, with a sensation of helplessness, he cast himself into the pit.

He let her go and held up before her the gloved left hand.

"And this? Does this inspire tenderness?"

"The hand of legend," she said.

"Yes. Didn't you believe me when I told you I wore the glove to mask a knife wound?"

"No," she said simply.

He turned his back, his face working in sudden pain. He had been moving toward this moment all along, this moment of shame and terror, for he had known she would see his lies in his face when he told them, this damnable seeress.

"Scars, too," he muttered, "scars, too. I was eight years old when I prayed to the gods to relieve the curse, and I hacked my own flesh to ribbons in the early morning of a feast day in Koramvis. Then Orhn came. I remember Orhn very well. He picked me up and slung me down in her rooms on a couch. 'Your mewling cub bleeds,' he said to her. She hated me for that. I was screaming, but I remember how she sent for a girl to clean the blood off the velvet before she called for the physician."

Amrek turned and looked at the woman who was to be his wife.

"She seduced my father in Kuma: it's common knowledge. She was thirteen but advanced for her years."

"Val Mala," Astaris said softly, but now she was only a golden shape imprinted on the lamp glow.

Shaking with his anger and his pain, he turned again, this time toward the doorway.

"I'll leave you, Astaris," he said stiffly. "You'll forget what I've said to you. It's dangerous to slander the King."

For her, such an empty injunction.

Yet he caught a glimpse of her eyes before he left her—those bottomless eyes—and saw the briefest flickering in them, as if he had stirred their depths with his anguish.

So he went out into the night garden, with his own insanity dogging him—a monster, a shadow shape from his own childhood nightmares, for he had terrorized himself in his dreams.

And she remained behind, the faintest despair on her, for she had seen the tortured animal in his eyes, burning there, and had been unable to communicate with it.

* * *

The garden was black as death, the moon put out in cloud. Two Dragon Guard fell into step behind, but he scarcely noted them, and they kept their usual respectful distance from him.

At the end of the avenue a figure moved out onto the path in front of him. He was barely aware of it at first, but one Guard ran by him, sword drawn.

"Keep still, whoever you are."

A light was struck, and Amrek saw then the yellow blazon of Kathaos's house guard, and after this, the face of a Dortharian prince. The incongruous apparition acted on him like an icy blow. His first thought was: "One of my father's bastards."

Then the man spoke.

"I ask clemency of the Storm Lord."

"Then ask it on your knees," the Guard rapped out.

The man did not move. He looked in Amrek's face and said: "King Amrek knows I honor him. He needs no proof."

Amrek felt himself reacting, not with anger, but with a peculiar excitement to this unforeseen thing. It cleared his head of shadows, and made him back into a human man, and a King.

"So you honor me. And you ask for clemency. Why? What have you done that you need protection?"

"I've offended your Lord Councilor."

"How?"

The man on the path grinned a savage and exultant grin. He might have been drunk, but not on any kind of wine.

"Ryhgon of Zakoris goes one-handed from this night on."

The nearer escort sucked breath sharply between his teeth; the second muttered an exclamation. Ryhgon had a certain reputation among the Dragon Guard.

"What made you come to me?" Amrek demanded sharply.

"Frankly because your lordship has more authority than Kathaos Am Alisaar."

The moon slid out overhead and sketched dim gray

ghosts between the trees. The man on the path blinked and shook his head as if the light troubled him, and Amrek noted lines of intense weariness on the extraordinary face. At this Amrek experienced an unexpected awareness of this man. As when he had seen Astaris for the first time, he felt himself confronted by a personality, a live thing— instead of the silken cutouts of people who generally moved around him, bowing and flinching, or else steeped in their own concealments and ironies as was Kathaos. And he sensed, too, a strange rearrangement of planes either inside himself or without. He felt that he was facing a part of his destiny. The insight was astounding. He looked hard at the stranger, this mere underling of Am Alisaar's soldiers, yet he could not shake the absurd conviction from him.

He waved the Guard back a few paces and indicated to the man a stone bench. They sat together, and it bewildered Amrek that this did not disturb him. "Well, and if he's one of my father's spawn, I suppose he has a half right to be at my side. Is this what I feel then? An obscure brotherhood?"

"Well, soldier," he said aloud, "what are you called?"

"Raldnor, my lord, Raldnor of Sar."

"Indeed. Then I know you better than I thought."

"The matter of your Guard, my lord. I humbly apologize for proving superior to the Chosen."

"You're playing a dangerous game, Sarite."

"What other game is left me, my lord? Either your Councilor hangs me, or you do. I would only draw your attention to one thing—something Kathaos of Alisaar has failed to see."

"Which is?"

"I've proved my excellence as a fighting machine. I could substitute for Ryhgon very well, and better, either in Kathaos's guard, which is unlikely—or in your lordship's."

"This is the proposal of a drunkard or a fool."

"And to ignore it would be the act of one. My lord."

"Be careful what you say to me, Sarite."

"One day, my lord, long after you've seen me dangle on

a gallows, a man may slip a knife in your back or a powder in your cup, which I, had I been there, would have prevented."

"You offer yourself as a bodyguard, then?"

Raldnor said nothing. The scents of the garden drifted about them.

"How did you find this place?" Amrek asked.

"I followed one of the Lady Astaris's women. She was returning from a tryst, I think, and didn't see me."

"You're too cunning, soldier. And you've too many enemies."

"I can deal with my enemies, my lord, if I live. And yours, too."

"I think," Amrek said slowly, "that you, Sarite, had the same father as I."

The face of the young man beside him seemed to harden almost imperceptibly, then relax.

"You don't have an answer to that, I see."

"My line is all Xarabian, my lord."

"Not in your eyes. You have the mark of Rarnammon there."

"Perhaps, my lord, we were honored, unknown, in some past generation."

Amrek rose; Raldnor followed him.

"From this moment your trial has begun. No, not the gallows. I'll give you what you claim a right to; then I'll watch you earn it, and I promise you, you'll be fighting for your life every inch of the way."

"Good morning, Kathaos."

Kathaos turned and bowed, and nothing about his attitude or his person betrayed his rancor or his unease.

"I called you to inform you of the whereabouts of a certain man—a Sarite. I think you know who I mean."

"Indeed, my lord."

"Indeed, Kathaos. He's here. Of course, you'd assumed

as much. Your hunter, who can defeat both your men and mine. Can you imagine what his fate will be?"

"I've a poor imagination, my lord," Kathaos said, without inflection.

"Yes, you've already proved that conclusively. Well, I'll tell you. I've pardoned your Sarite to save you the trouble. Look for him in a few days, and you will find he has become a Dragon Lord."

"You base your hopes a good deal, my lord, on the man's luck, which will one day desert him."

Amrek smiled.

"All luck, Kathaos, comes to an end. Think of that sometime, when you lie in the bed of my mother."

10

ON A BLUE XARABIAN MORNING of the warm months, the entourage of the Storm Lord and his bride left Lin Abissa.

It was to be a slow journeying—a miniature city on the move, equipped with all necessities and luxuries. Twilight found them between Ilah and Migsha on the empty slopes—a settling of tents like a flock of birds. When the moon rose, a herd of zeebas, galloping across the star-burned silences, fled from the red twinkling of their fires.

The messenger who had ridden all the way from Koramvis, and whose news had displeased Amrek, made inquiries over his meat.

"The light-eyed man in the Storm Lord's tent—who's he now?"

"Some upstart from Sar. He crippled a man and got made a Dragon Lord. That's how it is nowadays."

"He has the look of the royal line," said the messenger.

"Perhaps. He can handle his men—his division's the crack division they tell me. He gave 'em a name, like in the old days—the Wolves. Ryhgon trained him, Kathaos's dog, before his pupil turned on him. But the Dragon Guard spit on his shadow. He gave them a shaking up at Abissa—"

And across the lanes, in the owar-hide pavilion, Raldnor sat—at ease in the King's tent.

The surprise of power had long since left him. He had been too busy that month and a half at Abissa, busy with the network of bribes and threats and preferments that ensured those of his new rank their safety. And he found himself a leader, too, as he had boasted he could be. There had been a rebirth on that night in the garden. He had talked his way into the trust of a man he hated, had spoken to that man as if he honored him, and as if he himself were a Vis. And yes. He had *become* a Vis in that dark garden.

Sitting here in the tent of the King, he thought back over that scene for only the second time. The first had been in the delirious aftermath, when he had felt an exhilaration mixed with panic. He remembered coolly now Amrek's accusation: "You had the same father as I," and how his pulses had leaped and pounded in an insane moment of total confusion. For, having momentarily forgotten his Plains blood, it seemed his unknown father, too, might be a Vis, any Vis— even a king.

It amused him now to wonder where his looks came from—some past venture in his ancestry, he surmised, showing itself, as sometimes happened, several generations later. After all then, the Xarabian woman had left some birthright—royal blood—to pass on to him.

Amrek, his King and patron, sat brooding. The news from Koramvis had irritated him. The Council demanded that he leave his bride to travel alone, and ride posthaste to the Dortharian border of Thaddra, that wild and mountain-locked land, source of constant dispute and foray. There was fresh trouble there, and the Storm Lord must be seen as an ever-present power, not dallying with his woman in Xarabiss. So it was. He was the ultimate ruler of a continent, yet he must obey his Council. And he did not want to leave his scarlet-haired girl, Raldnor could see. Did he then love her? Raldnor, observing her in the distance of his life, acknowledged her beauty was astounding, but she seemed like a waxwork, a puppet moving very gracefully on strings. He had never been near enough to hear her speak, but he could imagine her voice—perfect, and quite without tone.

The question came suddenly to Raldnor, as he watched the King's dark, empty face: "This man I've allowed to give me every scrap I have; do I hate him as implacably as ever?" The white ghost sprang up into the tent but could not entirely materialize for him. Raldnor had lost half his blood, half his soul. The schism of divided race had finally resolved itself, and the Lowlander was eclipsed by the black-haired man. It was hard to hate now, and the pale girl who came in the night, still came, even between the silky sheets of Lyki's bed, was only a dismal dream, no longer accompanied by meaning.

"If an assassin ran into this place seeking Amrek's life," he thought with sudden surprise, "I'd kill him."

"Well, Raldnor Am Sar," Amrek said, "I'll leave the charge of this entourage with you."

"I'm honored, my lord."

"Honored? You and those Wolves of yours will die of boredom on the road. But my Karmian—keep her safe for me. Remember, I'm not a fair man. If she wants the moon, get it out of the sky for her."

He rose and put his hand on Raldnor's shoulder. It was unmistakably a gesture of knowing, not ownership. The King was at ease with him, and he at ease with the King. But then, there had been a strange sort of ease between them from the first.

"You can trust me," Raldnor said, and knew it to be true. "When does your Lordship leave?"

"Tomorrow, first light." One of the lamps flickered and went out. Amrek gazed at it and thought: "In a tent like this my father died on the Plains. A white woman with yellow hair killed him, and left her marks on my body before I was born. It always meant a great deal to me. Now less. Why is that, I wonder? Has she done it, the Karmian enchantress? I seem to see everything from behind cool dark glass. I vowed to erase the yellow scum from the face of Vis, but now I see only shadows, not devils. . . ."

He glanced at Raldnor.

"In your hands then. And be glad I didn't take you away from your own woman."

Lyki's body lay stretched in the black sheets like a star. A shaft of moonlight pierced the tent and blanched her flesh to fiery snow, bleached her hair to a negative without color.

"I think you never sleep," she murmured.

"I prefer to lie and look at you."

"Does Amrek still permit you to be insolent to him?"

"Amrek guesses, I think, who led me to him in Thann Rashek's garden. What lover were you coming from then?"

"A man I abandoned for you." She lay still, then said: "So Amrek rides to Thaddra. My lady will be even more difficult then, no doubt. I'm sure that she's deranged; sometimes she moves like a sleepwalker. She says the oddest things—" Lyki always spoke of Astaris in this way.

"You're very intolerant of the woman who provides your bread."

"Oh, what a banal statement. Such a betrayal of your peasant origins," Lyki said tartly.

But presently she said other things to him as he caressed her in the dark.

A storm rolled over the slopes near dawn. He woke from the dream and could not for a moment remember where he was. The dark girl was sitting up combing her hair, and she turned a pair of cool gem eyes on him in the half light.

"Astaris has dreams, too," she said with asperity. It was part of her character that she was sometimes sharp with him, particularly when he was vulnerable, as now: she knew of his recurring nightmare, though not the content.

"Does the princess, then, discuss her dreams with you?"

"Oh no. But she left a paper lying by her bed, and she'd written on it very clearly."

"And you read the paper."

"Why not? It said: 'I dreamt again of the white woman blown to ashes.' That was all. I remember very well."

He felt a cold wind pass over him, and the hair rose on his neck. He sat up.

"When was this?"

"Let go my shoulder. You're hurting me. It was a day or so ago. I forget. Is it Astaris you want now, instead of me?"

He shook the icy tendrils off him and pulled her down.

"You, you faithless bitch."

And tried to lose the incredible sense of fear in the core of her golden limbs.

There were partings at dawn—a private parting between the King and his bride, a public one among the tents. Troops presented arms; the Wolves showed well.

Raldnor had been drunk in his way when he had asked for a command among the Dragon Guard—his well-established enemies—but sober enough afterward. He had picked his men with care, his captains with more than care, and not from among the Guard. Kathaos's halls had taught him other lessons besides those of combat. He took his levy from the general bulk of the army—raw recruits, still young and inexperienced. It had interested and pleased them to learn they had been singled out from the mass; it was easy enough to have these newly enlisted molded to his specification, and to impress them. For he possessed, like Ryhgon, a reputation, and he used it better. They saw what he could do with sword, ax and spear, and when Kothon, promoted from the Chariot Corps, had taught him the ways of the flimsy Dortharian vehicles, they saw that here was a charioteer also. His veterans he selected cunningly. Like Kothon they were soldiers, intelligent in their particular trade, but in little else; limited men, who were contented with the good food and pay he saw they got and did not mind his increasingly long shadow cast over them. For he had walked by Amrek a great deal in Abissa and accomplished, in various ways, an admirable amount in the brief time he had there. He never questioned his abilities. His life had been inactive once; now he made up for those lost and useless years in a surge of judgment and power.

The Storm Lord, with his Guard and personal, small entourage, rode over the slopes, bypassing Migsha, and was gone. It was too early in the year for dust to mark their passing. And there was a good deal of mud on the first part of Astaris's royal progression.

The princess recaptured her solitude and lay bathed in it. She had responded to Amrek's inner pain with vague maternal stirrings which surprised her, but even these small tokens had been exhausting. He had leaned on her so heavily. She sensed his need, yet the impassable barrier remained to lock her in, away from him as from all others. She experienced the bewilderment of closeness without intimacy, understanding without knowledge, a blind communion through layers of gauze. And when he left, she felt herself emptied of the little she had achieved with him. Quite suddenly he became again a stranger. Yet the stranger had worn her out.

They passed through Migsha moving north. She sat like a doll at feastings and withdrew early. She did not notice that Amrek's new Dragon Lord watched her for a time very closely, for, as always, she scarcely noticed anything at all.

In the streets of the beautiful cities of Xarabiss, girls tossed early flowers, which fell in a rain about the procession and were trampled by the feet of men and pack animals and under the wheels of the chariots. To Raldnor the whole journey through Xarabiss came to be symbolized by this odor of crushed, bruised blossom, and by the eyes of women fixed on his face as he rode at the head of his Wolves.

In the warm humid evenings women would come to garrison gates, decked out in their various fineries, to request the pleasure of entertaining him. Sentries teased them, asked if they would do and finally divided the spoils among themselves. Something of Raldnor's past rose up and sickened him. The Vis woman was a harlot, everyone a daughter of the Red Moon. The easy victories after the aridness before had begun to cloy. And these dark ladies were jealous too, as he saw too often with Lyki.

They crossed into Ommos, and there also his past caught him hard.

A narrow land with narrow-towered cities, ruled by a cruel, perverse code. Scant honor for Amrek's bride here — she was a woman, merely the house of unborn men. The entourage kept to its own metropolis, the encampment, as it traveled. Only in Hetta Para, the capital, did they pause — etiquette dictated that they should. Uhgar, the king, had something of Yr Dakan in him for Raldnor; it was inevitable that he should. Raldnor took in the gaudy feasts, the fire dancers, the blazing-bellied Zaroks, the pretty simpering boys, with a grave face. Here, men, not women, importuned him. He was revolted but he had learned a sardonic tact along with the rest.

He slept poorly at Hetta Para.

On the second and third night in the capital he rose and walked along the bleak upper galleries of the palace, which were open to a sky full of enormous stars. He thought of Orklos, and of Anici. He became a Lowlander for brief agonizing seconds. It came to him at last, among the stones of Ommos, how pathetic Anici's life and beauty had been to her.

Then he saw something that was like an omen — indecipherable, yet charged with portent.

Across the walls and the gulfs between them, a woman with blood-red hair stood on her balcony, wrapped in a blizzard of untimely snow. Astaris, dressed in a cloak made from the pelt of one perfect and unmarked ice-white wolf, the gift to her of the lord Kathaos, who had bought it by proxy in the market of Abissa. Raldnor shuddered.

He turned away, back into the corridors. She had been like a phantom to him. And he could not forget that she dreamed dreams which were his own. Anici had become a curious property between them.

Lyki had come to his bed in his absence, and lay awaiting him with her expectant sensuality. He desired her only because she was available.

She lay afterward at his side in the dark and said: "I think I have your child."

The banality of her statement irritated him.

"Why assume it's mine?"

"It can be no one else's, Raldnor my love. With the others I took care not to conceive. Besides, I've been faithful to you. Can you say the same?"

"There are no vows between us. You can do as you like."

"Well, so I have. And I carry. Your seed. Does it mean nothing to you?"

He did not answer. Many Vis women bore their children without the accessory of a husband, yet he sensed in her a desire to bind him to her by her maternity, to show other women that he had put a piece of himself into her, as if he had chosen her specially for this purpose.

"You're angry," she chided him sharply. "Well, it's done now. I told *her*"—by her inflection he understood she meant Astaris. "She gave me a strange look, but then she's always strange."

Three days after, the rolling caravan crossed the river into Dorthar.

The suns were dazzling that day. Under a white metal sky he made out a land like a woman's dark hair drawn through a comb of blue mountains. There came an unexpected and unlooked-for quickening. Oddly, he felt he had seen Dorthar before.

Koramvis disturbed him deeply. Part of him had wished to remain unimpressed. But then, he knew from his reading, there was no city like her in all Vis. Never a city with such architecture, such grace, such splendor, such legends.

A man met them on the road.

"Val Mala, mother of the Storm Lord, sends fond greetings to her daughter Astaris Am Karmiss."

And this would be all the greeting Astaris would get, Amrek being in Thaddra.

As with the city, Raldnor had expected and wanted something different. He had pictured Val Mala in the light of what was said about her: a woman in her middle years, prone to rage and terrible cruelty, a whore and a villainess. He visualized a dragon woman with lines of age and evil living on her face.

His Wolves flanked Astaris and her attendants into the Storm Palace; so he saw Val Mala for the first time.

She had twice his years, yet her vanity and wealth had retained for her the long youth of the Vis. She had a voluptuous, vibrant beauty. Compared to Astaris's own it might seem a sort of vulgarity; yet conversely, set off by Val Mala, the Karmian seemed more than ever like something fashioned from wax. The Queen of Dorthar wore a gown of flaring liquid scarlet, and on either side of her chair was chained a long-necked scarlet bird with a spreading tail. One thing startled him, even though he had been told of it: the whiteness of the unguent on her skin.

"Astaris, you are to be my daughter from this moment."

She did not bother to conceal her dislike, and the ritualistic words accentuated this. She embraced the Karmian as if she were poisonous.

"We have allotted you apartments in the Palace of Peace."

It was an insult. A brief murmuring went up from the room. This palace, not its subsidiary, should house the future consort of the King. But the King was absent.

Astaris said nothing. It occurred to Raldnor how her immobility would infuriate. It amused him to see these two astonishing women locked in a form of mortal combat, and one of them so uninterested.

A steward tried to smooth the way with mutterings at the Queen's ear. She spoke to him softly, and he paled.

It was to be a day of strangeness for Raldnor. When they passed through the gate of the Palace of Peace, he felt a dark bird fly over his brain. Kothon, his charioteer, jerked a blunt thumb at old black markings on the walls.

"See that, Commander? That's part of the history of Dorthar. Have you heard of the Lowland woman, Ashne'e, the yellow-haired witch who killed Rehdon?"

"I've heard of her."

"The soldiers came to take her, and found her dead. There was a crowd behind them, and they dragged the body out and burned it in Dove Square. The brands they carried made those scorches."

A sickness came over Raldnor. Kothon did not notice. "This is what he plans for them all, all the people of the Plains, that man I sold my soul to," Raldnor thought.

Then the cool bowl of the palace appeared among the trees.

And he knew it. Knew the pale color of the stone, the sound the leaves made through windows at certain points of the interior. Inside—what? He searched his mind in a cold frenzy. A mosaic floor—a picture of women dancing—and above, there was a room in a tower. . . . No, what could he know of all that?

Yet when he was inside, he saw the floor before him. He did not search the room in the tower, for the thought of it filled him with a peculiar dread.

"Up there," Kothon said, applying wine to his grizzled chops, "that's where *she* lay, the Lowland woman. They found her dead up there."

A woman presented herself at the apartments of the princess. She was tall and sour-faced, her hair, the lifeless black of ebony, caught back in a snood of golden wool.

She answered Lyki's challenge with an arid smile.

"I am Dathnat, the Queen's chief woman. I am here to assess your mistress's personal needs."

She went about her task with few words, and her looks were as barren as her words and as unwanted as her person. When she was gone, Lyki mimicked her, screwing up her face and compressing her breasts with her hands.

Dathnat was a Zakorian, a strange custodian of the Queen's beauty. Lyki guessed that Val Mala employed her as much for the service of her sharp ears and her bitter disposition as for her talents as handmaiden.

A scented lamp burned softly in the Queen's bedchamber.

Val Mala had retired early. Two attendants worked, one on either side of the couch, painting and shaping toe and finger nails, and the Zakorian, Dathnat, had begun the kneading movements on her flesh. She was a skilled masseuse; the little creeping lines fled before her iron fingers.

Val Mala sighed.

"Who is this man all my women are chattering of?"

"The Dragon appointed by my lord, your son, madam."

"What excellent hearing, Dathnat. This is the man from Sar? Amrek's favorite. And what do they say?"

"They prattle about his body and his face. They say he has pale eyes, and a jealous mistress who guards him, though they've got from her that he is —" Dathnat paused distastefully, "remarkable between sheets."

Val Mala gave a drowsy laugh.

"I've seen him, Dathnat. I don't doubt his lady's estimation."

When the women were done with her, she sat for a long while by her mirror. It was her glory that she could still do this unafraid. Yes, she was a match for the Karmian, though twice her age. She pondered upon the new Dragon Lord, the upstart—he had had something in his face which reminded her of Orhn. She regretted the loss of Orhn still. She approached sadness when she thought of him. But the power she had given him had made him many enemies.

When the grooms had brought his broken, battered body from the hunt, she had had them flayed and pinched with red-hot tongs, but could discover nothing. How should he fall from his chariot and be dragged by it till he was dead, he who had mastered chariots at the age of ten along with his first woman?

Oddly, she thought of Amnorh, too, on this night, for the first time in years. Amnorh the too-clever, whose body lay on the floor of Ibron. She did not regret him. It had amused her, long ago, when she had been told of his death.

Dathnat crouched at a clothes chest, inserting perfumed sachets among the robes. Val Mala had a sudden, strange hallucination; it seemed another woman's figure—younger, graceful—was superimposed upon the Zakorian's. Lomandra. Lomandra, who had fled in revulsion when she had completed the Queen's task and dispatched the Lowlander's bastard. Lomandra, the soft Xarabian fool.

"Dathnat, you should get yourself a lover," Val Mala said. It was her pleasure to taunt the woman thus. The expected blood-burn appeared on the averted bony face. "A man like Kren, of the River Garrison, perhaps. A man with the shoulders of an owar."

In the dark corridor a woman's hand snatched his. Raldnor turned uneasily and found Lyki, with a bloodless face, at his elbow.

"Raldnor . . ."

"What is it?"

Her eyes kindled.

"You used not to be so brief with me."

"There used to be no need. What's the matter?"

She leaned against the wall.

"There was a message for me—a man waiting by the gate—"

"Did he muss your hair, then, this man? If you wanted a quiet night, you were a fool to go."

"You!" she flared at him suddenly. "You don't trouble

yourself what happens to me. You put your child into my body and then you're done with it."

"By your account, Lyki, the child was as much your doing as mine."

She would not look at him, or leave him either. She stood immobile, her eyes on the ground. When she raised them, they glittered with sudden spite.

"Am I dismissed, then, *Dragon Lord?* Would you rather spend your nights alone, dreaming about the little Sarite girl who didn't want you?"

She had touched him nearer than she knew. Seeing his expression, she fell back a step.

"You delayed me to tell me something, Lyki. Tell it."

"Very well. The man at the gate caught my arm, and he said: 'You're Lyki, Raldnor of Sar's bitch.' He had an ugly scarred face, and his right arm ended at the wrist, so I don't think there's any need to give you his name. He said: 'Tell your bedfellow that I've something I owe him for my hand. Because of what he did, I've nothing better to do in life except watch him, and wait until his gods forsake him. When they do, I will be near. Tell him that.'" Lyki smiled lifelessly. "Then he spat. And let me go."

She turned and walked away.

She did not come to his bed again, but he found no shortage of lovemaking when he desired it.

11

IT WAS A VERY SOCIAL LIFE at Koramvis. Raldnor found that he was fashionable, an asset at the supper tables of rich men and beautiful women. His birth in Sar fascinated them. He became a practiced liar. He knew that for the most part it was taken for granted that he was a bastard of the Imperial line—either Rehdon's work or that of one of Rehdon's lesser brothers. They amused Raldnor, these nods and fawnings, but he had made Kothon his bodyguard. He, like all men of rank, considered now he had a need of one.

His fame gave rise to weird anomalies.

At a dinner in the Storm Palace he met an officer of the Queen's guard, Kloris by name—a handsome boastful fool. He made it clear that he detested Raldnor and his meteoric ascent, and also that he coveted everything that was Raldnor's, from his post to his woman. The man had been wooing Lyki in trite, unoriginal ways for the whole month that they had been in the city, simply because she was Raldnor's. Raldnor wondered if she would lose her allure for Kloris now they had parted.

After the dinner the Queen made a brief appearance. She wore pleated white linen and a wig of gold silk. From a distance she was white-skinned and golden-haired. He had heard of the enmity between Val Mala and her son—was this some secret jibe at him, something she would not dare in his presence, yet which would be repeated to him in Thaddra?

She moved graciously among the important guests, her ladies drifting after her. The Zakorian was absent, he saw, but then that one was hardly for show.

Behind him, Kothon jerked to attention. Raldnor realized, with some initial surprise, that Val Mala had singled him out.

"Good evening, Dragon Lord."

He bowed to her.

"Do you guard the princess well?"

He met her eyes then, and words caught in his throat. In her face was a meaning and an invitation quite apparent. Her sexuality breathed out of her, and a burning hot shiver crept along his spine.

"Koramvis is a safe city, madam," he said presently.

"Not too safe, I trust. I've been told you're something of a hero. A young hero shouldn't become bored."

Confronted with her like this, many men had grown afraid, he had heard. She was too potent, perhaps. But not for him. He had reacted to her already and the promise in her eyes. Besides, she was a power in this land, as Amrek was. He decided at once, and a cool, ambitious logic ruled the illogical ambition in his loins.

"One word from Dorthar's Queen has dispelled any possible boredom forever."

She laughed, the frivolous false laughter of a woman engaged. How old was she? She seemed only a few years his senior, even this close. She took his arm lightly. People marked their progress as they walked.

"You invest me with an unfair amount of ability. One woman compared to so many, Dragon. You can pick and choose, I hear."

"Alas, no. The gods would make me happy if I could."

"Who is this that you desire, then? This unobtainable one."

"I wouldn't dare, madam, to pronounce her name."

"Well," she said. She smiled at him, pleased with the little play. "You shouldn't despair, my lord of Sar, the gods may be kinder than you think."

Leaving him, she gave him her hand to kiss. He encountered her smooth, scented, painted flesh. Her rings were cold on his lips.

In the guest palace that night he slept poorly. A girl with a red wig shared his bed—half of them wore red wigs since Astaris had come here. He no longer wanted her. He wanted the white-skinned bitch queen. Zastis would be in the sky within a month. How long would she make him wait for her, or would she change her mind? He felt cast back to his uneasy beginnings by this uncertainty, and the palace, which the women said was full of ghosts—more specifically one ghost—oppressed him in the dark.

But Val Mala, as she lay under the Zakorian's hands, had no intentions of delay.

Dathnat herself could have told Raldnor how brief would be his waiting. She knew this sleekness, this restlessness in her mistress from before. She was a student of Val Mala and had been taught well.

"Tell me, Dathnat," said the sleepy, throaty voice, "what's your opinion of Raldnor Am Sar?"

"Your majesty knows I am unqualified to judge."

Val Mala laughed. Her spitefulness, too, was always at its sharpest before a new affair, and Kathaos had been long away—first in Xarabiss, now in Thaddra.

Dathnat hated the Queen, but her heritage had made her stoical and very patient.

She thought of the Queen's pet kalinx. Once so beautiful, that creature, and so dangerous. It had lurked about these apartments, Val Mala's second self, equated with her name in the city. Innumerable lovers had gone in fear of it. Now the cold blue of its eyes was filmed and rheumy, its fur molted, its teeth rotten with age. It smelled. Val Mala could not bear it near her, though neither would she have it killed.

Dathnat understood, even if the Queen did not, that to Val Mala the ruined cat represented her own person—age which she had cheated and the deformities of age that would one day invade her body.

In her stony soul, Dathnat smiled. The gods, who had given her nothing, had nothing to rob her of. She was younger than her mistress and would see the ending of her.

She worked upon the Queen's skin with relish, striving with her iron hands to preserve, her eyes watching greedily for the first signs of Val Mala's punishment.

A man came to him, wearing the insignia of the Queen.

"Dragon Lord, Val Mala, the royal mother of the Storm Lord, requests your presence at noon," he said. His eyes said other things.

The day was very hot. The Storm Palace seemed to burn with dry white fire. A mask-faced girl with glinting eyes took him to a suite of rooms and left him there.

Smoky draperies shut out the harsh sunlight, and incense rose in eddies from ornate bowls. When she came in from behind the heavy curtains, she wore a plain robe, her black hair loose on her shoulders and her breasts. She looked incredibly young and incredibly knowing and certain of what she could do to him, and his eyes blackened for a moment in an irrepressible torrent of desire.

"Please sit," she said. "No, beside me. How restrained you seem. Have I called you away from some important duty? Some—further heroism?"

"Your majesty must know by now the effect of her loveliness."

"Do I affect you, then?" She poured wine into a cup and handed it to him. He could not drink it, and set the cup aside. The servility of her gesture had been intimation enough. He lifted her hand to his mouth, caressing it in quite a different way from before. He felt the pulse in her wrist quicken. She said: "Are you daring to insult me?"

Part of his cleverness as a lover was that he had always

understood with every woman, except one, her basic needs, her sexual requirements, and had responded to them intuitively. With Val Mala he sensed what she asked him for, and took possession of her mouth before she had finished speaking, and when she stirred, he held her still.

But she was, after all, the Queen. At length he let her go. He had no doubt she would give them what they both wanted, yet the decision was to be hers.

She rose and held out her hand to him.

"A little walk," she said, very low.

In the colonnade she ran her teeth along the edge of his hand.

"How did you lose this finger, my hero? In some fight?"

He had lied, too, about the circumstances of his birth, as well as the geography. Enough rumors had already accrued. Yet he had kept the falsehoods as near the truth as possible; it was easier that way. He knew nothing of the damaged finger, so he said now, as he had said before to many of the nobility of Koramvis: "I lost it in infancy, madam. I've no recollection how."

The carved door slid open; beyond lay her bedchamber. This symbol struck him—some hint of permanence to come, in that it was not merely a couch he was to have her on. But she had halted in the doorway, and her face, though still smiling, had become suddenly altered, as if the smile were only the garland left behind after the feast. She looked as if—he could not quite be sure—as if she had abruptly glimpsed another person standing in his place.

"In infancy," she echoed him, and her voice was strangely colorless. "I've heard it said you have the blood of my husband. Do you think it likely?"

Her coldness infected him. Desire fell away; his hands grew clammy. He felt himself on the brink of a fear he could not even guess at.

"Most unlikely, madam."

"You have yellow eyes," she said. She said it as if she spoke of something quite different, something horrible, obscene—a murder. All at once she seemed to shrink and shrivel. He saw in her face the weight of years which would eventually find her out. He no longer wanted her, she appalled him—why, he was uncertain. But he had been so close to the power she offered, still wanted that—

"Madam, how have I offended you?"

"You have the eyes of a Lowlander," she hissed.

His blood turned to ice. He found himself trapped, confronted unaccountably by a terrified old woman, and beyond them both, a waiting gold and silver bed of love.

"What did you want from me?" she shrilled. "*What?* You've no hope of anything—anything, do you hear? Reveal yourself and he'll kill you."

He felt himself back involuntarily away.

"Yes—go—go! Get out of my sight!"

He turned, he almost ran from her, driven by forces of hate and fear he did not understand.

Val Mala fled inside the door and pushed it shut. The room was full of shadows.

"Lomandra?" she asked them. Nothing stirred. No, it was not ghosts she had to fear. It was the living.

The *living*.

Strange, she had never doubted, never allowed the intrusion of doubt. She had thought the Xarabian had fulfilled her promise and smothered Ashne'e's baby. She had not dreamed the finger she had flung into the brazier had come from the hand of a living child. When Lomandra vanished, she had been unsurprised. The woman had been sickened and had run back to Xarabiss. It did not matter, for her work was done.

And yet now, never having doubted, she knew without hesitation, *knew* that the child had survived and grown into a man. A man with the face, the body, the very stance of a king.

She had thought herself rid of Rehdon.

But it was Rehdon she had found suddenly beside her—Rehdon in his youth, at the peak of his beauty and magnificence, as she had known him in Kuma when he had seemed to blind her like a sun. She had always believed the child was her husband's seed, despite her accusations; the gods had seen fit to prove it to her. And simultaneously he had given her the key to what he was.

Had Lomandra died before she could tell him his history, or had she lived and spoken? It seemed not. Would he be so stupid as to intimate to her in such a forthright way, if he had known? Unless, of course, he had meant to frighten her.

He must be killed. But how? They said Amrek loved him. Raldnor's curious, swift ascent seemed to uphold this. She would not dare have him assassinated out of hand. Inform Amrek, then, that his favorite was a Lowlander — but that would reveal her part in it, what she had tried to do. She hated her son, yet she feared him. Who could tell which way he would jump? Perhaps she would suffer as much as the bastard.

Sheer terror clutched her heart. What was his purpose here? A yawning gulf seemed to open at her feet. She glimpsed her face in a black mirror beyond the bed, a face for this moment stripped of beauty, and old — old as the mummy dust of tombs.

Zastis was in the sky, a red wound at the moon's back. There was a joke abroad in the lower quarters of the city. It concerned Astaris and the star and the color that her hair must be, surely, between her thighs.

There were rumors about Amrek also. He would be home shortly, Thaddra's barbaric insolence settled. There had been a skirmish or two. A few women would weep for their lost men, but that was nothing besides the prestige of Dorthar. And the worst was past. Kathaos was already in the city, attending to various council duties that must precede the Imperial wedding. The rites would be held at their traditional time — the peak of Zastis.

There was also Kathaos's personal honor to the bride. He had been ever mindful of this, though not vulgar: two or three expensive, unique gifts, as was fitting. Now he arranged a royal hunt in the hilly forest land—the acres of cibba, oak and thorn to the northwest above Koramvis. Kathaos entertained certain thoughts concerning Astaris. He appreciated the beautiful and the rare. His childhood at the court in Saardos had taught him to admire and value things, and, at the same time, systematically deprived him of them. Now he would pay handsomely for an exceptional piece of enamel work from Elyr, and be prepared to wait anywhere up to a year for a silversmith to achieve the required perfection in some lamp stand or set of plate. He had had to wait a lot of his life—be patient and be slow to get anything he wanted. It had become an acquired skill. So, in the same way that he saw the Karmian as an art object, he was prepared to maneuver, most of all to wait to have her. He had attained several high beds—Val Mala's not the least. And he had enjoyed the preliminaries as much as the prize—in some cases, more.

The royal hunt today was all part of the exercise. He did not think Astaris would enjoy it, if she noticed it at all. But there would be intervals when he could discreetly engage her attention.

Amrek was too demanding for her. It was subtlety that breached her remoteness, or so it seemed to him. It would be a game he liked to play, and which he was good at.

She looked like some exquisite pastoral goddess for the ride. He wondered who dressed her so well; she herself he could imagine taking no personal interest in such things. Lyki, perhaps, the Sarite's discarded mistress, chose her wardrobe.

And the Sarite was there also. Kothon absent from his chariot, he was handling his team himself.

The man was still a thorn in Kathaos's side. He had had an intermittent watch set on him, but Raldnor was probably aware that such a thing was possible and accordingly careful. It seemed he had done no specific damage. As often before, Kathaos pondered his origins and his purposes, achieving no solid answers. There was the story, too, of

Raldnor and the Queen. Certainly it had been a brief enough liaison. And now Val Mala had shut her doors to all comers, the lord Councilor included. He had heard she was ill. Kathaos sensed many threads leading down into some furiously productive yet hidden loom.

He saw that Raldnor had raised his hand to him in formal salute. On impulse, Kathaos trotted his team level with the Sarite's vehicle.

"I trust that you'll enjoy the hunting, Dragon Lord."

"I'm here to escort the princess, lord Councilor, not to enjoy myself."

"It's praiseworthy that you take your duties so seriously. But I assure you the princess will be quite safe in this company." The light eyes, so reminiscent of past royalty, were full of ironical disdain in the impassive face. "Your rank becomes you very well," Kathaos said. "Perhaps I did you a service, indirectly. And how is the Queen these days?"

The look in the eyes altered, and for a fleeting second Kathaos saw he had touched a nerve. With the polite friendly nod reserved for useful underlings or merchants, Kathaos turned his chariot.

Noon had brought unexpected heat to the still, windless day. Cloud masses were already building for a storm.

Grooms flushed orynx from their shallow lair with burning pitch; the kalinx pack was unleashed and the chariots rumbled after.

The hunting was not to Raldnor's taste. It was the old Lowland ways which troubled him again. A man hunted only for food or clothing or in self-defense. It was another mark of the effete and the sadistic to take life as a sport. He had detailed three of his captains to trail Astaris's chariot. It was privacy he wanted in these woods. Once he had been too much alone. Now he felt crowded. Always a man at his door, Kothon at his back, the bickering court, the soldiers' gossip. Even the women in his bed with their post-coital questionings.

Like all men forced consistently to lie, he felt now the pressure of being absorbed by his false self.

Heat beat and blazed through the forest roof. He thought of Val Mala and what she had cheated him of. The pang of his sex strove in him to make itself a strange component of his fear. For he feared her, feared her words to him. A hundred times each day he reasoned them away—over wine, at drill, lying snared in the satisfaction and arms of some woman after love. And she had done nothing, the white-faced Dortharian woman. Was she mad, then? At worst, even if she spoke, Amrek hated and distrusted her. When he thought of Amrek, he was filled now with abrupt uncertainties. He felt that absence had estranged what he had known. Amrek was once more stranger; and legends, ghost stories had come between. He recalled his moment of burning loyalty in the tent between Hah and Migsha with discomfort, almost with shame.

All light suddenly drained from the sky. The chariot team quivered the length of their bodies and stopped still. The whole scene seemed to congeal in soundless stasis. It brought Raldnor from his thoughts. He glanced upward through the carved boughs into a breathless mahogany overcast. Not a whisper of wind or rustle of life. It occurred to him that there seemed to be no birds. Then the light blackened totally and was gone; the sun had been put out. In the preternatural midnight, a gust of primeval terror swept over him. It had nothing to do with actual fear. It was something older, more intrinsic.

His head ringing with silence, he jumped from the chariot and slashed the team free. They ran at once, their shod pads making no noise.

The thunder came then. Not from the sky. It was under his feet.

The grass parted without wind. The trees began to creak and shake their leaden flags. The earth pitched. He was thrown against iron limbs a moment, but the ground was trembling and sliding. He rolled helpless across a landscape upset on its side. A large cibba sprang up with a victorious scream and appeared to bound in great hops across the forest floor. Other trees fell in ranks. He could not rise. He lay scrabbling at the soil like a terrified animal. There was nowhere to run or to hide.

The last spasm, when it came, was almost gentle. It rolled, like a sea wave, languidly, over the ground, and settled.

He lay there, holding on to the still land with his hands. Presently he got to his feet and spat earth from his mouth. He might have been in a different place. Dragon oaks leaned sideways; others lay across their own chasmic uprootings. One had smashed the back of his chariot.

He began to walk through the leveled forest as the sky lightened to cinnamon. He negotiated fallen things and the places where the rock had split and spewed up underlying humus.

There was a clearing ahead of him, a clearing that had not been there before. He glimpsed what remained of a chariot and its team. A man lay on his side—dead. There was a woman standing not far off. It was so dark still that he did not make out the color of her hair until he was near.

Her face was like parchment, her eyes wide open and completely blank. She might have been dead though still somehow standing, like the warriors in ancient Vis tombs. In a moment of enraged sanity he wondered where in damnation were the captains he had sent after her. He stopped half a yard away and said: "Princess." She did not answer or look at him. "Are you hurt?" he said. She had never been so physically close to him; neither had he seen her so empty. She had seemed before only vacuous, hidden away, closed in, but now she was hollowed out. She might have been cauterized to her very soul. It was no longer applicable to treat her as something royal and untouchable, though any man who laid a finger on her, without prior consent by the Storm Lord, would lose the hand as well. That was their law. But this was only a woman, a living creature in need. He put his hands on her shoulders, but her eyes did not even flicker.

Conscious of holding back his strength, he slapped her

face, then caught her as the blow toppled her. He felt all her sinews loosen, and so continued to hold her up. Her eyelids fluttered. The film left her eyes, and suddenly she was back inside them, looking out.

"I've never seen death before," she said in a cool and rational voice. "They kept it from me."

"Are you hurt?" he asked her again.

"No. I am alive."

He knew from her tone she meant something other.

A growl of storm thunder ripped the shattered clouds. The sky began to weep, a long drowning sheet of cold tears.

"Who are you?" she asked suddenly.

With a certain irony he said: "The Commander of your highness's personal guard."

The rain beat down. Her fabulous hair seemed full of fires.

He had never thought to desire her before. She was too beautiful, too unalive. But now, still holding her shoulders in the lashing rain, he met for the first time, and fully, those unsurpassable wells of her eyes. And though her face still reflected serene abstraction, there came a thrust of pure ego in him—his reaction to her and against her. And abruptly he had bridged the depths of her eyes and found their floor, and she was in his skull like a flame and he in hers.

There was a moment of shock and utter fear between them both, but each knew the other totally.

She said aloud: "How—?"

"You know."

"Wait—" she cried out, "wait—" But there was a wild joy in her face, and in her mind a conflagration. He knew all the internment as she had known it, as she knew all of his.

He pulled her against him and she moved to him as frenziedly. The longing came swift and devouring and fed on itself in each of them.

In the black ruin of the forest, under the spinning sky, they came together in a coupling like beasts in the aftermath of horror, and as if they had awaited it all their lives, like the last man and the last woman in the world.

*   *   *

The pulse of the rain had slackened.

He looked at her face and said softly: "This was insane. Anyone could have come here and found us. I shouldn't have exposed you to risk like that."

She smiled.

"You didn't think of it. Neither did I."

There stirred between them that communion given to their minds. He kissed her mouth and lifted her to her feet. He might have known her always, she him. The visions of her life before were nebulous, locked in; she had experienced no great yearnings or doubts. His own ambitions, dreads, desires had faded. At this moment she was all he wanted. He could not see beyond it.

"We could find a wagon in the hills, travel over the mountains like peasants. We'd be safe in Thaddra," he said.

"They'd find us," she said.

"What then? What? Amrek takes you and I waste my life in his armies."

"For now," she said, "for me, this is enough. I have no gods, but She, perhaps, will help you."

Knowing everything, she knew also his race. He did not fear her knowledge or resent it. In a way, she had made him back into what he was, but it was the best of him, not the least.

There came a shout from the trees. It came from another planet. He did not at first believe in it. But she cast at him one long glance, full of sadness and regret. And then they were apart and she was quite still, an icon again, the nadir of her eyes dissolved once more in subterranean amber.

Four of Kathaos's men had found them. They looked askance at Raldnor, embarrassed that they had known him before his circumstances altered. A captain of the Wolves was with them; the other two were dead, crushed in the deep gut of an earth crack.

She looked no different when she mounted the chariot and was driven away. Only the echo of her thoughts remained, like music carried on the wind.

Seven milk-white cows were slaughtered before the altars of the Storm gods. Did the steaming blood appease their anger? Who knew for sure, though the auguries improved when groped for in the entrails.

Half a forest felled, great rocks displaced. Ibron had boiled like a caldron.

For the most part Koramvis had escaped. Some dwellings in the lower city came down and a whorehouse, killing ten of its best girls. It was a religious city for many days.

Kathaos, sitting in his carved chair, an open book before him, let them wait a little, shuffling their feet; let them see, these two dragon soldiers, that it was not his custom to give time to such as they. In the corners twilight thickened stealthily.

"You requested an audience with me," he said eventually, "you have it. I understand that you're oppressed by some problem regarding Raldnor Am Sar."

"Yes, my lord," one spoke. The other kept silent, staring at the ground.

"If this is so, why come to me? Should you not seek out the Dragon Lord himself?"

"*Dragon* Lord!" The man looked ready to spit but remembered where he was in time. "Your pardon, my lord, but I'd not have any doings with him."

"If you've some charge, soldier, you should try the public prosecutor."

"I thought the matter better brought to you, my lord. As the Lord Amrek is away."

A cunning look revealed itself. This lout saw personal advantage in backing Kathaos against Amrek.

"Very well," Kathaos said, "I will listen."

"My lord, it's dangerous for me to speak—"

"You should have thought of this earlier. Already you've said enough to give me the right to detain you. Proceed."

"The quake," the dragon said unexpectedly. There was a mixture of craft and superstition on his face. "The gods were angry. I think, I think I know why. I was with the Storm Lord's garrison in Abissa, my lord. The Lowland muck still creeps in and out there— Rashek cares more for trade than a clean city . . ."

"Keep to the point, soldier. Your slanders are inept."

"Pardon, my lord. I'll be brief. There was a Lowland rat without a permit. He pulled a knife on me, but the damned Xarabians got it off him and swore he never had it. I remembered him after, went looking for him with Igos here. We got his girl, but King Amrek found out about it and took her off our hands—kept her too, I reckon, till he got tired of her. We never had a taste—"

"Are these sordid grievances all you have to tell me?"

The soldier muttered and said: "I had another look for the Lowlander after, my lord. Traced him to a Xarabian's house—the Xarab said he wasn't there, only his own brother with a fever. Couldn't find a sniff of him then—thought he'd scuttled back to his cesspit in the Plains. But I'd know him again, my lord. So would Igos."

"Indeed. And what has this to do with me?"

"He's here, my lord. In Koramvis. He calls himself Raldnor of Sar."

Kathaos's expression did not for a moment alter. He said: "Such an accusation is as stupid as it is absurd."

"Oh, no, my lord. I remember him. Same build, same looks—Vis blood somewhere. The Lowlander was missing a little finger on the left hand. And this Raldnor has pale eyes, my lord—that's rare in a Vis. And easy to dye his hair. At first I wasn't sure, but he's been about a lot, since the King took him up. In the end, I was certain, and Igos, too. If the Storm Lord knew it—"

"So you came to me."

"Your lordship took him on first—not knowing. And he maimed your Guard Lord—"

"Does anyone else know of this?"

"No, my lord, I swear—"

"Very well. The information may be useful to me. Go downstairs, the servant will show you. I'll see you get a meal. And some form of monetary reward for your time."

Kathaos's servant took the grinning dragon and his sullen mate below, having recognized the brief sign his master had given him. The two would be drugged with their drink and then disposed of. They were not the first voluntary spies who had gone that way into the dark, and would not be greatly missed, for soldiers, even dragons, deserted all the time.

Kathaos sat locked in thought. He had killed from caution, for an extraordinary idea had come into his mind. He knew the story: the yellow-haired woman, Ashne'e, who slew her baby, and devoured it, so the rabble believed. In more sophisticated circles, the disappearance of the child had been laid at several doors—Amnorh the Councilor's, Val Mala's, even Orhn's. Yet, if it had lived—

A yellow-eyed man, part Lowlander, part Vis—*royal* Vis—Rehdon's blood. . . . How often that resemblance had troubled Kathaos. Could it be that here lay the missing piece of the puzzle?

Raldnor. Raldnor, Rehdon's bastard by a Lowland witch.

Did he know it? No. Neither his actions nor his demeanor indicated knowledge.

Kathaos reflected upon the ancient law—that law which held that the last child conceived of the Monarch before his death was his heir. He visualized the throne of Dorthar. It had fascinated Kathaos, shining in the distance all his adult life. And now, here was the means of realizing the mirage—an insane yet feasible means, which would use Raldnor as its pivot.

"Even my father," Kathaos thought, "consented to a regency."

For the regency was the penultimate step toward the throne itself. And in the end, a King, tainted with Lowland blood, would be easy to be rid of.

12.

THE LONG SOFT SUNSET of the hot months rested on the mountains and the hills in chalks of red and lavender and gold. Raldnor rode the chariot above Koramvis, using the little-known tracks, the byways. But he was too skillful—the management of the vehicle did not take up all his mind. It left him free to think of her.

Amrek was expected in three days. Raldnor had not been near her since the day of the quake. He had seen her, as before, far off, a moving doll on strings. Sometimes, but not often, he felt the moth flicker of her mind in his, but rarely. She did not trust him among strangers, or else she did not trust herself. Sometimes in the dark he would feel her insubstantial presence close enough to touch. Even in these brief contacts, the speech of their minds had gone far beyond words, into those abstract yet specific concepts which are the soul of the brain.

And he was mad for her, and she for him. He knew this much. The Star tortured both of them. He took no women into his bed now, wanting none of them, only her. He seldom slept. He burned, as once before. "She has made me a Lowlander again," he thought. She had been a virgin. It had not surprised him once he had so completely known all her life. She had never desired a man before him. Now her passion was as exclusive as his. Yet neither sought the other. They were hemmed in by codes—they, who were unique.

He had driven beyond the lake. The way grew treacherous, then impassable. He tethered the animals and began to walk. Some instinct drove him upward. The sun was almost down, a smudge of savage light on the mountain crests.

He came unexpectedly on a hovel and a wretched field. Behind it a preliminary flank stretched up toward the blackness of a cave mouth. He paused, staring up at it. He had heard of men drawn by the edge of a precipice to leap down into death. Something about the black hole of the cave drew him with a similar chilly compulsion.

A woman came suddenly out of the hut. She seemed to see him; she waved to him and hurried up. She moved in a coquettish way, but, coming close, he saw her dirt, her age and her pathetic idiocy.

"Would you like to come in the house?"

Finding him silent, she pulled down her dress in a dreadful and revolting parody of allure, and he saw the brilliant jewels about her neck. She must have stolen them. Nothing of the hovel or herself proclaimed any wealth and these violet gems—clearly she had no idea of what they could bring her.

"Where did you find your necklace?" he asked.

At once she clutched her throat.

"I have no necklace—no—no—none at all."

He took half a pace toward her. She began to scream, and out from the hut burst a great brute of a man. As he raced up the slope, the woman caught at him, but he thrust her off and she fell headlong in the withered stubble.

Raldnor drew his knife.

"I'm the Storm Lord's man. Watch yourself."

The creature checked. With bewildered accusation he said: "You shouldn't've made her yell."

"I did nothing. I asked her about her necklace. Did you thieve it for her?"

"I? No, lord. She's a fool, an insect. I have to beat her . . ."

The woman whimpered as she heard him.

"Ask her where she got it."

The man lurched to her and pulled her up. He stared at the jewels as she made little sounds of terror.

"Where'd you get this glass, slut?"

"There—up there—a man came out and I took them when he slept."

Raldnor stared up again, where she pointed, into the solitary, ink-black nostril of the rock. A feverish coldness filled his body.

There had been a legend. Eraz had told it to him when he was a child. The jewel of the goddess, the Serpent's Eye . . .

He took a coin from his belt and threw it to the man. Then moved on up the slope towards the hole of night.

Near midnight, certain lovers strolling still in gardens, or human vermin abroad on their various business, heard a chariot pass them on the road. Women glanced from saffron windows and sighed theatrically, for it was the Sarite who drove beneath on the streets of Koramvis.

On the terrace of the Palace of Peace two or three late watch ceased laughing together and stood to attention. When he came, he had a look about him that kept them very quiet. They discussed it after—perhaps some pleasure drug of Xarabiss, or some woman who had at last proved too much even for Raldnor Am Sar . . .

In an inner room an officer of the Queen's guard was lounging—Kloris. Raldnor's mind moved sluggishly. He supposed the man had been after Lyki once again, but Kloris bowed with insolent, exaggerated courtesy and said: "Her majesty sent me to relieve you of your post. That is, as guard to the Princess Astaris. Here's the relevant paper and the Queen's seal. My men escorted the royal Karmian at dusk—she now occupies a suite in the Storm Palace." He smiled, promoting conspiracy. "No doubt the Lord Amrek would expect to find her there."

Raldnor stirred within himself a little way from the stupor of the mountain. He had sensed her gone. He took the
ornate scroll, glanced at Val Mala's seal. Kothon would already have done as much. He had half expected this sudden
reverse of tactics because of fright at Amrek's return. He
said what was necessary, but Kloris did not go.

"There's another matter—I discovered a creature skulking about by your apartments an hour ago, while I was
awaiting your return."

Kloris's insufferable smile wavered a little as Raldnor
looked at him.

"Well," he said, "I apprehended the man for you. He's
dumb, but your—er—Wolves—ascertained from his signalings that it was you he wanted. They have him now."

Raldnor gave him the briefest nod and went below to
the guard room. Kloris, summarily dismissed, continued to
idle about the place with a great show of nonchalance.

Like a shade come from the dead, the dumb man gazed at
him with torpid eyes. He was a beggar, his feet scarred and
dusty, yet he held out a little pouch of black velvet. In the
pouch was a strand of blood-red silk—hair that could only
have come from one woman's head.

Raldnor, the drug dream of the cave still on him, responded to this new urge like a sleepwalker. Pausing only
to wrap about himself a black anonymous cloak and not
once to think, he followed the mute out into the midnight
city.

They passed behind the Storm Palace, on the broad
white boulevards, under a cyclamen moon.

Soon the streets became narrower. Pole lights were in-
frequent here. At last he grew uneasy. A woman's lazy voice,
calling to him from one of the timbered doorways, brought
her for a moment nearer death than she knew.

The dank, foggy odor of the river seeped into the air.
Raldnor's guide turned into a street of villas, on whose tall
leaning gates broken escutcheons of ancient houses showed.

Water snakes and rats were the present tenants of these crumbling palaces, and probably the robber, cutthroat and procurer.

The dumb man hurried down the pavement and went under the ebony shadow of an arch.

An ideal place for a murder, Raldnor thought, but he followed.

There was a wild garden beyond the high wall. He stared at the overgrown lawns, the pallor of toppled statuary. The dumb man had halted. He stretched out his arm, pointing through a tangled growth of trees toward the ruined hulk of a mansion. It had blind-eyed empty windows, and beyond its ivy-webbed towers lay the iron gleam of the river.

Raldnor's guide slipped sideways into darkness and was immediately gone.

Raldnor drew the knife from his belt. It had been her silken hair, none other, yet the ruin filled him with a sense of leaden distrust. He went forward through the blowing grasses.

The garden was empty. Whatever shadows proved to be assassins searched for smaller prey than himself.

He passed between the fallen columns. The moon sent spears in intermittent pale hot shafts through the damaged roof. Ahead was a hint of the faint topaz glow of a lamp.

He threaded the dilapidation toward it and came out into a rectangular salon, open on one side to the Okris and the river-sounding night. Across the water temple lights burned on the far bank; here a little bronze lamp flickered on its pedestal. There was a great bed with transparent curtains. He touched them, and a fine powder of dust and rotten gauze fell from his fingers.

He felt a cool, soft, searching question open in his brain.

He turned swiftly. There was a woman in a hooded cloak standing in the doorway. He crossed to her and gently pushed back the hood and slid his hands into the flames of her hair.

"How did you discover this place?"

"I've been listening to gossip at last. This has been a lovers' trysting place for many years. The old caretaker is blind."

"So he says. You should never have exposed yourself to danger in this way."

"We have so little time," she said quietly.

It was an expression of despair, yet not uttered in sadness. It was so unarguable, he answered nothing. Then she touched his face and said: "Your goddess spoke to you."

He held her back a way and the river silence settled round them.

"No, Astaris."

Very slowly he opened his mind to her and let her see what he had seen. The shock, the numbing fear; the exaltation he lessened for her, partly forgetting that some of its impact on him had sprung from the beliefs of his childhood and the inherited memories of his race. He gave to her the stumbling dark cave, the tingling of the water drops, the singing soundlessness and the inner region where the light swelled from some unimaginable source. And then the soaring whiteness of the giantess with her whorling golden tail. Anackire, the Lady of Snakes. His bones had seemed to melt.

But the awful ecstasy was brief. He saw her for what she was, the magnificent symbol, not the thing itself. Even her serpent tail was damaged, some of its golden plates displaced and lost. Yet She had stood in Dorthar, the heart and hub of Vis, for uncountable centuries, this yellow-haired, white-faced Lowlander. How many other men had found her and fled? Not many. Only one, it seemed, had looted her, and there was no word of her in Dorthar—only those legends of mountain banaliks and demons so common to all lands.

He felt the woman tremble in his arms and drew her closer.

"I thought you had been granted a vision," she said, "but She, too, was only an image."

"No, She gave me something, something too subtle for me to understand as yet. But it will come. Besides, you're all and everything I want. And there'll be an answer for us. I know it."

Beyond the terrace Zastis had flushed the river like metallic wine. It brought them the first consolation of passion, and soon a fire to consume them. The mansion was a quiet and secret place; it muffled the whispers and the cries of lovers, and the anguish or the joy which lay between each joining through the long embers of the night.

Kloris crossed the still garden of the Palace of Peace. He had had a good deal of wine, and it was very late—or early, he supposed—near dawn. By a little ornamental pool sat a girl in a loose pale dress.

He still pursued Lyki simply because he had not yet had her. It had occurred to him, after his fourth cup of liquor, that he now possessed a piece of news which might alter things.

He stumbled on a root. In the tree to which the root belonged, a bird woke and let out a single piercing argent note. Lyki turned.

"What a clumsy spy you are, Kloris."

He chuckled.

"One day you'll cut your mouth on your tongue. What makes you think I've been spying on you? I don't need to, do I, to see how your belly's rounding?"

He was pleased when she flinched and looked away. Reaching her, he slipped an arm about her and fondled her breast. She thrust him off.

"Still hoping your virile Dragon Lord will do that for you, Lyki?" She made no reply. "The Sarite," Kloris said, very carefully, "has found himself another repast. A strange eccentric lady, who sends mute beggars to conduct him to her."

He saw he had caught her attention.

"What do you mean?"

"A mute came, and Raldnor followed him out. Where else would they be going on a Zastis night?"

"A dumb man—" she said. She seemed bemused.

He leaned on the tree casually.

"A dumb, tongueless, speechless mute."

Moving then, he thought, with unexpected speed, he blundered against her and caught her close, but she twisted away and, before he could stop her, raked his cheek with needle-pointed nails. As he shouted and staggered, she shot across the level lawns.

Going back through the garden, Kloris passed the night patrol with their lamps.

When he was barely past, one turned grinning to the other.

"Kloris found a kalinx in the shrubbery tonight."

The dawn was cold with the ashes of the Star, as cold as burned-out fire.

Cold eyed, Lyki halted at the gate of the Palace of Peace.

As she had thought, the iron chariot stood a little way up the white road, waiting for her. There was a veil of mist, and the chariot seemed to grow out of it, heavy and black as an old anger. She set her hand on the rail and looked up. He had learned to drive and control his team with his left hand. It must have been hard to do.

"Your little urchin messenger found me, as you see," he said. "It seems now you're as anxious to harm Raldnor of Sar, in your woman's way, as I am. I thought the time might come."

"I'll tell you something to make you happy then, Ryhgon. And after that I'm done with it." She looked down at her hand on the rail, then up again. "Your enemy has spent the past night with the Princess Astaris."

The scar on Ryhgon's face seemed to catch light. A grimace of pain or savage pleasure twisted his features.

"Do you know what you've said, woman? Are you speaking the truth, or what your wicked tongue suggests to you?"

"The truth. Would I dare make such an accusation otherwise?"

"I remember," Ryhgon said, "he was never out of the beds of the whores at Abissa. It seems he hasn't lost the habit."

"I'd thought for a long while there was something between them," Lyki continued, venom in her eyes. "Yesterday a man came begging for bread. He was a mute, and she happened to hear of it. She ordered me to fetch him, and then sent me out. That was before the Queen's escort came to take her to the Palace. When she went with them at dusk, she left all her women behind to see to her clothes and jewels. That was unusual, but she's always strange. I thought no more of it until I learned that a dumb man came here at midnight and summoned Raldnor away with him, as it's fancied, to some tryst."

"You're a jealous little bitch, Lyki. The gods will see you suffer for it." But he grinned at her. "Now you'll come with me and tell the lord Kathaos all this."

Startled, she drew back from the chariot.

"I said, I'm done with it."

"You're not."

She turned to run in sudden panic, but he caught her up and thrust her in beside him. A jeweled comb fell from her hair on to the road.

The chariot lurched into movement and the sky broke into a fiery race.

They came to Kathaos's villa, stone-still above the city in the morning.

Ryhgon pulled the chariot to a halt and tethered the animals. He looked back at her only once.

"Stay here. If you run, I'll come after you, and I can be tenacious."

He went in through a wall entrance, and the door was shut.

She did not dare flight, though she waited a long while. She recalled too well the angry scar, igniting with its own purple life. Eventually she opened a round of mirror in her bracelet and tried to repair her face paint. The comb she had lost on the road had been worth a good deal; no doubt some thief would find it and be grateful.

At last a servant in Kathaos's yellow livery came to the wall door and beckoned her in. She followed him through the tasteful and opulent rooms until she found herself facing Kathaos across a length of icy marble.

He was quite expressionless, as usual, but Ryhgon stood on his left, his face congested with impatience.

"Well, madam." Kathaos's coldness offset the demoniac elation of the man beside him. "I've heard a curious story. I believe you've been Raldnor's mistress."

"A while since," she said sharply.

"And now you're telling tales about your lover."

"I wasn't brought here willingly."

"Were you not? Did you speak unwillingly to Ryhgon, too? What prompted you, madam—your sense or your spite?"

Tightly, and with acid dignity, she said: "I don't think the gods of Dorthar would spare me if I allowed the Storm Lord's bed to be soiled."

"Very well. I'll hear your story again. I'd advise you to choose your words with care. I wonder if you understand what you'll be sending Raldnor to. I see you think you do. Then you can bear in mind that if you lie to me, you yourself will go to it."

Val Mala poised a jewel in the hollow of her creamy throat.

"Poor Kathaos," she murmured, "I've been neglecting you."

Kathaos smiled.

"That's your privilege, madam, and my misfortune. But not the reason I've sought an audience."

She raised her eyebrows. Amrek had returned this morning, and any signs of her rumored illness had been put from her. Their meeting, he had heard, had as usual been turbulent. Certainly, Val Mala would not have gone to it in any state of vulnerability.

"I've been made the master of some strange information that will doubtless bring you much grief." He paused only for a fraction. "The information is unfavorable to your son's bride." He marked her interest. She did not attempt to disguise it. "Nevertheless, the facts of the matter are uncertain. I require your jurisdiction, madam, to prove them true or false."

"Tell me what she's done."

"I hear that she's kept an assignation with the Storm Lord's elected Commander, Raldnor of Sar."

He was unprepared for the excessive excitement with which she greeted this statement. Eyes burning, she demanded: "You mean she's given herself to him, made herself his whore?"

He concealed a smile. Ironically he supposed she too had made herself Raldnor's "whore." She seemed to guess his thought.

"The Sarite has never been anything to me, Kathaos," she said. "He's an ambitious upstart. I shan't be sorry when Amrek's rid of him."

There was no intimation in Kathaos's face of his own opinion. He would regret bitterly the necessity of Raldnor's death — Raldnor, who might have been the key to so much. If there had been more time to plan. But the circumstances and the betrayal had been unforeseen. He had been forced to play for the lowest throw — Val Mala's spite against Astaris — simply because the man he had been prepared to back was a fool. He regretted, too, that nothing better than the fire would sample the exquisite Astaris's body.

"Majesty, if the Lord Amrek understands I'm working against the princess, he'll try to stop me, perhaps find some way to remove me. If the investigation were undertaken in your name, I can apprehend whatever treason there is, unhindered."

She nodded her gold-tiered head in unequivocal assent.

"Do it. What plans have you made?"

Concisely he told her. In a curious way he recalled Amnorh to her then—Amnorh, who had promised her Rehdon's death and whose reward had been his own. But, as she heard him out, she smiled, for she saw the host of her enemies overthrown, the fall of bright stars and the exorcism of ghosts before her eyes.

A man bowed to Raldnor on the terrace of the Palace of Peace and slipped into his hand a jewel.

"Do you know this gem, my lord?"

"The Princess Astaris's seal ring—how did you come by it?"

"No need for anger, my lord. My mistress could assure you of that. She asks you to attend her this evening."

"Who is your mistress?"

"You know her well, Dragon Lord. Her last servant gave her request no tongue."

Raldnor stared at the man, and in his heart feared for her. The speech seemed brashly put. She had chosen this time a poor messenger.

"You're too open. Take care."

"I beg your pardon, my lord. I only do as I'm bid. Will you go where you found her last?"

"She knows I will."

"Do you remember the way? This time there'll be no guide."

"I remember it."

"Leave here two hours after sunset then, when she's left the feast."

He bowed again and departed.

He himself, being master of a certain trade plied along the river bank, knew the old mansion on Water Street. It seemed they had questioned the princess's women as to where their own trysts were taken, then wrung from the old imbecile of a caretaker all the rest—the hooded woman and her lover, the priceless jewels that had been given in payment. Then Astaris's chief lady had stolen her seal ring. It had been easy enough to do, and the villain, as he slunk across the garden, felt scorn for their stupidity, these great ones who had everything and who thought themselves so beloved of the gods they would never come to grief. Well, let them rot, the pair of them.

Raldnor almost guessed the trap that had been laid for him. Not consciously—it was a prickling in the core of his bones. Yet he neither analyzed nor hesitated, for at that time he seemed to live in a limbo of desire. Besides, he had feared treachery before and found none.

As he left the gate, a figure, cloaked and hooded like himself, slipped out after him, unseen.

In the old unpaved alleys of the city, his dark intuitions came to the fore. When he reached the street of villas, his skin was crawling without apparent reason. He crossed under the arch, his knife drawn, and went through the rustling garden to the portico of the great house. Somewhere ahead the lamp was burning. Yet it did nothing to still his glittering nerves. He paused and reached out for her with his mind through the gloomy, river-smelling palace, and there was no answer.

He experienced an instant's icy clutching dread that she was no longer living, yet Anici had taught him that this at least he would have known. He went through the shadows and into the salon.

The lamp shone as before, yet more dimly, and the river washed beyond. On the bed there was a dark muffled shape, which rose up suddenly and poked out its scarred and grinning face.

"Not such a dainty repast as you thought, Sarite."

Ryhgon. He barely noted him. He knew abruptly that the shadows of the hall outside had been full of men. With a single leap he crossed the room and the narrow strip of terrace. Poised in the air, he saw the Okris gape for him, sprinkled with lights, until his passage cleaved them.

In high summer, in the streams of the Plains, he had swum to wash away the day's dust. But this water, now, in Koramvis was sluggish and very cold beneath. When he lifted his head for air, he rose against a stone wall, viscous with muddy weeds, where an old cooking pot floated on the scum.

The terrace of the ruined palace lay some way back now, and lights had flared up there. They knew he was in the river, but he had been too quick for them. They had assumed that he had gone the other way, for this was where they pointed. A partially submerged plank had caught their attention, and one man flung a spear at it. He dived again.

Red moonlight filtered down to him, and the river gods hung on his heels.

He rose a second time; the mansion was now far off downstream. A stairway lifted itself brokenly out of the water. He climbed up onto the desolate wharf, and rats scuttled to shelter. Beyond, black alleys opened out. He chose one at random and moved into it.

Soon he heard the sound of men's voices, the dull chink of scale plate. Then the color of the torches rose behind a row of hovels on his left. They must have recognized the plank for what it was and split their party in two. He gripped the pole of a street light and pulled himself up it to the level of a house roof, then dropped silently and lay flat on filthy clay still warm from the day's heat.

They passed beneath him with flare-lit faces, thrusting spears into dark areas—doors, alley mouths—but never looked up at the parapet.

"Must have headed for the gate!" a man shouted below.

The hunting party made off northward up the narrow street.

His mind in turmoil, he lay on the roof. Besides himself

and them, nothing seemed to be stirring. He lifted his head. He could still see the tawny lurch of their torches, off to the right now, and the hovels standing out like black paper against it. Yet beyond those, thrusting up like a pale marker in the uniform flat of the slums, he made out the battlements of the River Garrison.

The half-formed plan took hold of him, a madman's plan as once before. Reach Kren's hold and he could use his rank, perhaps, to commandeer a chariot, then drive across the searchlines to the Storm Palace—who could predict he would run that way? Then he must find some means to get to Astaris. He had had a moment's chilling leisure now to understand what had happened, and to see what would be done to her. But he would pry her out of whatever imprisonment they had allotted her, however meager his chances or strong the jail. He would sell his life and freedom for hers, if he had to, without thinking, for it was impossible for him to imagine that he might lose her to the fire, and he infinitely preferred to envisage his death rather than her agony. It was a new wine that filled him. As in the garden at Abissa, impulse ruled him and drove him on.

He swung over the parapet and dropped noiselessly to the cobbles.

And saw, too late, the individual patrol lurking in wait for him. As they thrust from cover, the Star painted their eager faces. He doubled back and a shout went up. Torchlight converged behind him.

He sped up the narrow alley, doubled a second time into Date Street and emerged onto the open and unsheltered square that fronted the high Garrison gates. Two red-cloaked sentries stood leaning on their spears on the raised walk before the gate. They were at ease, expecting, until now, nothing special this night. The baying of a hunting pack and the glaring brands jerked up their heads. They leveled spears.

A figure ran below, and after it, into the square, a group of fourteen or fifteen of the Queen's guard. There came then an abrupt cessation of all movement, each man poised like an actor in a tableau, scoured by the raw light of the flares.

Raldnor stared up at the sentries on the walk. He drew in his breath, hard, and prepared to speak with every shred of his authority. It was to be his throw of the dice against death, but he saw only her in his mind's eye.

The air parted with a hiss behind him, and he felt something thud against his back. He thought they had flung a stone at him, but there was no pain. He turned half around to face them—it had been part of his earliest training never to turn his blind side to an enemy, and he had forgotten it. In that moment he found he could no longer see. It took him suddenly, too swiftly to make him afraid. His hearing went next and after that, everything. The last conscious thought left him in the void was a woman's name, shining like a red jewel, but he could no longer recollect to whom it belonged. A moment later there was nothing.

The guard who had driven his knife into Raldnor's back moved to one side to allow him to fall on to the square. He grinned at the watchers above and bent to wipe his blade on the fallen man's cloak.

"Do you have the authority to kill?" one of the sentries called.

The guard finished wiping his knife and pointed to Val Mala's blazon.

"That's my authority."

The sentry turned and bellowed back at the gate, and into the courtyard beyond. Almost at once an alarm bell began to toll.

"You can tell the Dragon Kren all about your authority when he comes."

The guard spat out: "What's to keep us here?"

But the gates had rolled wide, and a phalanx of Garrison soldiery moved out, fully armed, even to their shields. A man was quickly sent for Kren.

The Dragon Lord followed his officers out into the walk

and showed neither displeasure nor irony at being summoned to this brawl. With his steady and appraising eyes he took in the scene and said at last, quite evenly: "Who is this man?"

"Ours," the guard snarled, "by order of the Queen. Cause us no further trouble, Dragon Lord."

"No one has answered my question," Kren said with the utmost politeness, his eyes like polished steel. "I asked you who the man was."

"The Sarite who calls himself Raldnor. King Amrek's Commander."

"And his offense?"

"That, Dragon, is the Queen's business."

Kren bent over the man named Raldnor and turned him gently. He had been swimming in the river, this one, and he looked near death. Kren lifted the lid of one eye, then took the limp wrist. He noted with a curious sense of imminence that the man's smallest left finger was missing. He had heard mention of Amrek's favorite but not paid a great deal of attention to what was said. There was a look of Rehdon in the face. And Val Mala's rats were hunting him, were they? Kren had no great love for the Queen's intrigues, and this piece of Koramvis, after all, lay within his personal jurisdiction. He traced the faintest flicker of pulse bedded in the Sarite's wrist, but he was losing blood fast.

Kren straightened.

"You've done your lady's work admirably," he said shortly. "This man's dead."

A barely detectable signal drew the phalanx in close about himself and Raldnor. Two Garrison soldiers lifted Raldnor on a shield and carried him quickly in under the gate.

"You've no right—" the Queen's guard cried out.

"I would remind you, gentlemen, that you're within the limits of the River Garrison. I have every right. But if you'd care to wait on our physician, he'll no doubt confirm the news I've given you."

They had no choice but to do as he told them.

His hospitality was faultless. He had wine brought for them as they paced, cursing, about the hall. Eventually an old man in a stained robe came nervously in. He glanced at Kren, then murmured: "Quite dead. The blade pierced the lung."

The guard's response was immediate.

"There'd be blood on his mouth if the lung took it. Do you think I've never seen a man die? You don't know your trade, Aarl take you!"

An unexpected severity possessed the physician. Lying at Kren's direction had disconcerted him, but this layman's lecture drew his temper.

"My trade? I know yours—to damage what the gods made; mine is to patch up what I can after your blasphemies. You butchered your victim, and if you know the method a man employs to live by after his heart's stopped, I'd be happy to learn it. As to Aarl, he knows more of that place than either of us."

13

AMREK TURNED A JEWELED collar in his hands. A beautiful thing, a fitting gift. Yet would it please her at all? She seemed never to notice what she wore. He nodded to the goldsmith and his assistant, his eyes fixed on the gems flashing in the lamp shine. He was troubled and constrained. He had seen her at the feast, at his side, and she seemed to him as remote as ever—and yet, strangely different. He could not be sure of the change, only sensed it. In the ante-room he had embraced her and found on her the hint of a most curious new physical mood, like a scent without substance. Though he had not inspired it; it was neither because of, nor meant for him. He felt he had lost anything he might have achieved with her before. Damn Thaddra. He had craved for this woman every night alone in the mountains. Where must he begin again?

The slightest of sounds came from the open doorway. Amrek glanced up and saw Val Mala standing there.

"My lady mother. An unexpected pleasure."

"Send these men away," she said. "What I have to say to you is not for their ears."

He set down the collar and stood up.

"What's the matter, madam? Has Kathaos disappointed you tonight?"

She said nothing, but there was a kind of blankness on her face, a mask she held badly; behind it he saw an impossible triumph. He stared at her, and a premonition laid its clammy fingers on his skin. He waved the two men out, and they scurried, bowing, away. He barely noticed.

"Well, madam? What's your news?"

"My son," she said, "what I have to tell you concerns your bride."

He felt the dark roaring of a sea engulf him.

"What's happened to her? What have you done?"

"A good deal has happened to her, and I've done nothing but discover it."

The hate that boiled up in him disfigured her and made her very ugly. He seized her shoulder. It seemed incredible to him that once he had been curled up inside her, at her mercy—and, now he was free of her, able if he wished to choke the life out of her, still he was mewling and helpless.

"No more games, madam. Tell me what you came here to say."

Then he saw the smile; she could not keep it back.

"Your Dragon Lord, Raldnor the Sarite, has been teaching your bride bed manners."

He let her go as if her flesh had burned him.

"Don't lie to me," he got out, knowing quite well that even she would never dare lie to him on such a matter, and tasting suddenly, once more, that new, unnamed, scentless perfume on Astaris's flesh.

Val Mala composed her face and held up the mask again as she told him everything.

While she spoke, his eyes never left her mouth. He seemed to watch the words that came out of it as if watching rats emerging from some stinking crevasse underground. By the time she had finished, his face had become quite fixed and quite empty, like the painted face of an idiot in a carnival.

He turned away, shutting his eyes against the painful light, but her relentless voice followed him down the black corridors of his brain.

"Surely, Amrek, you'd rather discover before your marriage than after it what a whore your princess is. Do you want a slut in your bed, coming to you every night from the couch of one of your soldiers?"

Her eyes glittered, yet something in her flinched slightly, waiting for the lash of his anger, at her spite. She remembered how he had flung himself at her once, when he was a child and she had thwarted some desire of his; he would have killed her then if he had had any weapon to hand. Yet now there was nothing. A sense of the ultimate victory braced her.

"Did you prefer, Amrek, to be deceived?"

"Yes," he said, and his voice was toneless.

"It seems then that others are more sensible of your honor and the honor of your rank than you. Perhaps, had you taken your betrothal rights, Amrek, she might have been satisfied and not turned her eyes elsewhere. It was a woman they gave you, not a piece of glass."

He had moved beyond the light of the lamp. She heard his silence in the darkness.

"You fool," she hissed, "think how this Karmian has slighted your throne. Make sure she suffers for it."

He came through the palace, half blinded by the soft light of the lamps. In the anteroom of her apartments, her women, having seen his face, curtsied in terror and fled. He threw open the inner doors and found her facing him, as if she had been waiting for his coming.

He thrust the doors shut after him and stood staring at her.

"I was betrothed to you at Lin Abissa, madam. I've come for my betrothal rights."

"As you wish, my lord," she said, without either reluctance or readiness. Whatever he did to her now she would accept, for he was superfluous to her existence. The fury rose into his throat like bile. He felt impotent, sexually and in all other ways, before her insane serenity.

"Did he force you?" he said to her.

There was the moment's briefest response. As once before, he saw a stirring in the depths of her eyes, yet no fear.
It was distress for him. She pitied him—*she* pitied— Did
she know what would be done to her?

"No, my lord. I was willing. I'm sorry to cause you pain."

"Pain? I think you need instruction, Astaris. By the laws
of Dorthar you'll go to the stake for this, and burn."

"And Raldnor?" she asked, as if not noticing her own
fate.

The congestion in Amrek's throat almost choked him.

"Whatever I order. At least, castration and the gallows."

She looked at him, but there was no sort of entreaty in
her face. She was resigned for both of them. He thought of
the men pinning her against the wooden pillar, and the
flames eating upward through her feet, cracking her ivory
bones like tinder, the uncurling leaves of her golden flesh
and the black petals blowing on the morning wind, and the
cloud of her hair on fire, which was fire, and he shouted
aloud, a great hoarse scream, his hands across his eyes to
shut out the million little separate flames of the lamps.

"I can do nothing," he cried out, *"nothing!"* and found
that he was weeping. Blindly he took hold of her, but could
not bear to touch her hair. "No," he whispered, "I won't let
you die because of a tradition. I'll find some way."

Dimly, as if far off, he felt the soft touch of her hand,
the bitter aloe of her consolation, this woman who had
betrayed him, who should expect only death in return.
And the thought came then of Raldnor, hunted now
through Koramvis, the man he had chosen to serve him.
Would he die on the knives of the impatient guard, or be
left for the rope he had evaded in the garden at Abissa?
Amrek kept still a moment, accepting her touch, then
drew back.

"I'll send someone here," he said. "Go with them. I can
offer you nothing but your life. Take nothing with you."

"Am I to go alone?" she asked.

He felt the armoring of years creep over him.

"Madam," he said, "don't ask too much of me. The mob will expect something. Besides, your lover is most probably already dead."

He did not know if she meant to say more. He turned and left her in the lamplit room. It would be easy after all to cheat the flames and still to lose her. He felt a terrible lightness. He could never have been meant to have her, he had always guessed it; his body, holding back, had known. Now he was returned to a point in time before her coming. He was himself again, the powerful madman, the monster, the cripple. He had reentered his own legend. All he could do now was to live there in the rabid dark.

"I must be true to myself," he decided.

Near dawn a man came, a nervous hurrying man, who led her through the lower corridors of the palace, having first wrapped her in a patched and musty cloak.

The gardens were gray and deserted, and a little boat bobbed below the steps at the river's edge. She passed between two stone dragons to get to it and among half-rotten lilies. There were no guards. There had been no guards at her door.

The sun rose and flooded the Okris with gold as the sweating man rowed them untidily downstream. The white morning city slid by on either bank. She did not ask where they were going. Destination had no meaning for her.

Since their coming together, she had felt Raldnor in her brain, however faintly, always somehow there, not a definite thing, yet conclusive, unobtrusive as a memory. And before ever Amrek came to her, she felt that presence snuff out. There had been death; she had already known it. His Anici had taught her too.

Now she also returned to what she was, that inner core, with all about it the empty vistas of her life. She did not weep. Her sorrow was not separate enough that she could analyze and be moved by it. Sorrow had become her flesh.

The nervous man rowed on, carrying his dangerous

cargo. By the banks men were cutting reeds. It was a day like any other.

Five days passed after it.

With great secrecy, the lord Kathaos, cloaked and reticent, came to the River Garrison on the sixth. The seal he had shown at the gate had been Val Mala's, but once inside, he pushed back the hood and put the seal away. Certainly the Queen had no notion that he was there.

Kren came in and bowed to him, showing no particular surprise—but then that was not this Dragon Lord's way, so Kathaos had heard. The man had been a commander in Rehdon's time, but kept his rank all the years since, which required some cleverness.

"I am honored, lord Councilor, by this visit. My soldier didn't know you."

"Yes. Well, we must all employ caution occasionally. The city's in an uproar."

"So I heard," Kren said.

"The Princess Astaris is believed to have taken poison," Kathaos murmured. "Certainly there'll be no public execution after all this time, though I gather an effigy was burned yesterday in the lower quarters. The mob are always hungry for a spectacle. They lost the Sarite, too. At your very gates, so I hear."

"The Queen's men were impatient and stabbed the man in the back. My own physician saw to him, but it was far too late."

"And you had the body buried here?" Kathaos allowed himself the most inoffensive of smiles. "Of course. That would be prudent in this heat. I believe the Queen sent someone to inspect the grave." Kathaos paused. "There's the strangest rumor abroad, Lord Kren, that the Sarite may still be alive."

Kren looked him in the face and said with matchless courtesy: "Your lordship is kind to tell me of these unfounded stories. Naturally the rabble will believe anything."

Kathaos acknowledged the man's wit. He saw he must fall back, at least in part, on the truth, though it did not please him.

"Shortly before Raldnor was stabbed at your gate, Lord Kren, I received certain information. Would it interest you to know that the Sarite had Lowland blood?"

He saw the change in Kren's face, and how he mastered it, but it told him altogether too little.

"Lord Kren," he said, "no doubt you recall Rehdon's unlucky union with the Plains woman, Ashne'e. The child vanished and was never found. If it had lived, it would have been informative to see how far the Council of Koramvis would have adhered to the law and upheld its claim to the throne of Dorthar."

Kren did not speak and his expression was schooled.

"I hope that you understand my meaning," Kathaos said. "Waste is always distressing."

"Indeed, my lord, but as no doubt you've heard, none of us can argue with death."

As Kathaos rode back across the city, he pondered the conversation. He was unsatisfied, and yet uncertain whether the man was lying to him or not. It seemed, in any event, that Kathaos had lost the game entirely inasmuch as it related to Raldnor. Whatever Kren purposed to do, there would be little detection or hindrance in the Garrison, that inner room of Koramvis. And it was plain besides that he intended no help in other quarters. Yet neither would he spread secrets; he had not kept his position through gossip but because of that persistent strength and cynical integrity so apparent in his person. So, it was finished.

Kathaos, who had grown accustomed to waiting, settled in again to wait. He, too, had been put back into an earlier skin, yet in his case at least the fit was not unkindly. He had lost a game piece, that was all. There would be others.

In the narrow room at the tower's head, Kren stood looking down at the unconscious man he had saved from death, simply out of a sense of justice. Nearby the physician clattered his instruments, and the girl servant was clearing up after him. He was a competent but messy old man, scrupulously clean with wounds—very few soldiers contracted festering or rot under his care—yet he was villainously untidy, with even a soup stain on his collar.

"How's your patient today?"

"Rather better. The worst of the fever's past and the back's healing well."

No other than the three in this room knew of Raldnor's continued existence. The Garrison had seen something buried in a bloody sheet and assumed it to be a man. In a way, Kren was a king here; the soldiers, armorers, cooks, grooms and their women and children lived within these walls as if inside a minute city, and he ruled them in his own fashion, which was one of discipline tailored to human needs. They gave him their fierce loyalty, and so he put a bundle of old rags and goat's flesh into the earth, not in fear of betrayal, but to protect his people.

As to what the lord Councilor had just told him, that could be shared with no one—except, that was, for the man lying on the bed, for it was obvious to Kren that he could never have known.

The maimed hand had made Kren uneasy, he could not at first think why. When he recalled at last the woman he had helped fly Koramvis and the baby she had taken with her, he had never thought to bring the two together—the man and the unseen child—as one. Until that moment in the room below, when Kathaos Am Alisaar had overreached himself in his machinations.

Now the weight rested on Kren. It troubled him that soon it would rest more heavily on Raldnor. With an unerring judgment he had already gauged Raldnor's inner fragility, which bore no relation to his physical strength. And it was indeed a burden for any man to bear, this knowledge of the undisputed past, the impossible frustration of the future. For here was a King who could hope for nothing.

*   *   *

Raldnor woke in the dark to a girl's anxious face.

"Lie still," she whispered at once, although he had not moved at all. "You're in the River Garrison," she added, although he had not asked her.

Soon after the physician came. He muttered and seemed pleased with himself. Eventually Raldnor began to question him, for he could remember nothing beyond the moment he had pulled himself from the Okris and into the hovels and the dreadful night. His long sleep had seemed haunted with dim shouts and torches. Now the physician told him why.

"However, you've mended well. Though you'll have a splendid scar to impress your next woman with."

It was hard now to wait out the captivity of his weakness. As the girl and the old man seemed to know so much, he asked them for news of Astaris. The girl blurted out at once: "Why, she poisoned herself!"

At which the physician took her shoulder and shook her, calling her every foul thing a garrison full of soldiers could have taught him, and perhaps a few more. He had heard the young man mutter a name in his delirium—the name of a scarlet Karmian flower—and guessed at deeper emotions than pure lust. Nevertheless Raldnor only said: "Better than the fire."

In his mind he felt a curious aching and turning, a search, but not for something dead. With an uncertain prescience he sensed her still alive, but far away as the stars. When they left him, he wept, but more from illness than despair. He experienced a strange mixture of hope and desolation, for he was once more in a limbo of the soul.

Soon there were days when he was sent to sit on the roof of the tower to take the air. It had been put about that the brother of the physician's girl was visiting her.

He wondered when he would see his benefactor, Kren. And wondered also what the man's reasons were for giving him life. There was nothing given for nothing, so the Vis had taught him. He was therefore not prepared for Kren.

The wide-shouldered man, long past youth yet obviously still strong of mind and physique, came onto the paved terrace at sun-fall and nodded to him courteously. Raldnor saw a scarred, lined face with unexpected eyes. There was nothing wavering or stupid in them, and nothing masked either.

Raldnor rose, but Kren signaled him back to his chair and sat also.

"Well, sir. It's very pleasant to see my guest so much better."

"I owe you my life, my lord. It's my disgrace I've no means to repay you."

"There you're wrong. There are a few matters I must talk to you about. It may take a while, so bear with me, and I'll be well repaid enough."

Kren poured himself and the young man wine from the jug set between them. He tried to be easy with him, yet he found Raldnor troubled him—too many ghosts sat at his elbow. Kren remembered suddenly how she had drooped before him with her tired unpainted eyes, his poor Lomandra, with the millstone of Val Mala's infamy on her back. His glance strayed to Raldnor's severed finger, and he thought incongruously: "It mended well. I never thought it would."

"Raldnor," he said, "who was your mother?"

The young man stared at him.

"No, I've not gone mad. I asked you to bear with me. Please do so. This will be a difficult conversation at best, but necessary, I assure you."

Raldnor looked away, his hollow invalid's eyes burning oddly.

"Then she was a Xarabian—"

"You must hear some talk, Dragon Lord."

"Please, sir, do me the kindness of dispensing with my rank. We're cursed with the same title. Yes, I've heard about your beginnings—a mother dead in childbirth at Sar, the father dead soon after, then adoption by a widow, your aunt. Is any of this true, or merely a convenient alteration of the facts? No, please, I'm not intending insult. May I propose another version of your story? You were the foundling of Sar, perhaps, but you weren't born there. Some traveler discovered you as a baby on the Plains outside the town . . . with a Xarabian woman. Was she alive or dead?"

Hoarsely Raldnor answered: "Dead. Your deductions are excellent. A hunter found me in my mother's cloak."

"Not deductions merely, Raldnor. I knew your—mother. Her name was Lomandra. She was a court woman and, for a long while, my mistress." Kren paused, seeing some irony in what he had said. "But, of course, I'm not your father. One of your parents, as you know, was a Lowlander."

The flaring eyes in front of him seemed to burn upward out of their pits.

"You're my host, my lord. I can only wonder at your humor. No man can think himself safe when he's named one of the Plains people."

"I know that. You see there are no witnesses to what I say. Let me go on and things may become clear. Lomandra had a good reason for taking you from Koramvis. She was making for the Lowlands, and she required my help, because her errand was dangerous. I gave her an escort—two of my captains. One of them loved her; I thought it might bring them luck. She would have sent me word when she was safe; it was her way. No word came. So I detailed a man to track them down through Xarabiss to the Plains. He found the wreck of the chariot and its driver on the Xarabian border, and, some way off, what was left of the other man, although the tirr had picked him fastidiously clean. It was only by chance he found the shallow grave, small enough for a woman. He unearthed her for me, to be sure, and there was no child. I didn't know then if whoever took you had found her dead or had killed her. As for you, I thought some slave master had carried you off. The caravans go all ways. There seemed no hope of finding you. Besides, I had then my grief for her."

Raldnor leaned forward and said: "You knew my mother. Who was my father? Do you know that too?"

Kren's level eyes darkened with their unhidden trouble.

"The gods play some strange tricks on us, Raldnor."

Overhead the sky was deepening toward dusk, and a flight of birds, catching the last of the invisible sun on silver wings, soared and swooped toward the river. Raldnor was acutely conscious of their passage.

"Raldnor, have you heard of the Lowland temple girl Rehdon took on the night of his death? He put a child in her, though it's been suggested it was the bastard of the lord Councilor, Amnorh."

"I've heard of her. Ashne'e. The women were always saying they saw her ghost in the Palace of Peace."

"Raldnor, Ashne'e was your mother, your Lowland mother. Rehdon, the Storm Lord, was your father. Val Mala feared your birth because it threatened her status through her son. She instructed Lomandra to kill you, and she demanded your smallest left finger as the token of your death. Ashne'e cut off the finger while you lived. Lomandra took you to the Xarabian border and died there, so you knew nothing of what you are." Kren studied the young man's face but could discern no trace of emotion. There was only that blankness in his eyes which spelled an inner turmoil too frenzied to rise to the physical surface. "It's the custom of the Vis that the last child conceived of a King is his heir. Amrek was plowed before you. You're Rehdon's last child. You are the Storm Lord, Raldnor. And if you leave this Garrison, your own Dragon Guard will hack you to pieces."

BOOK FOUR

Hell's Blue Burning Seas

14

IN THE SUNSET THE mountains were crusts of flame.
After sunset the darkness came slowly, spreading like
ink in the crevasses. Once its work was done, the great spires
were entirely featureless, except for the distant red dots of
hunters' fires or the occasional eyes of what was hunted.

Each time, as the light went out of the mountains, some
reflected meaning stirred faintly in her mind. But she was
mainly dead. Once it occurred to her: "I am a slave." But
this meant, on the whole, very little.

Astaris never wondered if Amrek had planned this fate
for her in lieu of the stake. In point of fact, the merchant
had taken matters into his own hands.

There had been a cloaked stranger in the market in the
dim hour before dawn.

"Are you Bandar the merchant?"

"What if I am?"

"This, if you are," and the amazing bag of gold was put in
his grasp.

"For what am I given this?"

"You're taking your caravan over the pass to Thaddra,
now the trouble's settled? Well, there's to be a passenger for
you. A court lady. One of the Princess Astaris's women. A
Karmian."

"For what do I want a passenger to eat my food?"

The cloaked man had shifted a little, and somehow the edge of his cloak slid aside and revealed the silver lightning which was Amrek's personal blazon. After that, Bandar ceased arguing.

It was a dangerous task, running through the lower ways of the palace, first alone, next with the—court lady. Oh, indeed. He knew well enough who she was once he had seen her hair. At first he had been terrified, his bowels scalded with terror. But once he had her safe away, other emotions came to him. He had heard, by then, the tale of her adultery, for Koramvin gossips had briefly joined his caravan on the road. Bandar and his woman dyed the princess's hair black in the secrecy of their wagon. The old fool was probably too stupid to guess what was up, but to be sure, he swore her to silence on the name of one of the ten thousand gods she believed in. Bandar knew now exactly what he had in his possession, and it was more than a bag of gold. She was adrift, without a prayer, this Astaris. Whoever had got her safe away—could it *truly* have been Amrek?—had no claims on her now, and she, she seemed living in a listless dream. Perhaps the shock had unhinged her. At any rate, her looks would fetch a good price in the markets of Thaddra. For want of inspiration, he had renamed her Silukis, after his Iscaian mother, and considered the bitch honored. In any event she answered to it obediently, as if her own name meant nothing to her.

The trek over the pass took a month. No robbers attacked or came to gather tax. The Storm Lord's men had incidentally cleaned out most of their nests for the present. All told, it was a propitious journey.

The morning the wagons moved down into Thaddra, the mountains were hot and hard and blue.

It was a dark land—humid black jungle forest and still heat without much brightness from the sun. Rarnammon had built a city here once, but it lay in ruins. Now each area had its own guardian, or little king, all giving lip service to Dorthar and to Zakoris, and all bickering between themselves. It was a land to be lost in, and not found. A dark land indeed.

They came to a place called Tumesh, where there was a large and ugly town of squat swarthy buildings which resembled perfectly its inhabitants. Tumesh, as Thaddra went, was wealthy. She had, therefore, the money for Bandar's goods—mostly ornaments and women—for metal ore, gems and prettiness were rare in Thaddra.

They settled in the great marketplace, and the old fat woman came puffing into the wagon. She stripped Astaris, and adorned her in a dress of mauve gauze and copper bangles, with paper orchids for her black hair. Astaris put up her hand and touched her hair, and smiled faintly. She was thinking of Raldnor and the dye that had preserved his secret, like hers. The woman, judging her quite insane, clucked at her and prodded her out on to the square.

There was a rostrum with a bell-hung awning. Under it Astaris was set to stand along with other girls who wept or smirked. Her surroundings affected her no more than a passing mist, for she was thinking only of him. It was her grief and her sustenance. She had no being except in what had gone before.

"You be careful, Bandar," the fat woman muttered to him. "Don't haggle too long over that one. She may have looks, but she's daft and they'll see it. And she's got a brat coming."

That last piqued Bandar's curiosity. Was it Amrek's child or the Sarite's bastard? Well, no matter. It didn't show in the gaudy dress, and she would probably lose it anyhow; she looked too fragile to bear, and she ate like a mouse, praise be.

The bidding began about noon.

A pair of Yllumite girls went first, sniveling, and a piece from Marsak next. Bandar began to be troubled. He led his prize forward and called out at the crowd. Had they no eyes for beauty—such a face, such limbs and breasts . . . and so meek. Had they ever seen so pliable and genteel a woman? She was built for pleasure.

It displeased him intensely that they still hung back. It never occurred to him that she might be too beautiful, too exquisite to appeal.

At last a big rough man came pushing through the crowd. He was tall for a Thaddrian, and heavily constructed, but under his matted hair showed a gold collar, and he wore a mantle of good cloth.

"You, sir. I see you understand the refinements—"

"Stop your squawking, merchant. I'll take her. Here's three bars."

"That won't do, my lord. This girl's worth much more. Look at this straight spine. Think of the boys you can get on her—"

"Three bars are my last offer. You'll be offered no better."

No one bid against him. Bandar began to have suspicions that the lout was bandit stock, secreted in Tumesh, on the proceeds of his garnered wealth, since Amrek's forays in the mountains. At last, with ungraceful resignation, he sold his wares and took the measly payment.

"What's her name?"

"Silukis," snapped Bandar.

"Seluchis," said the man, corrupting the name at once with his Thaddrian-Zakorian slur.

Bandar, even his mother affronted now, thrust the girl into the brute's keeping and wished them both ill of each other as he pocketed the silver bars.

His name was Slath, and he had made his money in robbery, as Bandar supposed, and also in hiring himself out as a cut-throat to the various lords of Thaddra. He bought the girl because she represented a form of elusive culture. He had seen it sometimes in old wall paintings in the ruined city of Rarnammon, where occasionally he holed up when things were uncomfortable for him. He was a romantic villain, and impulsive, and he knew he had made a mistake with her as soon as he got her into his house.

He gave her some wine and meat nevertheless, which

she scarcely touched, and afterward he took her to his bed-room. She was as dull in that as in everything. Slath liked a woman with some spirit—a grunting bandit mare or a clever whore who pretended.

"A pleasure slave are you, by Zarduk! You'll have to try harder than that."

He reduced her position. She swept out hearths and carried water. After three days he whipped her for her negligence. She was simple and he had been cheated. She did not even wail and weep at his blows. He contemplated the blood trickling down her satin back. She was useless, fit only to be looked at. He held off the lash then and considered another possibility—perhaps some Thaddrian lord would buy her. She would look good beside a supper table in some little kingdom—a king's ornament. Slath hung up his whip and sent one of his aides running for a salve.

There was a lord in the jungle forest, many miles northward. Slath had been meaning to hire out to him, if he wanted men. Slath disliked being long idle and, besides, had a certain reputation among his kind which would stand him in good stead. The lord was a great one for conquest, he had heard, a man of vague beginnings, like all lords in Thaddra it seemed, who had built his power from a store of treasure and gold, displaced the petty king and thereafter annexed five other kingdoms. Such a one offered good pickings. His shadow had been growing for years.

Slath did not travel light but with servants, to show his essential rank. After four days' riding they reached one of the nameless rivers of Thaddra and poled upstream into the thick wet gloom of the forest.

At this time Slath kept his girl Seluchis on his own craft, under a shady awning, and tried to see to it that she was well fed. She sat like a statue, never moving, and seldom ate. He had not laid a finger on her since that first time. He pampered the bitch; nevertheless, he expected she would lose her looks, damn her. Somehow she did not. She seemed unaware of the languid heat, and once he observed a butterfly settle undisturbed on her wrist for nearly an hour. On the whole she made him uneasy, and he would be glad to be rid of her.

They were five days on the river. On the sixth there was a challenge. Slath, who had once bought a certain password in the ruined city, with a knife, was conducted from the creeper-grown jetty to a hacked-out jungle road.

By evening they had reached the walls of a large Thaddrian town with, clustered about them, an overspill of rough hide tents and wooden huts. Cook fires spangled the dusk, and in the untidy streets dogs ran and women stared. At the far end of the town rose the Guardian's palace, a three-towered mansion of stone.

Astaris raised her head to look at it. It seemed to have some meaning for her, though what, she could not understand as it reared out of the twilight of her brain. For some time past there had been a curious glimmering, a disturbance in her mind, as if he were there, alive once again. But this could not be. She had felt his passing from her, and comprehended it. Raldnor. She suffered the false expression of his life in her, therefore, as if suffering the pain of a long-healed wound, something which stirred without reason, and for which nothing could be done.

In the wild garden at the palace's foot ruby blossoms drooped and ruby birds slept. One of the blossoms opened its petals and flew away into the forest.

It was an old palace, rough built but strong. There were massive but unornamented pillars in the great hall, and a smoke hole in the roof to serve the fire pit, there being no hearth.

Slath was well received, given a couple of no-more-than-average drafty cells for himself and his servants and promised an audience after dinner with the lord Hmar. Slath used the hour before dinner well, strolling about among the gaudy hangings and the snarling dogs, casually questioning here and there. When the meal was served, he found himself at one of the lower tables, and the food was plain but good. No one began their meat, however, until the lord was seated at his upper place.

Slath observed him closely and with a practical cunning. Hmar was a thin, oddly elegant man in his middle years. He ate with a niceness not common to the lords of Thaddra and seemed to expect those at his high table to do likewise; for the first time in a decade, Slath took care with his food. The face of Hmar was strange. It was like brown polished bone, of light complexion for a Thaddrian, and it gave nothing away—except, that was, for the eyes. They were narrow and flickering. They seemed in an eternal motion of search as if he quested for someone in the hall, some visitor he expected might be there at any moment. Slath recognized them as the eyes of a man in fear or very great unease.

And there had been talk. Slath had heard that Hmar had claimed, once or twice, to be the son of a goddess.

On the whole, Slath was pleased with the two aspects of Lord Hmar. If he was afraid, a little unbalanced, he would appreciate a strong and ruthless man to protect him, and, if he was so elegant, he would appreciate also the man's slave.

He noticed then the woman standing at Hmar's shoulder.

A swarthy Thaddrian, short and wide-hipped, with wiry black hair constrained in two plaits that fell below her waist. No woman in Thaddra or Zakoris would sit by her lord at table except the King's High Queen at Hanassor. To stand at his side showed rank enough.

"Who's the girl at the lord's elbow?" he inquired of a neighbor.

"Not for your plate. Panyuma's her name, the lord's slut for five years."

Slath took her in properly then. She was the sort of girl he liked himself, despite her sullen, haughty eyes. But there were bits of gold winking on her sandals and in her plaits, and she filled the lord's cup with a proprietory air.

"A tasty lass," Slath remarked carefully, knowing what

he said might be repeated to her if she were powerful here, and that he could afford to be insolent but not derogatory. "But doesn't Lord Hmar have more than one? It's usual."

"Oh, there are others. Ten or more, I've heard. Even some of those tall narrow females from the south. But he keeps them well hidden. Panyuma's the only woman seen about him."

Later, when Slath was summoned to the lord's presence, he went with a cheerful mind. The interview was brief and to the point. Slath had done well and foresaw doing better. In the campaigns to come there would be swift promotion, and Hmar seemed indeed to be all he had judged him. Slath restrained his after-dinner belches in deference to the graceful manners, and grinned inwardly at those nervous flickering eyes. At the last he spoke of his trouble, the genteel-born girl he feared was going to be a nuisance to him in his quarters here.

"Of course, Lord Hmar, I'd throw her out without a second thought, if it weren't for her remarkable looks. I saw her by sheer luck at a private sale—" He went on to say how he had been certain she was some noble's sister reduced through a decline in family fortunes, and how he had paid fifty bars for her.

Hmar looked at him, and the restless eyes leveled for a moment.

"I've been told of your girl already. If you wish to sell her to me you may bring her, and I'll consider the proposition."

Jolted by this bluntness, Slath shouted at the door for his servants, and Seluchis was hurried in. She had been bathed and dressed in a robe of thin red silk; the pungent scent of cibba wood emanated from her flesh.

Her eyes lifted and came to rest on Lord Hmar.

Slath was startled. It was the first time he had seen any life in her eyes at all. For an instant a look seemed to pass between Hmar and the girl—the robber sensed a bizarre recognition on both their faces.

"Yes," Hmar said shortly, but there was a curious tremor

in his voice, "you may ask my man outside for fifty bars' payment."

Unnerved already, Slath had anticipated argument over the price; shocked again, he bowed himself feverishly out and left his slave to her new master.

It was as if, drifting for miles over a faceless ocean she had come suddenly in sight of a marker in the sea. Nothing good in it, nothing to bring her joy or peace, for these could never be hers again, yet something oddly recognized. She did not comprehend how she knew him. She did not know him as a man. She knew him as all things know their own death, and with as much despair.

He said tightly: "She is here. I sense Her here. How can She be here, because of you, you Vis woman?"

By this she understood that he too sensed his death, and she was his death. They were to be each other's.

"So be it," she said to him.

He started violently, then seemed to master himself—all but the darting eyes, which, instead of raking the room, now explored her intensely.

"You inspire me with fear. This should be amusing. You're nothing. A slave. Offal. Whatever you once were has been obliterated. This is how it devolves upon us all. Once I was other than I am. Now I am Hmar, goddess-born, Guardian King of six ant heaps of Thaddra. Panyuma!" he cried out suddenly, and almost at once a curtain parted and a small dark woman slunk through on glittering feet. She looked directly at Astaris, but her broad-boned face was empty. "Panyuma," Hmar said softly, "take her and prepare her."

"Yes, lord," Panyuma said. Her aspect was of a malignant nurse humoring an evil child. But Astaris felt no protest at what was to come. The Thaddrian woman took her arm and conducted her out, and up long flights of ancient stairs.

The last metallic stains of sunset were fading from the sky.

The woman dressed her in a black robe heavy with gold, and wound jewels in her hair. Gold was put around her throat and on her arms and fingers and ears. Astaris grew aware of a curious coldness piercing her where the gold touched her skin.

In the orpiment twilight Panyuma led her through deserted corridors and finally to a granite wall. There was a mechanism in the floor which the Thaddrian clearly knew well. Bare stone parted and revealed a dim-lit gallery beyond. With a swift thrust Panyuma pushed her through, and the walls grated shut between them.

It was a place of the dead.

Here, past Guardians had been buried in the immemorial manner of Vis kings. Vast carved boxes contained their bones, with silver cups and bronze swords heaped up on them, and all about them their warriors frozen forever on their feet, shrunk to black sticks in their armor, with glass gems winking in their eyes. The air was heavy with dust and with the smell of those old embalmings.

But at one end of the gallery was something different. A lamp burned on a stand, and Hmar was sitting on a couch to face her. Behind him ranked ten women with gold burning on their hands and throats, and violet jewels in their hair. Astaris understood three things at once. The women lived, but they did not move, would never move and she was to become one of them.

"I see you comprehend," Hmar said to her. He rose and came forward and there was a gold cup in his hand. "You're to be a gift to my mother. I put her gold and her jewels on you, and then I make you as still. She hunts me in the dark. I angered her. But she loves me too, my mother Anack. Fear and love. Here, take the cup. Drink it down. A poison of the jungle, but without pain. A living death. And it will make you immortal. And you've no choice, I assure you, madam."

When she smiled at him and reached out immediately for the cup, he paled. She had reminded him again of another woman, years before, whose name had been Ashne'e.

Astaris emptied the cup. Still smiling, she asked him: "How long must I wait?"

"Not long," he said.

And it was true. Already she felt the cool passage of the liquor through her body, and presently she ceased to blink.

"Now I shall be what I have always truly been," she thought.

After a time he picked up her inert body and laid it on the couch; it was still malleable enough for his purpose. She observed his frenzied ecstasy remotely. It was a preliminary and she felt nothing of it. When he was finished, he set her up beside the couch like a doll, arranging her hands as he had arranged the hands of those others. He seemed to be speaking, but she could no longer hear him, and soon her sight also began to fade from her wide open eyes.

She was drowsy, near to the black sleep he had given her. She thought: "Now I am the icon I was always. This is fitting; only the shell and nothing left within." Then came the stirring in her womb, troubled, seeking. "Be still," she thought. "You were his and mine, but we are nothing now. Be still."

The dark came suddenly after that and took her away with it.

In the night, as so often, Anack came for him. He heard the dry rustling of her scales like dead leaves blown about the floor. The white moon of her face crested the foot of the bed. On her head the serpents hissed, and he saw her snake teeth gleam like fire.

He screamed for Panyuma, and woke.

The woman held him in her swarthy arms, but at first he did not recognize the corruption of his name when she spoke it.

"I am Amnorh, High Warden of Koramvis," he thought, bewildered, as she muttered her dark forest magic to keep spirits at bay. But then he remembered who he was, and how the incantation could keep him safe. For he had come to believe in these things, being no longer independent of their terror.

15

ALL NIGHT LONG HE heard the oars crooning in the water. They had for him the sound of death.

The boat was a narrow, shallow sea-skimmer carrying oil and iron into Zakoris. Raldnor slept, as did all the occasional passengers, under awning on her deck.

The crossing from Dorthar to the Zakorian port of Loth took a day and a night, and the day had been full of his own hope, his own sense of searching, because he had known at that time that she lived, and he had heard of the wild stories in Koramvis. Astaris had not used poison. Powerful friends had got her away, and where else should she fly but to the secret wilderness of Thaddra, which so often had swallowed up men and their histories. And Raldnor himself had a need of secrecy and hiding.

Kren had financed his passage through obscure routes of Dorthar in the dying glare of eastern summer, and from Dorthar to comparative safety in the west. From Zakoris he would travel over the mountain chain into Thaddra. To Kren his debts were numberless; he would repay them when, and if, he ever could. But he had been made to understand that neither repayment nor guilt were expected of him.

As to what he had lost—a mythical throne, a power he had never dreamed before was his—after the first turmoil, it had seemed unimportant beside that need, that tearing rending need, to find Astaris.

The sun sank, twilight clouded the sea. An hour after twilight he felt the almost imperceptible presence stir and slip softly out of his brain. No violence this time, as with the white-haired girl; this was a quiet, serene death—the black sleep came gently on her, for all it was final. But she left him empty.

And this was what he felt in himself—not anguish or pain or a compulsion to weep. Only emptiness. It seemed that in leaving him, she had taken also his soul.

Dawn came, and Loth. He left the ship, but no longer with a purpose.

Beyond the harbor was a broad stinking fish market, and threads of cobbled streets slippery with oil; at their back were clamorous jungle and the black treacle of the swamp.

Raldnor sat through the morning in a steamy hovel where wine and meat were sold. Runny-nosed children banged about the place, and two Zakorian soldiers glared silently at their own thoughts.

At noon he joined a caravan of Ottish merchants. They were traveling to Hanassor, the capital, and they made a great noise which somehow dulled the emptiness in him. He was afraid to let them go, to remain in the humid silence of the town, immobile, with his loss.

On the uncertain jungle road they chattered and sent up clouds of birds screaming in alarm.

After three days they took to the bridges and causeways that crossed the swamp. A foul black stench hung in the air, and the colors of the jungle were distorted before his eyes.

The swamp fever fastened on him with a steady and inexorable grip. By the time they had reached Yla he felt so ill, he thought he would die.

He lay in the dark hot inn, and a physician was sent to him—either by one of the Ottites or a Ylian, fearing plague. He was a smelly old skeleton in an animal skin, probably some journeying holy man, but with sharp, bright eyes and teeth. He stared at Raldnor and said: "You were ill not long since. I tell you, the god of death sits on your shoulder and you must shake him off."

"He's welcome to me," Raldnor said, but he drank the poisonous medicine. He thought in any case that he would die in the night, and was glad of it.

He dreamed of the cave temple above Koramvis, but the statue there was no longer of Anackire but of Astaris, a creature of enamels and rubies, with cold, unquickened eyes.

In the morning the fever had left him.

The Ottish caravan had left also, unable *to* wait on his recovery. So he was trapped at last in his limbo with despair.

He walked about the ramshackle town, stopping at leprous taverns with walls the color of yellow vomit, asking for news of traders going in any direction. Everything he did was the act of a sleepwalker, his relentless searching quite meaningless.

At noon, exhausted, he sat like an old man on a stone bench in the square and watched the Ylians. Soon the square emptied, leaving only the great slices of white heat and black shadow and the monotonous screech of birds from the surrounding jungle. And then came a lone figure on foot, walking in slow easy strides and whistling.

Raldnor observed him—a brass-burned man with shoulder-blade-long black strings of hair—with no interest as he came nearer. A few yards off he came to a sudden halt.

"By all the gods and goddesses—"

Raldnor glanced in his face.

"Raldnor," the man grinned, showing his salt-white teeth. "Raldnor of Sar."

"I beg your pardon," Raldnor said stiffly, "you seem to know me, but I—"

"Yannul the Lan. We served together, you and I, under the yellow fox, Kathaos Am Alisaar. There, you know me now. And I can see that you must be the sick traveler who came with the Ottish caravan. You've a look as though the goddesses took you out of the oven before you were properly baked. And some trouble too. Do you still serve Amrek?"

Raldnor shut his eyes and gave the briefest of smiles.

"I should imagine not."

"Well, we get little enough news of Dorthar in this place. . . . And you look as if you make room for a mug of black beer. Come with me. I know a halfway decent inn—"

Raldnor opened his eyes and looked hard at him.

"Why should you want to share my company, Yannul of Lan? Ryhgon broke your hand at Abissa because of me."

"As you see," Yannul said, "he didn't make a good job of it. I healed. And besides, you paid him back for me in full, I heard. The taverns of Abissa were noisy with it."

"You heard from the taverns, too, that I became Amrek's man?"

"So I did. It was a good joke, though I doubt if Kathaos laughed."

"And now," Raldnor said, "having exercised my good fortune too far, I've fallen from favor utterly. Because of me, a woman has died. The second woman to die because she loved me. And I, Yannul, am an exiled man, without home or hearth. If I were recognized, I should be killed immediately, without trial or any kind of nicety. You should be more careful who you drink with, my friend."

"In Lan, Raldnor, we judge a man as we find him, not by what he tells us he's done. I'll be glad enough to drink with you, but if you find me wanting since last we met, then say so, and I'll leave you in peace, you Sarish fool."

On the flat roof of the inn, under the black awning, it was cooler and almost deserted.

They drank at first in silence, but near the end of the first jug, Yannul told Raldnor what had become of him in Lin Abissa. Wandering about the midnight city streets, sick and delirious, he had finally propped himself against the court-yard door of a house in the merchants' quarter. Here two girls discovered him—the householder's wives on their way home from a supper party, as it turned out—and they expressed at once a wish to keep him. He was nursed back to health by a skillful physician, who later informed him that, as a bonus, his master Kathaos had also had him poisoned.

"My iron constitution had luckily expelled the muck along half the gutters of Abissa," Yannul remarked, "and the old man's drafts ensured my survival. Don't let it trouble you. You see I live and breathe."

As for his hand, the physician had set it faultlessly—at the absent merchant's expense. The two ladies, it seemed, thought a lot of him, and he soon found himself repaying them by service in their beds. Hearing, however, of his unwitting benefactor's imminent return, Yannul prudently took his leave.

He secured work on a ship bound for Zakoris, and thereafter labored at various occupations until he took up with an acrobatic troupe. They were of little ability and a quarrelsome disposition, and, having spent a few days with them on the road, he decided to desert in the first town, which turned out to be Yla. Here he toiled at the ledgers of a timber merchant, accruing enough coin to buy a passage to Alisaar. Zakoris was too stern a land for Yannul, though he had no plans as yet to return to his own. But in Alisaar jugglers and body dancers were liked well enough. Besides, he had once known a beautiful Alisaarian contortionist. . . .

Raldnor found himself stirred to anger and icy dismay by the first part of the narrative. Further on, he laughed here and there. It surprised him. He had imagined himself in all ways emotionally, if not physically, dead. In turn Yannul did not press for information, and Raldnor told him nothing. His grief, and the burden of his grief were terrible; to relate them would be a superfluous, useless agony. Yet he found he needed Yannul; after all, the anchor of human company dulled his pain.

In the afternoon, Yannul settled his affairs at Yla. The following morning they were on the road to Hanassor and the sea, riding with two or three vendors and a cage of snarling black swamp beasts.

At a hostel on the road, they heard some news from Dorthar.

Amrek had seemed dead with his faithless bride; now he had left whatever emotional grave had held him. He returned with vigor and determination and set about that burning plan of his adult life—to sweep Vis clean of the sorcerous and defiled race of the Lowlanders. Already the edict had gone out: death to any Plains people inside the limits of Dorthar. His dragons were hard put to it to find them. They had scoured the minor towns and villages for their prey. Only a few remained, and these were the old, the sick and the unthinking. Execution had been haphazard, though total. A casual, ultimately competent butchering.

The twist to the story—what interested the Zakorians in the hostel much more than the Lowland slaughter—was the reaction to it by the King of Xarabiss, old Thann Rashek, sometimes called the Fox. Surely a fox should be more sly?

He had sent word to Amrek that he deplored the act. "Is it your ambition, Amrek, son of Rehdon, to make known your name by a shedding of blood? To begin with the death of my daughter's daughter, Astaris Am Karmiss, whom you slew without trial or certainty; continuing with the massacre of virgins and babies?"

There had been an answer, too. The storm gods of Dorthar directed Amrek in his holy war—they would no longer brook the scum of the snake goddess. The earthquake which shook Koramvis had been their warning. Indeed, Amrek understood quite well that Xarabiss indulged herself in trade with the Lowlands, which enterprise must instantly cease. As to Rashek's charge that he slew virgins, the Xarabians could set their minds at rest. There would not have been a single dead girl who could legitimately have claimed that title after capture by the dragon soldiery.

There was some laughter in the hostel over Amrek's wit,

though, on the whole the Zakorians thought him a shallow King, chasing after his phantoms like a peevish child.

To Raldnor, hunched by the murky fire in the cool of the jungle night, the discussion and the mirth came like a far-off baying, a cry of despair carried on the wind out of his past. A new pain pierced the old. He felt the wondrous agony come on him. "My people," he thought. "*My* people." The images crowded close as the chill night: Eraz, his mother, the men and women of his youth, the dragon, too, spitting in the snow, and the soldier who had hunted him through Lin Abissa; last, Anici, white as winter, a pale bone of death. And he had walked at Amrek's side—Amrek, his brother, the murderer and the madman. And then came the final turn of the knife in him. He had taken that man's woman. If he had never done so, would Amrek, in the shade of her serenity, have forgotten to wreak his vengeance on the Plains? It came too late, the guilt and the knowledge and the shame.

He saw Yannul looking at him in the red shadows.

"Black news for the Lowlanders," Yannul said. "Perhaps their snake lady will strike Amrek down."

"Like her people," Raldnor said, "she has her teeth, but never uses them. And a thing grows rusty with disuse."

And remembering how he had lost his naivety and his faith in Abissa when he read of Dorthar's gods, he half smiled and thought: "And now I have lost everything."

Hanassor. The Black Beehive of Zakoris, whose bees were known not for their honey, but their sting.

Built into the conical cliffs, the sea breaking on its lower walls red as wine in the sunset, not a light showing, everything encased, a city like a brain in a black granite skull.

Igur, the old king, was dead, and the brief period of mourning done. Igur's eldest sons had fought for the throne, as was customary, for Zakoris had not forgotten her heritage of war. Yl had won the contest by breaking his brothers' backs. He took three hundred wives to his throne with him, and crowned his first queen for slitting the throat, while heavy with his child, of a swamp leopard.

All this they learned at the gate.

It was always night in Hanassor under the rock, always torchlight and shadow.

They ate in a stony inn, where a fire-dancer scorched her gauzy clothes off her body with two spitting brands. There was a blue scar on her thigh. She had been careless once.

They made enquiries of the landlord, who spoke of a ship making for Saardos and offered to direct her captain to their table. Later, a black-burned man with a gold stud winking in his left nostril came and sat by them.

"I'm Drokler, ship lord of *Rorn's Daughter*. I hear you want to buy a passage to Saardos. I don't take passengers, as a rule, you understand, excepting slaves."

They bargained half an hour with him over the cost of their fare. In the end it was settled and a clerk called in to draw up their agreement, this being Zakoris and life and liberty on the whole rather cheap. Drokler could write only his name, but this he did with brutal flourish. They pocketed their deeds, paid off the clerk and sought their beds.

At first light a sailor came to guide them to the cellars of the city, and the great caverns where the ships of Hanassor lay at anchor. The man rowed them through the arching caves, among the frozen, albescent dripping of stalactites, and the dusky flickering forests of spars, into the morning and the wide mouth of the ocean.

Rorn's Daughter was out, showing herself a tower ship of the western seas, triple oar banks spooning already at the glassy water, her sail bellying on the early wind, bright with the double moon and dragon device of Zakoris.

"She's a fine thing," Yannul said.

The sailor only grunted; he was an unenamored man, well used to his wife.

He got them aboard and showed them to their boxlike accommodation in the guts of the tower. They would be eating above in Drokler's hall, he said, and gave them a

sourly congratulatory look before going off about his duties.

Minutes later there came the judder and swerve beneath
their feet that told of departure. The oar banks churned,
and she sprang out from the bay, a great wooden she-
animal, staring with the scarlet eyes painted on her prow.

It was a pull of fourteen days to Saardos, a leisurely, un-
eventful voyage, marked by the groaning of timbers and the
crack of the sail, the screams of sea birds and the occasional
brawls of the sailors, under a sky as clear as painted enamel.

Women worked with the crew, the ship's prostitutes, for
trade did not stop for Zastis. They were a tough, wild lot,
willing and able to fight like swamp cats. Their hair was the
same bleached-out gray-black as the sailors' from the scouring of the acid salt winds.

By day Yannul and Raldnor indulged in those immemorial pastimes of the passenger—the book, the dice or the
flagon—or walked about the deck. At dusk they ate at
Drokler's table in the tower, along with Jurl the oars master,
monosyllabic and mannerless, and Elon, officer of the deck,
a quiet unremarkable man, who studied at table a succes-
sion of dark-bound, apparently entirely similar manuscripts.

In the night a woman might come stealing to their box.
Yannul accepted what was offered him, and with any whose
lovemaking proved inartistic, took it on himself to teach
them Lannic methods. So Raldnor lay alone through the
groaning, spume-sounding nights, listening to these activi-
ties of lust. He did not want their women and could not
sleep. He took to prowling about the ship in the moonlight.
In the moon's path the water was like milk. He thought of
the ruined city on the Plains, the white wolf and the white
girl. He felt a kind of drawing exerted on him.

"Where is home? Is this then my home, after all I've
done to escape it? The Lowlands and the shadow of Amrek's threat. Why not? I am hated like my land, and believed dead and toothless like my land. Ashne'e, my mother,

puts her ghost hand on my brain and turns it to the south. Perhaps, then, not Saardos but the Plains. Perhaps I will go home."

A day out from the bay of Saardos, Drokler honored the brass Rom god in the prow with a pound of incense.

The blank god mask stared back at them through the pall of sweet blue smoke. It was an ugly rough-hewn thing, without the passion or the delicacy of a Xarabian Yasmis, and with none of the cruel magnificence of the dragon-headed icons of Dorthar. It gazed in myopic stillness out over the long shock of the waves, ignoring their words, their presence, their costly offering.

A blazing magenta sun sank, apparently steaming, in the sea. Black towers of cumulus clouds were rising in the south, and the heavy pulse of the wind pressed like a hand on the trembling hollowed sail.

The narrow craggy strip of coast which was Alisaar receded into darkness.

At dinner, Jurl was absent from the board.

"Poor weather to make harbor in," Yannul remarked.

The wind kicked at the ship, and plates slid in their scoops. On their iron chains the low-slung candle wheels clanged dismally, and hot wax dripped.

"Rorn has a bellyache," Drokler said.

Caught in the high window of the tower, the sky blushed black. The ship, as if sensing the maturing of unseen forces beneath her, leapt like an animal in fear.

"Can you make Saardos in this?"

"Oh, indeed, Lannic gentleman. We run before the wind and use our oars. This place is free of rocks. No need to be alarmed. Eat your meal, or have you lost your appetite?"

Elon rose and put aside his book. He went without a word, and when the door to the deck was opened, the room seemed filled by the plunge of the purple gulf all around them and by sudden lightning.

Drokler got to his feet.

"Continue with your food, gentlemen."

Simultaneously, *Rom's Daughter* tilted on her side in a horrifying yet almost frivolous movement. There came from every quarter of the ship the sound of unsecured things rattling and cascading. One of the great candle wheels, flung sideways with enormous force, struck Drokler on the temple with a sick, dull clash. The ship lord collapsed across the board without a sound. The two junior officers, who had risen with him, gave vent to cursing. One ran for the surgeon and left the door flapping on the crow blackness outside.

Yannul and the remaining officer eased Drokler on to the floor. He was breathing thickly, but otherwise looked quite dead. The officer made a clumsy religious sign to one of the many rough and uncaring sea elementals of the Zakorians.

Yannul got up.

"Look for me later," he muttered as he passed Raldnor, "I'm about to give our dinner to the sea."

The water-rushing, intangible darkness of the deck enveloped him. Raldnor moved out into it and passed the surgeon in the doorway, a man with swimming eyes and a look of terror ill-concealed on his face. It was not good to lose a captain while at sea, for the Zakorians carried their own factions and wars with them on their ships. Lightning speared the deck. Raldnor saw the livid shapes scurrying about the sail, and the yellow spindrift cast up from the oars below.

The oars.

Jurl still had them row, then, even against this. And yet, what hope could there be now, other than to ride the tempest out? Besides which, the hatches would be taking in the sea with every lurch of the waves, and there would soon be broken ribs or worse among the rowers, administered by bucking oar poles.

Raldnor swung aside and through the narrow, low aperture leading to the below-decks rowers' station.

The dismal, gloomy, stinking dark of the place was accentuated by the odor of fear and the flickering lanterns smoking from the damp. There came the hiss of the ocean—already the lower positions were awash—and the creak of the iron-bladed oars and of men's cracking sinews. Jurl sat on the master's platform, spume spurling at his feet, relentlessly drumming the oars' beat, his face an ugly, carven, immovable mask. He had a look of Ryhgon. Certainly he was of Ryhgon's breed. Raldnor took a breath of hate from the fetid air and shouted: "Lay in, oar's master! She's drinking the sea."

Without turning or faltering in his beat, Jurl spat through his teeth: "Empty your damned guts somewhere else, Dortharian. We run to Saardos."

Raldnor sensed men straining to hear him even as they strained at the oars.

"Lay in, Jurl, and close the hatches before you sink this ship or kill half your oarsmen."

"I'll take no orders from you, you mewling bitch-birth. Get out before I break your back."

Rorn's Daughter seemed suddenly to spin beneath them. There came a cacophony of impossible thunder, and gouts of white water burst through the hatches, splintering them like broken glass. Men, up to their necks in the water, screamed and dropped their oars, which veered and struck others from behind. The compelling rhythm fell apart.

Raldnor leaped to Jurl and hit him in the ribs, then seizing the beater's hammer, struck him between neck and shoulder with a blow suited to his bulk. Across the confused cries and shouting, Raldnor roared for them to draw in the oars and secure the hatches. Presently he went down into the chaos and pulled with them. These rowers were paid men—only war fleets or pirates used slaves—and therefore had none of the hypnotized discipline of helpless chattels. He sensed them on the verge of panic-stricken mutiny and formed them into a baling chain before it took them. A man's voice called from the back.

"The wind'll blow us beyond Saardos into the sea of hell—we'll fall into Aarl!"

"Stories for women and children," Raldnor shouted back. "Do we have someone's wench down here, passing for a man?"

There was some crude laughter and no further complaints after that. He had learned what Zakorians feared the most, and it was not death.

When they had cleared the galley levels of water, he left them to Elon's orders, and took Jurl over his back to the oars master's quarters near the stern.

The fury of the storm seemed to be lessening. Rifts had appeared in the cloud mass, though the sea tossed them up and down like a ball. It had gulped men and supplies from the deck and left them, in barter, a host of flopping sea creatures.

He found Yannul with a paper face in the tower.

"Perhaps my sacrifice did us good," he muttered. "Oh, to be in Lan, where the hills are blue and, above all, motionless."

Overhead the sea had shattered the window, and glass and broken plates floated on the inch or so of water on the tower's floor.

Elon came in from the deck and said: "Is the surgeon still here? I've some men with smashed bones."

The surgeon came quickly and went out. Drokler had no further need of him, being dead.

The sea lay down and seemed to smoke. The smoke formed a gray twilight that crept coiling on the deck. They baled and slung off the water, and cooked the dead fish on damp fires to replace the provisions the sea had taken.

"Sir, it was good of you to help us," Elon said to Raldnor. "With Drokler dead, it will be a serious business getting her to Saardos."

"Jurl will cause you trouble, then?"

"Oh, indeed, yes. And he doesn't like to fall asleep across

his oars. I warn you to be on your guard, sir, while you continue to ride *Rorn's Daughter.*"

"My thanks for the warning. But we're only a day out, aren't we?"

"No longer," Elon said. "The storm blew us off our course, and how widely this fog holds, only the gods know."

Later, the gray thickened and became a swathe of black velvet wrapped about the ship. No moon, no star pierced the velour curtain.

A woman came with fish and a flagon of wine. Yannul, now much recovered, kept her through the night.

All next day they drifted through the fog. It was a silent ghost world. Shapes emerged from it resembling galleys, mountains, or great birds, all melting before impact, folding in on themselves in charcoal subsidences.

In the polished metal that served as mirror, Raldnor saw how the gray tinge had invaded his hair. For a while it would mimic the hair of any of the crew, that pale black common to the sailor. It was the salt in the winds. Soon the salt would scour out the last of the black dye, and there would be no replacing it from the broken bottle he had found among his things after the storm. He would be then naked among his enemies, a yellow-haired man, a Lowlander: Plains scum. Yet curiously, in the regions of the fog, none of this seemed greatly to matter. He, like the ship, was adrift without compass or sight of land. There being no remedy, there seemed also no great distress.

Men lowered the body of Drokler into the iron water. The short, harsh Zakorian prayer was spoken. He sank like lead, for weights had been put in his boots to make his going hasty.

About an hour after this makeshift burial, the insubstantial prison around them began to break up. Inside an hour the waves were empty of anything but themselves and the night.

Not a trace of land in any direction could be seen. Such instruments as the ship had owned to divine her position, had been lost. The night had provided neither stars nor any moon.

A slight wind moved *Rom's Daughter*.

Toward midnight the watch horn sounded. Ahead and to larboard there was a red flickering on the horizon.

"By Zarduk, the beacons of Saardos!" one of the officers cried out. A cheer went up. They had all feared some kind of disaster, adrift in the ghost world.

The wind was against them, blowing for the west, so they set down where they were to wait for morning. There were beer casks breached and emptied. Raldnor saw Jurl drinking in the shadow of the king mast—that peculiar and specific drinking which showed neither pleasure nor intoxication. His rowers would take them into Saardos tomorrow, and no doubt he would drive them hard.

Saardos. And after Saardos, the Plains. Raldnor thought of it in the dark of his cabin. And somewhere in the dark there came to him a sense of incompleteness—this ending was altogether too provident. It was an intimation of destiny which he neither knew nor answered.

Dawn woke him, a dawn like the cinders of a rose. Also a sound that had no place in a man's dreams.

Yannul still slept, without a girl for once. Above, the levels of the ship creaked and settled. The sound pierced through wood and flesh and bone and exacerbated his ears.

On the deck the ashy crimson light that had squeezed in at the cabin slit below the tower was one great indissoluble wash across the sky and sea. Everything else was black in silhouette—the huge king mast with its slightly bloated sail, the bulk of the tower, the sweeping prow, the groups and huddles of men and women, all quite still, standing gazing out across the water to the scarlet flickering of the horizon, listening. It was a low, unhuman droning note, like some enormous pipe sounding far down in the crust of the world. But it had no definite location—rather it was all around them, ambient as the morning.

One of the women began to wail abruptly, crying of

devils in the sea. A big man came hulking from the rail and struck her hard across the face as he passed her.

"Shut your mouth, trull."

It was Jurl. He made for the galley hatch without a look to either side, his grim, sneering face devoid of any feeling. Somewhere on the deck, Elon's voice rang out. Men jumped to their work, the women scuttled to ropes. The anchor was drawn up, the sail set. Abruptly the ship lurched into life as the oars below struck water. She began to move, straining, before the slight warm wind, with every semblance of life. Yet she only seemed living. The dawn was stopped still. No sun rose and no darkness fell; only the rosy grayness persisted. And with it the demon's piping that seemed its vocal expression.

Raldnor stood at the rail.

There came a sudden crack of thunder beneath the sea, which did not surprise him, though his guts turned cold with an automatic fear. The piping ceased. A great roiling turmoil of movement below the ship pitched him down across her deck, as a lightning erupted from the sea. The light grew big, swelling from crimson into savage white. A rain fell on his face and hands and neck, a black burning rain. Men screamed. There came a wind over the ship like the rustling wings of a great bird composed of fire.

He pulled himself up against the rail and stared over the plunging sea.

The ocean was tumultuous with the pangs of birth, but it was a monstrous, a terrifying child: smoldering ebony, the cone stretched up to spit into the sky. Breakers burst in white steam against its molten buttresses. From the gaping mouth spewed lightning and a blazing vomit.

"Mountain of Fire!"

The frenzied cry racked across the deck. It was the legend of Aarl, the burning stacks that rose from the sea—dragons' mouths belching up pyrotechnic blasts. The Zakorians yelled their horror. They were in hell, and the eternal agony had begun.

Raldnor stumbled back along the deck and pulled wide the doorway in the tower. He tried to shout to them to seek sanctuary inside, but men turned their blanched faces and their blind wide eyes on him and away, their mouths extending cries. A glittering needle hail of embers fell abruptly into their midst. There was a rush for the hatches, and now some came for the tower. They collided, fought and cursed each other at the entry. Beyond their struggling, Raldnor saw the sky split over the sea cone's maw, and white explosions burst in the water. *Rom's Daughter* bucked the length of her body. Men rolled shrieking down the deck, over the rail, into the boiling waves. A plume of fire appeared like a miracle on the sail.

Beneath them all, he felt the motion of the oars stagger to a halt.

The picture came to him, disastrously clear, the panic that had seized them once again in the dark and personal hell of the rowers' deck. He thrust through the press at the door and at the hatchway and somehow got down into that reeking place. They were in uproar, and there was no beater on the platform. Where Jurl had taken himself was beyond questioning at this time. Raldnor seated himself at the oars master's station and took up the hammer, as once before. With thunderous strokes he began the rhythm. A half lull came; they were slaves in their own way to that inexorable beat.

"Row!" he shouted at them.

"The ship's on fire!" a man yelled. Others cried out in unison.

He brought the hammer smashing down.

"Do I use this on the block or on your heads? Put your backs into it, you sniveling fools!"

They cringed and held to their places. He had assumed Jurl's voice and manner. Almost as one, they snatched back their oars.

A crash came from above, dim screams, the bald flare of fire.

He increased the strokes of the hammer. It was the speed of war he used, for ramming or for flight. He left them no room for their terror.

When the first breath of safety came, he knew by instinct only. Beyond the hatches the ocean was like blood and ink, yet the judderings had left the ship. He slowed their speed, then ceased beating. They sank on their oars like dead men.

He went up the ladder, but the hatch was hard to lift. When he got it open, he found the dead lying across it.

The dead also lay about the deck. The planks were thick with them and with a fluttering violet ash. Little fires trickled here and there; a few men were creeping from cover to deal with them. The sail flamed. Cinders swirled like moths. The air was thick and turgid with smoke.

Behind them now, the volcano was fading in the murk, still a blare of red or white. The distant rumbling filled the sea.

For miles the water was full of burned things. They cast their own human corpses down to join them. This time, there were no prayers.

16

THE WIND HUMMED IN THE PATCHED SAIL.

"We no longer hold a course," Elon said. "Our instruments are smashed. The stars indicate we're far from Alisaar, but their configurations are strange and altogether untrustworthy. Tullut tells me he thinks the dust from the fire mountain distorts the size and pattern of things in the sky. Who can doubt it? Last night the moon was huge, the color of a blue plum. No, we can't judge our way by star charts."

"Turn back," Jurl growled, facing him across Drokler's table.

"And pass again through the Gates of Fire? We lost half our crew to the storm and the burning mountain, and ten oarsmen. There'd be mutiny if I told them to risk that way again."

"You're too soft, too gentle altogether, Elon. They'd mutiny because they know you'd let them. Resign your position to me. We'll see things settled then."

"It would seem you resigned your own position to the volcano," Raldnor said.

Jurl swung about.

"Why does this landsdog sit at council with us?"

"Because, Jurl, he has twice proved himself a better oars master than you," Elon said.

"Where were you, Jurl, when we passed the fire?" Tullut, the younger of the two officers, cried out.

"Below, about my own business."

"Saving your worthless, diseased and filthy skin!"

Elon banged on the table top to silence the altercation.

"The wind blows us southeasterly," he said in a sober and dispassionate voice. "The watch have seen flocks of birds, which should mean land of some sort."

"There's no land in these seas."

"Probably an island, too small to have been charted. Nevertheless, we may hope for fresh water, and perhaps meat. We'll rest the men there. After that we can decide on what to do with ourselves and our ship."

They cut a notch in the door lintel of the tower at each sunset. The sea was exceptionally, searingly blue; sometimes patches like blue fire moved over it. The skies were strange colors by day; at night men made superstitious signs against the amethyst moon, the vitriolic lemon of the stars.

The food, rationed since the storm, began to bear hard on them. No longer were there dinners at Drokler's table — only the fish stews and dried biscuit common to all.

The burned men lay under awning on the deck, groaning, muttering, weeping; howling for water, the dull-eyed women tending them as best they could. In the predawn gray of the fifth day past the volcano, Raldnor woke from a deadly sleep and, going up on deck, became aware of a peculiar and ominous silence. Not a man cried out, not even a whisper sounded.

Yannul, coming after him, stopped still and said: "Can they all have died?"

"Indeed they can," a man's voice said sneeringly, almost with amusement. "With a little help."

Jurl stepped out from under the awning. He carried his knife flamboyantly, letting them see the blood. A couple of sailors slunk out after him, making less of it.

"You've butchered them," Yannul said. His hand went to his own knife, then fell away uselessly.

"Why let them go on eating our share of rations?" one of Jurl's men blurted. "They'd've died tomorrow—the day after. Better off dead they were."

"Shut your mouth," Jurl rapped. "Do we need make apologies to land scum?"

He swung past, his acolytes hurrying after.

Dawn tinged the sea.

Yannul swore in a virulent undertone.

"Will you refuse an extra share of the food?" Raldnor said softly, gazing out at the rim of the sun. "As Jurl's friend told us, they'd have died anyway, and in great pain. Now they rest, and we eat."

Yannul turned to stare at him, but in the expanding light a new surprise usurped the first.

"Raldnor," he said, "your hair—is *white*."

Raldnor did not look at him. His eyes and face were quite blank.

"Sea salt," he said quietly. "It bleaches out the best dye. I'm a Lowlander, Yannul."

Yannul swore again, softly.

"I thought in Abissa . . . I *wondered*— But, Raldnor, all that time in Koramvis—you dared that deception with *Amrek?*"

"An irony worthy of the annals of the old myths I used to read. Yes, I was Amrek's nearest Commander. I stood at his right hand. I nearly bedded his mother; certainly I took his betrothed. I fell from my office because of simple indiscretion, not race. There was no hint of my blood. I was Dortharian, and my crimes suited me excellently. I am Amrek's brother."

"His brother—"

"Rehdon's son. Not by Val Mala, as you will surmise. Ashne'e carried me, the amber-haired witch. She accommodated me in the womb which killed my father." The words had come flooding from him, yet he felt no release at speaking, or any pain. On the horizon a dark cloud was resting against the sea, blotting out the lower hemisphere of the sun.

"Then, by the law of Dorthar, you're their King," Yannul said. There seemed to be no doubt or query in his voice; both the situation and the curious blank face of the teller carried their own conviction. Besides, Yannul had always sensed some vein of mystery in this man he had called a friend.

"The King of Dorthar."

Raldnor smiled blindly at the sea, at his own thoughts. "There's the island Elon promised us," he said.

Yannul, startled, turned about and saw it. Simultaneously the watch yelled from above, and men came running to the deck.

It was a mere small silhouette lashed by the sea. It had no look of home. Yet men shouted and pummeled each other's shoulders.

Only the dead men under the awning continued their silence, as if they were wiser, or more content.

The island.

It was formed in the shape of a flat platter; at its center steep-built rocks, smoking with white falls, splayed above into a broad plateau. Jungle rose in blue-black tiers from the beach, noisy with birds. They flew in flocks, wheeled screaming in the sky, vocal with alarm at this invasion.

Rorn's Daughter cast down her anchor in the bay and the boats put out; only the women and a handful of the men were left behind with their officers to watch the ship.

Their legs were uncertain on the ground. Men rolled and played like babies in the nacreous sand.

Elon split them into parties to fetch water or food. Tullut and Ilrud fashioned slings and brought down the bright birds for meat. Others splashed in sapphire pools, scooped gourds full of these sapphires, then spilled them, tossed them over their heads, yelling. It was a land of plenty indeed, this place where things could be wasted.

No men lived here—at least, they saw none.

Yannul plucked an orchid and tucked it in a rent in his shirt.

"Do you think I could persuade a few of these to grow in some earth on the ship? This sort of flower would fetch coins from the ladies of Alisaar."

Many of them were talking of Alisaar now, and of Zakoris. Even this little ground had made them optimistic. They looked less narrowly at the bluer-than-blue fiery sea.

As they sat on the beach with their grilled meat and fresh water, a group of men came running from the forest, carrying yellow fruit. There had been a deal of craziness, but these men looked wild and mad, garlanded with flowers, laughing uproariously.

"What's this?" Elon asked them.

"A rare fruit—a wonderful fruit," a man cried out. "It goes to your head like a wine of Xarabiss."

Tullut clicked his tongue disapprovingly.

"Did you eat it? Foolish of you. None of us know what grows here. It might be poisonous."

"Might be—might be—"

Men mimicked him. They were drunk indeed, juice dribbling on their chins, throats and chests as they scrabbled again for the yellow fruit.

Elon turned away. Men capered up the beach.

Raldnor saw Jurl emerge from the nearest tree line, two or three of his followers trailing after. He came to the fruit pile and picked about in it.

"It's good then?"

"But not necessarily good to eat," Elon said. "I thought you were to stay aboard the ship, Jurl, to keep your rowers in order."

"Only the Aarl lords will trouble Rom's bitch in this sea. I rode the boats as you did, deck master." Jurl took a bite at the flesh of the fruit and ate, grinning open-mouthed. "The men are better judges of the table than you, Elon." He hefted a couple of the fruits and went to eat them at another fire about which the drunken men were dancing.

Gradually, one by one, some uneasily, some swaggering, men went to join him. They were of his faction, believing in his brutal authority, or else excited by his lack of scruple. There had been several cries of approval over the dead men under the awning.

Soon the group about Jurl grew murderously loud. They began to push out the boats again, skipping and guffawing.

"They'll bring in the watch off the ship," Tullut exclaimed. "Deck master, she should have some guard, whatever deserted sea we're in."

Elon stared at the white hem of the water.

"Do I have authority to stop him, Tullut? There seem to be few men about this fire."

"They're drunk on the fruit, woman-weak—"

Elon got up without another word. Stiff as a plank, he walked down the beach toward the crazy garlanded men and their boats. Raldnor rose; Tullut, Yannul and a few others followed, falling into step behind him as he went after Elon. The wheeling birds embroidered the sky in slow persistent circles.

Suddenly Jurl came thrusting out of the press. The fruit had intoxicated him, though he had not adopted the other men's garlands or mannerisms. Like a man accustomed to wine, his character had not been blurred or altered, but rather sharpened, accentuated.

"What are you doing, Jurl?" Elon said.

"Bringing the last men and oars-pigs, and the whores from the ship. You wouldn't deny them the island, would you?"

"They'll be denied nothing. I'll send a relief party shortly, when the men are rested."

"The ship needs no guard, Elon. Not here."

"I haven't ordered you to disband the watch."

"You. You no longer order anything. Go chew your bread and water, my lady, while we men enjoy ourselves."

"You'll answer for this in Hanassor," Elon said softly into the silence.

"Hanassor." Jurl spat. He had not caught their faith. "If and when is good enough. And I'll have charges of my own. Against that landsdog at your shoulder, for one. By Zarduk, Dortharian, can't you keep your nose out of anything?"

"The beach is as much mine as yours," Raldnor said, "and your voice carries a good way."

Jurl's hand flickered at his belt and came back with the knife. The silence crackled.

"Put away your blade," Elon said.

A man giggled, high like an excited girl.

"Let's them fight—Ten draks on the oars master."

Voices cheered raucously.

"Well, Dortharian, do you take me? You've seen this blade used before," Jurl said. *"Milk hair."*

Raldnor's hand moved in its own practiced manner, and produced a knife. One or two men noticed the professional intimacy of the gesture, and some of the cheers broke off.

"Yes, you've used the blade before—on half-dead men," Raldnor said. "I'll take you."

Jurl started forward, but somehow Elon interposed himself. Jurl turned snarling and slashed into the deck master's body. Red splashed on the white ground. Red licked up Jurl's knife like flame. Jurl jumped sideways for the nearest boat, men leaping after him. They pulled for *Rom's Daughter* and were out in the bay moments after Elon fell.

Tullut ran forward and took Elon's head on his knee, but Elon's eyes were already filmed over and opaque with death. His blood soaked in the sand.

They buried him in the sand and shingle at the fringe of the jungle, but it was shallow soil. They struck stone too soon. There were animals, too, not seen before and not showing themselves now, only little rustlings in the forest, bright blinks of eyes, to intimate their presence. And the birds flew round the darkening sky, wailing their greed. So the man raked off the sand and piled on twigs and creeper, and fired them. It was a cleaner burial, but the stench of burning flesh drove them far along the beach.

Tullut moved away from them all and stood alone in the twilight as the charcoal ashes that were Elon blew and smoldered. It was not a man's part to weep, and, if he must, he grieved in hiding. It came to Raldnor, with sudden remembered pain, how he too had once restrained his tears as he walked behind Eraz's bier at Hamos.

A huge moon floated over the trees.

A red glare spiraled and smoked from the plateau above, and sounds of singing and pipes and noisy calls came over the wash of the sea and the small muted thunder of the falls.

The boats had come back to the island as they carried the tinder to Elon's body. Laughing men and screeching women had exploded across the beach into the trees, carrying lanterns and casks of beer from Drokler's private storage hold. Now they drank, and ate the fruit, and sang around their fires on the rock.

Tullut came walking slowly back across the sand, his face in shadow.

"Tullut!" A sailor caught his arm, "Tullut, let's take a boat, get to the ship and sail her. There must be some safe way home. We can leave them their island."

"No," Tullut said.

The tide had climbed higher up the sand, hushing in slow pale whispers, like a mother with a child.

"By Zarduk," the sailor said, "it wouldn't make me sad if the fruit poisoned them as you said it would, Tullut. That'd be justice. I shouldn't trouble."

The last glimmer of light sank in the sea. A woman's voice burst out in high song on the plateau.

Yannul stirred uneasily. He said to Raldnor, very low: "They're hard bitches, most of them, they can take care of themselves. But there was a little girl—from Alisaar, I think—a Zakorian pirate took her when she was a mite. She was tough on deck, but she got scared at night. There may be too much fun up there. Would you object if I went up and got her back?"

"Your gallantry does you credit. But the getting may be slightly harder than you suppose. I'll go with you. Two soldiers from Ryhgon's school should be a match for twenty or so drunken Zakorians."

They sidled away from the group on the beach and abruptly took to the indigo channels of the forest.

It began in a sort of grim humorousness, that climb through the jungle. It eased the tension in both of them, brought back certain pleasant memories of conspiracies at Lin Abissa. Yet, as they moved steadily upward, the presence of the forest began to steal on them, to overpower them with its flat, dark essence.

The gut of the jungle was all shadow, with edges of icy blue where the moon tipped its leaves. It purred and rustled and throbbed. Those small numerous eyes that had ignited below at the edge of the beach winked like stars in the undergrowth. The grasses crackled with the flame of unfelt winds.

"Spies everywhere," Yannul whispered.

But neither of them smiled. To Raldnor it seemed the whole forest pressed close, all of it animate, watching, hostile. He felt for the first time the coldness of the shadows that were not cold in any physical sense, the oppression, the almost psychic smells of age, of something ripening on its own rottenness. The island, quiescent by day, stirring at nightfall, had breathed into its own dark life and found itself penetrated and deflowered. They had disturbed its primeval dusk. It hated them.

The plateau leaped abruptly into orange nearness through tall fern.

On the bald rock men and their whores shouted and sang, eating their fill and drinking from the broached barrels. A great bonfire flapped its skirt at the sky. Two or three women were dancing naked, holding burning twigs in their hands in imitation of the fire-dancers of Zarduk.

"Do you see your girl?" Raldnor asked.

"No. We'll have to move closer."

A few steps more and a female figure jumped up.

"Yanl of the Lans—and Ralnar," she slurred, immediately knowing them both, particularly Yannul, but she was not the one Yannul sought. She led them to the fire, nevertheless, and gave them beer, and wound her arms about Yannul. At this, a man came staggering up, his eyes bloodshot.

"You're with me, Hanot. Don't waste your time on that landsdog. Jurl'll want to know you've seen fit to join us, *masters,*" he jeered and careened off, dragging the woman with him.

"There she is, little Rella or Rilka, I forget her name," Yannul said, "and having trouble, too."

He ran toward a disturbance in the shadows, with Raldnor following. They pulled up four sailors and dealt with them swiftly. Yannul half-lifted a struggling, clawing girl, and convinced her, at the cost of almost losing his eyes, that he was not part of the prolonged rape which had been planned, but Yannul, to whom she had told her secret fears in the dark. She was small-boned, with a fine straight profile uncommon among Zakorians. She might indeed have been an Alisaarian. She smiled at him uncertainly, but her trust quickly gave way to a look of pure fright.

"Well, so we're to be honored after all," Jurl's voice said behind them. "The dogs have come to fill their bellies."

"Back to back for the fight," Raldnor said to Yannul, "like the training floor at Abissa." He found a savage grin on his face. "But first an appetizer. This man's Ryhgon's breed, and we both have a score to settle with him."

He could not make out Jurl's face against the fire. It did not matter. A sudden seething and intolerable hate came on him. He knew abruptly that it did not belong to him, but had filled him like an empty vessel. Hatred—the island was alive with it. It crawled in his blood, in his brain.

He felt the dead places of his mind tear open in a swift,

unlooked-for agony. Not Anici or Astaris to enter them now—no sweet woman with thoughts like splintering crystal, no otherself all warm fire. Not now. This was an alien, a dreadful and unstoppable thing. A possession. He felt the entity collect itself, focusing through the jungle's purple eye, yet seeking expression incredibly through his own. He felt something break out of him. It was horror and fear. But it made him grin and laugh in an impossible madman's triumph.

Jurl suddenly shuddered and clutched at his throat, his belly. A sharp cry burst from his mouth. He fell and screamed and clawed, and rolled into the fire.

All around them panic dropped on the feasters. They grew silent, heads raised like the heads of animals snuffing the wind, tensed for the first feeling of pain.

It came swift, that retribution. They leaped and shrieked like demons in the glare of the flames, all caught in a pattern of terror and death.

Yannul said urgently to the girl: "Did you eat the fruit?"

"They gave me beer and fruit," she whispered, her eyes wide, "but I hadn't had food for three days. I sicked it up."

"Good girl," said Yannul, proud of her, his face very pale.

"There's nothing we can do here," Raldnor said.

He turned back into the trees, shaking like an old man after fever, and they followed him.

The forest was very silent as they made their way back through the shadows. No eyes opened. There was only the sound of the falls, the sea.

On the beach Tullut's men sat huddled at their fire.

"The fruit was poisonous, Tullut," Yannul said, "in the end."

His Alisaarian girl began to cry. He comforted her.

They slept by the fire. At dawn Tullut took two men with him to the plateau to see if any had been purged of the poison and still lived—as did Yannul's girl. They came back inside the hour. They did not say what they had seen on the plateau; certainly no one returned with them.

They took what was left of the bird meat and barrels filled with fresh water and rowed for the ship. There was a full wind blowing—a warm, not an angry wind. It blew them out of sight of the island. They were glad enough. Ten men and one woman were all that remained to crew this tattered, burned hag-ship, once a beautiful thing, riding proud on the western seas. They were not enough to take her oars; they could only let the wind push them as it wished. They were all tired out, immobilized and drained by what had been done to them. Many days passed; they did not cut notches and lost count of them. Overhead the position of the stars was strange. There came a lull.

"I'm finished, Ralnar Am Dorthar," Tullut said, addressing Raldnor by the name he had chosen to go by. "The food is gone, the wind's stopped. This blue sea has no end. We're becalmed in hell. The voyage was cursed from the beginning."

"You took ill luck with you," Raldnor said. "Don't you say it's bad fortune to carry a felon or a wanted man?"

"Oh, some sailors' yarn. Most of our men were felons, Ralnar. They've paid for it, I think. There's some talk among us—to make a death pact. It's our custom. This is an arduous way to reach the gods."

"There's been too much death," Raldnor said.

"I know it, Ralnar. Elon was my father—Did they tell you? He got me on a girl at Hanassor, only a Zastis mistake, but he saw me schooled, bought me my commission on this ship. This damned ship. I inherited too much of him. He was a good man, but it's weakness in me."

Raldnor said gently: "I guessed your grief, though you hid it very well. I, too, once held back grief so no one should see it. A man should have no shame in weeping."

"No, Ralnar. But then our customs are different. How is it your hair turned white after the burning mountain? I've heard it happens from shock or fear, but you're a brave man. You were braver than that bastard Jurl."

"It's the mark of another fear," Raldnor said, "an older fear. A fear of betraying who I was."

Tullut looked at him but asked no question. He took Raldnor's hand in a gesture of friendship.

"Well, you must do as you wish, Ralnar. Yannul too, and Resha will do as he does, no doubt. We have our own way. I hope your luck may change. I doubt it will."

He went below as had the other Zakorians. They did not come up again.

So she lay, a ship of death, and at dusk three birds came flying over the mast.

"Land near," Yannul cried. "Perhaps better than the last."

The moon swam cold into the sky and brought a cold wind. It blew them through the night, and there were big fish leaping silver in the water.

Resha fell asleep at Yannul's side. At last only Raldnor still watched. He saw the black shape of the land come up out of the ocean like a huge beast.

As the sun rose, the heights of the land were drenched with carmine, while its valleys were black, as if in retention of the night.

He thought of Tullut. "None of us," he thought, "wait long enough. Whatever god, whatever destiny, is at work must have time." And in the midst of death, he felt the surge of hope in him, and leaned and woke Yannul out of sleep.

17

HAVING BROUGHT THEM WITHIN sight of land, the wind abandoned them. There were dark forests along the coast, rocky inlets, a backbone of crags. It seemed a turbulent landscape, and untenanted by men.

The heat of the day came down from the sky, up from the ocean.

Raldnor, as he sat alone at the rail, made out a movement in the sea, and thought it was a fish. But the fish swam on the surface, never dipping in the water. Shortly he realized it was a narrow boat, made of some hollowed black tree, similar to the fishing canoes of Zakoris. One figure occupied it—a man, rowing with strong easy motions. As he drew closer, coming quite obviously for the ship, Raldnor saw his sunburned face, empty of surprise or curiosity, a face quite closed in on itself, yet at peace. The man's hair was very long, lying over his shoulders, chest and back.

In color it was corn yellow.

The pulses kicked in Raldnor's body. He lifted an arm and hailed the rower. In turn the man raised his hand briefly; he did not call.

The narrow boat came alongside where the ladder trailed in the water. The man climbed up on deck and stood facing Raldnor. They were of an equal height, but the

stranger's body, though muscular, was thin almost to the
bone. He wore only a cloth about his middle; the rest of him
was tanned, but with that pale clear tan of the white-
skinned, which fades with the cold.

"You're a Lowlander," Raldnor said, and he laughed, his
eyes extraordinarily full of water.

The stranger clearly did not understand his speech, did
not attempt to speak himself. He gestured to the boat below
and indicated that Raldnor should follow him. Raldnor
shook his head, pointed to the tower and called Yannul and
the girl.

The man showed no concern. The boat did not seem
large enough, but somehow he placed all three of them in it
and took up the oars, rowing in the same easy movement as
before. Little patches of the blue fire ran before them, almost playfully. The ship fell behind, a ragged skeleton, black
on the sky. Ahead, the land drew closer. The boat appeared
to be making for an area of thick forest where a rocky
promontory stretched out into the sea. There were no signs
of life there, but faint blue smokes rose from the tree-
covered slopes above.

The man never spoke or moved his lips. His mouth had
an indefinable strangeness about it, as if it had never been
used to form words. Perhaps he was dumb. A dumb Lowlander, Raldnor mused in surprise.

The canoe was beached. The stranger moved to the first
line of trees. There was a clay vessel set in the shade. He
gave them water, then led them up into the forest.

It was a house of wood—a tall, wide hall built of mud clay
over a frame of staves, with its black knotty pillars and
mainstays the great trees themselves. The roof was full of
leaves and nesting birds, which shook off their droppings on
the floor, and sang in sweet fluting voices, and flew inces-
santly in and out of the high window spaces. The forest people lived in the wooden house, bathed in the clear streams
below, cooked at innumerable fires on the open place above.

They ate neither meat nor fish, most of their food being raw: berries and fruit, plants and leaves and milk from their small herd of black goats. They were a yellow-haired race, and light-eyed. None of them spoke. It came to Raldnor at last, as he lay in the shade of the wooden house near sunfall, that they did not speak because they had no need. They, like the Lowlanders, came together in their minds, and being more at peace, more content with their life, saw no need to express themselves in any other way. He felt a sense of angry despair, finding himself again with this key of communication, which should have been his birthright, freshly denied him. He was once more a cripple, a deaf mute among the hearing, speaking ones.

Yannul and the girl Resha seemed more ill at ease than he, though they were all well enough looked after. The silence troubled them, though for different reasons.

An indigo night settled, like the birds, on the wooden house, glinting with white bird-eye stars. Raldnor rose and went out into the cool. Fireflies darted a gold embroidery from thicket to thicket. Below, the soft thunder of the sea.

As he stood there, someone came walking through the trees toward him, light as an animal. He sensed rather than heard her come. For some reason his skin prickled.

At once there was an old woman, near him, in the starlight.

She was dressed, as were all the forest people, only in a cloth tied about her middle; yet, despite her age, there was nothing ugly in her body, though she had neither the smooth skin nor the firm breasts of the young women. Her hair was faded and streaked but still fine, and very long. Her eyes were strange, large and yellow as an owl's. She seated herself cross-legged on the grass with a suppleness that gave him pause; she indicated that he too should sit, facing her.

She stared in his face. After a moment there came a startling, fearful flicker in his brain. He flinched; sweat broke out on him. It was to be hard this time, though without pain.

"Cease struggling," a voice said suddenly and quite distinctly in his skull.

He lapsed, shivering, against the bole of a tree, and the voice said: "There is nothing you need fear."

He did not comprehend how he could understand her, for they did not know the language of the lands he had come from. That much had been plain. He strove for expression. The voice said: "I use no language, only thought. You interpret in your own way, which suits you best."

It had no gender, this voice. He tried to question it, blindly. An answer came.

"There are many in this land. Not all live as we do. Yet all could speak within, at need. You are of our people, yet you could not speak within. Some of us are more sensitive and more strong—we are the delvers. We seek out pain in the sick mind, and cure it. I am sent to you to cure your pain, so that you may speak as it is your right to do. I see now there have been others. Both women. Lovers. Ice hair and fire hair. To these you could speak; such a thing has its logic. Have no fear of me; I see your grief. Let me see all. I will help you to be yourself."

But his mind cried out at hers in angry hurt.

"So there is another land," the voice said, "and dark men who rule it. We have old stories of such a place. Do not fear your half-blood. It is your strength and not your trouble. I see your mother, back down the long corridors of your memory. Look, there is your mother. Do you see her? That is how you saw her as a newborn child. Thin she is, sick from bearing you. But how beautiful. There is strength, true strength, hard as the forest tree. Think what lay behind her, and before. Would you call this woman weak? Do you think she left you nothing of herself? Yes, weep, poor child. Know her, and weep. She is your spirit, and the other half is a King." Then there was a curious inflection in the voice, a kind of sorrow. "You imagine yourself so little, Raldnor, son of Ashne'e, son of Rehdon, Dragon King. So little."

There was a lance of fire in his skull, yet no pain. A darkness swirled like the sea, but there was no fear. Now the voice, which led him like a guide through the unknown dark rooms of his own brain, had assumed a sex and a name. It had become Ashne'e's.

Yannul whistled as he crossed the clearing behind the wooden house at noon. Resha sat, as she always did, outside, staring dejectedly down across the slope at men and women moving in the thin forest below. They had been here ten days and had adopted the forest people's mode of dress. Resha looked very well in it, and, certainly, she had worn little more aboard *Rorn's Daughter*. Yannul lightly ruffled her hair. He thought of her generally rather as he had long ago thought of his sisters, with a protective amusement, tempered by occasional slight irritation. Their sexual unions did not disrupt this attitude, for in Lan, where farmsteads were remote from each other, it was neither uncommon nor frowned upon for sisters either to couple with, or even marry, their brothers, or sometimes their sires.

"Well, Resha of Alisaar, I told you I would communicate somehow with them, didn't I?"

"You did, Lannic man. In Alisaar, boasters are whipped."

"Are they, indeed? Well, well. No wonder you jumped aboard a Zakorian pirate rather than stay to lose your skin—No, don't clout me on the ear! Hear me out. I have had a little conversation with some of the men. Truly, a simple method. We drew pictures on slate and waved our arms about. I've learned a good deal. Over these hills there are cities—great cities, with kings and palaces and taverns and entirely suitable whore shops. Ah! Bite me now, would you? Listen, little banalik, when Raldnor comes back from wherever it is he went with that old woman, you and I and he will seek our fortune over the hills. They talk there—by mouth. We can soon pick up their tongue. Imagine a city ruled by a yellow-haired king."

"We'll be outlanders—scum," she grumbled. "They'll

burn us or stone us as the Vis of Dorthar do the Plains people."

"No, Resha. Judge by these. Are we outcast here? Yellow-haired men, I've observed, have more justice. Did you know Raldnor was a Lowlander?"

"He was brave," she said. "I did my best to win his favor on the ship, but he was celibate and pure. A good man."

"And the son of Rehdon, the High King. Yes, that makes big eyes. It whets your appetite even more, doesn't it, you shameless piece? Up now, and I'll teach you to juggle and stand on your hands. We'll need a trade where we're going."

The dusk came on, and little black bats fluttered among the trees.

Yannul and Resha lay in the shade. She had worked obediently, and her body—strong and supple from ship's labor—was quick to learn, though far too enticing. In the red slanting rays of sunfall he had pulled her down for other lessons.

Now, in the lengthening shadows, a man came walking through the trees toward them.

"Ralnar," Resha said.

Yannul looked up and studied the figure. Yes, he knew it. Skin burned almost black by the sun—the tan of the Vis— and hair salt-bleached to white, long now as Yannul's own. Yet, as the man came nearer, Yannul hesitated to greet him and checked again the physique and face, as if uncertain after all. They had all suffered and all been changed on the nightmare voyage, and then had come this nine-day absence, during which Raldnor was hidden with the old wisewoman. But did any of these things account for the vast, oddly inexplicable differences Yannul saw in Raldnor? He crossed the little clearing and came to a halt by them, looking down. His expression was remote, as if he saw them from a long way off, still—as if he did not know them well. His eyes were wide, burning, clear. Yannul thought, with uneasy amusement: "That old one, she's been feeding him incense leaves. He's been having visions in the forest." But this did not seem applicable. Yannul fathomed it suddenly. "He's been emptied, scoured, cauterized. Then filled. Filled with something better." But he said aloud: "You look strange. Were you ill?"

"No, Yannul," Raldnor said. Even his voice was somehow altered. Now it was the voice—Yes, of a king. The forest fell peculiarly silent all around them. "For the first time in my life," Raldnor said, "I am at peace with myself. A rare and wonderful gift."

He turned and walked away from them, toward the wooden house or the sea.

Resha whispered: "He's marked for a god."

Her fingers fluttered in a swift religious sign. Yannul cursed her.

"Don't be a fool. He's had misfortunes. Perhaps the old woman helped him bear them."

"No. I've seen that look on the faces of priests before they jump from the rocks into the sea, to honor Rorn."

"Do you mean you think he'll die? Be quiet, you stupid girl."

Resha looked at Yannul in scorn.

"From now on, Lannic lout, all men will be to him only like dust on the wind or blowing sea spray. None of us could harm him. He is his god's. And the gods protect their own."

In the morning there were new men in the wooden house. They, too, were of the forest people, almost indistinguishable in coloring and style of dress. They had brought with them three riding mounts—milk-white zeebas of unusual size—and linen garments suitable for two men and a woman.

Yannul marveled.

"They're very prompt to supply our wants. How did you get them to understand you, Raldnor?"

"I can speak with them now," Raldnor said.

Yannul said nothing further. He had heard the stories of

the Lowlanders' telepathic abilities, and, having already seen evidence of it in these alien forests, accepted Raldnor's part in it with a shudder of unease. To Resha, nothing Raldnor did at this time was too wonderful. He was his god's, which accounted for everything.

They left the wooden house before noon, leading the white zeebas up the narrow forest tracks, with one of the yellow-haired men walking ahead. The tree shade grew intense, then diminished. They reached a rocky summit, and below stretched rolling ocher grassland under a cobalt sky. Their guide pointed down and away. Raldnor nodded. The man turned and vanished back among the trees.

"Where are we headed for?" Yannul called, as they left the rock and mounted. "A town? Or that city they mentioned?"

"There are three cities here in the Plain. I shall make for the first of these, but naturally, you'll have your own plans."

"I planned to ply my old trade," Yannul said, ill at ease as they rode. "A city would be a healthy place for it. And you?"

"I have business with their king, whoever he is."

"Their king! You're ambitious."

"I always was, Yannul. I obtained status but no direction. Now, I'm driven, obsessed."

"To do what?"

"To get my birthright. My second birthright. Already this land's given me the first."

"High King of Vis," Yannul said. "A difficult task."

"No, Yannul. That essential thing is merely secondary. My kingdom is in the Lowlands. They had their own lords in the past. Now, they have a lord again."

Yannul glanced at him. Raldnor seemed calm, remote, his passionate words untinged by emotion. Then Raldnor turned in the saddle and looked full at him. For the first time the Lan felt the force of an incredible personal power stream like light out of the Lowlander—a power that seemed alive, fathomless, indestructible. It was an awesome thing to witness in a man he had known only as a man; for now, Yannul saw, whether at the whim of a god or not, Raldnor had become something more.

"What did the wise-woman do to you?" Yannul said, trying to grin.

"Removed my blindness, woke me out of sleep. Gave me the purpose I was born to."

The passionless voice was, nevertheless, filled, like the face before Yannul, with the same vast strength.

"You look as if you'd eat these cities to get what you want—swallow the sea to reach the plains of Vis."

"A harsh diet. Yet, whatever I have to do, I will do," Raldnor said.

Yannul let the reins slacken a little. Raldnor's zeeba moved ahead of him. It had a certain aptness. The white-haired man seemed to have outstripped them all. Yannul drew in a deep breath of the alien summer air. Whatever fire burned in Raldnor had scorched him, too. He knew he was no longer a free man. If any of them were any longer free. Even in the quiet, insect-humming afternoon, he sensed forces of disruption, of retribution, stirring underground. A cataclysm was coming, a leveling, a wind from chaos. They would all be caught in it, like fish in nets. And there, riding before him, was this unknown man, this comrade once called friend, who was to be the fisherman.

18

IT WAS A THREE DAYS' JOURNEY. They passed first through a scattering of villages and two small towns, all paying tax to the city, which in turn protected them from bandits by means of troops. Though physically resembling the Lowlanders, the yellow-haired people of the Plain were quite unlike them in disposition and intent. They were busy, outgoing and, on occasion, sly. There was no mysterious unvoiced code—they had their robbers and malcontents, and had had their battles, too. Only five years before, the city had been at war with its nearest neighbor. Who knew how many corpses under the soil helped now to nourish the grain?

Raldnor seemed able to speak their tongue fluently. Yannul, by dint of hard labor, began to learn. He learned also, as did Resha, to pull up the hood of his garment when they approached populated areas or passed travelers on the roads. The Plain dwellers did not seem hostile in the least to the strange phenomenon of black hair, but their curiosity and surprise grew irksome. Of their mind speech there was no great evidence. It seemed as if prosperity and worldliness were letting that inner art decay.

They reached the city on the afternoon of the third day: a strong-walled, high-towered pile built on an ancient man-made hill some eighty feet or so above the Plain. It did not have the beauty of a Vis city. There was something crouching and squat about it despite the towers. Vathcri it was called. Various houses and taverns sprawled down the hill and over the Plain beyond its walls, and there were soldiers about in the dark-blue livery they had seen in the towns. Despite this, discipline at the gate was lax. A polite answer to a brief challenge got them through. It was a Justice Day—a day when the king gave public audience, settled disputes and tried offenders in the open-air court before his palace.

"We have such things in Lan," Yannul said, "and the Am Dorthar call us barbarians."

The city seemed to rise in terraces toward its citadel, its winding streets clothed with crowds, wine sellers and pickpockets. Resha's hood slipped away, and an excited babble went up. The girl stared haughtily about and stalked on, the crowd parting to gape at her. Yannul pushed back his own hood at that, and they moved more easily afterward. When they reached the audience place, the press was at its thickest.

"These peasants," Resha hissed with profound contempt. "What King of Alisaar or Zakoris or Dorthar would demean himself by talking directly to a pack of clods?"

They got down steps and emerged in the bowl of the court. The palace which rose behind it pushed up tall spires, and painted friezes glowed on its red walls. Black shade trees had been planted where the King's platform stood. The King himself sat in an ivory chair, before him were two kneeling supplicants, all around him the clutter of his court, advisors, clerks and military officers. Something caught Yannul's eye—the banner held up behind the King's chair.

"Raldnor," he said, "do you see—?"

On the light-blue ground, an embroidery of a woman with ice-white skin and golden hair, a woman with eight serpentine arms, her body ending in the coiling rope of a serpent's tail.

"Is that their King?" Resha asked superfluously.

"I imagine so," Yannul answered, still staring at the banner. "And that woman? Would she be his wife?"

Yannul looked again at the platform and saw the reason for her interest. The King was young and very handsome. To his right, a little behind him, half hidden by the drifts of tree shadow, sat a woman in a white robe. About to reply that this was most certainly the King's favorite and only wife, to whom he had sworn forever to be faithful on pain of inexpressible divine torture, Yannul checked himself, for he saw abruptly that Raldnor was no longer with them. Yannul gazed about him, then swiftly ahead. Even in the blond crowd that salt-white hair was easy to discover.

"By the gods—he's asking audience of their King."

Taking Resha by the arm, the Lan pushed his way further forward until he stood at the very fringe of people, looking out across the flagged space at the handsome King. The two supplicants had moved off, one grinning, one sour, as was to be expected. Now a clerk hurried to the King, spoke to him and drew back. The King was frowning. His eyes skimmed over the crowd and found out Raldnor. The King said something. The clerk turned and beckoned.

Raldnor stepped out onto the open space and went forward. There was a burst of exclamations, then total silence. Even in this gathering of racial brothers Raldnor was remarkable. Without seeing his face, Yannul sensed again that incredible, almost physical, emanation of certainty and power.

"Kneel," the clerk rapped out. In the stillness words carried well.

"In the land I come from," Raldnor said, "one King does not kneel to another." His voice was quiet and very level, yet there was not a man there who did not hear it.

The crowd murmured, then became quiet.

"So you claim royal birth," the King said. "Of what city then are you King? Vardath and Tarabann, I believe, might dispute your rights."

"There is a land beyond your seas, King. My rights are there."

The young King smiled.

"Are you a dreamer, I wonder? Or are you mad?"

There was a deeper silence then. Standing behind Raldnor, unable to see his face or his eyes, Yannul nevertheless saw the effect they produced on the King, whose own eyes widened and flinched. His tanned face paled. He snarled through his teeth, midway between shock and anger: "You dare to try magicians' tricks on me!" And to the clerk in fury: "Who is this man?"

The clerk whispered. The King again looked up; this time he made out Yannul and Resha. The King seemed unnerved. He stared at Raldnor.

"You say you come from another land, a land where there are dark-haired peoples. The man and the woman there—are they your proof?"

"I am my own proof, King. Read my brain. I open it to you."

The King flinched a second time.

"Such things are for the priests of Ashkar. Do you ask to be examined by them?"

"My lord," Raldnor said, "my kingdom is a small one. Men there resemble the men of Vathcri. But there is a black-haired tyrant who hates my people simply for their color. Every moment that is wasted between us sees the shadow of their persecution and anguish thrown farther."

The King gave a violent cry. He leaped from his ivory chair. Guards ran to him. He thrust them aside. Even the white-gowned women started up in the shade.

"Don't try to breach my mind with your own sick dreams!" the King shouted. The guards now ran to Raldnor; they came thrusting through the press and seized Yannul also, and the girl.

As the blue-liveried soldiers dragged the Lan across the court, he had one last glimpse of the Vathcrian King, and saw the fury and the terror on his face. Behind, the crowd milled in uproar.

The sands of twilight drifted on the floors of the red palace.

Jarred of Vathcri paced through them, up and down before the great hearth. He was a young king, very young. His father had died in early middle life, abruptly, and left him the ivory chair before he was ready for it. He had ruled half a year; now, confronted by the stranger, he saw it had not been enough.

"Who is this man?" he asked again. "Where does he come from?"

The pale-haired girl in the white dress sitting in the light of the one lamp in the room said gently: "Perhaps he is who he says he is, and comes from where he says he does. Shouldn't you consider that eventuality, my brother?"

"Impossible," Jarred snapped. Her demure, uncluttered wisdom angered him.

"Why impossible? There's always been a legend of another land, a land of dark-haired men. And don't you remember the maps of old Jorahan the Scholar—the sea routes that lead out of Shansar, in the north?"

"He breached my thoughts. In our father's time that would have earned him death—to dare speak within to a king—and he did more. I couldn't shut him out. He thrust aside the barriers—mind-spoke me against my will. How many men can do that?"

"Some of the priests," she said.

"Some of the priests tell us they can," Jarred sneered. "How many have you known do it?"

She said musingly: "It was said to be the greatest gift that Ashkar gave us—the ability to speak within. Now few of us use it, or could we use it if we wished?"

"You and I, Sulvian," he said, "since childhood."

"Oh, you and I. And we talk with our mouths at this very moment. No. Mind speech has become a hindrance to prosperity, because it's hard to practice dishonesty when your thoughts are accessible, difficult to steal and murder and grow rich. Only the forest people mind-speak now, my brother. She must pity us."

"Ashkar is honored daily in the temples of this and every other city. I doubt if she objects to that or to the gifts laid on her altars."

"Who knows," Sulvian murmured, "what a goddess would prefer to have from us. Our gold or our integrity."

The door opened. The High Priest of the order of the Vathcrian Ashkar entered—a thin, straight man in the dark robe of his calling, the violet Serpent's Eye on his breast. He did not bow or in any manner prostrate himself, his status, in certain aesthetic and still recognized ways, being superior to the King's.

"Well, Melash, you've come in time to rescue me from a lecture by my lady sister. She takes her duties as priestess too seriously."

"I am delighted, King, that she does. We shall need Ashkar's guidance in the days ahead."

"What do you mean, Melash?"

"I mean, King, I have just come from questioning the stranger and his two companions as you asked."

"And?"

"And, my King, he is all he says. And more."

Jarred's face whitened.

"You're mistaken, Melash."

"No, King, I am not. I discount the insult you render me in doubting my mental capabilities. I understand the stranger breached your mind and made you afraid."

"Not afraid!" Jarred shouted.

"Yes, my King. No shame in that. He has made me also afraid. He has been very honest with us. He has shown me that before he reached our land, he had neither purpose nor direction; his mind was closed. Now the capacity of his mind is greater than any I have ever encountered or heard spoken of. And his purpose is likely to upset the balance of our world."

"Well, tell me what he showed you. The whole story. Let's see if it's at all credible."

Melash told him.

"You're speaking like a fool, Melash," Jarred cried when he was done. "Have you lost your reason? This is some romance made up in the bazaar."

"No, King," Melash said, "but if you are in doubt, you should question him yourself."

"Then bring him," Jarred said stonily.

Behind the priest the door immediately opened. The stranger came through, but only his white hair caught the little lamplight. The rest of him was shadow.

"Did you call him with your mind?" Jarred rasped.

"There was no need," Melash said quietly. "He can read all our minds, whether we permit it or not."

Jarred felt himself tremble, and stilled it. He retreated into the aura of the lamp, and sat down in the ivory chair, near Sulvian.

"What are you called, outlander?" he demanded in a dry, harsh voice.

"Raldnor, King."

"Come here then, Raldnor. Where I can see you."

The priest bowed his head and stood like an effigy, disclaiming without words the actions of his lord.

The stranger moved up the room. The lamp caught his face and his extraordinary eyes. The eyes fixed on Jarred.

"Melash, the High Priest of Ashkar, has told us everything you told him, Raldnor. I must congratulate your vivid and inventive imagination. You've missed nothing, even the goddess has been put in, Ashkar, who you claim to worship in this—*other country* of yours, under another name. Please tell me now what you hope to gain by such a fantastic mishmash?"

"Help for my people," the stranger said. "I have learned of the other cities of the Plain, their river outlets and their ships. And there is Shansar in the north."

"Don't think you can make a fool of all of us," Jarred spat at him.

Sulvian's hand gripped suddenly on his arm.

"Listen."

Outside a wind had risen; it moaned and sawed about the palace towers. Distant shutters banged in an irregular tempo. The priest raised his head. It was the dust wind of the Plains, but not the time for it. The room seemed suddenly full of omens.

Jarred shut his eyes, but already he saw, and the inner darkness was alive with pictures. He witnessed the smoking ruins, the slaves driven through the snow in chains and the wind blew among the yellow hair of the dead. It came too fast, he could not contain it. There was a black-haired man, with burning madman's eyes—a man composed of hate and the desires of hate.

Beyond the palace walls the dust wind scoured down the winding streets of Vathcri. Men muttered, children woke and screamed in fright, women hurried to the temples. In the great pillared place of Ashkar, where it overlooked the sacred groves below, the serpents hissed and thrashed in their pit. A gust blew wide the shutters and doused the lamps on the altar. A cry of superstitious terror arose, and sleeping birds clouded up from their sanctuaries on the temple roofs.

Sulvian left her chair.

The lamp had smoked and flickered out, but in the darkness she could somehow find her way. She glimpsed Jarred huddled on the ivory seat and the gray-faced priest. But she *saw* the stranger, as clearly as if the lamp still burned, not on him but from inside his flesh, behind his eyes.

"You trap our city in a vise of fear," she said. "Let go."

"You trap yourselves," he answered. "Are you afraid, Sulvian, priestess of Ashkar Anackire?"

"No," she whispered. Then: "Yes. I saw myself dead in your mind. The Black King had killed me."

"Not you," he said, "though she resembled you."

She saw herself abruptly in his brain; he showed her herself as he saw her: pale as pure light, her hair as white as his, yet blown by the wind into a tinsel of ice.

"Anici—" she said. "But there is another—"

"No longer," he said. "Amrek, the Black King, has caused both their deaths."

"You must hate him a great deal," she whispered.

"I pity him."

She heard the terrible power behind his voice, the thing so invincible that it could pity the enemy it would destroy.

"Did you call the wind?" she asked him.

"No. I am not a magician of Shansar."

"But the wind came."

"Yes, Sulvian. It came."

"Jarred . . ." she said. "By the laws of the cities, you've challenged his rule as King."

He said nothing.

Beyond the windows, the wind fell suddenly quiet. The horn of a gold moon pierced the tangled clouds.

In Tarabann of the Rock the wind came funneling from the southwest. Priests, as they stood on the high prayer-towers of Ashkar—raised up and built to resemble striking serpents— saw the wind coming like a long-tailed cloud, itself a python made of dust and storm.

It smote on Tarabann for two days and a night between. That night's moon was dark blue as sapphire, the days' sun the color of old blood. The waves reared up and flooded the salty flats that stretched out two miles from the Rock to the sea. Ships were wrecked and roofs blown off. The priests had different prayers to attend to. They smoked their incense and laid bare their minds, and became troubled. On the day after the wind dropped, the High Priest of Ashkar of the Rock came to Klar.

"It seems, lord, there is a new King in Vathcri."

Klar, who was the King of Tarabann, who had fought at

his father's side in the last battle with Vathcri five years before, put down his gilded book.

"A new King, you say? What's become of the young pup, Jarred?"

"He lives, King. You must understand that thought and things of the mind are as mist—we comprehend as best we may—"

"So you fumble at your tasks. I understand very well."

"Indeed, King, you do not. There is a—power—in Vathcri. I have no other means to explain what I have felt. A vast power. Greater than the King's. Not, I would judge, the power of a man. It has to do with the wind, yet is dissociated from the wind."

"Riddles," Klar snapped, snapping, too, the clasps of his book.

"Once gods walked on earth, King. So our fables tell us. Once She talked with men, like a kind sister."

"You're trying to say there's a *god* walking about in Vathcri?"

"I would not pledge myself so far, lord, as to say such a thing."

Klar was wary of the magic of the priests. He was two things: one was mostly merchant, the other all soldier, and neither had time for mysticism. The inner tongue had been dead in him since his brother—the only man with whom he could so speak—fell in the siege of a Vathcrian town. Nevertheless, he respected the priests, though he did not like their business to overlap into his own forthright and uncomplex world.

"Very well, sir," he said, "I'll send people to Vathcri. We'll see what's up, eh, old priest? Don't fret. You did well to tell me."

But Klar's men were only away two days. On the third day they returned, and with them the six Vathcrians they had met on the road. They had a curious look about them, these Vathcrians. Klar could not gauge it. They brought a message not from the king, Jarred, though it bore his seal. Klar read it and looked up amazed.

"There is a man here, commits himself to paper, calls me brother in the manner of a king and bids me come inland to assembly in the Place of Kings at Pellea."

"King," the chief Vathcrian said, "that is the old place of assembly, used by our ancestors."

"So it is, precisely," Klar said, "but our ancestors, and not since. The last meeting there was a hundred, a hundred and fifty years past. By Ashkar! And is the rest of this correct: I must decide, along with the other Kings, whether or not to go to the aid of this Lowland country, never before heard of or seen?"

"Yes, King. Lord Jarred has sent men also to Vardath, and up into Shansar."

"By Ashkar. I thought it was this Raldnor sent you, not Jarred."

"They're bound as brothers," the Vathcrian said. "Raldnor also is royal, son of a High King and a priestess." He did not look abashed, but rather, proud.

"Well, well," Klar said. "Well, well."

To blue-walled Vardath the wind came only for a night, stirring up the fishing boats on her broad river. A tree fell in the King's garden. It had been planted at the hour of his birth, and the omen alarmed him. His wife, Ezlian, High Priestess of the Vardish Ashkar, went herself to the goddess, and returned to him in the dawn, pale, but smiling in a certain way she had.

"Rest easy, Sorm my husband. The omen was not your death."

"What then, for Ashkar's sake?"

"There's change coming. The wind brought it. We must neither resist nor sorrow; both are superfluous and quite futile."

"Change for the worse?"

"Simply change," she said and kissed his face.

Sorm loved his wife and trusted her. He was neither weak nor unmasculine, yet in things spiritual, he leaned on her. From a child she had possessed aptitude and could speak within to most who were willing. In adolescence she had gone to live a year with the forest people, since when she had eaten no meat and shown particular cleverness in healing, both physical and of the mind. He himself had seen her somehow communing with a lion in the yellow hills above Vardath, while drawn knife in hand he trembled in every limb with terror for her. The snakes in the temple pit she called her children, and they wound like bracelets round her wrists and throat, and snuggled in her hair.

The Vathcrian riders came ten days after the tree fell.

Sorm asked, as others had similarly been moved to ask: "Who is this man?"

Ezlian seemed puzzled, searching inside herself. Presently she said: "There is a Vardish fable of a man born of a serpent, a hero. His name was Raldanash. He had dark skin, pale hair. The legend says his eyes were like Her eyes."

"Yes, priestess," the Vathcrian said, using the title generally considered to be more important than queen, "this man is dark, and very fair. His eyes burn."

"Is he then some sort of god?" Sorm said, his mouth dry as ash.

"We must go to Pellea and find out," said Ezlian. Then smiling in her way, she added: "But naturally, it's as my lord wishes."

In Shansar no wind came.

Mountains divided it from the fertile plains and forests of the south, and mountains thrust up inside it. There was a great deal of water in Shansar; it was a land of rivers and lakes and marsh, with the great rock stacks and steeples jutting in marching lines across it, like jagged stepping stones discarded by giants. It had a hundred or more outlets to the sea. Jorahan, the Vathcrian scholar, who had lived out his old age in a little-known town of the south, had left

maps to show these mostly unused ways. There were many
kings in Shansar and many tribes. They built ships of necessity. Sometimes they sailed around the coasts to pirate in
the south. They worshiped magic, but with them also only
their holy men spoke within—or lovers, or families. They
had a goddess. Her name was Ashara. She had a fish's tail,
and her arms were eight white cilia such as they occasionally discovered on lake creatures.

Three Vathcrians, one of whom was a guide, rode into
the mountains, crossed an ancient pass, came down into
Shansar and bartered for a long narrow boat. There was a
fourth man with them, not a Vathcrian, a tall man with
white hair. They deferred to him as to a king, but he had
come to be his own messenger in these lands that answered
to no call from the south. There was a hosting place here,
too; Jorahan had marked it on his maps. It also had been
unused for centuries; only tradition and superstition had
seen to its upkeep.

They rowed up great stretches of pearly water, the
stranger-king taking his turn with the Vathcrians under
skies purple with heat. In villages, women washing clothes
stared at their southern garments. Men challenged them.

"I am making for Ashara's Breast," the white-haired
man told them. That was their name for the old meeting
place. They let him go. They had certain antique ritualistic
truce laws concerning men who sought Ashara's Breast. Besides, the warriors who spoke to the white-haired one became convinced that he had reason and purpose. Long
boats began to trail a mile or so behind the Vathcrian canoe,
not in hostility but mainly out of a desire to witness whatever the white-haired man intended to do.

They reached the place at evening and climbed up its
shaggy, moss-grown steeps. Despite its name, it was in no way
like a breast, either of woman or goddess. Near the summit
stood a ramshackle priests' dwelling, which housed five or six
old priests, stiff in their joints, yet with fierce, dangerous eyes
for visitors. One stood in the path of the white-haired man.

He held out his staff, then threw it down at the man's feet. The staff convulsed and became a black serpent. The Vathcrians jumped back, cursing; the Shansarians, who had moved up the mount after them, made signs of religion and magic.

Raldnor looked in the old priest's face. He said very quietly: "Is the child afraid of the limbs that bore him?"

He reached and took up the serpent, which sprang instantly straight in his hands. He held out to the priest a staff. The old man's eyes watered. He said: "Do you claim, outlander, to be Her son?"

"How does a man reckon such things?" Raldnor said, looking into the old priest's eyes. "It would be fairer to say my mother was Her daughter."

"You blaspheme," the priest said. He trembled. Then he shut his eyes and tottered. Raldnor gently took his arm to steady him.

"Now you know me," Raldnor said.

The old priest whispered: "I have seen into his mind. He must have his way, whatever it is to be."

A murmur went up, like the wind stirring.

"There is a beacon here which summons the kings of Shansar," Raldnor said. "I have come to light it."

They led him up to the top of the mount. There was a vast crater there, and in the crater one tall dead tree. None of them knew who had planted it; certainly it had lived long, before death. Its white wasted branches seemed to reach into the apex of the sky. Raldnor struck fire and let the fire have the tree. The flames ran up and up, springing out on the bony boughs. It appeared that the tree was abruptly, miraculously living and in scarlet blossom. Men muttered and fell silent. There had been a legend in Shansar of a change which would alter the world when a dead tree bore red flower.

Night came on, and the tree burned like a red spear dividing the night.

Then, the wind rose.

It blew in black and scarlet gusts. The smoke and the colored sparks filled the sky. For uncountable miles the beacon showed; for uncountable miles they smelled the smoke on the wind.

It was too ancient a sign, too magical a sign for a land that worshiped magic to ignore. Tribe spoke to tribe, forgetting feuds or caste. Kings met up in the barren black rocklands, or in the watery dawn of the lakes. They gathered, and they came toward the ancient place, toward the magnet of the burning tree. For a night which would see the firing of the tree in Ashara's Breast had been itself a myth and a prophecy.

"How will he speak to them? What will he say?"

It was the third night on Ashara's Breast. The three Vathcrians sat at their own separate fire, a little down the mount from the priests' house. There were many fires on the mount that night, and below the mount fires spread out like a million ruby eyes across the dark plateau. Above, the tree still smoked. It had proved good timber.

"How many have come?" the Vathcrian asked again.

"She knows," another answered. "Half the kings of Shansar, at least, and more on the river road, Url says. As to what he'll say—he's a King, and more than that. By Ashkar, I'd fight for him. It's a fever in me; why, I don't know. You feel it too, all Vathcri felt it before he was done with us. It's a fever. They'll all catch it, those tribal men down there."

"I love him," a man said.

Another man laughed and said something witty and crude, poking at the fire.

"No, not love that sits in the crotch, you damned midden-brain. Like love of the land, of the place you were born in, the thing you ache to get back to, the thing you'd fight to hold, die for your sons to keep it."

"Ah, you romantic. No, it isn't love I feel. But he wants justice—only that. And he's a King's son, yet he'll take his turn with us in the mountains or on the boat—I value that in a man. He can lend his hand, yet lose nothing of what he is. The old Kings were like that. Besides—this land of black-haired men is rich and ripe for the taking, I'd say. They'll see that too, those pirates below."

Later, they rolled themselves in their blankets to sleep.

In the yellow dawn the priests burned incense. The kings came, powerful savage men, each with his two or three personal bodyguards, his eldest son, his magician. They crowded down into the crater, packed together. It was a good place for treachery, but here was no treachery; their laws had no room for it at such a time. The tree was almost done smoking.

Raldnor spoke to them; his voice carried to the edges of the crater, yet the voice was not merely in their ears. It spoke to each of them in their brains. They grew uneasy; the magicians chanted and made passes in the air. There was a humming of chants, like bees.

Then a silence came—gradually, a little at a time. There was a surge, like water bursting from the ground, swelling, filling the crater, spilling down the slope, to take in the rock, the plateau beneath. First one man, then another. Each had a chink, a crack in the adamantine crust which had submerged his mind. Each felt invasion at that chink, that crack, yet it came too swift for any fear. They felt in those moments neither greed nor pity, for he eclipsed their thoughts with his own. He made them, for those moments, himself. They saw his ambitions and his aims, his anguish, his passion and his power—all as if they had been their own. They felt grief and anger and great purpose. Then it was gone, fading like the color from the sky, like moisture in the heat.

There was talk and superstition after. They shouted among themselves and set their sorcerers to work. But the storm had come and gone. They provided an aftermath with no meaning.

"How can one man communicate with so many merely by use of his brain?" The Vathcrian, who had spoken of the pickings of Vis land, wondered, hushed, "Is he then a god? Look at them argue."

"Let them. Their decision's made. He made it. Beasts that run to the sea to drown themselves may discuss what they're doing on the way, but the sea still has them."

In the sanctuary the old priest sat with his serpent staff across his knees. He too, with all the rest, had felt the solitary brain command his own. But with his inner knowledge and the harsh training of his calling, he had seen, too, into the depths of Raldnor, known the past, the desolation, guilt and pain, now set aside forever, but marked indelibly, like deep scars.

"We ask: is he a god, that man?" the priest thought. "But lie is no longer anything we know to put a name to. He has found his soul but lost his self. Raldnor, or Raldanash in the myth. He said his mother was Her child—Yes, I saw her. She had Her face. And his Lowland race I saw so clearly in my mind when he conjured them. Across great seas, yet they worship Her—How can this be? A strange race, asleep now, but he will wake them. And he is theirs, an emanation of his people. No longer a man, but a collective being. Yes, that is what he is. Not king or god, but essence, expression."

The staff twitched in his hands. He smiled but not enough to stretch his narrow mouth. He had practiced the illusion so often that now it seemed sealed in the wood. The staff believed itself a snake. This was how he explained the phenomenon.

Outside, the day gathered itself and fell away. He sensed them alter course and begin to persuade themselves to the direction they had already had chosen for them.

"But whatever he is, have we ever known such power?" the priest thought. "How can we contain it? At some time the fight will finish. Will he simply burn away then, like the magic tree? What then can turn him back into a man?"

Summer was descending from its golden summit at Pellea when the three kings came there with their households, and the lords of their holdings and their towns. They came for their several reasons, with their several curiosities, fears and impatience. They spoke with Jarred, and stared at the dark-haired man and the dark-haired women walking in their elegant Vathcrian clothes. It seemed the stranger, Raldnor, had taken his demands to barbaric Shansar, and had been gone two months of the Vathcrian calendar.

"You've lost him," Klar said. "The sorcerers have eaten him up, and good riddance."

Yet Jarred was not the youngster he recalled; here was poise now, and calm, alongside the good looks. Klar noticed, too, how Sulvian was.

"She fancies the stranger-King, whoever he is," Klar mused. "She'll cry if he doesn't come back."

Klar had been at Pellea two days when the sentries rode down from the hills. They had seen riders on the upper passes—Vathcrian livery and arms, a white-haired man at their head, at back some two hundred Shansars on skinny marsh horses. Klar concluded the stranger was bringing down an enemy force to overwhelm the civilized men of the south. He called for action, but got only one. Ezlian of Vardath laughed at him—not rudely but affectionately, which was worse. He dragged his own few men into shape. When the force appeared on the Pellean plain four days later, he rode out and challenged them. And then his skull seemed full of things—bright, amorphous, pleasing things. It was like some drug. Klar was reminded irresistibly of that brother he had mind-spoken with, and grit tormented his eyes. He pushed emotion from him and stared at the stranger.

"I see you're all they said. You were well suited where you went—the land of magicians. And you've brought your brothers with you, by Ashkar."

But he rode with Raldnor, side by side, into Pellea. Something had touched him, touched him in a deep way, yet he was soothed.

The assembly was formed in the morning.

The five Shansarian Kings who had come with Raldnor from the lakes sat ranked behind him, grim-faced. It was clear they had assumed their stand already. The Vathcrians had spoken of a vast communion, mind with mind, on the beacon place of Shansar, but if any were alarmed or welcomed that here, it did not come. Raldnor spoke to them as a prince, cleverly, and fairly. He made them see what was to be gained—but also what might be lost if ever men of the dark races found them, men more willing to make war than they.

"Not so much a mystic as you hoped," Klar said, "eh, Lady Ezlian?"

"We have already had our omens," she said. She had spoken with Raldnor a long while as they walked with Sulvian in the old ruined gardens of Pellea's crumbling palace. Snakes and vermin had lurked everywhere, Klar supposed, but that would hardly have troubled those three.

At dusk the torches in the ancient hall were lit. Light flared on hollow eyes and silent faces.

"What you ask, Raldnor of Vis, is immeasurable," Sorm of Vardath said. "Not merely in terms of battle or of supremacy. I ask you only what we lose when we bow utterly to you?"

Ezlian rose. She lightly placed her hand on Sorm's shoulder.

"If you are to lose anything, my lord, then it's already lost."

Jarred also rose.

"I put my force of arms at disposal of your will, Raldnor, King. I pledge you here and now that your battle is mine."

Sorm said: "This woman at my side speaks for me. Count me your captain, Raldnor, King."

Klar glanced about. He caught suddenly the dark eye of the black-haired man seated at Raldnor's right hand, the one they called Yannul.

"You," Klar bawled, "what've you to say when this fellow traveler of yours takes us off to pillage your racial kin?"

"My sword arm is Raldnor's," the man said, "as will be the sword arms of several of my countrymen. None of us are kin to the Dortharians."

"Then, damn you," Klar said, "I'll take my chance with the rest of you. That's the best omen of all when wolf eats wolf and swears it's jackal."

In the dark Sulvian walked about the garden, where fireflies reflected in the stagnant pools. Beside a broken urn she paused, sensing the quiver in her thoughts, then turned and saw Jarred.

"You shouldn't roam about unescorted," he said.

"Oh, here it all seems very safe. So old and so peaceful. I'm glad that you spoke first with your mind to me."

"I'm rusty. It will improve, I expect. Klar's still planning his campaign with Urgil of Shansar, discussing Jorahan's sea routes. The lower halls are in uproar. It seems they like each other because they can both hold their beer. We must start the levies. Odd that our men will fight so willingly."

"You understand why," she said.

"And you," he said, "are you happy, my sister?"

"Happy?" The intermittent fireflies spangled her hair. "Happy, do you mean, because I shall be betrothed to him, married to him to seal the alliance between his land and ours? Happy, perhaps, that I resemble a woman he once loved?" Jarred was silent. She said: "Oh, I know he will be kind to me. I know he will give me pleasure—that I shall bear his child. Somehow I see all this. I see, too, that he can't love me. It would be impossible. He is beyond love. I shall be the wife of a demon, as if in a story."

"But," Jarred said, "you love him."

"Yes. Of course. I shall never love anyone else now. He made me into that other woman—Anici. He reincarnated her in my flesh. It wasn't intended; it simply happened when I saw myself in his mind."

"This is absurd," Jarred said. "We'll let go this match for Vathcri. Let him have one of Sorm's daughters."

"A child of eight years? No. He must leave his seed here in this land when he leaves it. I think that he will never come back. No, Jarred. I want to bear his child. It's something, if not very much. Oh, this land," she said. "She made us the last part of his journey—only a fragment, a means."

The moon emerged, rising out of the foliage of a tree and opened the garden to its light.

"There's something harsh in moonlight," Sulvian said. "It

scours every shadow. Jarred, when this is over, will we still remain, or will the harsh light scour us away?"

A night bird began to sing somewhere among the overgrowth and ruined terraces. After this, silence hung on Pellea. And on the beaches of the wide lands, south and north, only the sea was moving.

BOOK FIVE

The Serpent Wakes

19

A S HE CAME NEAR the city he saw smokes rising
from it, up into the red drought of the early winter
sunset. Despite the smoke, it was a ruin, a desolation; already the shadows had it. Yannul noted the strip of banner
over the gate—the black dragon of Dorthar. So, she was
occupied, as the vague rumors had suggested out in the
wilds of the Plains. The ruin had been invested with malignant, alien life. Yannul was reminded of certain sorcerers,
mountain charlatans no less evil for being frauds, who
claimed to be able to animate the corpses of the dead with
demons, and make them eat, drink, copulate and dance.

He cursed softly, but his companion kept silent.

They had had a zeeba apiece till the last village, some
twenty miles back. Since then, Raldnor had gone on foot
while Yannul rode. It was a logical expression of their supposed relationship—Vis master and Lowland serf. Yet the
"serf" seemed composed enough with whatever thoughts
he had, whereas Yannul was uneasy, his whole body tense.
The situation fitted him imperfectly, or perhaps it had simply been the long journey with this man, inland from the
dark sickle bay where the Shansarian ship had left them.
They had come by another route from the far land of the
yellow-haired men—a route marked on their ancient maps,

free of fire mountains and fiery water, and dotted with small islands. Yannul had diced and wrestled with the pirates, cracked jokes, drunk and exchanged histories. At the primeval bay, the edge of the Lowlands—unfrequented because it was too near the mouth of Aarl Sea—he had found himself alone with a man who was no longer a man in any human sense. He felt great loyalty to this being. Also compassion, admiration and even a desire to serve him—that ancient tribute inspired by true kings, so legend had it. Yet the old liking and the old companionship were dead. It had been hard on Yannul to travel in this silence and awe across the cold and lonely Plains toward a city of despair.

There were soldiers in the gate.

He swore again. The menacing incongruity worked on him like acid. Amrek's jackals. Yannul spat to clear his mouth of a taste of sick anger.

They reached the ruined walls. Two sentries stepped out and peered at them through the dim vermilion dusk.

"Rein in, traveler. What's your business here?"

"Not mine, my master's. With the Ommos Yr Dakan."

"Oh, yes? Your hard luck then. Who's your master?"

"Kios of Xarabiss," Yannul said. He drew out and showed the nearest soldier a forged letter and seal.

"Hasn't your master heard the Storm Lord's forbidden all trade with the Lowlands?"

"I told you, sir dragon. He's dealing with the Ommos pig." The soldier laughed.

"And who's this ape trundling along with you?"

"My slave," Yannul said. He spat again, in Raldnor's direction. "It saves an extra pack animal."

The soldier, still grinning, drew aside.

"Pass through. And watch out for your needle in the pig's house."

The gateway was black. A weight of years and abysmal solitude pressed on the Lan, yet he, too, grinned, pleased at his acting.

The terrace and the wagon way beyond the gate were

slippery and stinking with decayed fruit. Traders, venturing to ignore Amrek's new trade laws, had had their merchandise tipped out at the gate. The dragons took what they wanted, left the rest to rot. Under this stench came a cold, dull, tomblike odor, the perfume of the doomed city.

There was no sound but the zeeba's hoofs in the long, unlit streets, over which the sunset had suddenly gone out. Yannul saw no lights. The smokes rose in the distance, all in one place. This place, he deduced, was the Dortharian Garrison.

A bell began to toll onerously.

"We will separate here, Yannul," Raldnor said. "You recall how to reach the Ommos?"

"I remember. And you? What if they catch you on the streets when the bell's finished?"

"This spot is close to Orhvan's house," Raldnor said.

He turned and moved off up the street, becoming a shadow among other shadows. Yannul rode left, along the stony, empty roads. The bell rang itself out. No moon rose to alleviate the dark.

Orhvan's house.

No lamps burned. A ceramic vessel lay broken on the steps.

The tall man struck the door with his fist. And on the silence of the place was overlaid a second silence—listening, with fear in its mouth. The man did not knock again; he sent his mind, instead, into the dark house.

Presently a hand drew back bolts. A figure opened the door a little way and beckoned him in. Then the door was closed and rebolted. Not a bar was left out of its socket.

The figure, guiding by mental signals, led across the round hall in the blackness, up stairs into an upper room. Two or three candles flickered here in a candlebranch, giving off the palest, most insubstantial glow. By it, the guest made out his host's face, which had become the face of an old man.

The old man spoke now aloud.

"You're welcome, sir. We've little to offer you. You see we hide like rats up here, afraid even to light a fire. But you were wise to knock on our door once the curfew sounded—lucky, too. This may be the only inhabited house left in the street."

The guest looked about him. An old woman sat in the shadows. On her brocaded flesh was suddenly imposed the memory of a young, pale, beautiful mask.

"Orhvan," the guest said. He pushed back the hood of his cloak and looked full into the faces of the old man and the old woman. "Do you know me now?"

"Why—why—" the old man stammered. Tears, either of emotion or shock, welled in his eyes.

"You are Anici's death," the old woman hissed. She tensed, fluttering like a fragile insect; the venomous pain of her thoughts pulsed in the room. "The death of my daughter's daughter. I only saw you once. That is how I remember you." But she could not meet his gaze with her own. Her hatred guttered before him.

"Now you can speak with your mind," Orhvan said, as if he had not heard her. "Ah, Raldnor, how did it come to you?"

"I was well taught, though in a distant place."

"Oh, what joy to see you." Orhvan took his hand, struggling with the moisture in his eyes. "And yet—why come back at such a time?"

"At such a time, where else, for one of our race?"

"Raldnor, Raldnor—where else indeed. Where else. Have you seen the dragon men?" Orhvan let go his hand and stared into the black corners of the room. "Every night, when the bell finishes, they split themselves into parties, draw lots for which house to visit. They fling in live brands at the windows. If there are women, they use them in the street. Men are flogged to death every day. They invent reasons. Once they caught a man after the curfew. They cut off his hands and feet and nailed them up where he could see them as he bled to death."

The old woman whispered a name like a curse, from the edge of the candlelight: *"Amrek Snake-Arm."*

"No, no," Orhvan said, "Amrek's lying ill at Sar. He sees devils, so they say. No, these are the whims of the Koram-

vian soldiers. They have a commander, a man from Dorthar.
He lets them do as they wish. No matter. We are only cattle
waiting to be butchered. Before the year is out, every hovel
in the city will be emptied. The old will be slaughtered without compunction. The young and the strong they'll take to
the mines of Yllum, to the galleys and the refuse pits. That
was Amrek's promise to us. We shall be his invention—a
race of slaves."

Through the chinks in the broken shutters there came a
spurt of red fire igniting far off across the city.

Orhvan, shuddering, turned from it toward the faint,
flickering candles.

"We have a little food—you must eat—"

"I need nothing," Raldnor said. "Are you alone in this
house?"

"Alone ... yes, Tira and I. ... Yhaheil died—died of a
chill, like an old man—up in the tower room, staring at the
stars. We are alone."

"Then you will be the first in the city to hear me. I did
both of you a great wrong in the past. I have not forgotten."

"Ah, Raldnor, there's too little time to eat bitter bread
together. We've put aside that past, haven't we, Tira?"

Then he felt the current stir and sift in his brain.

"I no longer know you," he suddenly thought. "I wasn't
mistaken. No longer that anguished boy pulled both ways by
his blood, the angry sullen boy whose mind was shut. Now
here is a stranger who commands me, a man I've never met."

The old woman, glimpsing something, whispered in her
mind: "You have come a long way to us. Somewhere your
guilt was purged or lost. Does she rest quiet, then, my little
white-haired baby, my Anici?"

But the man had begun to speak to them. The tide of his
own thoughts bore theirs away like leaves on the wind.

The Ommos was big, a strong-built man succumbing now to
fat. Rings cluttered his hands; a ruby bled on an upper
tooth.

"Well, Lannic traveler, what is it you wish?" The voice was smooth, without a modicum of interest.

Yannul stood his hard-won ground in the hideously frescoed hall. There had already been considerable trouble with the porter.

"I've told your man. I want to speak to your master, Yr Dakan."

"The Lord Dakan is at dinner."

"Splendid. I'll join him. I've eaten nothing since this morning."

The Ommos smiled, snapped powerful fingers and waited while two thickset house guards sidled in from the porch.

"I suggest to you, Lannic traveler, that the dinner might not be to your liking."

There was a smash of timbers a few streets away, the sound carrying harshly over the silent city. The Ommos's slothful eyes shifted involuntarily to the door, and Yannul, tearing aside a curtain, strode into the hall beyond.

Red light submerged the room. A massive Zarok statue dominated the center, its belly flaring poisonous flame. A memory of abominable sacrificial rites griped in Yannul's guts.

Yr Dakan, seated at a low table, looked up startled from his food, a tidbit held halfway to his mouth.

"What's this? Am I not to be allowed to eat in peace?"

Yannul halted in front of him, gave a short bow, and handed him the letter from the imaginary merchant stamped with the false seal.

Yr Dakan set down his meat and took the letter in his greasy fingers.

"Explain. Who sends me this?"

"My master. Kios Am Xarabiss."

Dakan broke the seal even as the Ommos servant appeared between the curtains. Before the man could utter a word, Dakan waved him peremptorily to silence. Yr Dakan read, grunted and looked up.

"You know your master's mind?"

"The lord Kios has considered in some depth the imminent termination of all trade with the Plains."

"A few months, a season, and the Plains will be no more."

"As you say," Yannul smiled, "and what a lot of good things will go for waste—assuming the Dortharians don't find them."

"How perceptive of your master. He is thinking of the village temples, perhaps? Yes. Well, I have a little knowledge of such things. If he is prepared to find means of transport, as he suggests he can, and to see that I am recompensed for my trouble.... He mentions a reasonable sum, but I think my services may be worth more—We shall see. But I will take no risks with the Dortharian rabble—this is to be understood."

"Perfectly, Lord Dakan."

"Orklos," Dakan said, half turning to the servant at his back, "before you shut guests out of my hall, you will inquire into their business."

Orklos stretched his mouth and bowed.

Dakan waved toward the several dishes.

"Eat if you are hungry, Master Lan."

He bent to the letter and reread it.

Yannul took a cup of wine. His hunger had been curbed by tension and fatigue. And it was to be a long night yet, discussing business with the greedy Ommos, upping his fee, assuring him he need have no part in the smuggling—for the merchant clearly understood the Dortharians despised his race almost as much as the Lowlanders. He had not reckoned on a long sojourn in the city once the dragons came there. Some night they might burn his house as readily as the serfs'.

The wine scorched Yannul's throat. Dakan began to amuse him, sinuously avoiding all manner of dangers, not realizing the secret agent at his table was using him and making sure of him for the struggle which was coming.

At midnight Dakan allowed him to seek a bedroom on the upper story. A man led him there, guiding him with a lamp. Yannul had noted several Lowland servants about the place, and this man, too, was a Lowlander. Yannul studied him with a certain uneasy curiosity. He seemed almost entirely fleshless in the creeping lamplight, his eyes craters. At the low-linteled door the man went by to light the lamp beside the bed.

"You serve Yr Dakan, do you?" Yannul asked. Something about the man prompted him to exploration.

"As you see, Lord Lan."

"Do you think you'll be safer from the dragons with a Vis master to look after your hide? Not that there's much of a hide. Do they starve you in this house?"

"Yr Dakan is a good master to those who serve him well," the Lowlander said without expression. The lamp caught suddenly in the pits of his eyes, and Yannul saw a surprising welter of emotion in them; thoughts slid like fish—unrecognizable, yet forever revealed in motion. Yannul sensed pain, a capacity for hate.

"What's your name, Lowlander?"

"Ras."

The dull sibilance disturbed Yannul.

"Well, thanks for the lamp, Ras. I'll say good night."

"No need, Lord Lan. I am only the merchant's slave."

A smile, or some sort of stillborn bastard sister to a smile, briefly altered the Lowlander's mouth as he turned away into the passage.

The blackness dwindled into a gray winter dawn. The Dortharian bell sounded over the city; the curfew was finished for another night. There had been no bells in the Plains, or any other warning. They had brought this brass voice from Marsak, and had repaired the city walls, also, for their own purposes as jailors. Beasts still roamed the streets at night, but on two legs now. Day, a day of cold sun, drew the creatures of the city out of their lairs. The little albino house snakes, on whom the Dortharians stepped when able, slid on the palely sunlit stone ruins. Light-haired men moved in the shadows, dropping back into darker places when soldiers passed on the roads. Trade still persisted—barter, the stuff of life—yet very silently. The whole city smothered beneath its silence. Only the Dortharians made sound.

Of the other races—those part-Lowlanders with the blood of Elyr, Xarabiss, Lan—some, capable of passing as Vis, had fled back to the lands their half blood opened to them, and lived there with a sense of horrified estrangement and precarious safety, and nightmares. Others went to earth in obscure villages of the Plains, or into the deep cellars of the city, even, to exist as brothers to, and in the manner of, rats. The soldiers killed a few for offenses various and bizarre. They were the mark of an ultimate shame and had no right to remain as proof of it Some died without assistance. Yhaheil, the Elyrian astrologer, had done so, seated before the wide, star-filled windows of the icy tower. Despair, not fever, had eaten him—but it was an impersonal, spiritual despair, for he had seen Amrek's genocide written over the sky, and intimations of chaos following it.

With the day, women began to gather at the ancient watering places, carrying their jars, lending to the morning with a sort of normalcy.

On the steps of a well in the northern quarter of the city, they moved aside to let the old woman draw her water first. They were courteous to her age, also to her sorrow, for Tira had outlived both daughter and granddaughter—an almost mystical grief—and lost, too, the companions of her age to illnesses of the hot months and the maladies of fear. Her weed-grown court no longer susurrated to the brittle, moth-wing flutter of their movements, the dry grasshopper rustle of their old women's voices. Nor indeed to anything, for the dragons had long since burnt it out.

Tira bore the brand of these things, and yet today Tira was different. She moved differently; her mind emitted pulses of a curious and definite strength. At the head of the steps she gestured aside the young women's hands offering help, and drew up the water herself. Then she turned, the brimming jar balanced on her hip and by her bone-thin hands. She looked at the women, and suddenly into the mind of each of them fell a single pure shining drop, like a tear of molten gold let fall into the dark water of the well.

There came a rattle of wheels. Down the narrow street galloped a light chariot with two Dortharians in it; it reined to a halt at the watering place. The soldiers called out obscenities at the women who stood there. Their immobility melted, they vanished as swiftly as the night had done. Only an old woman balancing her water jar on her hip was left at the well's head.

"Give us a drink, old bitch!"

The soldier grinned when she came down to him and handed him the jar. He snatched carelessly, pretended to lose hold, and dropped the vessel on the roadway, where it broke. Water gushed out. The soldiers laughed. A bronze whip cracked, and the chariot rushed on.

Tira stood still. They did not see her extraordinary smile. She had dealt in symbols once, and now, changed by the man who had come out of the night, she saw Dortharian blood, not water, running self-spilt down the street.

Four winds howled like demons through the streets of Sar.

On the hill's head a black bull was slaughtered to appease them. A priestess of the shrine, found thieving from the votary offerings, was taken to the sky-stung hill and whipped. Her blood mingled with the dead bull's, but the winds continued to rage. The day was blown away.

At dusk the Guardian of the town bowed himself into the chamber where the Storm Lord sat—had sat, in fact, since he had come here. The walls were hung with thick, dull velvets of a miasmic crimson. Shutters were clamped at the windows, yet the wind spat through and the marble candles guttered. The Guardian's eyes went nervously to his royal guest. Amrek's face had a waxy, fixed pallor, and the lankness of illness had invaded every part of him. He slouched in his chair like a distorted doll, but his eyes had the vivid dangerousness of an animal looking out of a cage. For the thousandth time the Guardian cursed the fate which had struck down his High Lord in Sar, bringing such anxiety and trouble to a peaceful life.

"My Lord," the Guardian ventured, "may I humbly ask you how you're doing? My physician tells me—"

"Your physician is a sour-breathed fool," Amrek said. "You want me away, do you? Out of this refuse pit you're pleased to call Sar. Your weather is a foulness. I can't sleep for the wailing of your filth-laden winds."

"My physician is preparing a draft to encourage your slumbers, my Lord—rare herbs from Elyr—"

"Damn his potions. Let him take it himself and omit to wake up until I'm gone. Besides which, insomnia has become more pleasant to me than my dreams." Shadows and the sickly wavering candlelight fluttered up and down his face like ghastly birds. "The gods," Amrek said, "torture us in our dreams. Has this ever occurred to you, Guardian?"

"My Lord—I—"

"They make sport of us, Guardian. Last night I slept long enough to dream the sky was full of blood. A rain of blood falling on the towers of your wretched little palace."

The Guardian stood staring at him.

"Shall I send for a priest to read the portent of it, my lord?"

"Portent? There's no meaning, Guardian, beyond what is obvious. Men don't dream of what is to come, but of what has been, what's finished." His head dropped forward on his chest as if it were too heavy for him. "That's how the gods make fools of us. By showing us a million times those things we long to forget, those things we aspire to alter and have no power to change. That, Guardian, is how it is done."

The Guardian of Sar shuffled out of the close chamber. The irony that beset his town had not escaped him—the misfortune that Astaris's seducer had named it his place of birth, however fallaciously. In the corridor the man caught himself making the old sign against evil intent, and shame filled his sallow cheeks for fear some underling had seen him.

*   *   *

The yellowish winter dusk filled the city. The bell clanged
dismally. Having emerged at dawn, like the little snakes, the
Lowlanders vanished with the snakes at the first suggestion
of darkness—only the feet and the torches of the Dortharians moved on the empty streets. They played their games
of rapine and death less frequently, for now the ruins seldom yielded prey.

Inside the garrison, fires smoked and voices were loud.
It was an old palace they had put to their use; the wide halls
were well suited as a barracks. Yet age leaned on them in
that place—the crushing presence of time and the accumu-
lations of time. Men drank heavily, and dicing led to brawls.
Overtaken by boredom, they became the meat for bad
dreams. Superstition stirred. How hard must you beat a
Lowlander before he would cry out? And their pale women,
lying in their own blood with eyes filmed over like the eyes
of the blind. By the gods of Dorthar, they would be glad
enough to pack the slaves off into the mines and galleys,
and be done with them. Fear, the begetter of all hatreds,
recalled old tales of Plains witchcraft. They remembered
Ashne'e the demoness, and the curse on Rehdon's line.
Here, in a black box, with the keening of the wind as lulla-
bies around the box's towers, and the icy fingers of drafts
stroking their limbs, the dragon men tossed and muttered in
their sleep, struck at the whores who shared their couches,
fell sick and fell out among themselves.

Three days after a Dortharian had let fall an old woman's water jar in the northern quarter, a patrol in the eastern
sector saw some ten or twelve yellow-haired men talking
together on the steps of a roofless house. The Lowlanders
had a certain gift, an ability, to slip swiftly and unexpectedly
away. Partly, the Dortharians had taught them this art. Only
one man failed to elude them. They cuffed him and dragged
him to the garrison, and into the presence of Riyul, their
commander.

Riyul was a man of Marsak, a soldier fourteen years

since, a mercenary by trade to any land that would buy him, until the profits of his homeland army tempted him. The command of the Plains's garrison had come to him unexpectedly, with Amrek's illness. It made him both imperious and uneasy. He subdued the city by terror, out of deference to Amrek's hate, but also because it came easy to him.

He questioned the Lowlander for an hour, between the strokes of the whipman, as first snow drifted by the windows. Meetings of more than two men at a time were prohibited. The restriction had been a matter of course, until now either observed or unnecessary. The Lowlander bled, but said nothing. Riyul had him slung at last into the cellars of the palace which made such an excellent jail, and left him there to rot. There were no further gatherings, at least none the Dorthanians spotted. There seemed no need to be troubled. The Plains people were a passive, servile race— everyone knew it—with livers pale as their skin.

There was a Lannic juggler in the hall that night, a clever devil who had struck up an acquaintance with a soldier at the garrison gate and wheedled his way in. Riyul threw him a silver piece.

It seemed he had legitimate business of some kind with the Ommos, Dakan, but the interesting thing about him was the talk he started of Lowland whores. Such a creature had never been seen, either in the city or out of it, yet the Lan claimed he had laid skinny blonde bitches galore, who, for a fee or a false promise of safety, would teach all manner of interesting bed tricks.

Riyul's curiosity was whetted; his loins began to disturb him at the thought. Had there not been old stories of temple prostitutes?

Riyul's name day fell in the gray time of the thaw. He had planned to have himself honored then by a makeshift feast in the palace hall, in the manner of a conqueror. He was playing at greatness, a dangerous silly game, in Amrek's absence. Drunk, and lusting for white flesh suddenly in his smoky chamber, he sent the juggler word that if he valued garrison

pickings, he had better make good his boast and provide it
with some Lowland whores on the evening of the feast.

Yannul slept very deeply in the stagnant barracks that
night. A cheerful madness had come on him with the con-
tinuance of the crazy acts he must commit. Vague thoughts
of horror, of blood to come, he set aside. He had no choice.
He had known as much when he rode across the alien summer landscape behind Raldnor, and sensed the stirrings of
chaos underground.

His head heavy with the garrison wine, his last thoughts
had also been of women, though in a temperate vein. Resha,
his Alisaarian girl, for one, who had gone with a Vathcrian
noble to live an unaccustomed life of order and fine clothes.
She, who had initially feared racial enmity, had surprised
Yannul by taking complacent refuge in camouflage. The
Vathcrian had begun to pay her court in the last month at
Vardath, when the nights were red from forge smoke and
the roads rumbled with the passage of the great trees felled
for ships. She must have learned early to survive and ride
her chances aboard the Zakorian pirate. Now, a schooled
opportunist, she accepted her suitor despite all obstacles,
and the matter of his age, for he was well into his middle
years—it made him a safer proposition, clearly. If it was her
novelty that attracted him, however, the noble was to be
sorely tried, for, once their union seemed likely, Resha had
turned like a chameleon. She bleached her hair and began
to use a face paint much like Dortharian Val Mala's famous
white unguent. Yannul rendered Resha all applause, and
hoped her shaky house would stand. There had been no
romance between them but a deal of liking. He only trusted
her stout lover could keep pace with her through the dark.

Whatever else, he guessed she might be happier than the
pale-haired girl, Jarred's sister, they had wed to Raldnor at
the altar of Ashkar Anackire. She had already the look of a
woman who loved deeply and forever, but went unnoticed
in return. Raldnor had been gentle with her, no doubt, but

it would be an impersonal, automatic gentleness. And once the solitary month was up, he had left her and would probably never go back. A great pity, for she had been worth a second look, had Sulvian of Vathcri.

Asleep, Yannul dreamed of the farm in Lan. Snow thick on the hills, icicles stabbing from the roof. His mother happily heavy with child as she seemed perpetually to be, his sisters singing and squabbling at the loom, or nursing birds which had fallen, half-dead from the cold, beside the door. In the second thaw, three thin large-eyed girls holding out handfuls of wings. White birds soaring up from brown hands without a word of thanks; white birds turning black against the blue sky.

On the narrow pallet, Yannul dreamed of home. The ghosts of the palace left him alone.

Over the city the snow moon burned like a lamp of blazing ice. Sentries passed on the wall of the garrison, shivering and cursing.

"Do you hear that sound?" one asked the other.

"What sound? I can only hear my guts freezing."

Yet he sensed also the electric movement of the air, less sound than vibration, a deaf thrumming under their feet, the twanging of a silent harp.

Somewhere, a wolf howled, sharp as a spike.

The sentry grinned.

"Do you remember that old man with the pet wolf—the black bitch Ganlik got with his spear? Lucky devil, Ganlik, with that pelt to wrap up in of a night."

"I've heard Ganlik's sick," the other said.

They separated and moved on. A cloud choked out the moon.

And in Sar, Amrek dreamed of Astaris on the back of a white monster. Her hair bled over her shoulders, and her face was a golden skull.

20

SNOW FLAMED ON THE wind. The wind was on fire with snow.

When the snow stopped, the Plains lay in unbroken whiteness under an exhausted purple sky.

The detachment of soldiers wound in a slow black rope across the blank whiteness of the land. Their business—the urgent provisioning of the garrison—was one they cursed in their various fashions. The makeshift pens, originally packed full of Lowland cattle stolen by Dortharians in warmer months, had grown progressively roomier as the occupation dragged on. Now the snow had come, while Amrek still took his ease in Sar, and the second Siege Snow would not be far behind it. There was talk they might even have to spend the winter here in this stinking verminous hole.

The detachment's captain snarled out his orders and chafed his hands. Frozen to his very bones, he was thinking of a particular woman he had left behind in Dorthar, a bitch he was sure would find other amusements in his absence, and now had all the cold days to catch some filthy disease with which to present him on his return. In addition they had passed one farm holding and a village, both of which had been empty.

The second village showed itself to them two hours after noon, when the sky was already darkening drearily.

The gate in the stockade was wide. They rode through, and up the broad street, the men fanning out, stabbing open doors, peering into the musky gloom of stables and barns. Neither human nor beast remained. Shutters flapped and slapped at windows.

The hooves of the animals pushed the track into mud, and the swinging braziers spat pink phlegm.

A shadow ran suddenly out between the houses, its eyes a leap of flame. With hoarse nervous shouts men leveled spears at it.

"Wolf!"

But the thing vanished like a spirit.

"Ride on," the captain bawled.

They overtook no one and found no footsteps in the snow.

The next village, the third, was nearer—only a mile or so.

Some plates lay broken in the road, partly covered by snow. A heavy silence welled up to meet them. They searched and found nothing. Once there came the whirr of a wheel on a loom, but it was the wind that turned it.

"They're running," the captain grunted. "Where?"

This time a few men slipped aside to see what might be picked up in the way of loot—people who moved in such apparent haste must surely leave valuables behind. They did not find a single metal ring. In the gloomy temple building not a golden scale remained.

Leaving the abandoned village, they strained their eyes for any sign of movement across the aching white waste of the Plains.

A luminous dusk soaked into the sky.

Far off, over the shadowy mirror of land, the captain glimpsed a thing, a shape, that might have been two men on zeebas, or only a trick of the gloaming. Fresh snow began to fall.

The captain sneezed and wiped his nose. He ordered the

column back toward the deserted village and a chilly comfortless night's camp.

On the scarp the two pale-haired men sat still on their zeebas, watching the Dortharians trample back through the stockade and, presently, the mauve smokes rise up.

The snow did not trouble them. The childhood of each had been spent in some holding of the Plains—their later life in the ruined city. For bread they had become the servants of Dakan the Ommos. They were well used to the raw cold and eternal hunger, and hardship of a hundred sorts.

One man glanced at the other, speaking without words. They turned the heads of their mounts.

The Ommos thought they were at his work, gathering gold for a nonexistent merchant of Xarabiss with Yannul the Lan. The Ommos had therefore provided the pass that enabled them to leave the city and roam the Plains at will. Certainly there was a tiny priceless statue and a heap of gems in their saddlebags as proof of their supposed errand. Yet their mission was a different one.

There had been an old woman, and a single shining thought dropped into dark water. Ripples had spread from that drop, ripples of the mind across the black stagnant well of the city. Only they knew what the golden thing meant to them, but such was its purity that it was totally communicable. At each village, each farm, the two messengers passed on their vision, Raldnor's vision, unaltered, still perfect, through the unclouded medium of mental speech, passed it like fire from torch to torch, until the whole surface of the Plains would be burning. The change, where it came—and soon it would come everywhere— was entire. A sleeping serpent, coiled in the brain, always present, never until now awake, had been wakened, as if it had been foretold. Promontory slid into recess; groove fitted with groove in a jigsaw of destiny, abruptly engaged.

Through the falling snow, the two Lowland men rode over the scarp and silently on into the night with their invisible fire.

*   *   *

Under the city's ancient gateway the host poured, from dawn till dusk. The Lowlanders came with their wagons, their livestock and their belongings piled in carts. The Dortharian wall guard was doubled. They sat their animals in the deadly cold, working off their anger on the Plains people. They snatched bits of amber and thin gold chains off the necks of the women.

They assumed the snow had caused the sudden influx— also fear of the soldiers of the provisioning detachment. Certainly the scum had brought food enough for the garrison with them. If any starved, it would not be the Am Dorthar.

That day, too, Yannul came back to Yr Dakan's house, the Lowland men riding behind him with their bags of jewels. The Ommos examined the treasures greedily. He ran his pudgy fingers over the breasts of the Anckira statue, but their coldness seemed to repel him.

"Little enough in stones," he said, "but She—She is worth something."

"So Kios will think," the Lan answered.

"And when will your employer expect you?"

"Not till the Snow's done, the spring thaw. There may be other stuff I can lay hands on besides, at the bottom of all those wagons that have come into the city."

"Don't forget that I have helped you, Master Lan."

"Indeed, Lord Dakan, you can rest assured."

Under the snow, time paused in the city.

In the white-crusted ruins wagons camped about the stone-ringed fires. Smoke rose more frequently, for the Dortharians seldom now troubled the dark. The cold of the Plains was too bitter for them. Besides, they were sullen, trapped in this tomb with their captives, and discontent robbed them for a while of pleasure in their sadistic sports.

There came a night of iron stars.

Long after the curfew had fallen, a piece of movement

came silently through the streets. It was a thing of shadow, like a ghost; avoiding the routes of the Dortharian patrols, it slid at last into the inky porch of Orhvan's house and sent a mind like a pale blade searching through the walls.

Orhvan soon came and led the shadow into an upper room, where a small fire now burned and flickered. Firelight fell harsh then on the bone-white angles of hands, and fell back from the hooded face. It was a priest.

"Raldnor," Orhvan said.

Sparks ignited briefly within the hood as the priest's eyes turned and fixed on what was sitting perfectly still before him—a figure as dark, as enigmatic as his own.

"You call this man Raldnor," the priest said softly, "who claims to be our King."

A voice came from the figure.

"Call any man a king; it will not alter him. Call a king by some other name, he is still a king."

"I speak to you with my mouth," the priest said, "because your mind is too expressive for my needs, and conveys too much. You have let fall a thought, woken a snake in the brain of our people. They have never seen you, but their minds visualize you as a myth, half king, half god. I dispute nothing of this. Nor the vision of another land, which I too have been shown in that chain of minds which has spread from yours. For all the years of our race, we have been passive, meek, submitting rather than observing the rules of war. The Vis set their heel on our necks for centuries. The heel crushed us, but taught us to endure. You have found out our secret—the serpent coiled in our soul. By this abstract yet entire thought you have implanted, you have said this: They who endure more, are more; they who suffer most can accomplish most. You, who master yourselves, can master others. You who possess the speaking mind should not bow down beneath the yoke of the deaf, the blind and the dumb. You have given us hubris. That was the unborn serpent in our core. You have hatched the serpent's egg; you have woken us. But it is the double-edged sword. After you have taught us to be cruel, can you teach us to be humble once again, in time, thrust us back inside the broken shell and seal it, before we rend ourselves?"

"We must live for each moment as it comes," the voice said to him, "neither in our past nor in our future. Should we fail to wake at this moment, we shall be destroyed forever. Those who sleep will die in their sleep. There will be no survivors of Amrek's scythe."

"You are the dual child, both bloods. This is very clear."

"I am an amalgam that had eventually to be formed," the voice said. "The era has called forth both myself and Amrek, the black tyrant. We are figments of the destiny of our separate peoples. No more."

"They who said they were your messengers summoned us here from the Shadowless Plains. They said tonight you will speak to us, your mind encompassing every other Lowland mind in the city. Can you do this? I, too, have felt it to be so."

A coal burst suddenly in the fire. The priest caught the glimpse of a face that seemed cast from dark metal, and two burning eyes of a strangely colorless icy gold. The eyes appeared to be without soul. Only purpose, only power was behind them.

"Indeed," the priest thought, "you are no longer a human man."

"I am the golem of the goddess."

The terrible jest filled the priest's brain. He lapsed by their fire to wait.

At midnight there came a peculiar intensity over the city, like the brittle contraction, the unseen shimmer that precedes a storm.

The Dortharians spoke in loud, broken whisperings about the streets. In the garrison, men swore and swilled their wine. The air hummed. Yannul the Lan lay stiff as starch in the Ommos bed, feeling the city moving as though a torrent rushed under its roads.

The rain broke early as the snow had been late. Yet it was an uncertain, fickle thaw; flakes still met in silver spirals, though the gutters ran with mud.

These bright spinnings beat on the shutters of Yr Dakan's chamber as Ras moved noiselessly across it and swung down the bronze candle wheel and snuffed its lights. On the floor an erotic painting of young men throbbed in the glow of a plum-colored lamp.

Yr Dakan lay in the big bed, eating sweets. Sometimes a girl would lie beside him awaiting his intentions, or a boy, or possibly both. Tonight the space was empty.

Ras crossed to the bed and stood looking down.

"What do you want?" Dakan demanded irritably.

"Lord Dakan," Ras said softly, "since I came to you I have been an obedient servant."

Dakan said lazily: "You'd have felt the lash otherwise."

"Lord Dakan," Ras whispered, his face unchanging, "tomorrow night, one of this household will kill you."

Dakan started up, letting fall a nibbled delicacy.

"Who?" he rasped. His eyes glittered with shock. "Who?"

"Any one of us, Lord Dakan. Perhaps Medaci, the girl who bakes your bread. Perhaps Anim, who looks after your stable. Perhaps myself."

Liverish anger rushed into Dakan's sickly face.

"Zarok has burnt a hole in your brain. You're mad. I shall have you whipped tomorrow."

"A good measure, Lord Dakan. Don't spare the thong. Beat me senseless. Cut off my hands so I can't grip a knife to harm you with."

Dakan caught Ras a blow across the face.

"Tomorrow I will have Orklos deal with you."

Ras said expressionlessly: "There is talk of a king. Do you remember Raldnor of Hamos? He's instructed us to murder every Vis in the city, Lord Dakan. Tomorrow, on his signal, at the seventh hour after sunset."

"Zarok has scorched you," Dakan repeated, but his

heavy face was heavier with fear. Eventually he said: "How do you know all this?"

Ras's smile was a stillbirth which scarcely altered his mouth.

"My mind. Have you never heard the tale that the people of the Plains talk inside their heads?" He turned and walked to the curtained doorway and looked back. "Kill all your Lowlanders, Yr Dakan," Ras said. "Kill us before the snake stirs in us. Then bar your door."

It was still very cold.

The two soldiers who set out every five days for the gust-battered town of Sar, taking Riyul's report to the Storm Lord, kicked their beasts into a lather, and damned the mail that clung to them like a second skin of ice. Those who remained in the garrison slept badly at night; by day they hanged Lowlanders in an ancient marketplace.

On the morning of Riyul's name day the clouds were lined with a thin skim of gold, as if a split wine gourd had spilled over.

Yr Dakan came late to the table.

"I hope you're in good health," Yannul said.

Dakan did not look well. He grunted.

"Tell me," he muttered, "do you think there is something abroad in my house—some conspiracy against me?"

"Who would dare such a thing?"

"My slaves—my Lowland slaves . . ."

Yannul let out a sharp laugh.

"Lord Dakan—you leave me speechless. The lily-livered rubbish are incapable of violence. Besides, how could they escape punishment if they had such a plan? Amrek's soldiers would be only too glad of the excuse to butcher the lot."

"One of my servants has told me that there will be an attempt upon my life tonight," Dakan said.

"Who?" Yannul knew at once his question had been too

ready. He added swiftly, "Whoever told your lordship such a thing's a madman."

For some reason an instantaneous picture had formed in his brain—of the thin, strange-eyed Lowlander who lit the lamp on his first night in the city. "But no matter," he thought. "Whoever blurted, there's no stopping now."

Dakan's face relaxed.

"Yes, the man who told me this is mad. I have long suspected it. I will bar my door," he added to himself, "a mere precaution . . . where will you be beyond sunset?"

Yannul, who had never seen fit to speak of his second role in the garrison, slyly drooped one lid.

"A little Elyrian," he murmured, carefully not stipulating his invention's sex, "has offered me entertainment for the night."

By noon the Dortharians were in the streets, selecting Lowland girls for Riyul's feast. Their acts of rape had taught them to be generally unafraid of the old reputed sexual magics of the Plains women. They were, it was true, all bones— frigid, unwilling bitches. But part of Riyul's wine ration had already gone round in the garrison, and the soldiers regarded these skinny makeshift wenches cheerfully enough.

The women collected in the chariots with an expected pathetic docility. Some wept—slow tears without sound. The Dortharians did not notice that their eyes held a crystalline hardness in them, like zircons.

The men pulled up their skirts, cuffed them, and laughed at them, and eventually left them to the mercy of the garrison whores, who spat in their faces as they wound ribbons like colored weeds through their hair.

At last they huddled in the dark like dolls made of rags, in their gaudy anklets and glass beads, and with blank faces and trembling bodies. Their hard, cold, wise, and terrible eyes were fixed on the flags.

Night fell and thickened. A thin layer of snow gilded the streets. In the fifth hour after sunset ice formed like glass.

Inside the palace hall the torches had blazed since dusk, and carcasses turned on the great hearths, spitting fat. Three quarters of the garrison was present, lolling at the tables, steeped now in the plentiful wine and beer. A troupe of dancers, of mixed Elyrian and Lowland blood, had been caught lingering in the city at twilight. Brought in to entertain, they turned somersaults with anxious eyes, while their girls tremulously shook strings of bells. They understood well enough that they might be given money tonight, but flogged into pulp in the morning. Amrek had no mercy for their kind.

Riyul sat in his place in tarnished finery—a couple of defaced gold armlets, loot from an old war in Thaddra, and a grease-spattered scarlet shirt. A soldier had died the night before, and Riyul had appropriated the black wolf pelt from among his belongings, and wore it now on his own back. He was very drunk, as were his men. It was late that he recalled his new lusts.

He looked about for the juggler.

"You there, Lan," Riyul shouted, catching sight of the man at a lower table, "you've been gorging our meat, but have you kept your word, eh?"

"My word, Lord Riyul?"

"These temple trulls you idle with—where are they?"

The Lan grinned.

"Outside, my lord."

A ragged cheer went up. Men banged their wine cups on the board.

One of Riyul's aides was sent lurching to the hall's single entrance. When the big door was opened, into the oppressively close air blew a gust of the vicious night. The torches curled and smoldered.

"Bring 'em here!" Riyul roared.

The silence of curiosity fell on the feasters.

The little Lowland girls, employed until now as servitors, turned their pale faces and stared. The garrison whores muttered spiteful sarcasms.

The three women the tipsy officer now shoved into the hall wore saffron shifts, slit at the sides from ankle to thigh. Their arms and legs were bare gleaming whitenesses, each naked limb painted with the golden rope of a serpent. Their flaxen hair hung down their backs in coils; their lips and the lids of their eyes were stained with gold. They grinned as they came up the room to Riyul and thrust out their breasts. No man there had ever set eyes on a Lowland prostitute. There was an odd wickedness in their paper faces, leering mouths, and shimmering skin.

The Lan had edged over to Riyul's chair.

"Temple girls," he murmured. "I told them your lordship might be disposed to save them from the mines if they pleased you sufficiently. Whether you do so is your business, but have no doubt they'll supply their best tricks for you tonight."

Riyul gave a low drunken laugh.

"Engaging sluts."

The first girl had reached Riyul's place. She set her hands on the table top and vaulted lightly to sit among the gravy-crusted trenchers. Despite her full breasts, she was thin. Yannul saw the sharp bones of her hips stab momentarily through her shift. Curiously, the contrast stirred him, and he also, in that macabre instant, hardened for her core. His lust disconcerted him, knowing, as he did, what was to come.

She sat there, smiling, her eyelids flashing, while Riyul maneuvered his paw under the flap of her skirt. Suddenly she raised her long arms and began a sinuous torso dance, stretching and weaving like a snake. The two other girls drew narrow pipes out of their saffron. A formless, wandering melody came from their fingers and slid about the big room.

In Dakan's hall, the Zarok god waited, like a beast that must be fed.

Yr Dakan had taken it into his head to eat in his chamber, and the hall was in darkness save for the coals in Zarok's belly. Lit by its own flame light, the thing glared through the shadows, the long points of its teeth seeming to drip blood.

Orklos came late with the tray of slops; behind him the slave girl Medaci carried in narrow hands a vase of wine. The glow out of Zarok's oven stained her hair bright gold, like the glass in a palace window. It showed a bruise mark where someone had struck her across the mouth, and her glistening eyes, boring into Orklos's back.

With the stone shovel, Orklos replenished the coals and waited until flames sprang and crackled. Then he threw in the rinds of his master's meal and watched the fire consume them. Orklos turned and took the vase, thrusting the shovel into Medaci's hands.

He began to pour wine into the fire, lazily, aware of nothing save his task. His back to her, he did not see the sudden shudder that ran over the girl's body.

She raised the shovel and struck at Orklos's skull.

Stunned by this first blow, the Ommos staggered and the wine vase shattered at his feet. Raising herself on tiptoe, Medaci struck a second time with all her strength, and again, and again, until blood ran. Then, as the man tottered, she dropped the shovel and pushed at him with both her hands. As he fell, his head went into the oven.

Above, there came a crash and splintering of wood.

On the table top, the Lowland girl glared down at Riyul with her golden eyes.

Riyul was prepared to be good-natured.

"Look all you want at me, bitch," he encouraged. "You'll see more of me later."

He raised his cup and was drinking deeply when the girl's hand shot forward and buried a dagger to its hilt in his chest. Riyul grunted at her stupidly while wine spilled out of his mouth; then he fell into her lap, splashing her with crimson.

Yannul moved back from the table. Expectancy had not been enough. He tasted bile, for what he saw was nightmare.

The dragons had brought only women to their feast, planning to use them, when the festivities were at their height, in the orgiastic manner of the ancient feasts of Rarnammon. And these women had struck simultaneously, with daggers, with knives from the table, with heavy stone drinking cups. Thick blood ran on the flags and smeared the walls.

Those men still living were too drunk and too dumbfounded to retaliate. They watched the Lowlanders run toward them and did nothing to prevent the swooping blades, like beaks of thirsty birds. The thing was too sudden, and too terrible and too unlooked-for. In death, their faces were masks of surprise. Those who staggered toward the single door, stumbled on the heaped bodies of their officers and subordinates. Those who reached the corridors beyond the arch screamed out in frustration and fear.

Lowlanders had killed the sentries at the same moment that the women struck inside the garrison and were now bounding through the complexes of the building, seeking further prey.

All through this Yannul stood rooted to the spot. There was something unutterably horrible in the sight of these Lowland girls, their faces blotched, their hair striped with hot blood, killing and killing, without thought or hesitation, like machines with eyes of blanched steel.

Yet their hatred was discriminating. They did not touch him or the group of Elyrians at the center of the hall. They ran round them and past them, as if they were no more alive than other furniture which must be avoided. In honesty, neither he nor the Elyrians moved at all. Dazedly, he watched their own dazedness.

He had never shirked a fight in his life, but this fight was not his. For a long while he would remember every detail and, it seemed, every red-stippled face.

The garrison sentries who, unlike the men in the hall, had worn scale plate, lay with their throats open. A new soft snow fell over them and dropped into their wide eyes and mouths.

In the garrison there was a sudden quiet.

In Riyul's hall, the Dortharians' whores were too fearful to set up the keening that betokened death. They huddled by the fire pits, idiot-faced from fright.

In the web of streets that stretched away from the gate, dragon soldiers lay on their faces like broken toys under the falling, falling snow.

Yannul made his solitary way back toward the house of Yr Dakan. Frequently he passed the dead, their torches smoking on the paving, which was marbled with their persistent blood.

Sometimes, but not often, Lowlanders went by him, silent as wolves in the snow. Their eyes gleamed at him like icy moons, but they left him alone.

He was sick, and to his very soul. Not only because of what he had seen, but because of his part in it. He had hated and despised the Dortharians. Now, with an abrupt disintegration of purpose, he discovered a massacre of drunken babies, and discovered, too, the color of his skin and hair in this place of the yellow-haired men. And he had come to fear the Lowlanders, these people he had so pitied — to fear their awful certainty and efficiency, and their union of minds.

When he came to Dakan's house, the guards were lying under the porch. The doors were wide open, but no lamp burned in the foyer. There was a faint glow seeping out of Dakan's hall, presumably from the belly of the fire god.

He entered the archway and mounted the stairs to the upper apartment. Another Ommos lay here, a vicious boy whom Yannul recognized as one of Dakan's playthings.

Dakan's door, bolted as he had promised, had been forced inward, the iron bar torn out of its socket. Dakan himself lay across the bed, his eyes accusing the ceiling.

Yannul turned, taking with him the small lamp at the

bedside. It threw gesturing shadows on the walls. Apart from the dead, the place seemed unoccupied.

Then, in the foyer again, he heard the sound—long retching sobs—and he smelled too, suddenly, the disgusting stench that hung about the entrance to the hall.

He went in, past the drawn curtain, and held up the lamp to see.

An indescribable thing hung, half-in, half-out of Zarok's oven, smoking still. Nearer, crouched by the table, was Medaci, the kitchen girl. Her hands were clutched at her stomach, and her eyes were shut until the new light struck them. She stared at him, then jumped to her feet and ran at the doorway, trying to escape by him into the foyer beyond. When he caught her shoulders, she screamed out, although he had been careful not to hurt her. After a second her eyes cleared. She seemed to recall who he was. She flung herself against him and buried her head in his chest, yet she was so thin he hardly felt the impact of her flesh.

"Why was I made to kill him? Why did Raldnor make me kill him? He came into my mind, and I beat and beat with the stone shovel—"

Yannul stroked her hair, and she wept like a child after a bad dream, longing only to be comforted.

"It had to be done," he said. The words came without thought, answering his own question as well as hers. "It's over now, and you're safe."

"Don't leave me," she said into his chest.

Did she remember, as he had, the color of his skin and eyes? Or had these things become irrelevant for her in the aftermath?

When he felt the tension slackening in her body, he led her out into the street and lifted her onto one of Dakan's zeebas and took her to Orhvan's house.

The one dragon soldier left living in the city strained his eyes toward the dawn. He had spent the night trussed to a pillar in the vault under the garrison, where a crack of a window looked out of the earth bank into a paved court. In the night the window had not proved friendly. The wind had haunted him through it, and bloody arms and hands had snatched at him, whether in hallucination or reality he was not sure. He had seen his comrades die in the hall, and in his drunken terror had run out into the stone corridors, hearing the ghastly din behind him. He had hidden himself under the cot of a sick soldier, whose throat, he had time to notice, had been sliced from ear to ear. Here he vomited up Riyul's wine and lay in the stink of his own sickness, afraid to move or search for weapons.

About an hour later, two Lowland men had come into the room and pulled him out, gibbering with shock. It was as though they had known of his presence there for some time.

He thought they would run a blade into him and be done with it, but instead they dragged him down into the black cellars of the palace and bound him to a pillar. There was a dead Lowlander lying by another.

When the dawn filtered in to him, he heard them at the door. The dim light fired their pale hair; their eyes were like splinters of flame. He could not read their faces, but he knew that they were no longer slaves.

One of them loosed his bonds.

"A pleasant day for a hanging," he remarked, swallowing nausea.

"You're not to die," said the Lowlander. "The Storm Lord has asked for you."

"Amrek?" Incredulous, the soldier felt he had, after all, lost his wits in the night.

"Raldnor," the Lowlander said, "Rehdon's son."

They took him by alleys to a dark house and left him in the circular hall. He thought of chancing an escape, but could think of no refuge in this hostile city. He had seen them dragging the bloody corpses into an open place, and burning them. The Lowlanders always burned their dead.

When the man came, the soldier was astounded. A Vis, he thought at first, until he saw the hair. Then something struck him—a name, and a face. He started violently at the crippled hand.

"Dragon Lord!" he exclaimed.

"You know me."

"You're Raldnor of Sar, Amrek's—" The soldier fell silent in horror. Here stood the dead, for Amrek had had this man killed, had he not—the seducer of Astaris Am Karmiss.

"You will do me a service," the undead said to him.

The soldier trembled and mouthed words which never came.

"You will carry a message to my brother Amrek." The eyes leveled on the soldier, held him trapped and unpleasantly aware, burning the words into his skull. Irrationally, intolerably, yet without a doubt, the soldier knew that whatever mission this man gave him must be accomplished. It was inescapable as a geas. "Tell Amrek that his father Rehdon is my father also, that my mother was Ashne'e the Lowland woman. Remind him of the laws of Dorthar, that I was sown two months later than his sowing in Val Mala's womb, that therefore I am the Storm Lord. Tell him that I freely lend him the months of the second snow in which to put his affairs in order and to relinquish his throne. When the snow is ended, if his place is not mine, I will drown Koramvis in the blood of his people."

The soldier shuddered and half began to weep. This man was no ghost who could make these demands of the living.

"If I speak to him as you say—he'll kill me—"

"Dragon," the man said to him, "it will not trouble me if you die."

The soldier cringed and covered his face against the phenomenal eyes. Here was no hatred, and no mercy either—nothing. Nothing in this man sought vengeance. Similarly he contained no mechanism for pity.

Men and women crowded to look down from the snow-rimmed towers of Sar.

The winds had abated, yet there was little enough to

amuse them with half the theaters respectfully closed, and the wine shops full of Amrek's Guard. Now there was a rumor, a wild story—they watched the solitary Dragon ride into the square before the Guardian's palace, a train of about twenty camp whores trailing behind him. Abruptly Amrek appeared at the head of the outer stairway, a startling black figure against the vivid snow.

"What's your news, dragon?"

The soldier fell to his knees.

"Storm Lord—the Lowland garrison has been destroyed, every man in it killed except for myself."

"What?" The dry voice rang with an unstable, hollow derision. "A whole garrison gone and only one worm left to crawl out of it? Who did this miraculous thing? Banaliks?"

"My Lord, I swear—it was the Lowlanders. They struck all together in a space of minutes—How could we know, my Lord, that they'd find a leader?"

"A leader." Amrek's hands twitched at his sides; his mouth curled. He came slowly down the stairway into the square.

"They let me live—to bring his message to you," the man cried. Amrek stopped still. There was no sound. "They took me to this man. He said—he said his father was also yours— Rehdon, the High King. His mother, the Lowland witchwoman. He says—says he was conceived after your lordship—that by the old laws this—makes him the Storm Lord—he demands the throne of Dorthar, or else . . ." The man faltered on the rash, impossible threat which, in that round dark hall, had seemed so immutable, so certain. "My Lord, he swears he will drown Koramvis in the blood of her people if he isn't acknowledged by the snow's end."

Amrek laughed. It was a melodramatic, insane noise to fill the dead silence.

"This man—this *King,*" Amrek said harshly, grinning, "who is he, this lord of scum?"

It was a rhetorical question. Yet it had, so curiously, an answer.

"Raldnor of Sar," the soldier choked out, unable to help himself. "Raldnor of Sar, your Dragon Lord—"

Amrek's blow split his lip; he tasted blood in his mouth.

Amrek screamed at him: "You're lying to me! Who paid you, you filth, to lie to me?"

The soldier lay on his face. Amrek turned, and turned again, screaming at the high walls: "All liars! Damn you! Damn your lies!"

He circled the court, yelling at them, beating the air with his hands. Suddenly his eyes rolled back. He fell and twitched on the ground, writhing and sprawling in the middle of the empty space. No one approached him. They were too afraid to help him. He seemed possessed by an ultimate and inescapable demon.

Then, abruptly, the fit was finished. He lay quite still.

To those watching from the towers, he was a black cross against the snow.

21

THE HIGH COUNCIL HAD been formed in haste in the palace on the Avenue of Rarnammon. Many were absent, keeping to their beds on this chill and inauspicious day and sending word their physicians would not let them rise. Mathon, the Warden of the Council, rubbed nervously at his cold hands. He was an old man who had been elected for his safe vacillating and his well-known lack of ambition— and this situation was quite beyond his ability.

Sharp-faced and sick-eyed, Amrek sat in the dragon-legged chair. He had recovered from the terrible spasm at Sar, only to ride to Dorthar with all the frenzy of a madman. The treacherous thaw had ended, and the snow was falling heavily by the time he reached Migsha. It did not dissuade him. He tore across the caravan tracks of the Plain lands and the hills, camping at night in a sodden tent and traveling through blizzards that sent him blind for two days in the Ommos town of Goparr, his chariot clogged to the wheels in snow. His Guard fell behind. He lost them and left them to the wolves and the deadly cold, and to struggle after as best they could. He crossed the Dortharian border with ten men at his back. He rode unknown through Koramvis and came immediately to the Council Hall. The mud-stained cloak he had worn lay on the floor behind the chair.

"Well, we are agreed then," Amrek said. "No army of Dorthar can march until the snow is done. Word must go to Xarabiss. She's a lazy land, but has enough troops to quell a Plains rabble."

"My gracious lord," Mathon said, "I fear Xarabiss will evade such work."

"She's a vassal," Amrek said, "and will obey. Send a messenger to that effect."

The Council was silent. They had heard rumors out of the Lowlands, even ahead of Amrek's crazy race. They did not care to exacerbate him further.

From the edge of the room came a man's voice, a voice made unmistakable by its Zakorian slur, that gift of his dam.

"There is one small matter which disturbs me." An uneasy movement ran over the chamber. It was like Kathaos Am Alisaar to touch baldly upon a point which, until now, they had so scrupulously avoided.

"Your Lordship's soldier claimed that the Lowlanders' 'king' was Raldnor the Sarite."

Amrek's black eyes glared unseeingly.

"The fool was mistaken."

"A mistake of unusual magnitude, my lord." Kathaos paused, allowing the Council to see, by inference, how Amrek permitted his judgment to be clouded by his jealousy and shame. "My lord, surely it should be considered that if the Sarite lives, suspicion falls on a Commander of these same armies we all trust to defend this city. You'll recollect that Kren, Dragon Lord of the River Garrison, informed us, without a doubt, that Raldnor was dead."

"I recollect."

"Then surely, my lord—"

Amrek was on his feet.

"We'll have Kren here to answer your charges."

The Council sat frozen.

"Damn you, Mathon, move yourself! Send a Council guard to escort Kren here."

"Storm Lord, you've not yet rested—"

"Rest be damned. Do as I tell you."

"And if he declines to come?" Kathaos murmured.

"Then I shall make him come."

Nevertheless, this Amrek could not do. Garrison it was, and fortress too, built, long before the wharfs and hovels had grown up about it, as a defense of the river. Battlements surrounded the buildings inside; the place was stocked with food and drink and a community of men and women entirely loyal to Kren. It could withstand a year of siege, but the streets and houses around it could not.

To Amrek's demand, Kren returned the courteous message that he was sick and could not leave his bed, but that he would welcome the Storm Lord's person at any time he cared to approach the gates.

Mathon paled on hearing this, fearing some endless strife was about to tear the city in half.

"We must send a party of Councilors to the Dragon Lord. We must try to persuade him to reason."

Amrek thrust past them and, with his improvised escort, rode to the Garrison gate.

He stood in the chariot like a supplicant, his face yellow with fatigue. The red-cloaked sentry saluted him and presently led him in.

Kren was waiting for him on his feet, and without a trace of subterfuge.

"You seem in excellent health to me, Dragon Lord," Amrek remarked.

Kren smiled.

"Shall we say, my lord, the sight of such an illustrious visitor has done me good."

"Kathaos suggests that your reluctance to present yourself before the Council proves your guilt conclusively."

"All suggestions, perhaps, should be considered carefully, my lord. Do you believe the Sarite lives?"

Amrek's glance faltered like a candle.

"You must tell me that, Kren."

"There is a grave within these walls, my lord."

"Yes. I believe my mother sent her guard to make sure of that. She was very anxious for my honor at that time. Is it the Sarite's grave?"

Kren's steady eyes met his own.

"Indeed, my lord, it is. Is there some proof I can offer you?"

"Your word will do, so I've heard."

"That, my lord, without hesitation, you have."

And yes, he had buried the Sarite there, the invention that had been the mask of a man he had enlightened and made whole, and broken at the same instant.

When his royal guest was gone, Kren stood some time alone in the shadowy room.

The early dusk was numbing the bitter whiteness of the palace courts. The mountains loomed on the distant sky like threatening clouds.

The cold dazzled Amrek's eyes. Coming from the chariot, he stumbled and seemed to hang above a gaping vault of blackness before one of the Guard caught his arm.

Crossing a room where the lamps were already lit, a woman came rustling toward him in glimmering brocades. He looked up from his stupor and saw his mother, Val Mala.

He pushed away the supporting arm and glared into her white painted face. How beautiful she was still, this mother. Would her arms have been a comfort to him if they had ever spared him a moment's solace when Kathaos and Orhn and the others had done with them?

"Well, madam. You've heard."

"Yes, I've heard everything. I've heard that the Lowlanders sent you packing from their dunghill. I've heard that you rode like a peasant across three lands, and after that went begging to Kren. What a son I've made. The midwives must have turned me in my labor so that I lay on your brain and crushed it."

He watched the diamonds glittering in her hair and ears. Their refractions made him dizzy and sick.

"You tell me you hear all these things, madam, yet you've never heard what happens to a woman with a Lowlander's face. You'll use another unguent, madam, before I see you next."

"What faith you have in my obedience, Amrek. I am your mother," she said with spiteful sweetness.

"And I, madam, am your King, distress you as it may. If I chose, I could send you to the fire for your whoring."

For a second he saw how afraid of him she was; a bitter triumph surged through his veins, like a poisonous yet refreshing drug.

But she said: "No, Amrek. This is your sickness. You confuse me with another."

In the black ruin on the Plains, anvils rang, and the makeshift forges turned the night clouds red. Into the melting pots went iron caldrons, brazen bowls, the accumulated metal of the villages, the bolts from city doors; in went the armor taken from the bodies of dead dragons, those eight hundred men who had perished in a single hour. New swords lay stacked in empty houses—also shields and metal plates to guard the chest, back and limbs.

All the while, like an ally, the three-month snow fell into the cup of the Plains.

In those first white days, six men left the city. Three rode northeast, to Lan.

They were many days on the Plains. It was hard going in the snow, yet not impossible. The two Lowlanders bore all difficulties stoically. Yannul the Lan, exasperated by their silence, cursed and sang in his saddle. On the whole he did not feel too bad, yet nervous as a boy going to his first woman, riding back home on this ironic errand.

When they crossed into the little land of Elyr, the snow was falling fast. In a matter of miles, they passed five or six dark towers—astrologers' roosts, each with a single dim light burning high up.

It was not a long passage through Elyr. Near dawn, on the border of Lan, Yannul saw two wolves, their smoking jaws clamped in some edible death. They stared with red eyes and red drooling mouths, and their spit steamed in the snow. Yannul thought unpleasantly of omens.

The King was young, only a child. He held a kalinx kitten on his knee as he listened gravely to what Yannul said, and, at his side, his sister-wife listened also. Yet it was to the King's advisors that Yannul spoke in actuality as they stood behind the bone chair, toying with pieces of quartz.

When he was done, however, they waited on the boy to speak first.

"You are a Lan," the King said, in his high boy's voice, "yet you'll fight for the Lowlanders. Why is this?"

"The man who sent me, my King, has inspired me to fight for him."

"How? By promise of reward?"

Yannul smiled wryly, seeing the child was wise beyond his years.

"No, my King. His cause is just, as I've explained to you. Also he was a friend."

"Was?"

"Now he's a king, as you are. It makes it harder to be close to those around you."

The boy nodded. Clearly, this much he had already learned. Then, in a controlled but eager tone, he asked: "And this other land—tell us, Yannul, about that place."

Later, the councilors went away to discuss what should be their policy, and the boy talked seriously to Yannul, while the little girl Queen smiled serenely. His heart burst with absurd pride in them. When he was an old man, or even if he did not live to be one, this pair, full grown, would rule well in Lan.

"You must understand, Yannul," the King said to him, "that if I were older, I would lead my people to fight for the

Lowland King. But I know what they'll say. They will say that not only Dorthar, but Zakoris and Alisaar hate the Lowlanders, and will also attack them; that Dorthar herself is our neighbor, separated from us only by a little stretch of water. She would turn to us and destroy us, and we have no army."

"The Lowlanders have no army, but they're making themselves one. They've had to."

"Yes," the King said. His eyes shone. "Many men will go from Lan to fight with them. I heard two or three on the stairs talking about it. Amrek isn't loved here. The Queen thinks he's a demon."

The serene girl lowered her lids and giggled.

The policy was to be as the King had said, yet not harshly put. As to the passage of other-land ships along the western flank of Lan, no harm would be offered them. It was intimated, if not spoken, that men who rode to the Plains would go unabused. At supper in the hall, four young nobles came to Yannul and talked with him at length, with bright fierce eyes, of justice and struggle—at which the councilors never turned a hair. Questions were also asked of the Plains men who had ridden with him. Until now there had been a sort of restraint; yet the Lowlanders seemed strange and silent to the people of Lan. They did not question them overlong.

Once, in the indigo hills, Yannul and his brothers had boasted that they would eat at the King's table. The memory smote him that day. Ringed by familiar things, he yearned to ride deeper into his country and be lost there for a while. But there was no time.

Three men rode to Xarabiss in the snow, to Xarar, where, eleven years before, a hot spring had erupted out of the earth. A new palace had been built to encompass the spring—a winter house where the king and his wives might warm themselves in the cold.

Thann Rashek, whose name in certain circles was still Thann the Fox, had been dozing by the ornate hearth, while two pretty girls played and sang eight-stringed melodies of Tyrai. He was an old man who liked beautiful things about him, professed himself indolent and appeared deceptively docile. When the man leaned to his ear and whispered his news, Thann Rashek's eyes expanded, and he began to display symptoms of unnerving wakefulness.

The three cloaked figures entered the room and bowed simultaneously, like puppets.

"Lowlanders. How interesting," Rashek remarked.

"We carry a letter from our King," one of the men said.

Thann Rashek's steward intercepted the paper and brought it to him. The wax bore no imprint. Rashek broke the seal and read. Presently he looked up.

"Your King has signed himself Raldnor Am Anackire. Does he claim to be the offspring of the Lady of Snakes?"

"It is a method by which all of us now make ourselves known. Our land has no name—therefore we claim our descent from Her."

Rashek smiled.

"An elegant fancy. Poetic, yet apt." His voice did not alter. "Does your King imagine I can defy Dorthar on his behalf? With my weak, my idle land?"

He had sent a similar message to Amrek regarding the Plains city: "Alas, my troops are indifferent: pleasure lovers and braggarts. They would not survive the snows."

Amrek's answer had been swift.

"Your open unhelpfulness angers us. We have not forgotten your previous words concerning the scouring of the Lowland filth out of Dorthar, neither your persistent trading in Lowland goods long after our edict forbade it. You will set your house in order, my lord, before the spring."

The Lowland messenger seemed to read Thann Rashek's mind. Perhaps this was even possible, for they read each other's, did they not?

"You may be forced at last to engage in war with Dorthar, lord king."

"So I may. But not before I'm forced, I think."

"Then you will march against the Plains?"

"I?" Rashek smiled. "I was never a warlord, sir. And my land is a courtesan, willing only for luxury and love."

"After the thaw, lord king," the messenger said, "we ourselves move against Dorthar, and our way lies across Xarabiss."

"I deny access to none. We are a hospitable and friendly people. No doubt you'll find generosity here, particularly from our liberal women."

The messenger bowed; so much had been implicit in the nonchalant words.

"One thing," Thann Rashek said. "I've heard your King is the man from Sar—the lover of my granddaughter Astaris. Val Mala's men had killed him, I thought."

"He is the man, Lord Rashek. He did not die in Koramvis."

"That's very wry," the Xarabian said. "Perhaps he will avenge, then, your King, the red-haired woman Amrek destroyed."

But the Lowlander made him no answer.

He thought of Astaris when they were gone. She had been, of all beautiful things, the best. A strange, rare woman. And beyond the high windows the snow fell into the mouths of icy fountains, and he felt that coldness creep in his old man's bones.

Before the third month of the snow had ended, the ruined city was full once again of Vis.

They came in chariots, wagons, carts, on zeebas and on foot, not for purposes of occupation, but out of fierce new loyalties to a barely known cause and a lesser-known people. Easygoing Lans, handsome Xarabians. Elyrians who proved withdrawn and mainly silent. It was a fever running in the lands to north and east. Even soldiers came— mercenaries from Xarar and Tyrai with their officers, carefully defacing their Xarabian insignia around the fires at night to save Thann Rashek's name. Even the slurred accent of Corhl was heard about the streets, and in the encampment outside the walls, two itinerant Alisaarians who had found nothing to love at home. Also, for some reason more slowly, those of mixed blood returned, those men with light eyes and dark hair, and the blonde-haired, black-eyed women. They were perhaps more lonely then, seeing that King, who was like them, and yet had become so different. But the old suppressed pride, the frustrated angers welled in them. They were as ready for the struggle as any paid fighter of pure Xarabian blood or stargazing Elyrian.

The newcomers brought their own squabbles and problems. They stole each other's cattle and zeebas and equipment. They composed their own individual ballads, too, and dreamed nostalgically of their homes, now they were no longer safe and dull in them.

It was a strange time, for already the forces of disruption were at work, and men felt that weird quickening, either in their bones or in their souls. Even so early, no single thing could stay quite as it had been. Soon everything would be altered, swept away; only in realignment and great change could anything remain.

In Koramvis, in the third month, the snow held like stone.

In this bitter weather, the Queen's woman, Dathnat, her own face pinched and wooden, worked longer upon the Queen's flesh with her creams. Val Mala, sensing in the snow an enemy, kept much to her apartments. She no longer wore the white unguent. In the harsh, pale light of the winter days her golden skin seemed brittle and papery. Nothing amused her.

"I begin to tell myself old tales, like an old woman," she thought. "I. *I*."

She had been thinking of Rehdon, not so much as a man, but as the personification of her disappointment in him. It was a sour taste in her mouth when she recalled how he had come to her father's palace at Kuma.

Her father was the Guardian of the place, a small and

unimportant merchant town with squat towers like squashed cakes. It lay in the path of one of Rehdon's progresses; otherwise, doubtless, he would never have considered entering it. Val Mala had hated Kuma, and she had hated her carefully preserved virginity. Her countless lovers did their best to serve her, in their own way, and after every Zastis her nurses came, with their prodding fingers, to ensure that matters had not gone too far. Such were the sexual customs of her house.

On the evening before Rehdon's arrival, her women had chattered ceaselessly, hysterical with excitement. They had all manner of tales concerning him. Tales of his power and beauty, and burning eyes that could strip a woman literally quite naked—a magic thing which they had been assured he had once done. For the occasion of his visit, Val Mala had been made a dress of glassy stuff sewn all over with golden flowers, and her hair had been plaited in twenty stiff braids woven through with pearls.

The sun rose. The palace woke and grew frenzied with anticipation, and Val Mala, accompanied by thirteen ladies in matching gowns of blush-red silk, had been taken to the head of the city wall. From here, she was told, she might look down and throw flowers decorously to Rehdon's chariot. She had been instructed in everything, but she waited at the wall, breathless in her anxiety that he should look up at her.

The long brazen river of men seemed to wind endlessly in through the gates of Kuma. At last she saw his vehicle, quite unmistakably ornate. She leaned forward and flung the blossoms from her hands, and called out to him—only his name, which was enough, as it turned out.

Above the hubbub, her clear high youthful voice had reached him, and he lifted his head and looked into her eyes. In those days Rehdon, though many years her senior, had been a giant—handsome, almost godlike, a magnificent product of his line. The sight of him struck her deliciously dumb. Her whole body ached for him with sudden wild longing.

Later, she lay in the dark, watching the lights of passing sentries quiver on the domed ceiling, and she imagined, with uncontrollable intensity, the ecstatic delight she might feel at Rehdon's hands if he took her as his wife. She vowed to herself that if she could make him desire her enough, he would marry her, and take her from dreary and provincial Kuma to the splendor of Koramvis and the agonizing rapture of his bed.

It became plain to her, in the days that followed, that Rehdon was fascinated. He could not keep his eyes away from her and would stare at her for long spaces of time, during which she affected not to notice his scrutiny. At last she contrived to be alone with him, in a marble chamber where stood the ill-carved statues of her ancestors, and where no servants, who had made their own analysis of the situation, would dare to intrude.

"Ah, my lord," she had sighed, "how beautiful Koramvis must be. How you must long to return to her."

As always, his eyes hung on her face and body, and when she went forward to him, he caught her hands in his.

"Would you like to see Koramvis, Val Mala?"

"Yes," she whispered, "oh, yes, my lord."

He slipped his arms about her.

"You're no more than a child, Val Mala."

She pressed herself against him.

"I long that you'll teach me to be otherwise, my lord."

He could have had her there and then. There was money enough to recompense for her defloration. But her extreme beauty had ensnared him, and her trust, which was really her unthinking foolishness. In some ways he was a sentimentalist, and in the matter of women and his reaction to them, his understanding was limited.

So seduced was Rehdon that he married her, and set her higher than his previous consorts. In the wonderful white palace, at the feet of the Dragon Comb of Dorthar, he lavished a million gifts on her, but her marriage to him destroyed her expectations.

In the great, gold-embroidered bed, he had hammered himself into her, but such was Val Mala that the pain pleased her more than anything else he might have done. She had endured so long the arts of love without their culmination that agony was a delight in itself. When it was finished, she must have more of it. It was her avidity that frightened him. Rehdon was not a master; for all his mass, he preferred to be the seduced rather than the seducer, which was the reason for her success with him in the first place. Now he taught an unwilling pupil the role she must play, and taught her to hate and despise him in so doing. Despite all this, she was adept and skillful, and he grew to rely upon her. Presently she became his chief Queen.

It was ten months after their marriage that she began to withdraw her favors from him. When he craved her the most, she proved the most evasive. She forced him to cringe for the benefit of her body; she made him fearful, taking a wicked pleasure in the enterprise, all the time hating him the more because he succumbed to her whims. She was a child of fourteen, he a man and a king. She longed for him to silence her, take her and use her, although she did not truly understand these desires.

At last she turned from him to the riches her position offered—to the temptation of power, and to lovers, the most ingenious of whom was Amnorh. He proved very useful to her, not least as an assassin. But the best-loved was Orhn Am Alisaar, for he treated her as a whore and so, in some curious and appropriate way, fulfilled her utterly.

In the fourth month the snow was cracked like marble by the rain. Nine days later, under yellow plumes of rain-cloud, an army rode out of Koramvis with all the paraphernalia of war.

Atull of Yllum had been picked to lead it—a Dragon Lord formerly in command of one of the mountain strongholds set up on the borders of Thaddra. He was a man of some experience, tough and forthright, well used to fighting, yet in reputation obscure. To deal with a peasant rabble in the Lowlands he was the ideal choice.

That Amrek should lead the punitive force was barely considered. No king was required to swat this fly. This was as well, perhaps, for Amrek had been often ill (something seldom alluded to), and his rulings indecisive. It had seemed to some that he would have been afraid to return to the Plains. Was it the old shame, the cuckolding that made him sweat? Or did he believe the tales of Lowland magic and dread the lingering curse of the Plains woman Ashne'e? Believe that the Lowland King was indeed his father's son?

Amrek, as he stood on the great stairway to watch them go, felt a nameless horror and despair whisper in his core. "I am impotent before a ghost," he thought. He glanced at the woman behind him.

"Well, Mother, our brave captain rides out."

"We shall pray to the gods," she said without inflection.

"You think Atull will fail," he said to her, coming close. The faintest of lines were etched on her forehead, which troubled and pleased him. "Have no hopes the Lowlanders will ultimately kill me."

She turned her head.

She remembered Raldnor, and she remembered the fair-haired woman who had sent the snake to her in Rehdon's tomb.

"Did I mistake death a second time?" She thought of the grave in the River Garrison. No. She would not have them unearth whatever lay there. She no longer wished to know, for if she had lost him yet again. . . . Lamps burned softly through the nights in her bedchamber. She had begun to fear the dark.

Atull's force moved across Ommos. The Ommos had taken to throwing yellow-haired dolls made of rags into the fire bellies of their Zarok gods. The sky blew and thundered.

When they crossed into Xarabiss, countless mishaps befell the march. Wheels ran loose, trees crashed in their path.

Between Abissa and Tyrai, as they bridged a river, now rain-swelled and foaming, the timbers gave under them. Chariots, men and animals floundered and were swept away. At night came disturbances in the camp; running figures made off into the hills. Supplies were pilfered, beasts unshod. There was frequently some burning tent, blowing its ashes down the wind.

Atull sent his dispatches home. Word came shortly to Thann Rashek: "Your people hinder us. Prevent them."

Thann Rashek's reply was very courteous. Xarabiss had suffered a hard winter, and a poor harvest before it, and hunger had inflamed her robber population. If Rashek knew a means to govern bandits, he would be a happy man; he entreated the Storm Lord to instruct him how it might be done.

Atull's command reached Sar, under beating heavy rains, and found the place in uproar. The Sarish watchtower had sent up a scarlet signal half an hour before. At dawn goatherds had spotted a force moving northward on the Plains.

The population of Sar was afraid, both of Atull's soldiers and the Lowlanders. They began to evacuate the town in droves, burdened with crying babies and bleating domestic animals. Even if the stories were true, they were sure that Raldnor, for all he had claimed himself one of her sons, would not spare Sar.

The dragons advanced on to the Plains and crossed the border in the late afternoon. They saw no signs of an army on the march, rabble or otherwise.

"Those herders were drunk, or asleep and dreaming," one of Atull's captains remarked. "My guess is the rats are still skulking in their ruin."

As dusk fell, they made camp on the banks of a narrow watercourse, where a small wood provided some shelter from the rain. Soon the dark was jeweled by their cook fires. Sentries prowled on the perimeter. They were not uneasy. They expected nothing.

Just before dawn, a sentry on the western rim of the encampment heard a movement in the dripping brush and went to investigate. He did not return.

"Fire!"

The yell burst across the tent lanes. Men sprang up, cursing and coughing; animals screamed and kicked at their pickets, broke free and ran, lathering with fear. The rain had eased in the night, but there was little dry enough for a blaze to take hold of. Nevertheless, the waterlogged undergrowth smoldered and stank. A thick, choking flame-fog enveloped the camp.

Atull pushed from his tent, his eyes weeping. There was no hope of orderly retreat. Men and animals burst from the wood.

Beyond the trees, back-lit by the first white rays of the sun, unexpected figures materialized. Swords clanged with a dull iron sound, spears sung. The Dortharians, who had looked for nothing in their pride and ill-fated assumptions, were cut to pieces as they erupted in confusion from the smothering trap. The enemy were half their strength in number and, by comparison, indifferently armed. Smoke and surprise, however, turned the balance. There was an absurd and bloody slaughter. Atull himself, fell heavily, an obscenity on his lips, a Plains man's shaft in his guts.

They had been smoked out of their lair like orynx in the hills above Koramvis. It was a trick well remembered by the man who had once hunted with Koramvians, on the day the earth shook.

A few men evaded the red blades and fled. It was an ignominious flight and ended in death anyway. Some perished oddly in Xarabiss. Those that reached Dorthar were hanged to the last man.

Also unlooked for, like black swans, there came out of the north sudden ships.

They crept over the laminations of the sea: vessels of Shansar and Vathcri along the shadowy coast of Lan toward

Ommos; a vast fleet of Shansar and Vardath edging behind barbaric Thaddra, making for Alisaar and Zakoris. And, far off still, behind the Dragon Crest at Dorthar's back, Tarabine galleys with blood-red sails.

They had been a long time building. Vathcri had stripped her forests of their huge trees, turned her army into a navy at Vardath and manned the wide decks under Jarred. The Shansarians, eager to despoil the Vis lands, leaped about their own black sails, which bore insignia of countless different kings, and sang their pirate songs. There were pale goddesses with plated tails leaning out from the up-curving prows that had the carved beaks of birds or the wide mouths of water snakes.

The spirit which had departed with the white-haired man still moved them in their various ways.

They hung, a few miles out from Vis, waiting, like the shadow of an evening soon to fall. It was not yet quite the time. There would be a signal; their priests would know it — an emanation, a Sending. It might come from the holy men of the Plains — a magic communion from one group of sensitives to another. Many believed that he alone would order it, the man they called Raldnor. Especially the pirates observed his name with awe. To some extent he had been deified among them.

The days passed. Storms broke at Dorthar's back, and the red-sailed ships of Tarabann withdrew to a farther horizon.

"He is in Xarabiss," said Melash the High Priest of the Vathcrian Ashkar. And a muted, half-troubled cheering rose from the wide decks.

To forty Shansarian pirate ships in the twilight off Alisaar came the first injunction.

The priests cried out with white faces. The sails opened; the iron oars ripped the glass surface of the sea and churned the bay of Saardos, capital of Alisaarian kings since the time of Rarnammon.

Their decks were straddled by their armament. The

spoons of catapults barked on their leather buffers, and spat white flame among the towers and walks of the seaside mansions and the merchant quarters. Flame lodged and gouted and lit up the sky. The pirates, wild with their blood frenzy, leaped down among the blazing wreckage of the docks, running on the spines of smoking fishing smacks and up the fire-bright wharves, to butcher the unprepared soldiery massing from the garrison.

Saardos burned that night, a horrible example to the dark-haired races. The ancient palaces collapsed in rubble; the garrison gave out at dawn. The city showed a gutted skull's face to the pitiless day as the howling invaders ravaged her corpse. Her king fled by a back gate to the fortress at Shaow to muster troops. In the confusion and fiery dark his commanders had learned nothing of the enemy. They surmised Zakoris or Thaddra had attacked them, and the world had gone mad.

The Lowland army had left Sar lying untouched, yet virtually abandoned behind them.

The warm, half-fetid perfume of summer was on the wide Xarabian plains. Towns lay in their path; they passed them with a mile or so between. They skirted Xarar, and no warning smoke rose from her garrison tower, though patrols had noted their passing from the woods above the road. Sometimes men rode to join the march—in twos or threes mostly, sometimes alone.

Often the wayside fields were empty and the farmsteads quiet, but full of anxious eyes. The Lowlanders took little and despoiled nothing. Near Tyrai the land was red with flowers, and men intercepted them with carts laden with beer and bread for Raldnor's troops. There were women too. They threw the red flowers at the soldiers. The Lowlanders watched serenely. The Lans laughed. The Xarabians bowed and tucked the flowers in their collars. Flowers trampled under the feet of the animals sent up a smoking fume. For Raldnor it was like the summer a year before.

The dark-eyed girls still stared at him. But he was different now, no longer an adventurer from Sar, but now a god in a hero's body. Their sighing was altered, but no less.

Thann Rashek was at Lin Abissa, in the white palace with the twisted golden pillars. He sent word to the force in his land: "My city lies helpless before you. We open our gates and beg the mercy of Raldnor Son of Anackire."

That night the Pleasure City did a brisk trade, though not from the Lowland men. It was the Lans and Xarabians who were taken to its erotic breast, and loved and fleeced under the ruby lamps.

"The Lowlanders do not fancy women," the beautiful daughters of Yasmis complained. "Nor anyone else," remarked her beautiful sons in the Ommos Quarter. It was a disappointment to discover, as they had always suspected, the sexual reticence of the fair-haired race.

Raldnor dined that night at Rashek's table.

"Well, we are conquered," the Xarabian said. "How unfortunate that you should find us so poorly defended."

He had been very curious. Now he observed, with ironic delight, the Dortharian-taught prince's manners, but he noted, too, how the soul was drained by what drove it. Yet who could doubt this man was Rehdon's seed? "He will die, of course, in Dorthar," thought Rashek. "Amrek's dragons must outnumber them, in proportions so vast as to make assessment unthinkable. Their luck at Sar is unrepeatable. They will shortly be overwhelmed. And this extraordinary man will be led in gold chains through Koramvis and slaughtered in some unique manner of Amrek's devising; for who cannot believe that Amrek hates and goes in terror of my elegant guest? Well, Raldnor will follow where she went, perhaps. If the shades are capable of love."

As the Lowland troops rode away from Abissa in the morning, a man on a black zeeba came galloping after. The Xarabian contingent took him in gladly enough, but in the dusk, when their camp was made once again on the open slopes, the newcomer presented himself at Raldnor's drab, owar-hide pavilion, the impersonal erstwhile tent of some minor Xarish officer.

He was at pains to get in. The Lan he had heard of and one or two captains from among the mercenaries were drinking wine. Raldnor stood by the lamp, reading a piece of reed-paper.

"Well, my friend," the Xarabian said, glancing around, "who would have thought it?"

Raldnor turned about. The Xarabian, catching sight of his face for the first time in more than a year, checked himself and his humorous banter.

"Xaros," Raldnor said. "You are very welcome."

He held out a hand, his mouth moving in the exercise generally recognized as a smile.

Xaros laughed uneasily.

"Well, I've come to swell your number by one. No doubt a stupendous contribution."

Later, crouched by a smoking fire in the chill late of night, Xaros composed a letter to Helida, who had never for a moment expected him to think of such a thing.

"Oh, by the gods, my love, how he's changed. I suppose I should have anticipated something, but not this. I had feelings of sentiment toward this man, as you well know. But I might as well grasp the hand of an icon. Oh, he treated me excellently, when I'd have been happy to rough it and grumble, because, as you understand, I was never made to be a soldier. But he's no longer anyone I know. Look for me back any day, though I'll stick this fool's errand if I can. This damned zeeba I robbed your uncle of has devoured half my food as I wrote this. I have told it I shall eat it in return, if ever we reach Dorthar."

In Koramvis, Amrek had not stirred. There had come a rumor of fire and terror in the west—Saardos sacked by pirates with pale hair. As yet it was only a rumor, like so many of the wild tales born suddenly in the mouths of the fearful.

Again, messengers had ridden to Xarabiss and returned by circuitous routes in fear of the Lowlanders.

Thann Rashek's answer was, as usual, courteous, but this time with a barb in the tail.

"I exclaim once again that I have no able troops ready to defy the men of the Plains. Though anxious for Dorthar's honor at all times, I am an old man. Can I be blamed if my cities surrender in terror to the savage Lowlanders, when even your Highness's own soldiers were forced to fly?"

"He begs for war, and shall have it," Amrek spat.

The Council were silent. The Lowlanders also begged for war; yet Amrek made no move to arrange it.

"Storm Lord, can all defense be left now to Ommos? Surely some men must be sent—"

"Then see to it," Amrek rasped. His eyes were fixed upon the letter he still held. He raised it, showing them the crimson wax with its imprint of the woman-headed dragon of Xarabiss.

"Anack," be hissed.

The Council kept still, their own eyes darting.

"Anack!" Amrek screamed out. "He dares to use the snake goddess as his seal!" He sprang from the chair, pointed at the six personal guards grouped behind him. "A Xarabian—find me a Xarabian in Koramvis and bring him here."

Without expression, two of the black-cloaked men strode out.

They took a Xarabian tailor in the lower quarter. His wife ran after, screaming and imploring them, as they dragged him up the narrow ways into the wide white streets and under the obsidian dragons of the Avenue of Rarnammon. Amrek's Chosen grinned, and men laughed on the roads, for the Xarabians, who should have cauterized the running Lowland sore and had failed to do so, were not greatly liked.

The dragons pushed the whimpering tailor into the Council Hall and held him still.

Amrek caught a blade from the nearest belt and slit the tailor's threadbare shirt.

"Your master, Rashek, the stinking Fox of the Xarab midden, has sent me a certain token, which you will take back to him."

He slashed with the knife, and blood ran. The tailor screamed, and screamed again as Amrek carved on his back the crude symbol of an eight-armed image with a serpent's tail.

At last, shivering, Amrek dropped the knife on the flags. The Xarabian had fainted.

"Take the offal out. Whether it lives or dies, send it to Abissa as my promise."

The hall was thick and close with silence. The face of the Warden Mathon was gray and puckered, for the sight of the blood had made him ill.

Kathaos sat motionless in the shadows.

Surely now there could be no further doubt that Amrek was entirely mad.

There was plague in Ommos.

It came with the summer heat. Men suffered pains in their bellies, turned black and died. Of the garrison force of a thousand Dortharians established in Hetta Para, where the plague was at its worst, only two hundred men survived, and most of them greatly weakened.

The Lowlanders had at this time taken Uthkat, where a battalion of Ommos soldiery fought them on the plain of Orsh, and unaccountably fled in rout. It was reasoned that the ravages of sickness and a certain foolish superstition were responsible. The Ommos had left off burning yellow-haired dolls. Some, it was muttered, burned wax effigies of Amrek instead. The Lowlanders were magicians, in league with hell and the creatures thereof—with banaliks, anckiras, and demons.

News had broken through at last, even to Ommos. Saardos had indeed been gutted, and the Alisaarian king slain at Shaow by white-haired berserkers, who fought screaming and seemed to take no wounds. Alisaar at least could no longer offer troops for Amrek's expected offensive, though Zakoris had dispatched a generous vassal's guard of three thousand men—gladly, and with contempt. She had no fear of pirates. Hanassor, inviolable in her rock, laughed at the rabble of the seas, whoever they were: Let them chew up Alisaar and come on. Yet who were they? Ommos knew. Devils conjured from the Waters of Aarl by the sorcerer who infested *them* with plague.

The Plains army reached Goparr and sat down for siege. It was remarkable, despite the sickness raging in the barricaded city, that none of Raldnor's troops, Vis or Plains man, took the disease.

In the long hot blue of the nights, crickets scratched with their tinsel wings.

On a slope below besieged Goparr, a Lowland man lay dreaming in the dark. Sometimes he twitched in his sleep. The crickets troubled his dream.

He had found her face, her forgotten face. It was white, all white, and transparent, like crystal. It hung like a mask in the air.

"Anici," he murmured.

No one was near enough to hear him, or to pry into his mind; he was very careful to sleep alone.

High overhead, a violet lightning expanded the sky.

Ras started awake. This was his agony, for awake, he knew her to be dead and himself alive. Awake, he forgot her face, remembering only the faint image.

When the spear had opened his skull, and he had murdered Yr Dakan in the upper room, it had come to him, as a sudden revelation, what must be done.

He must kill Raldnor.

Never before had such a solution to his pain presented itself, yet, in the act of killing, he saw how easy and how nourishing to his bloodless soul that act of blood would be.

Yet Raldnor was no longer human. He was a golem now, soulless also, capable of dying, but, to a human executioner — impervious. Only events, not hands, could slay the preternatural creature he had become.

Ras got to his feet. He made toward the zeeba pens. Passing two Lowland sentries, he shuttered and locked up the sparkling fever of his mind.

He had visualized the creeping black swans sailing on Zakoris, waiting off Dorthar and the Ommos coast. A jumble of possibilities cascaded through his thoughts. As another had once done, he had been recently at great pains to learn of the Dortharians. Yet he did not see them as enemies. They had become a means to an end.

He took a zeeba from the pen and mounted it.

Musky foliage flashed past and overhead were glimpses of a faded moon. No one halted him. Such was Lowland unity that there seemed no reason.

Three miles from the camp, he remembered his hair and skin and pulled up his hood.

22

KORAMVIS, WHEN HE CAME to it, seemed composed of white flame.

The Zastian months had begun. The days were now very hot—heat of a dull sickening variety, heat like an omen, which to Ras meant nothing. The guards in the great gateway, expecting nothing extraordinary of a single man on foot, and oppressed by the sun and the Star, barely glanced at him.

Some miles beyond Hetta Para, Ras had become part of a great Ommos flight, intent on putting as much distance between themselves and the Plains people as possible. By that time he had darkened his hair and skin haphazardly with a sour water dye. Doing it, he had no sense of a perfidious irony—nor when he entered Koramvis. He had forgotten Raldnor's past, for Raldnor had become for him a target—no more, no less.

The dye infected his flesh; scalp and skin broke out in dribbling sores which he scarcely noticed. The Ommos, however, avoided him, fearing this disease of scabs to be a new variety of the plague.

Due to the plague, the sprawling caravan found itself halted at the river border of Dorthar. Soldiers menaced with spears. They did not want the sickness carried over.

Ras went downstream, forded the river in the deep of night and went on alone.

The journey slid off his senses; only the city awoke him—not to itself, but to his purpose. The pure white bird of Koramvis on her nest of fire left him unmoved. There was no room in him for curiosity; the capacity for observation had long since starved on the aridness of his soul. So he saw nothing beautiful, and neither did he see the turmoil which was eating like a worm between the whiteness.

In almost every thoroughfare there were soldiers— mostly mercenaries of Iscah and Corhl, or black Zakorians. In other parts, mainly the narrower, poorer byways of the city, families were packing their belongings in readiness for flight. Cooking utensils and piles of clothes and furniture were stacked precariously in carts. In a shadowless doorway a carrier was extracting his fee from a cow-faced whore.

Everywhere there was an aching tension, an absence of children playing in the streets. Wine shops had closed their shutters like pursed lips.

To these things Ras was impervious. He rode, gazing ahead of him, slow and dumb, an ugly apparition—a tangible form to some, perhaps, of the sudden, unlooked-for superstitious fear that held Koramvis. For here, too, they had begun to believe in magicians.

He crossed the Okris at noon and began to ask the road he must take. Men laughed at him and spat on the blazing pavements.

"*Kathaos!* Listen, Yull, *this* wants Kathaos, by the gods."

A woman crouched on the steps of a temple where sweet smokes rose into the sky glanced up and pointed in answer to his toneless query. Later, an urchin led him to the wall of a great villa and picked his pockets of all their little coins.

Above the gate, the dragon of Alisaar is worked in bronze. Two guards slouched with narrow eyes.

Ras hesitated. His mind saw only the immediacies of entry. He turned back a street to where he had half seen a well.

Minutes later Am Kathaos's two guards metamorphosed from their slouching with oaths, for a Lowlander stood on the paving, looking up at them with gelatinous, mosaic eyes.

Lyki straightened and idly began to rock the cradle in which her child was lying. Her child, and the son of Raldnor. Its nurses had taken to calling it Rarnammon, and she imagined they did so to spite her. Its hair was a series of coiled darknesses, like flower buds growing on its small skull. Its eyes were curious—neither dark nor golden but strangely both at once—and its face was sullen and apt to turn purple, like a bruised fruit, when its digestion or its emotions troubled it.

Lyki rocked passionlessly, and the child stared at her with an aloof distrust to match her own.

Several gems glittered on her hand. Her dress was of a rare embroidered silk. Her rank, since Astaris Am Karmiss had perished, was considerably improved. She enjoyed, as Koramvis had observed, the personal protection of the lord Kathaos. Many of Astaris's handmaidens had not been so fortunate.

Lyki herself was unsure of her position. While she had carried the child, Kathaos had made no proposition of any kind, save that she remain within his house, and she felt this gallantry due not to courtesy on his part either toward her or her condition, but merely to the fact he had no immediate need of her and yet foresaw a need at some future time. She knew that he would use her in whatever manner seemed good to him, and the knowledge made her nervous, even while she could discover no alternative. Once the child had been born and he had bethought himself of the matter, he had wooed her with all the lascivious pertinacity of a lover. Again, she realized, he did so with no sincerity, but because it amused him to do so. And indeed, his goal once achieved, his amatory interest had been brief.

She took her hand from the cradle. The baby kicked among the covers. She saw, with a strange and bitter gladness, that it would not develop Raldnor's beauty.

There was a sudden noise in the inner court. Lyki heard feet running and voices calling for Kathaos. With a swift start of terror, she envisaged the enemy already at the gates, but the quietness of Koramvis all around her instructed her that whatever the event, it belonged to this house alone.

She crossed to the long window and stared down.

The court was rectangular, laid with black and white flags and dominated by a curious fountain. The water and the spray were constructed from faceted crystal, and ivory lilies were set in. No doubt the deception was well suited to Kathaos's tastes. Sometimes birds would fly to the surface and attempt to drink, their claws clicking among the frozen flowers.

At the fountain were two guards, dressed in Kathaos's yellow, and between them was a small skeletal man, whose face and neck were splotched with sores. He was a Lowlander.

Lyki's head swam; she clutched the upright of the window to steady herself. It was not the man below who produced this effect on her, but the emanation of another man, suddenly conjured in her brain.

A second after, Kathaos appeared in one of the doorways which opened onto the court.

He was quite calm, apparently uninterested. She had expected nothing else.

"What do you imagine that you want?"

A series of shudders ran over the Lowlander. His voice, when it came, was cold and muffled, as if it rose from a tomb.

"I can tell you something that will help you, Lord Councilor. I can tell you something about Raldnor, Ashne'e's son, that will make Koramvis uneasy."

Lyki felt fear burn her throat, fear and something else, as she gripped the window and recalled Raldnor the Sarite. At the court, and in the streets, the Lowland king was never accorded any other name than this. The lower city knew him as Raldnor Bride-Stealer, for they had nothing to gain by forgetting Astaris. Only in the presence of Amrek himself did they desist. There, men did not speak of Sar. Many of the captains and commanders grumbled amongst themselves concerning Kren, the Dragon Lord, who had harbored an enemy of Dorthar, but their weapons of spite were compulsorily sheathed.

"It will take more than a visitation of rats to make Koramvis afraid, Lowlander," Kathaos said.

"But there are more rats than you think. Consider Saardos and Shaow. Raldnor doesn't work alone. There are ships and men stealing in from a place beyond the sea, of which Dorthar, in her magnificence, knows nothing."

"For an informer," Kathaos murmured softly, "you're notably arrogant. Why betray your own people? Can it be that it's your Raldnor who sent you here? For some obscure reason—to create panic, perhaps?"

The man in the court smiled, but it was like the grinning of a skull.

"I no longer have a people. I have a wish. I want Raldnor to die, soon, and when he is dead, I want you to kill me, Lord Councilor."

"On that point at least you can rest assured." Kathaos turned to the guard. "Take him inside."

As they moved in through the doorway, Kathaos said without raising his eyes to the window: "Follow us, Lyki. I shall expect you."

Yet when she obeyed him, trembling with vague fright, she found herself shut out, to wait, presumably, on the Lowland creature's mouthing.

Once she had heard a story in this house that Kathaos had long ago known Raldnor to be the child of Rehdon. Oh, how little she knew this devious man who now had such access to her life.

At last he let her in. The Plainsman was gone; she had no notion where—whether to reward or instant death.

Kathaos said immediately: "How is the child today?"

She looked at him without comprehension, startled at the seemingly irrelevant question.

"He does well enough."

"Good." Kathaos smiled. "I've been thinking it a great pity that Raldnor never saw his son."

At once, though still without understanding, she was overwhelmed by terror.

The streets of Karith were empty. Although the plague had not penetrated here, three days since had come the news of Goparr's fall, and the Ommos fled before a magician's shadow. Only a few abandoned pet animals wandered to and fro, searching for shelter or food.

In the brain of the watchtower, a Dortharian soldier gnawed on a stick of roast meat and scanned the sky. He scarcely credited Kathaos with sanity, however the Council at Koramvis had seen things. As much expect ships to whistle out of the clouds as from a make-believe land over the sea. He doubted greatly if any such existed. The thought of the doomed garrison at Hetta Para bothered him also. Who knew for sure whether or not plague germs lurked here? Damned Kathaos, certainly, had no concern for a private pushed every way on other men's business.

And he hated the deserted town, full of cold echoes and ghosts. It was hot in the tower, yet he felt the occasional urge to shiver. Zastis hung like a wicked scarlet rip in the night, and he wanted a woman; his need was distracting and imperative. He longed for the end of the watch. Every so often, from some hovel in the town, he heard a girl screaming. Most probably she was in labor, and her Ommos husband had thought her too cumbersome to take with him in his flight and left her to the will of Zarok. The soldier was not unduly concerned with her discomfort and certain terror, but whenever the cries came, they pared his nerves to the quick. He longed to go out and find her, and beat her into silence.

He finished with the meat, slung the bone from the open window and heard it crack on the court below. There was the patter of frenzied claws, and some small animal made off with it into the shadows. Beyond the court, the rock stretched down some forty feet to the pale smudge of the beach, where little ripples chased each other. On the sand he made out the stark line of catapults and, on the sea itself, the bobbing, anchored Ommos fishing boats extending away parallel to the shore as far as the eye could see.

Idly he looked farther out, toward the horizon. A dark, dimly smoking mass was moving there.

An instant's sheer panic choked his throat. He remembered Alisaar, taken unaware in her sleep, by a fleet come from nowhere; then he flung himself to his feet, plunged up the three steps to the cupola where the giant bell hung on its ropes and dragged it into life.

Faintly, over the water, they heard the bell ringing in the hot silence.

They were soldiers of Vathcri and Vardish sailors, carried together in the great beaked vessels that had once been forest trees; there were also Shansarian pirate ships, their black sails like gall in the light of the Star. They had come a long way to see this strip of land, this fortressed town, and waited a long while for the signal-sending of the white-haired man they called now Raldanash.

Jarred of Vathcri stared ahead.

"Ships, captain."

"So it is, my lord. But no men on 'em."

Eyes scanned for any movement on those low decks. The movement came instead from the rocky beach beyond.

"Catapults!" Jarred cried. His urgency possessed him. He ordered his vessel to fire, but the white streamer fell short and sizzled in the sea.

"By Ashkar!" the captain shouted. "My lord—their gods have driven them mad! They're not aiming at us, but at their own vessels."

Orange flame burst and arrowed from the shore and lodged among the little rigs and skimmers lying idle on the water.

Men cursed and marveled. The Shansarians laughed and roared their contempt into the flaring night.

The first explosion burst from the Ommos boats as if a monster had woken in the sea.

A column of pure flame gushed outward and upward, eighty feet in height, accompanied by a waterspout of scalding blackness that crashed down upon the foremost Vathcrian galleys. Red light bled across the whirlpool, and flame ran after. In the wake of the first convulsion, a second followed, then a third, a fourth, each one giving rise more rapidly to others, as the inferno spread from vessel to vessel. The whole sea thrashed and boiled.

"Oil—" The captain wept, kneeling, blinded on the deck.

Men screamed as the heat peeled skin from flesh.

Jarred's ship was the first to catch alight.

Her sail screwed itself into wizened papers, like a moth's wings caught by a huge candle. The figurehead of Ashkar began to melt, dripping its ivory like wax. Timbers blazed up. The sea was a pool of liquid gold.

Men jumped from burning hulks and perished in the burning water. The air was thick with smoke and screaming.

The ships of Shansar, more to the rear, fell back, taking what men they could, leaving the pride of Vathcri to split and fry.

No other menace came from the shore. There was no need. The raging wall of fire ran every way.

The casks of oil in the Ommos boats continued to erupt, blotting out the sky. The conflagration lasted through the night.

In the pink smoldering fog that came with dawn, small sea creatures lay dead at the foot of Karith, and the stripped corpses of men floated and rapped with half-bone hands against her rocks. One of these bodies was Jarred's. Of the enemy fleet there was no sign, save for those still-smoking ruined trees, with their curious charcoal prows lying broken sideways like the necks of swans.

"How does he know these things, Yannul my friend? Has this Raldnor I used to go whoring with become a sorcerer out of a book?"

Yannul shrugged. He and the Xarabian Xaros had struck up a wary camaraderie, partly to persuade the factious Lans and Xarabs in the camp that it might be done. At dusk the Vis sections of the army had been in good spirits. Goparr had fallen and was the first stronghold they had looted. She had tried treachery in her first surrender, and Raldnor had given her over to rape and sack with the merciless justice they had come to expect of him. The Lowlanders had taken no part in that. They sat silent at their cookfires, speaking no doubt in their skulls, Xaros sourly concluded. He too experienced that uneasy uncertainty about the Plains men and their mechanical, emotionless abilities.

Now the Sending had come, or whatever in Aarl it was. Somehow, by some mentally immoral method, Raldnor now knew that a segment of the allied fleet had been driven from Ommos, and more than half of the segment destroyed.

"Whatever else, one thing's for certain," Xaros said. "The Dortharian and Ommos soldiers at Karith will be out on the road to meet us, and no help from your otherland friends."

"Their young King died in the sea," Yannul said. For various reasons this had distressed him. He had come in some ways to equate Jarred with the boy-monarch of Lan.

"That's bad, but reaches all of us. I regret I'll never see my Helida again—a prize among women, who thinks with her brain more often than her pelvis, which is uncommon. Ah, nostalgia, Yannul. I wonder if she'll put up a shrine for me, or simply hop into bed with one of my damned father's rich and handsome younger brothers. And who is that girl you ache for these Zastis nights? Ah, yes, the golden Lowlander Medaci."

Yannul grinned.

"And what of the Tarabithybannion—whatever-god-forgotten-name-it-is fleet off Dorthar? If the dragons know the plan, there'll be trouble there as well. No, wait, I can surmise. Raldnor has *sent* to warn the ships."

"So he has."

"Oh, by the gods. I should have been resigned to it. I suppose he'll settle the Karith force by magic, too."

"Who knows, Xaros. The plague in Ommos was strange. And I told you of the dustwind at Vathcri."

"On the assumption that we should save our pitiful strength for Koramvis, what stands between us and Dorthar now, apart from Karith?"

"Hetta Para due north, mostly evacuated. And a small Dortharian garrison across the river to keep out possible plague carriers."

"I have a plan," said Xaros, "improbable only in its genius. Come with me to Raldnor, and let's show him what honest clods can do by a bit of verbal wrangling."

When they went through it, the camp was bright with fires and there were Ommos women still about in it, though Goparr lay some miles behind. These at least seemed to have preferred Lannic and Xarabian rapine to Ommos peace.

Forgis of Ommos, the bullock fat captain of the mixed troops from Karith, sweated in the early sun and stared where his scout had pointed. He did not like this work in the heat, nor the five hundred Dortharians who laughed at him—and not behind his back, though it was broad enough.

"Well, well? What am I to be looking for?"

"A rider, on the slope, coming from the direction of the Lowlanders' camp, sir."

"Plains man?"

"No. See, sir—he's dark."

Forgis wiped sweat from his eyes, but could not make this out. Nevertheless, he struck a spearman on the shoulder.

"Ride, you oaf, and bring him down."

The man plunged off in a wash of dust. But there was no need of him. The rider met with some sudden difficulty, his beast floundered and fell and the man rolled off, over and over down the scarp, to end in an untidy curl at the bottom.

Forgis rode up without undue haste. The man shifted,

groaned, sat up, and rubbed his face gingerly with long brown fingers. The zeeba had wandered uncaringly away and was cropping the grass. Forgis let out a slow laugh. The man turned and stared at him vaguely. The fall seemed to have jolted the wits out of him.

"Xarabian, are you? Where do you come from? The Lowlanders' camp?"

The Xarabian's mouth worked anxiously.

"No—I—" He broke off and appeared to be searching for an adequate excuse for his presence there.

Forgis spat.

"We cut up dogs like you and feed them to the beasts. If you want to live, be hasty. Where are you going? And why running away?"

"I—the gods of Koramvis—"

"Gods?" Puzzled, Forgis frowned. "What is this talk of gods?"

"They're dead," the Xarabian suddenly said.

"Dead? Who is dead? These gods? Gods cannot die."

"Sentries huddled at their fires, some in their sleep. All dead."

The scout said in a dry excited voice: "Do you mean the Lowland army?"

"No longer," the Xarabian said.

"If they're dead, who has killed them?" Forgis grumbled. The scout backed off.

"Plague, perhaps, sir. You, Xarabian, stand away. You may carry the disease."

The Xarabian slunk aside.

Forgis barked orders, then turned and said: "You will guide a detachment of one hundred Dortharian foot soldiers to witness this thing." He grinned at his own cunning. If there were sickness, let the accursed-of-Zarok catch it.

The Xarabian began to protest in terror, but a drawn sword quickly changed his mind.

So it was, an hour later, the Dortharians, emerging over a rise on the old Goparrian-Karith road, saw their enemies stretched out below them in the myriad ghastly attitudes of painful death.

The dragons went no closer and did not linger; neither did they retain their guide who had begun to clutch his belly and groan.

In a spume of dust they marched back along the road, and thence back to Dorthar and her white city, where, for a time, there were crazy rejoicings in the lower quarter.

There were rejoicings also in the camp of death once all the corpses had rubbed life back in to their stiff limbs, put out a burning tent and caught several strayed zeebas. It was the best and last joke of the march, and Xaros was a hero who would take his place thereafter in any decent saga, as a prince of deception.

"So much for magic," Xaros remarked. "And now I think of it, I was lucky they didn't turn the tables on me and grant me a quick death with a sword."

In Dorthar the laughter presently stopped.

News limped in of fires along the Zakorian coast and Hanassor besieged, while the remnants of the fleet driven off from Ommos had fallen in frenzy on Karmiss, and her nights also were now full of smoke.

From the river quarters on the Ommos border the dispatches were very late. At last a solitary man reached Dorthar and died of his wounds in the streets of Koramvis, like a warning.

The Lowland force was alive; he had seen them. They had razed Hetta Para and crossed the river, wiping out the small camp there with ease.

No trepidation or superstition had really prepared the Vis. It seemed unthinkable. The scum of the Serpent Woman had touched the soil of Dorthar with its feet, had drawn in lungfuls of her dragon air. Despite all hindrance and all probability, they had, at last, become all too real.

23

KATHAOS SMILED AT HIS GUEST.

"I hope the wine is agreeable to you, Lord Mathon. A subtle vintage from Karmiss, which I fear may never produce grapes again. We must make the most of it."

Mathon shivered and set aside the wine, which had the color and suddenly the taste of blood.

"Yes, this thing seems to have grown unstoppable."

"That, my Lord Warden, is because inadequate steps were taken."

"But a rabble, and so few of them—Ultimately they must fall before the strength of Dorthar's arm," Mathon concluded querulously.

"I am soothed to find that you think so, my lord." Casually Kathaos added: "Had you heard? Two days ago some of the Sarite's Vis troops rode east and sacked Kuma. As I ascertain, merely for provisions and exercise."

"Kuma. The Queen's birthplace."

"Indeed. A minor town yet a healthy one, and under the circumstance that it has produced royalty, worth repayment. But still, I believe, the Lord Amrek considers it unwise to meet the Lowlanders in battle." These words were spoken without inflection, but Mathon twitched, sensing an awkward drift in the conversation.

"It's near, then. Siege perhaps," he muttered.

"Such a thing seems incredible. But yes, my lord, I think it may even come to that. I gather that several of our most notable citizens are making for Thaddra, and the dregs of the lower city are already gone. In addition we have the soldiery which Yl Am Zakoris has so kindly loaned us, kicking its heels at every corner. Soldiers become bored with inaction and pick quarrels. They also eat a good deal."

"I'm certain, Lord Councilor, that Amrek will move when the time is right . . ." Mathon said uneasily.

Kathaos smiled at him again.

"Indeed yes. Besides, we have our own garrison, do we not?"

Mathon balked at this hint of Kren. He made some excuse about his duties and rose. He thought: "I am an old man. I cannot be expected to parry the thrusts of this intriguer. What does he want me to do? Very well, so he has saved us from the pirates by strategy, and is more clever than Amrek. Can I make him King of Dorthar? He has the Council already in ferment. Ah, why cannot Amrek rouse himself?"

In the taverns where they had been billeted, Yl's mercenaries boasted and swore, picked their teeth and spat out wine that was not to their liking. Occasionally they would clash with Amrek's soldiers, churning the byways into arenas of dust and blood. Their commanders agitated at the palace, seeking an audience with the Storm Lord. The streets became rowdy and unsafe after twilight. A well-born girl of twelve was raped near the river bank in the upper city by a Zakorian captain, and the matter hastily smothered. Dorthar had no wish to insult her benefactor, Yl, by a public whipping.

The great brazen heat of the warm months became unbearable. The sky pulsed like a tautened skin; clouds painted on it in white ink never moved. The Okris withered and shrank in its margin, sucked dry, showing its stagnant dirt now, and the harvest of garbage and discarded furniture thrown in by the people. A stench rose from the low water, and river things crawled up the mud and died on the paving at the top. Slaves were sent to clear the wreckage before the rotting plates and bedclothes bred an infection.

The priests in the temples raised their arms, spilling the blood of black bulls and pale birds. Rolling in trances, they declared that the drought was a sign of coming thunder. The Storm gods were preparing to strike the Lowlander down.

Crops burnt up in the fields like tinder. Slaves took their meager possessions in the night and fled to Thaddra, though sometimes their masters caught up with them. All along the white road leading through the plain before Koramvis, men and women were hung on poles to die.

Koramvis, the thinking jewel, the heart-brain, had become a refuse pit of dying things and their decay.

In the last month of Zastis a scarlet signal shot from the watchtower on the plain.

A man in Kathaos's livery rode through the shouting streets.

At the gate of Kathaos's villa a crowd of supplicants had gathered, pleading for his aid, shrieking for transport with which to abandon the city. Guards stood massed, keeping the hordes back with a hedge of spears. Men in despair beat their fists against the wall. The rider forced his way into the courtyard, flung himself down and ran in through the high doorway.

Kathaos met him in the striped shadows of a colonnade, and his face, for once, was as fierce as a leopard's. Beyond a filmy curtain, the messenger made out a woman standing with her hands pressed to her mouth.

"Well?"

"My lord, they're half a day's march from us."

"And Amrek—"

"—is sick, my lord, unable to leave his bed."

Kathaos nodded, turned without a word and thrust aside the curtain with his hand. Lyki stared up at him. The paint on her eyes and lips was too vivid, for she was suddenly very pale.

*   *   *

Into the small room where he sat the dusk came crowding, full of shadows and unheard sounds. It filled the corners and swirled about the chair like the sea. Beyond the high window only the mountains showed—vast looming blocks, with the color and apparent substance of the tinted sky.

"You are ours," the mountains said to him. "The son of our mornings, conceived beneath the shade of our bones. Come up, come with the dark. We will conceal you and keep you safe."

"No," Amrek said aloud. The noises and flickerings of the dusk flurried and resettled. "No. I am a king. My penance for that is that I must grapple with devils tomorrow, with the first-born of the Lowland serpent-witch. Yes, I've sent them word that we fight, that I'll lead them. And I'm afraid, afraid, *afraid*. And I can't keep from thinking it: Here is my doom, my destiny. A coward. Yes. What else? Last of the line of Rarnammon, and I have no son to follow me. Wait, Raldnor. Hold off until I've had time to marry and get myself a boy on her."

Amrek laughed softly. He shut his eyes. The room was suddenly full of a dark garden and the scent of trees. A voice at his elbow said to him: "One day, my lord, long after you've seen me dangle on a gallows, a man may slip a knife in your back or a powder in your cup, which I, had I been there, would have prevented. I can deal with my enemies, my lord, if I live. And yours, too."

"Well, Raldnor," Amrek said aloud. "Well. The enemy is at the gate, the men with their knives. How will you defend me?"

At the brink of the plain below Koramvis, Raldnor's army made its camp in the twilight.

Red smoke still floated in the still air over the watch-tower, a mile away down the valley. A road began among the burned-out orchards and wound off toward the elevation of the lower hills and the distant, silhouetted diadem of towers that was the city. There were no lights on the plain, but they had made out that marching line of poles where slaves had been hung, rotting in the fire of day.

There was a great silence on the camp. The Lowlanders moved as ever in their passive unemotional way; over the Lans, Elyrians, Xarabians and those of mixed blood a vast quiet had descended. Until now they had ridden on an adventure—with a stirring of the soul, with luck and trickery, with a chance, also, to turn back. Now, confronted by this ultimate symbol, Koramvis, they sensed what they had done, and they, like the Dortharians, were numbed by it. They had reached a supreme, an unthinkable goal. And thereby given it power to destroy them.

Koramvis, the beautiful and the strong.

Yannul, as he honed the blades of long swords in the glare of crackling flames, visualized the wide gates opening in the new day, spilling the might of Dorthar.

"They were waiting, lazy, letting us come to them for the plucking," he thought. "There should have been help from Shansar and Vathcri with us, Tarabine men marching over those mountains to take the Dragons from the back. But a traitor ran to Koramvis, and now no other man will come. Death in the morning. A few hours away. Gone beneath the hooves and the chariot wheels. Made into dung to fertilize their blighted fields, carrion for their birds to eat. Oh, creamy-breasted Anack of the Plains, why bring a man so far to die?"

Yannul glanced about. A Lowlander was at his shoulder.

"Come," he said.

"Come where, and for what?"

The Lowland man pointed. Men were leaving their fires. Lans and Xarabians, leaving their women and the spoils they had snatched from Kuma, moving up beyond a line of orchard trees, out of sight.

"What's up there?" Yannul asked, his scalp unaccountably prickling.

"We go to pray."

"To pray—ah, no. I'll spend my last night alive in other sports, many thanks."

The Lowlander said no more and walked away after the others. Yannul turned back to the pile of weapons.

The crackle of the fire became very loud. The sky darkened, and the last flush of flame on and over the mountains guttered out.

Yannul's back began to crawl. He slung down a sword with a curse, got up and stared about. Even the women had gone now. Only an empty slope remained, dotted with little fires.

He went up after them, in among the trees. In the dark, men stood in a union of vast soundlessness.

"Pray," Yannul thought, "to what? To Anack?"

Then he felt the curious whisper in his brain.

He started. Could they invade Vis thoughts now? But no, this was something different—an awareness only of the humming intensity all about.

Will. Why call it prayer? Prayer was their instrument; they used it like cloth to fashion a garment, like the stone he had used to sharpen blades.

"Well, I, too, can will to live out tomorrow."

It seemed quite natural then, the linking of his consciousness with those about him, in a common cause of self-preservation, though the air sizzled and thrummed as if before a storm.

Under the torch-lit gate of Koramvis, a covered carriage rolled toward the valley plain.

Within the musty dark, Lyki snapped shut her eyes. All this, she knew, was a game to Kathaos—more fascinating in the irony and skill than in likelihood of success. She gnawed her lip in a sudden extremity of fright. "May the gods damn him!" She felt her heart twisting in on its own raw blackness of anger and fear.

When she opened her eyes again, she saw Ras on the wooden seat opposite her. His face was like white enamel, and she wondered if he could see hers as well, for the darkness of her skin.

"Why are you doing this, Lowlander?" She had tried to keep all pleading out of her voice, but her tone betrayed her. At first she thought he would not answer, but then he said, quite gently: "I hate him. I hate Raldnor."

"Do you hate me too?"

"You?" He stared at her as if seeing her for the first time. "If we do what Kathaos wants, I'll die. They'll kill me."

"It doesn't matter to me," he said, but there was no malice in his voice.

"What about the child? The child will die too."

"Raldnor's child."

In a sudden gesture of defense, Lyki drew the child close to her, shielding it with her arms. She had carried it inside her and labored harder to bear it than she had previously labored at anything, and now a man who knew nothing of pregnancy or birth brushed away its little span of days as lightly as a feather. She looked down at its swarthy dreaming face, the black curls like wisps of fern clustering on its broad, low forehead. They had given it a medicine to make it sleep, to shut its strange, accusing eyes, and muffle its demanding mouth. She bowed her head over it, absorbed once more in her own bitterness.

Many years before, another court woman, whose name had been Lomandra, had come this way, down this pale road, from Koramvis, carrying a child in her lap.

Almost an hour passed, marked by the faint creaking of the carriage, the uncertain rumble of the wheels as they left the road and took to the hilly paths between the cibba groves and drought-blasted fruit trees.

At last the carriage came to a halt, and the silences of the plain gathered around them. Their driver jumped into the grass, dragged back the curtains and stood waiting. He put out his hand to Lyki to help her, and his mouth was crooked with contempt. She longed to spit her venom into his face. She thrust off his hand and pulled her mantle about her until it hid both her and the child. Beyond the trees she saw the red suggestion of firelight. Suddenly her limbs seemed to dissolve and she felt as weak as if death had brushed her—but not from fear alone.

The Lowlander took her arm—a casual, deadly touch. They began to walk.

At first the enemy camp seemed deserted. No movement or sound emanated from it. Then came a sudden burst of singing over the slope, and hands clapped in a Xarabian dance, and there was laughter.

She marveled at their confidence on this eve of death.

Suddenly there was a guard silhouetted in front of them against the fire haze; he was carving a stick with his knife.

"Who's there?"

"Peace, friend." Light slanted on Ras's hair. The Lan relaxed, showed his teeth and stood aside for them. He winked at Lyki's averted face.

"As good a way as any to wait for a battle."

Irrationally, Lyki felt fury seize her, because the sentry imagined that she had given herself to this thin pocked man. Then the camp was all around them. There was the smell of food cooking, and steam rose from iron caldrons slung over countless fires. It was now a place of dimly seen movement, vaguely heard voices, smoke going up, animals cropping turf at their pickets, everything blurred together by the smearing flame light.

No one spoke to them.

At the head of one of the tent lanes, a deserted fire was burning in a circle of stones. Cibbas grew thickly here, casting a dense shadow. Ras went to the hearth and seated himself. Meat bones lay whitely in the grass, and scraps of bread from a finished meal. All around the camp, the orchards and vineyards ran in seared acres under the blistering stars. Lyki thought for an instant she might slip away when Ras took his cold eyes from her. Yet she knew that he would never look away, would never allow himself to be distracted.

"Why do we wait?" she asked eventually.

"There will be men in the tent with him—Yannul the Lan, and the Xarabian; some of my people, maybe. When they leave him, I shall see them go."

She looked about them for some Commander's pavilion, but all the tents were the same.

"Which is his tent?" she whispered.

"There."

Her heart stabbed and she shivered in the boiling night. When the flap was opened, yellow light spilled out, shocking her. Men moved away across the camp, two of them laughing together.

Ras got up.

"Come now."

Lyki stared at him. She clung to the child and found she could not move.

"Come." He crossed to her and took her arm, pulling her slowly, without menace and without gentleness.

"There will be a guard," Ras said softly. "Walk toward him, and I'll take him from behind."

She nodded dumbly. Stumbling, she began to make her way between the cibba trunks. She saw the guard now, a Lowlander, leaning on his spear impassively.

He caught sight of her at once.

"How can I help you?"

Lyki opened her lips, but her mind had emptied. She knew that her terror must be evident in every part of her. While she stood there helplessly, Ras came from the dark and felled the guard with a stone.

"There's no one to stop you now," she hissed at Ras. "Go into the pavilion and kill him, and let me go."

He glanced up. His eyes were like the eyes of a banalik, scalding her with hate, and she knew her plea was useless.

"You must kill him," he said, "as Kathaos intended." He smiled, but without humor, probably without even realizing he did so. "He would never let me kill him. He would come into my mind and stop me. You must do it."

"Oh, but he's a sorcerer," she snarled scornfully, trembling. "Can't he look into my mind too?"

"You are Vis. Your minds are shuttered, even to Raldnor."

She turned away and took the flap of the tent entrance

abruptly in her hand, and it astonished her—the reality of the leather between her fingers. She held it open a little way and stepped through, and let the fold slap shut behind her.

There was only one man in the tent, reading beneath a lamp. He looked up slowly, without surprise, and the lamplight fell on his face.

She had not known how she would look at him, but she could not take her eyes away. She had not known if he would seem different to her, and she found him changed, utterly, yet indefinably the same. His sheer physical beauty she had remembered well, yet not well enough, it seemed, for now she was amazed by it. She found that she could not believe that this was the man with whom she had locked limbs, whose shoulders she had imprinted with the marks of her kisses, and her teeth and her nails. Those memories of passion which had tortured her through Zastis, became terrible, awesome in this drab tent, as though she boasted copulation with a god.

"Lyki," he said.

"Yes," she whispered, "I'm Lyki." She pushed the hood back from her hair and the cloak from her shoulders. She wore a black dress, without ornament, and carried the child pressed against her, wrapped in a shawl. She raised this burden now and held it out to him mechanically. "I've brought you your son."

Despite Ras's certainty, he seemed to see into her, piercing her brain with pitiless clarity. At last he came toward her, and his nearness made her afraid, as the eyes had done. He lifted the child lightly from her arms.

"Your son," she repeated. "I never gave him a name, but my women call him Rarnammon. A joke you will no doubt appreciate."

The baby in his hands awoke now, yet did not cry, and she felt a sudden fierce jealousy run through her and longed to snatch it back from him, and hide it again inside her cloak.

"Unfold the shawl," she said. "He brings you a gift."

The tiny gilded box lay on the child's chest, tied there by a ribbon.

"This?"

He eased up the lid. She caught the glitter of the golden chain inside. The blood stamped in her skull.

Raldnor turned, holding out the box to her.

"Honor me, madam. Take out the chain and put it round my neck."

"I?" She drew back. "No—"

"An Alisaarian trick," he said. "A razor edge, lacquered with poison. Kathaos?" He shut the box and set it aside. "The second time, Lyki, you have betrayed me."

"Don't kill me," she cried out. "I had no choice—Kathaos forced me to obey him—Let me live, for the sake of your son, at least—"

"If I were to say to you, Lyki, that I would spare your life on one condition, that condition being that I take your child and rip it open with this sword, you would let me do it, for that is how you are made."

She shrank away from him. Then, when he held out the child to her, she seized it and buried her face in its shawl.

"Your death would be useless," he said. "Therefore you shall not die."

She longed to weep, but her eyes were dry as if the drought had burned them up. She could not look at him anymore.

Two hours before dawn, Yannul and Xaros, coming from the tent of two sweet-natured women, caught sight of something revolving slowly beneath the high bough of a cibba.

Going nearer, they found a man had hanged himself in the night.

"This is the strange one from Yr Dakan's house," Yannul said, "the one with the serpent-hiss name—Ras. Why in the world—?"

"Our traitor, perhaps," Xaros said.

They cut him down and stowed him out of sight, for since the curious prayer on the slope, the mood of the camp had been too good to have it spoiled.

*   *   *

An hour before dawn the only coolness of the day lay in the burned gardens of the Storm Palace. Already white haze was forming on the shrunken river where decayed lilies stank, and on the river steps, before the palace temple, a flaccid water thing had crawled and died.

The man, dressed in black scale-plate, paused to look at this before turning aside under the portico.

A film of smoke still drifted in the huge and empty aisle. Amrek stood motionless, staring up at the black marble monsters which dominated the gloom. Their long irrids were slurs of dull radiance, their dragon features a blurred impression of some ancient and untranslatable nightmare, half lit by the cups of spooling flame beneath.

"Have no fear, great ones," Amrek said softly, "I'm here in observance of tradition, no more. I'll ask you for nothing, as I know quite well you will give me nothing."

He thought of the child on the morning of the feast, hacking away his flesh with the agonizing and incompetent knife. Pain and revulsion and terror. That hand, that hand with its layered silver scales, which he had slashed over and over again, screaming out to those black gods to accept his blood, his blood, but let the curse of the serpent goddess be taken from him. The screams had circled in the great roof, echoing, becoming one continuous scream. Then Orhn had come, his mother's bedfellow, the seal of horror and scorn, and later the scales grew back among the jagged scars.

Amrek touched now at the hand, covered by its black glove, the too-thick last finger held grimly by the dark blue jewel. He had known at eight years how potent was the Lady of Snakes, and how little the gods of Dorthar loved him.

"You have no admiration for the weak," he said to them.

Their very shadow crushed him, buried him, blotted him out.

He opened his eyes and saw the figure of a woman standing facing him across the great, flagged space. The light was attracted dimly to her exquisitely painted face, and to white glimmering points on her throat and hands. He smelled perfume over the temple musk.

"I forbade you to wear that unguent," he said.

"Did you, Amrek? I'd forgotten."

He glanced at the gods.

"So it is. My mother comes before me on the day of the battle, wearing the white face of my enemy. What do you want?"

"I shall need transport and an escort. I intend to leave Koramvis."

He turned to look at her fully. She was smiling, but her eyes were bright with fear, though she had done her best to hide it from him.

"I require the services of your guard, madam. For a war. I can't spare you fan bearers."

"Then I'll take my women and go alone."

"By all means. I wish you luck with the mob at the city gates."

Venom came into her eyes now, and into his. Each saw in the other a likeness of the flesh, none of the soul.

"What poor encouragement to the armies of Koramvis, madam—the Queen flying from the back gate while the lord rides from the front."

"You!" she spat at him. "A lord! A commander! You weren't made for war, neither for a throne. You should have been a priest, my son, with nothing to do except raise your arms to the gods and entreat their pity." She paused, and there was more than spite in her voice. "The Lowlander will kill you, Amrek."

He felt the blood draining out of his heart, not in horror or surprise, but at the perfection of the portent, coming as it did from her lips.

"Yes, Mother," he said, "I've long been aware that he would be my death. I've been evading him. Now circumstances have made it impossible for me to escape. Neither, it appears, can you."

"You coward! You resign yourself to dying and drag as many down with you as you can."

"It seems to have turned out an unhappy day after all, Mother, that you lay with Rehdon and conceived me."

He moved away, but she called out to him in a voice that was abruptly wild and fragile with excitement: "Wait!"

He stopped, his back still to her.

"Well, madam. I wait. For what?"

"To hear the truth from me," she said.

When he faced her, he saw she had again that look, that look she had worn when she told him that the one woman and the one man he loved, had loved each other in despite of him.

"Whatever it is, then speak it," he said.

Triumph and alarm lit up her eyes. Her words came quickly, one on top of the other.

"Very well. I will tell you. It was said that Raldnor wasn't Rehdon's sowing, but the bastard of Amnorh, his Councilor. But which of us doubts that Raldnor comes from Rehdon's line? It is you, my son, who bear no impression of the sire."

His mouth moved stiffly.

"I don't understand you, madam."

"Don't you? I must be more explicit then. Rehdon was afraid of me and could give me no child. Without one, I should eventually have lost my high place in favor of a younger, ostensibly more fertile girl. You've always called me a whore. Revel in the proof of it. I took Amnorh into my bed, and, unknowing, he got you on me." Her eyes went blank with old remembered hate. "And then my royal husband, who had no life in his loins for me, mounted a little white bitch-virgin in the Plains and gave her what should have been mine. Can you estimate the irony, Amrek? You, the fool and the cripple, are Amnorh's distorted seed. Raldnor, not you, Raldnor should have been my son."

She looked at him, and at that moment her years had caught her up. Cheated of everything, she supposed, she also had been given the power to destroy. But his face showed nothing. His eyes were fixed like the eyes of the blind.

He might have been dead already.

24

FROM THROATS OF RAW bronze the Koramvian trumpets howled—a sound of war unheard in this place for centuries. Every stone of the city answered it. It peeled white layers of birds from their roosts above the Avenue of Rarnammon. Only the clouds kept still—the transparent, shriveled clouds, little flat embryos of unborn rain on an indigo sky that was almost black.

Down the half-empty streets came the soldiers with their drums, rattles and pipes, rank on rank of them; the sun burned on their armored scales, cavalry and chariots, and banners bright as blood. Catapults and other machinery of war passed rumbling on their chains. Men and women peered from windows and galleries, and were heartened. The Lowland magician was outnumbered and greatly out-classed. Here came Amrek's personal Guard, the white lightning on their cloaks; and there the High King, the Storm Lord in his chariot. Black plate and gold; over that the wide collar and the tall spiked Dragon helm, at which they pointed, as if to remind themselves of Rarnammon, and history itself, which bristled with successful war. A few women flung down garlands, already withered in the heat. Amrek's face was without expression of any kind, but they noticed mainly his armor. After him came the Zakorians, forgiven now for their indiscretions, striding with their eight-foot maces, and masked in black metal.

At the wide space before the Plain Gate of Koramvis, three bulls were butchered on the marble altar.

Kathaos stood waiting in his armor, his chariot beside Amrek's. The Lord Councilor had many thoughts to occupy him. He did not know if Lyki had succeeded at her task; it had been a matter of chance, all part of the game, and she, like all the rest, a game piece, one he would not even particularly regret losing. The Council had approved the scheme, though not Amrek—it had been kept from him. If it failed, it would mean little. Confronted by this superior force the Lowlanders could not do much but die, their mercenaries with them. If it had been successful, however, Kathaos would become the hero of the city; it was as simple as that. They still feared the ravages of the pirates, but Dorthar, unleashed, could, they believed, quell such brigands; besides, for this moment, they were the problem of Zakoris and Karmiss, which would perhaps save Dorthar the trouble. Even those who spoke of demons from the sea understood quite well that Raldnor had conjured them—that should he perish, they would perish too. Yes, it was Raldnor they mostly, absurdly feared; his outrageous luck, his reputation and his mother had made him into a figure of ominous brightness.

The last bull bled.

Blue smoke wound upward and whitened on the dark sky.

"And in the coming fight," Kathaos thought, "if Amrek falls, I carry the Council in my hand."

He became aware that Amrek was looking at him.

"Where is Kren, my lord?" Kathaos asked immediately. "Do you anticipate the troops of the River Garrison will join us here?"

"I have left Kren to guard the city," Amrek said. His voice was toneless, empty.

"He has lost hold on life already," Kathaos thought. "He thinks Raldnor will kill him."

"But, my lord, there's some suspicion surrounding Kren. If he were to open the gates to an enemy—"

Amrek's eyes glittered for a moment with a curious vestige of life.

"You're blind, Kathaos, as I am. It comforts me to know that."

They stood under the molten sun, forming a shape dwarfed by the drought-blackened vastness of the plain.

Above, the Dortharians poured from the gate and spread their shining squares across the slope.

Men laughed and swore. If that were the Lowland army, how had they got so far?

A Zakorian roared: "Does it take a grindstone to squash a flea?"

Yet there came no fresh commands. The great mass of soldiery began to move toward the plain, and, from a rise, the first Dortharian catapult jarred and spat. The gobbet of flame fell wide and set the dry trees immediately alight. Smoke obscured the valley. With a sudden cry the foremost lines of Dortharian cavalry broke ranks and galloped down into the fog. Spears leveled, the foot soldiers ran after and the great chariots juddered at the rear.

Amrek felt the vast spasm of movement sweep him up. He was borne along with it, shouting bright men on every side, into the burning darkness of the orchards.

"Aiyah! Aiyah!" The yelling of the charioteers.

The smoke wrapped black across his face like a woman's veil.

To his left, abruptly, a man screamed and fell dead, an iron shaft through his neck.

Amrek stared at him.

More fire rushed through the air, lighting up the way ahead. Amrek saw a yellow-haired man come running out of the murk toward him with a masklike face, his sword raised.

"My first Lowlander," he thought. "The first Lowlander

I've seen this close." But no, it was not so. Raldnor had been
a Lowlander. Raldnor, his brother. And also—yes, a girl,
long ago. A white-haired exquisite girl who had died quite
literally at his touch, as if he were the incarnation of her
death. As Raldnor would be the incarnation of his own.
"This man running at me, this man should be Raldnor,
bringing my death," he thought suddenly, but the face was
unknown and the raised sword falling.

A Guard had struck the Lowlander down. He fell under
the wheels of the chariot.

Val Mala's women scurried about her apartments, shrill-
voiced with alarm, gathering up the costly clothes and
priceless jewelry.

The Queen sat in her chair, twisting her hands with frustration and fury.

Amrek.

She was consumed by a final hatred of her son, a clawing
paroxysm as she recollected everything—how she had carried him in discomfort and ugliness, her beauty subservient
to his needs, how she had borne him in indignity and pain,
how she had drawn back the birth robes and seen Ashne'e's
mockery irrevocably branded there.

It did not trouble her that she had at last destroyed him.
She had never credited him with humanity; it had never
been convenient for her to do so.

Today, she imagined, he would die, and after his death
she saw the abyss opening in her path. Other sons of other,
lower queens might take the throne, and their heads, and
the heads of their mothers, she had anointed with her malice since the morning on which she married Rehdon. She
visualized what they would do to her once Amrek's body
lay within the Hall of Kings. Already she had tasted the
poison on her lips, experienced the stifling velvet pillow
pressed to her sleeping face. This city could no longer be her
home. She must abandon it as the rabble had done.

Beyond the long windows, the city lay burning and

breathless in the coruscating sunlight. There seemed to be no sound in the world save the clamor which was all around her in this room.

Dathnat, the Zakorian, appeared in the arch-mouth.

"As you ordered, a covered carriage waits for you in the court below, madam," Dathnat said. Her tone, as always, was precise and clipped. It gave Val Mala an uneasy comfort to know that this woman was totally unmoved. The elements of confusion and distress seemed to shrink away from her, afraid themselves that she would find them unacceptable.

"These fools!" Val Mala said. "They can do nothing. They have the wits of lice. Tell them to be quick. Tell them I'll give them each a flawless jewel if they hurry."

"As you wish, madam." Dathnat's eyes touched hers for a second. Val Mala met in them the hatred that had amused her once and which now sank into her breast like a weight of cold metal. She thought: "I am surrounded by enemies," and saw no particular justice in it.

A smell of corruption breathed suddenly across the room. One of the nervous girls let out a shriek. Val Mala turned. The white kalinx stood in the arch. The Queen started; it was like an apparition of death to her.

"Take it away from me!" she cried. "Why isn't it locked in the court? Which of you fools let it out?"

The women approached cautiously. It snarled at them and crept to Val Mala's feet, staring with its glazed blue-bubble eyes. It rubbed against her, but she kicked it away.

The kalinx snarled again, aimlessly, showing brown teeth like rotten filberts. It was too old to defend the rags of its existence.

The rheum ran down its bald cheeks like tears.

The Lowlanders, after all, refused to die.

The Dortharians cursed the running fires and fog of smoke which their own catapults had created. The Lowland troops used the smolder as cover, ambushed out of it small groups of soldiers cut off from the rest and slunk away to hide in it when this work was done.

"They fight like tirr, the bastards. How many have we killed?" the captains demanded of their runners. No one knew. They came across bodies with yellow hair, yet there seemed somehow always more of the enemy among the trees, as if the dead replaced themselves by supernatural means.

"Banaliks come to fill their armor when they fall!"

A Dortharian was found screaming in a burning grove.

He whimpered that he had seen a thing pass—half woman and half snake. He had been drunk before the battle; nevertheless someone clouted him over the head to keep him quiet before the panic spread.

Somewhere, from the slopes, the brazen trumpets bellowed a withdrawal.

Sluggishly, the smoke-blackened, scale-plated men pulled themselves out of the trees, the Zakorians coming grim and orderly behind.

Amrek's commanders crowded to him.

"Storm Lord, we've lost few men. The scum must be crippled, but there's no way to tell in that trap. If we let the fires spread, we can drive them out into the open on the other side and take them cleanly."

"Do it," Amrek said. His Guard had served him well; there was not a scratch on him. Yet he seemed in a trance.

A last catapult delivered flame among the orchard trees.

The dragons drank wine as they waited above the smoke.

Glancing up at the blue-black sky, a man said: "No carrion birds. That's strange."

"Not enough to feed them of ours, and the skin and bone Lowland muck would stick in their gullets," his neighbor answered.

Farther along the line, a boy, ladling from the wine pitchers, fell abruptly behind in his task.

"Come on, you. Get a bit of speed on."

"It moved," said the boy.

"What moved, you numbskull?"

"There! Look—" The boy pointed, and, staring down, his sergeant saw a tremor disturb the scarlet liquor, ripple and run and flatten out into nothing. He laughed.

"There's a beetle got in, boy. Ladle up. One of our lucky lads'll get more in his cup than he reckoned on."

Yannul the Lan straightened and drew out his blade. The Zakorian, who had stayed behind to fight, crashed down into the bushes.

Now at leisure, Yannul glanced around. The smoke was full of dimly glimpsed figures moving all one way. The dragons seemed to have been called off to let them choke and roast at their own pace. He turned and ran with the general tide between the fires and emerged on higher ground where the smoke lay more thinly. Behind, trees crackled under their pall; beyond those was the glitter of the Vis troops in their immaculate squares, drawn up as before, and waiting.

A great stillness had settled over this place, though he could hear faint shouts and cheers from the Dortharian end of the valley, and the snap of burned wood in the orchards below.

"What now?" he said to the nearest Lowlander, wiping soot and blood from his eyes.

The man turned to him an ash-white face. "Now they die," he said.

Yannul's scalp shivered.

"You mean, I think, *we* die—once they leave off swilling and cheering, and come on."

Just then the sky turned black as night.

Some of the Vis sections of Raldnor's army let out cries and curses and stared up at it. The Lowlanders stood like blind statues, paying no attention.

Then there came a new sound across the valley. A sound like a colossal gong beaten underground.

The shadow of the black sky fell over the dragons, and their cheering stopped. In the thick stillness which followed, a man began to gibber. The animals tossed their heads, rolling their eyes and sweating.

"Storm coming," a soldier said hoarsely. "Look how the trees're thrashing about."

In the orchards the cibbas were swaying like dancers. Men pointed at them and made religious signs, for there was no wind.

Then came a great brass mooing, up out of the ground at their feet. Animals reared in fright; men cried out to their gods. On the upper slopes a creaking catapult tilted slowly and fell flaming among the Dortharian ranks. But the ultimate voice came from behind them — the voice of the city, where a thousand bells began to toll.

They turned, struggling with their mounts, staring back toward the white towers of Koramvis, and in that moment they saw the red spout and gush of powdered rock explode silently from beneath her walls, after which the hills ran together, and she was lifted like an offering to the ink-black sky.

Above the city, in the cave of Lake Ibron, the steep sands let go their immemorial hold. Deep down, where colors bloodied into purple, ancient laws of balance became subtly altered, and tidal urges swept the hidden caves.

The first shock cracked through Koramvis. The noise of it was a low metal booming, the single note of a monstrous heart. Lightning turned the sky to glass.

At the second shock, paving lifted by its roots, and fissures spread in a spilling stain. In the lower city, walls burst apart. Lamp poles fell in rows. The river came running sideways up its banks into the collapsing hovels, its water as red as blood. The fleeing wagons overturned, or ran out of control along the roadways.

The great bridge that spanned the river to the south broke at its center, as if under the impact of a gigantic axe, letting go its human freight into the boiling mud.

In the Avenue of Rarnammon the Dragons tumbled

from their bases, showering a rain of shattered obsidian across the streets.

Towers leaned and fell.

Fires burst into white flower.

Screaming, calling out to their tottering gods to save them, the terrified and the trapped wailed and shrieked in their agony.

In a celebration of doom, the thousand bells of Koramvis roiled and jangled.

Val Mala stood beside her chair in the tilting room, while gold lamps crashed from the ceiling.

"Dathnat!" she cried.

The bells seemed to beat inside her skull. Her legs were the feeble limbs of an old woman. She dared not cross the room. A girl lay dead before the archway with bloody hair, and in a moment she too would sink forward and the roof would come down across her back.

Miraculously, she felt iron fingers suddenly grasp her arm, supporting her.

"Dathnat—the ceiling will fall—"

"Lean against me, madam," the dry voice said, without a trace of fear.

Weak with terror, Val Mala could do nothing else.

Dathnat half carried her up the impossible angle of the floor and under the arch. The corridor was full of smoke, for a fire had started in the lower rooms. A stream of ocher gushed from above.

"We must find a way out, Dathnat. Quickly, Dathnat."

The Zakorian glanced about her, and ahead. The passage seemed blocked by fire; besides, there would be no time to reach the lower courts before the upper portions of the palace gave way. Even so, her gods had not been entirely unjust. Pausing beside an open gallery, Dathnat pointed.

"See how Koramvis burns, madam."

"Dathnat—have you gone mad? Find a way for me to escape this place before the roof falls and kills us both."

"There is the way, madam," Dathnat said.

Val Mala looked down. She saw a terrace laid out with colored flags that seemed from here as small as a checkerboard.

Presentiment came, immediate and undeniable.

"Dathnat!" she screamed.

Dathnat, with one swift and irresistible blow, thrust the Queen over the broken ledge of the gallery. That one thing her gods had left her time to do. Complacently she watched Val Mala spin shrieking to meet the empty stones beneath. After the meeting, she was silent.

In the depths of the rock, Anackire stirred.

The margins of the pool within her had long since widened and filled up the room, bursting the door from its hinges and flooding the stone temple. Now the foaming water had lifted her a little and was thrusting up against the roof of the cave.

Her golden head grazed on the granite above. Over this place huge clefts had already spread themselves as the quake dissolved the structure of the hills. Now the land slid and fell away. Out of the chasm emerged the massive milk-white torso with its burning eyes and hair.

The third shock, the final shock which flung down the last of Koramvis, spewed Ibron up into the cave. The full force of the water came gushing out from the fractured rock, lifting the goddess with it.

Higher and higher the jetting liquid took her. She crested the hills and rose incredibly into the pitch-black sky, a towering moon of incendiary ice and flame.

In the plain, floundering among the craters and the fire, the dragons witnessed that last and most absolute omen. Her eyes like stars, Anackire soared and blazed, crushing them with the eight maledictions of her serpent arms. Now the known laws of their world, which had supported and nurtured them all their lives, betrayed them and brought about the final inrush of Chaos.

They had seen Nemesis. Their world was ended.

The goddess shone like a meteor in the black air, then sank, as the wave relinquished her, out of their sight, into the torn mirror of the lake.

But Kathaos lived and was unchanged. He imagined nothing at the sight of the creature in the sky. Even at the end of the world he was rational, and a cynic. She was a device. He knew it, though her origins at this time held no interest for him. For he understood quite well, despite his logic, that the things he had labored at carried neither significance nor hope in this altered landscape.

Only one thing, therefore, was left. An act that was fitting, if no longer useful.

He rode his chariot along the broken lines, past men clawing in the contrary earth, through the churning flame fight and the purple smoke, and the weeping and the prayers.

He came to Amrek at last. Amrek, the Storm Lord, who had become, through the admission of Chaos, accessible. He looked at Kathaos blankly, without trepidation or violence.

"I beg your pardon, my lord," Kathaos said. He approached Amrek and stabbed him in the side where the mail was unaccountably rent, as if purposely for his knife. "It is an act compatible with our circumstances."

Kathaos remounted the chariot and turned the heads of his team toward the first and only break in the sky.

Amrek lay still in the dark. He was not quite dead. Only formless thoughts disturbed him. He was tranquil, until terror came abruptly out of the ground.

Terror had glittering eyes and came sliding and narrow from its black home under the boulder. Terror was a snake.

Amrek's body jerked helplessly.

The snake wove in circles, its head darting from side to side in frenzy. It, too, was afraid; the earth had also shaken down its world. Suddenly it discerned a refuge. It looped against Amrek's face and trickled to rest against his throat. He felt its living pulse pressed strongly to his fading one.

And abruptly terror stopped. Partnered with his flesh, the skin of the snake was dry and cool and layered like cameo.

"How can I fear this thing?" he thought quite clearly. "Something so beautiful."

Presently, the snake, restless and seeking now the earth was quiet, left the shelter of the man's dead body and shivered away across the slope.

BOOK SIX

Sunrise

25

THE HUGE, DULL-RED SUN, poised on the final edge of the horizon, blistered the mountains into coral. A black tongue of shadow had already covered the tumbled angle of hills below and the ruins of the city which had once been Koramvis.

There had come a season of snows and rains — after this, a season of heat, when the urge to growth possessed the fertile northern land. And the fruitings of the soil were not idle in the city. The deserted gardens overspilled their boundaries; young trees burst from the broken streets. Soon the corpse of the metropolis was entirely claimed by a loose mantle of vegetation. Birds screamed and sang in the wrecked palaces, and in the upheavals of the broad road-ways, orynx and wildcat established lairs. Of men, only the dead remained in Koramvis. Their tombs were haphazard and various. Others, clawed free by lovers, or discovered on the battlefield below, had achieved houses of earth and markers of stone. Of a King's mound there was no trace. If Amrek had found burial was unknown. Perhaps the earth had swallowed him at last, or the running fires ironically given him Lowland rites. Certainly, no woman or man had come weeping to carry him to the privacy of the grave. Such was his destiny.

It was on the plain below that men lived and went about their work, in a town of wooden houses, with a few roughly made stone halls—an ugly, sprawling, makeshift place. To the west of it, on the lower forest slopes, a temple was being built before any other thing—a Vis temple of white stone, with a high tower and many pillars and steps. Incenses burned on the altar, grapes and fruit were spread out and blood spilt. They never forgot to worship here, nor to bring Her gifts, for now She was theirs. Adopted in their terror, She had assumed the character of their own. The Dortharian Anackire. They would name the new city for Her, when they built it, and Her priests were dark-skinned men who praised Her with fire, smoke and cymbals, experienced visions and practiced magics for Her sake.

And there were other Lowlanders in Dorthar now.

In one of the stone halls on the plain, two councils sat down. The first comprised Dortharians. Kren, who had once been a Dragon Lord in the city, was included in its ranks. Mathon, the old warden, miraculously protected from death by an eccentric formation of the collapsing house beams over his head, still held his familiar office in unfamiliar surroundings. In the second council sat Lans and Xarabians, and yellow-haired men from the Lowlands and elsewhere. Warriors of Tarabann and Vathcri were seen about the streets; pirates from Shansar turned politician and hero overnight. Sorm of Vardath was detained in Zakoris, where the black beehive of Hanassor had capitulated, starved to its deepest cellars; and in Karmiss the Shansarian vengeance fleet, having drunk its fill of blood and wine, had set up Ashkar as goddess of the island and began the business of making Her sons into kings. Karmiss was a malleable and docile land. She showed them her ways of pleasure and her forms of joy, and bowed to the yoke gracefully. And it was whispered behind the ivory lattices that the conquerors were beautiful and brave, and women, like another woman in Vardath, began to bleach out their black hair and tint it gold, paint their dark skins white, as once the Dortharian

Queen had done. And amber, which had been of precious mystic value to the Plains people, now grew priceless as black Karmian pearls.

Across the breadth of Vis, alliances of the flesh began. In that second fading of the summer, the first crop of children was harvested from that first sowing. The obscure Sarish name of "Raldnor" invaded the nomenclature of those newborn sons whose blood was mixed.

And talk of the King who bore the name was rife as the weeds. He had wed a Vathcrian woman, but would he also take a wife of the dark races in the manner of the Vis? And would he live on, below the ruined city of Koramvis, or return to her ruined sister on the Shadowless Plains? Or did he live at all? There was a rumor that he had died in battle, for very few had seen him since the earth moved and shook down Koramvis.

As the last piece of the red sun slid behind the mountains, a chill breath of night blew down the wooden streets. The double council, seating itself in the dark stone hall, talked together, Vis to Vis, in stealthy whispers, while the Lowlanders merely kept still, as was their way.

The lamps were lit. A man entered and took his seat between them. He had never dressed as a king; now he wore a dark cloak, as if for traveling.

He heard their business out. Decisions were made, things settled. But there was a sense of the portentous in that place. At last he told them their responsibilities, and who he would leave in his stead as regent for the pale-haired son Sulvian had borne him across the sea.

There was clamor from the Vis. Men came to their feet.

"Storm Lord—the land is still in a state of flux—Where in the goddess's name are you going, that you feel you can leave us like this?"

The Lowlanders kept quiet, knowing already.

"My work is done," he said. "It finished when the city fell."

He looked about at them. His face was curiously altered. Some of the great and terrible light had gone out of it, and yet the eyes, which had been empty of everything except those fires of will and power, now contained an infinite closed in shadow. The thing which had cast out his soul and possessed him had now let him go. He was, in the most essential sense, himself again.

He paid no attention to their altercation. Kren, the Dragon, saw something in Raldnor which told him as much as the Lowlanders could tell, for he was an excellent judge of men, whether the gods had chosen them or not. Yannul the Lan, because he had known Raldnor once, formed a picture in his mind as clear as if Plains telepathy had come to him. Xaros was at that time in Abissa, feted as a hero for his trick in Ommos by Xarabians who wished their aid remembered. When he heard how the King had lived solitary for several days, then come to the Council and given his kingship back into their hands, he also guessed.

How Raldnor found his way to it, they never knew. Yet his mind to theirs was like a bright machine—it might be turned to anything. And so they glimpsed this vast complex of thought—this brain, so enlarged, so alien, striving in some secret and deliberate frenzy of search. What had been the trigger to the searching was equally hidden—some infinitesimal tremor or stirring. Perhaps merely hope, or the thrust of buried yet insuppressible pain and loss. For he was still a man, after all. Those who saw him in the Council could no longer doubt it. It was to them an unnerving thing to witness a god reduced. They preferred to remember everything but that.

Outside, the night was cool and still and lit up by stars. A few men watched him ride up the slopes into the ruins of Koramvis, making for the mountains.

An hour later, in his wooden house, Yannul said to Medaci: "She's alive then, after all. In Thaddra. Red-haired Astaris. And he's gone to find her."

There had been a child's voice, a child's voice calling across the black gulf, piercing his brain with its lost beseeching.

He had thought briefly of Sulvian's son in Vathcri, more briefly still of Karmiss, and the black-haired baby Lyki had borne him and finally carried there. Flesh of his flesh cried out to him—not with words, for it had learned no speech, yet in an abstract, intimate tongue of the inner mind he had spoken only with one other. A perfect equation constructed itself.

His seed.

Astaris's child.

Astaris.

When the thought was made clear to him, a formless presence gushed from him and was gone. He was emptied of the geas, the spiritual motivation which men explained as Anackire, that emanation of race which had possessed him. As in the past, the thought of a blood-haired woman took hold of him, flooding his brain like dawn, and left no room for any other thing.

The search was, at first, entirely of the mind. He had no different means to seek her or the thing in her which guided him. Through the medium of the embryo, he traveled dull continents, wide plateaus of darkness, and came eventually upon the flickering beacon, unmistakable in the featureless night.

The translation was made after, the nonphysical landscape processed into roads and mountains and forests. The magnetism lay in Thaddra, as he had once believed.

The rebirth of a race, the symbol of the shattered city, became distant. He left them without recognition or regret. At the finish of the fight, after all, his godhead had not consumed him, for something had come indeed to turn him back into a human man.

Across the wild garden of the Guardian's palace, the evening shadows drew close, like long cool fingers praying. In the jungle forest beyond the wall, birds squawked malevolently, and the orange Thaddrian moon was rising.

A man leaned on the wall, near the old gate.

Presently, a short, swarthy woman came slipping through the trees toward him.

"Well, Panyuma," he said and snatched her breast. She thrust him off.

"You're a fool, Slath. If Hmar heard of this, he'd kill us both. He understands the use of many slow and hideous poisons—"

"Be still, you slut. You know you come because you want. He's not man enough to use you, and I am, and never tell me you don't enjoy it. Besides, he thinks you protect him from this snake woman he says haunts him, and I—I protect him from his *mortal* enemies. In that last war we had up river, who brought him the heads of two lords?"

"You," she said sneeringly.

He thrust her back against the wall and pulled up her skirts, and the moon stared with its fierce eye at the choreography and conclusion of their labors.

"I must go back now," she whispered harshly. "He'll call for me. He's very fearful these past months—since the stories came over the mountains."

"What? The Dortharian war? Why should that bother him?"

"I think he's of their blood. And the snake woman—isn't there a goddess with a snake's tail, sacred to the yellow people? The traders said the yellow people took Alisaar and Zakoris and shook down the Dragon City, while their goddess sat on the mountains, watching," Panyuma muttered in the hushed singsong voice she used for her forest spells.

Slath laced himself and spat scornfully at shadows of night or soul.

"Stories for brats."

Panyuma said: "There are old things still, and strange things. Do you remember the slave you sold to Hmar?"

Slath nodded. A year since, Panyuma, irresistibly anxious to display her secret power, had shown him the hidden mausoleum, and, despite his casual brutality, his intestines had crawled at the row of undead dolls in their finery.

"I remember. A great waste. She was an ornamental bitch, my Seluchis."

"He goes there to gloat," Panyuma hissed. "He takes me sometimes. Their hair still grows, and their nails, and I must clip them, like a handmaiden. When the lamp fell on your slave, her hair had grown out red."

Slath swore.

"By Zarduk!" He struggled with his memory and said: "The Storm Lord's bride—didn't she have a red mane?"

"So I've heard the traders say. Do you know what Hmar did then? He sweated and muttered and pulled me out. Then, when it was the black of night, he left our bed and went there with an iron bar—I followed, though he didn't see. The thing in the floor which opens the stone—he took the bar to it and smashed it."

"Perhaps he thinks she'll come and strangle him with her red hair, like his snake lady."

"Now he keeps to his rooms," Panyuma said. "He has fever and screams all the time in his sleep."

"That's happened before."

"Yes," she said. Her black eyes glittered. "You were only a cutthroat mercenary when you came," she said, "now you captain Hmar's men. Since the war up river, they'd answer to you."

"What're you plotting, you bitch?"

"I have said nothing. Only woman's talk. Men think for themselves when they're men."

The gold bits sparkled a cold yellow in her plaits as she slunk aside and hurried back toward the three-towered mass of the palace.

After almost a month, the man called Raldnor crossed the mountains into Thaddra under an expressionless sky of weary blue. It was a dead yet living land, choked up with black jungles and arid fields where nothing grew.

He rode through Tumesh, where, in a gaudy marketplace, slaves were sold, and, passing northward, he came to one of the nameless rivers and gave his mount in exchange for a raft. He used no company on the river, but poled himself upstream.

On the sixth day there was a challenge.

He had no password; he simply stood looking at the three men, seeing them with more than his eyes, gauging them with his senses, which were finer and more numerous than theirs—and on them he found, like a faint scent, an intimation of what he sought.

They breathed out oaths at the color of his hair. Something in his demeanor and face made them loath to apply their knives to his back and prod him up the track, like any other trespasser. They told him they would take him to Hmar, guardian of the eight kingdoms, and he thanked them.

And then, somehow, on the overgrown jungle road, they lost him. As night came on, they searched and shouted in the forests. They came to believe a leopard had seized him just too quickly for their eyes to see and, swift with hunger, had dragged him into the undergrowth and devoured him whole.

By that time Raldnor had reached the bursting Thaddrian town and was walking the refuse-scattered streets toward Hmar's mansion of stone.

Amnorh, King's Councilor, Warden of the High Council of Koramvis, opened his eyes on a chamber of guttering torch smoke. Amnorh, conceived of a Dortharian prince in an Iscaian wine girl's reluctant womb. Amnorh, who had ridden Val Mala, the Storm Lord's Queen, but never known he sired her child; Amnorh, who had murdered Rehdon, High King of Vis.

"Hmar," he said, "I am Hmar."

He thought of the secret room, and the woman standing waiting with her bloody hair. Ashne'e's doing. Anackire rejected his gift.

"Oh, Mother mine," he crooned. "I regret most bitterly I have offended you," and he laughed crazily and in terror.

They had seen Her in Dorthar, too, in the sky like the sun, which had gone black. The city had been shaken down—it pleased him. Yet it was her revenge—Ashne'e's, Anackire's—the shadow of her vengeance had expunged Koramvis. Now it came reaching for his life—

"Who's there?" Amnorh cried out. He had heard a cold footstep in the premature dark of the room. Was the assassin here already? Shivering and sweating, Amnorh stared and glimpsed Panyuma in the torch glare. She had carried a quartz phial in one hand, filched from a great chest against the far wall as he lay sleeping in his insane dozes. But she had slipped the phial between her dark round breasts before he noticed it.

"Only Panyuma, lord. Will you rise?"

"Yes. Tonight I'll eat below. In my hall. You shall serve me."

"I'm your slave, lord."

He washed immaculately in the stone ewer, and she brought him his robe and the gold for his fingers.

When she went to fling the dirty water out from the window, she pulled free the phial from between her breasts and threw that down also a few moments later. It did not strike on the ground. Somewhere below a pair of hands had caught it.

Panyuma followed behind Hmar, descending the stairway into the hall. When he sat, she stood behind his chair and served him his meat.

Slath, Hmar's captain and bodyguard, was laughing lower down the table. He had learned the good manners Hmar expected and learned them well. He had even learned the mode and forms of table talk once prevalent in Dorthar.

"This wine's particularly good, Lord Hmar. I've had it in store for a year—Zakorian liquor. Can I offer you a cup?"

Hmar's darting eyes, moving as ever here and there across the length and breadth of the hall, skittered over the flask. He nodded peremptorily. Panyuma emptied his goblet and swilled it with water. She went to Slath, who handed her the flask. She filled Hmar's cup, let a swift trickle merely line the bottom of the captain's flagon and bore the brimming vessel back to the Guardian.

Hmar drank and nodded again.

"A bitter fluid, but personable."

He drained the liquor, his long fingers wrapped about the stem, his eyes once more in motion. Panyuma's face was blank. Slath noisily gulped nothing and was jovial with alarm. They had poisoned their lord, but he did not seem to be aware of it. And it was a slow agent. With luck, he would die in his sleep.

Beyond the high and narrow windows the last color left the sky.

At the far end of the hall one of the small doors opened. A man came through—a faceless, hooded man in a thick cloak. Hmar's soldiers made a good deal of noise at their dinner, the newcomer was not discernible by sound, nor by anything else tangible. Nevertheless, Slath felt an odd, additional unease. He glanced at Hmar and was troubled, thinking the drink was working too quickly after all. For Hmar's frenzied eyes had suddenly ceased their eternal search and were fixed on the stranger. Hmar's face was sickly. He gave a sudden hoarse crow of laughter. A peculiar horrified sense of fulfillment seemed to have taken him, like that of a man condemned for months to die and confronted at last by the gallows.

Amnorh remembered. There had been a water-singing cave. The woman had tricked him in that cave, and he had grasped her arm.

"Perhaps I should abort my child from you, and leave you to the gentle mercies of the Lord Orhn."

Incredibly, a smile rose like dawn over her white face. He had never seen her smile, nor any woman smile in this fashion: it seemed to freeze his blood. His hand fell away from her.

"Do so, Amnorh. Otherwise he will be my curse on you."

Amnorh stared down the length of the hall, hearing only the blue tinkling of the water in his head. The man was not seated, but standing by one of the lower tables. Amnorh could see no face within the hood, no gaze answering his own.

A curious sensation gripped him, so that he seemed to look at her, not with his open eyes but with a third eye set in the center of his forehead. And it was not her he saw. Standing where she stood was a young man, indistinct, spectral, yet Amnorh could make out that he had the bronze skin of the Vis and, at the same time, eyes and hair as pale as the Lowland wine with which he had poisoned Rehdon during the first nights of the Red Moon. . . .

"He is here," Amnorh thought. "She has sent him. Anackire's messenger—my son—"

He chuckled grimly. No, not his son. Rehdon's son, after all. Rehdon, whom he had poisoned with Lowland wine.

To Amnorh there came a vision. He saw Val Mala standing with her hand on his shoulder, staring with avid eyes at the liquor he had distilled to be Rehdon's death—a bright cameo of the lord's woman and the lord's man conspiring to kill him. And suddenly, it was no longer Val Mala he saw, or himself. It was Panyuma, the Thaddrian, and Slath the mercenary, and the wine they had mixed was for him.

Amnorh let out a hoarse cry. He picked up his empty cup and slung it across the floor. He thrust from his chair.

"I am poisoned!"

Men left off eating and stared up at him.

"Poisoned!" Amnorh shouted, his eyes starting. He flung about, and struck Panyuma in the face. She fell down and cowered. "These two have murdered me. This bitch, and Slath, there, my captain—"

At every table men leapt to their feet. Treachery, they knew, was not greatly discriminating. They drew their knives or snatched blades off the board. Slath's paid men began to roar for him; others began to strike about them in fear and anger. At once there was fighting. Blood and wine ran; a torch was knocked from its socket and inspired a blaze in the tapestry along the wall. Women shrilled.

Slath, growling with fury, pulled out a dagger, but Amnorh had spun round and fled—through the arch behind the dais, into the maze of corridors and stairs.

The stranger in the dark cloak, barely noticed now, began to make his way up the hall toward the arch, walking between the brawls and struggles as if unseeing. Near the dais a man jumped on his back with a crazy whoop of rage. The stranger gave a curious half turn, a sort of stumble and, as the man slid from him, cut his throat with a pitiless and accurate gesture. No others ran at him. Only the woman Panyuma saw him pass. His shadow fell over her as she crouched by the table. She made a magic sign against him, her eyes flashing dread, but then he was gone, silently, following dying Hmar into the dark of the mansion.

It was easy to find the place.

An unseen light, an unheard sound, an unfelt thread between his fingers—all guided him there. The way was half-lit by irregular banks of torches and the dim star-shine in windows.

Raldnor came eventually to a blank wall of stone and a broken machinery in the floor. It was here.

On the ground lay a narrow-eyed man, with gold on his hands, whimpering. He left off whimpering and said prosaically: "You've come, then."

Raldnor looked at him. The man smiled.

"You kept me waiting a long time, son of Rehdon. Is it her you want—the red-haired woman?"

"Yes."

"Retribution," mused the man on the floor. "You note, confronted by the inescapable, I've become quite lucid. You'll find the door inaccessible. The mechanism is damaged. I myself did this, in a fit of terror. But then, I've heard you brought an earthquake to Koramvis. Perhaps you can open the stone yourself."

Raldnor kneeled by the broken levers, examining them intently. The hood slipped from his head. Amnorh stared at him. He began a dialogue concerning Ashne'e, but this was interrupted suddenly when the man struck sideways at the machinery with his fist, and then again, and, with a rusty protest, the stone began to pull reluctantly apart.

"Well, well. And clever also with his hands."

Raldnor walked by Amnorh into the lightless gallery of the tomb.

A place of death, heavy with old embalming musk. Dead warriors and stone boxes of bones, and heaps of little treasure. At the far end of the gallery, ten women paralyzed in attitudes of marble. Their skin had turned to the texture of wood, their hair to wire. Soon real death would begin to eat their flesh.

His hands touched them and abandoned them. He came to an eleventh figure and found her suddenly, and her skin was as he remembered it, and her hair, with the frozen gems in it now, the Serpent's Eye of Anackire.

A deeper shade of silence fell inside the opened tomb.

Amnorh babbled his elegant delirium at the door.

Below, a dull explosion rocked the palace. The wild impromptu battle had run out into the ragged town, fire had spread and smoke obscured the rising moon.

In her brain there was only darkness, a deserted hollow void, the shell of a citadel stripped bare by the motionless winds of time. Yet the essence of her being was somehow present—one last ghost in the ruin, and the far-off whisper of life which was the child.

Astaris.

He moved in her mind, calling her, and received no answer.

Then the image came.

It formed and hardened, a familiar configuration, now altered to undertake new horror.

Astaris stood waiting before him; the wind was washing through her scarlet hair. A red moon, the Zastis moon, shone behind her. She raised her arms, and long cracks appeared in her body—ink lines on amber. Then she crumbled all at once in blazing ashes, and the ashes blew away across the moon.

He blotted out the image, but it formed again and again on the dark.

He put other images in its place. Images of love, images of passion, the sexual images of the body, the yearning images within the skull.

Initially, he alone peopled her brain with creatures. Then, like wraiths, the first memories that were truly hers came drifting up from the cobwebs to greet his.

Her mind filled itself, slowly, like a cup. Then came the deep dreams, the conclusions, the solitudes, all in great surges as if the doors had finally been broken down. She herself came last of all, behind a train of shapes and fantasies. The inner she, like a distant jewel, or rising sun in the core of the brain, opening its single eye and regarding him.

Raldnor?

In the dark of the tomb he felt her physical life return to her. She stirred in his arms.

"Are you here?" she said aloud.

"I am here."

Somewhere, a dawn rose over a forest and filtered between the drifting smokes. It struck a half note of color in the black gallery, through the open doorway, across which a man was lying.

Raldnor took Astaris's hand. They crossed the stone room, stepped over the dead man, went along the empty corridor.

Much of the palace had burned in the night. Many rooms were gutted. A few dogs ran yelping about the streets outside. The sun stained everything with nebulous gold and wine-red panes.

Only a child saw the wagon pass. He was to remember later, twenty years later, when, as the result of various promptings and by various means, he had crossed the mountains and assumed the yellow robe of the Dortharian Anackire.

A white-haired man and a scarlet-haired woman. He had thought they must be blind, for they seemed to see nothing at all, and yet, when they had glanced simultaneously aside at each other he had been aware, despite his lack of years and the terrors of the night, that they did indeed each see one thing, which was the other.

When grown, the child—then a man—discovered so many legends concerning Raldnor and the manner in which he had vanished from the world. The Lady of Snakes had taken him, or he had gone below into the earth, for gods cannot remain as gods; they can only transcend themselves, or in some inferno of mythology forget their power and die.

And so the Thaddrian priest would tell what he had seen, for it appealed to some streak of logic in him, that piety should not necessarily be coupled with conjecture and fable.

Raldnor, son of Ashne'e and Rehdon, Raldnor called Am Anackire, the Storm Lord, had gone with Astaris the Karmian, the most beautiful woman in Vis, into the great jungle forests of Thaddra on a rickety wagon, both of them riding like peasants.

And it was not legend, but the forests that had swallowed them. Though it was legend which would preserve their names thereafter, until some final chaos—not change but annihilation—sank Vis in ocean and pulled down the sky.

5495

Kari Sperring
Living with Ghosts
978-0-7564-0675-2

Finalist for the Crawford Award for First Novel

A Tiptree Award Honor Book

Locus Recommended First Novel

"This is an enthralling fantasy that contains horror elements interwoven into the story line. This reviewer predicts Kari Sperring will have quite a future as a renowned fantasist."
—*Midwest Book Review*

"A satisfying blend of well-developed characters and intriguing worldbuilding. The richly realized Renaissance style city is a perfect backdrop for the blend of ghostly magic and intrigue. The characters are wonderfully flawed, complex and multi-dimensional. Highly recommended!"
—*Patricia Bray, author of The Sword of Change Trilogy*

And now available:
The Grass King's Concubine
978-0-7564-0755-1

To Order Call: 1-800-788-6262
www.dawbooks.com